SUDDEN STORM

An Evans Novel of Romance

SUDDEN STORM

DIANE CAREY

M Evans
Lanham • New York • Boulder • Toronto • Plymouth, UK

M. Evans
An imprint of The Rowman & Littlefield Publishing Group, Inc.
4501 Forbes Boulevard, Suite 200, Lanham, Maryland 20706
http://www.rlpgtrade.com

10 Thornbury Road, Plymouth PL6 7PP, United Kingdom

Distributed by National Book Network

British Library Cataloguing in Publication Information Available

Library of Congress Cataloging-in-Publication Data Available

ISBN 13: 978-1-59077-374-1 (pbk: alk. paper)

☉™ The paper used in this publication meets the minimum requirements of American National Standard for Information Sciences—Permanence of Paper for Printed Library Materials, ANSI/NISO Z39.48-1992.

Printed in the United States of America

Chapter One

No one was saying anything. The question, though, was in all their eyes as she stepped off the ferry's gangplank. What was she doing stepping onto Straight Wharf on very proper Nantucket Island wearing a very proper poplin skirt and very *im*proper riding boots? The answer, she gave them with her eyes, was that these were her traveling boots and what she was doing in them was traveling. Add to that the fact that when one travels horseback for half the journey, one travels lightly. She doubted they would be any more pleased with the one other skirt she'd brought, which was buckskin, split and sewn up the middle for riding purposes, or her other shoes, which were—heaven forbid—moccasins. Then again, perhaps if she took short strides . . .

They looked, but they didn't look long. It was a busy place, this New England port, and everyone had affairs to tend to that didn't include Abbey Sutton. Good. That meant she did well to choose her dark blue jacket and skirt in Newport before she had set sail. Maybe she wouldn't look so out of place on Nantucket. She didn't want to be pegged straight off as the woman from the West. She'd be living here from now on, and had better try to fit in. If she held her handbag close to her body, just so, she'd seem as prim as any Nantucket lady.

A beaded handbag dangled from her wrist and bobbed against her hip as she strode down the gangplank toward the dock. Perhaps it would work; they wouldn't be able to tell where she was from or that she was a stranger to the east ever since her parents left their Ohio roots to homestead the western states when Abbey was eight years old.

Abbey was struck first and hardest by the colors of Nantucket. In Wyoming there were wide green valleys and long wheaty ranges, the broad blue sky and all the bright sparkles of winter under the far-reaching sun. Long, wide, bright bands of color that stretched way out. There were the browns of wooden branch houses and rail fences, the sooty black smoke of the once-a-week train, and the colors of livestock. Cattle colors, sheep colors, frontier colors. Grit colors.

Here there was nothing like that. Builder's hand and nature's ire had steadfastly created only gray—blue-gray skies, dove-gray houses and oyster shell–drab harbor shacks with eggshell trim, fog-gray clothing and pearl-gray faces moving about against an ash-gray sea. Little, tight, neat colors on boxy buildings tucked close together. Everything was so close! There would never be room here for indulgences like the twenty-foot bench that had run the length of Abbey's ranch porch out west, or the wide vegetable garden she'd tended behind the bunkhouse.

The sounds here were different, too. In Wyoming all the sounds were faraway sounds—the clang of the triangle announcing dinner across the range, the long low *moo* of a cow calling her calf, the *yip-hyah* of the cowboys urging their horses to move faster, then the hollow trammel of hoofbeats coming up through the very ground.

Here, there were close-by sounds. Hobnails clicking on the dock-wood, the sharp *dang-dang* of ships' bells, the unapologetic slap of waves on the pilings below, and voices—voices everywhere. There were more voices right here, right now, than she'd hear in a whole year on the ranch.

Out west, this—Nantucket—was the kind of place she'd only heard about. Now, as she stepped off the packet and put her first island step behind her, Abbey felt her spirits suddenly heighten at the sight of this storybook place. Even at the Newport wharf, there hadn't been this kind of feeling, this kind of singularity of purpose. Nantucket's port was a place dancing with mastheads and spiced with the scent of the sea and a heritage that was stuck deep in the lore of the sea trade, as majestic and as awful as that lore could be. All around her, in businesslike repose, were ships made of wood, docks made of wood, trunks made of wood—and all these woods carried the aura of the places they came from, woods with names that rang out—bangkarei, ironwood, madiera, blackwood, teak, ebony. During the sail from what the crew called "the Continent," Abbey had listened with care and a little caution to descriptions of what Nantucket would be like, and she'd taken those descriptions with a pinch of salt, assuming the crew to be filled up with themselves and gathering their importance from the tales they told.

But she did feel it! She wasn't imagining it. The seaside had something that felt like a memory, even though she'd never been in a place like this—never been entirely surrounded by the sea, except on the boat that had brought her there. It was a kind of reverie that touches all humans, whether they're ocean-born or mountain-bound. There was something fundamentally familiar. She knew she wasn't imagining it.

And just as she was soaking up these scents and colors and sounds, there came a sound utterly out of place here. Several sounds, in fact.

Gyves. Their chains clattered against the wharf wood—a terrible metallic racket that must have sent a shiver down every spine on the wharf. And the smack of a leather lash against flesh. Human whimpers.

Abbey spun around, her shoulders drawing in instinctively as the sound rang home in her mind and she put together what she was hearing with what she could now see.

Down the wharf, not twenty steps down, was disgrace itself.

A lash jerked backward, then came down hard on the shoulder of a cowering Negro woman. She huddled in a group of Negroes, but raised her hands, wrists bared, to be placed in shackles by a pair of white men in travel-weary clothing. These men might have been trappers in Abbey's part of the country, but here, evidently, they were bounty hunters. Slavers.

She held her breath, struck silent with indignation. There were seven Negroes in the group. Their skin color ranged from toast to roan, and the woman who had just been shackled had face and hands as dark as brown could be without being black. Not the same family, then. But possibly . . . the same plantation. Or a roundup of escaped slaves from several plantations. Abbey had seen roundups before—collections of cattle from several ranches gathered together for a drive. After a few drives, she'd found it easy to see the subtle differences between stock from one ranch and stock from another. There were cattle with thick legs from the range in the foothills; cows with black calves from the ranch with the two Black Angus bulls; the longhorns from across the river; the shorthorns from this side; the herefords from the county line; the thin heifers and steers from the poorly grassed range down-county . . . and so on. The astute eye could tell at a glance which came from where.

Abbey stiffened. She cursed herself for seeing them as cattle. Yet she could tell they were a gathered bunch, and not all from one place, perhaps not even from the same state. There was obviously a plot of some kind being forestalled here, an arranged, calculated escape being foiled, not just a family that slipped away on the spur of a moment.

But in Nantucket?

In Memphis, perhaps, or Savannah, but on this dot of New England dirt thirty miles out at sea?

Like her, most of the people on the wharf had paused to watch the sad sight as one of the slavers brought the whip down again on a teenaged Negro boy. Abbey read disgrace in the boy's eyes, eyes that knew disgrace as a way of life, eyes that carried a dread of what the boy knew would be awaiting him when he was returned to his owner. Abbey's stomach tightened at the discovery of a pocket of hostility and shamefulness in this clean, well-organized port. Her image of Nantucket shattered.

Bridled like mules, the group of slaves were hobbled together by a single heavy chain running through their leg gyves, and they weren't even on their feet yet. They were still huddled together in a lump, and the slaver with the whip was lashing them with a chilling lack of emotion. He barely seemed interested in what he was doing, so much had it become a matter of course for him to reduce other human beings to toadeating.

She sensed a person move at her side, and Abbey registered the presence enough to make use of it. She reached out, caught a heavy woolen sleeve and gave it a hard tug. A face swung into view, and she turned to meet it.

A strong face—boyish in its way, but full of experience. A long nose set over full lips that parted slightly in puzzlement.

The man's monk-brown eyes locked on her immediately and didn't fall away. Beneath an uncombed thatch of blond hair, his face bore the unmistakable glower of surprise that she'd touched him at all, much less given him such a yank.

Abbey hesitated only an instant at the strike of those eyes, then said flatly, "You, sir. Won't you stop that behavior?" She swung a gesture down the wharf.

The blond man's glower deepened, and he snapped his gaze to the offensive scene. There was a flash in those eyes, a flash that Abbey recognized. It was a flash of pure indignation at what was happening on the wharf.

Abbey blinked, momentarily disarmed by the rage in the young man's rosy face. Amazement hit her. Out of the crowd she had somehow plucked a compatriot! There was sudden fellow feeling with the stranger in the moss green woolen sea coat. She felt he was seeing what she saw, the same way she saw it. He saw slavery as the corrosive insult it had become to the country as a whole, saw the brutality in it and the poor judgment of deciding freedom based on color. A few things had changed in the past hundred years since the more brutal 1740s, when slavers hunted the wilds of Africa to bring back chattel to work the plantations and farms. Oh, that still occurred, but it was much less necessary now, in times when the slave population had produced a few new generations and many working slaves were native-born Americans. As American as anyone else.

When she saw the flash of insult in the young man's eyes, Abbey knew this man understood. By his clothes and his hands she could tell he knew what it was to work an honest day for an honest wage. He was probably a sailor, perhaps a whaleman—strong, then. Perhaps now something would be done!

The blond man held his breath as the whipping continued and the young Negro male was brought to his knees. Then the sailor took a step—backward.

5

What? Abbey sucked in a gasp. As her mouth hung open, the sailor stepped past her and strode away. She spun on a heel and demanded, "You can stride away from that, mister?"

Straight shoulders pivoted, and the brown eyes were on her again. "Leave off, miss," he said.

"Coward," Abbey snapped back.

His weathered fists balled up, and his voice took on a steaming tolerance. "Look, miss, on a little island like this, we can't be messing in other folks' affairs."

Abbey raised her nose just enough for punctuation. "I hope I'm never assaulted within earshot of someone so polite."

As she turned away from him, enraged, she was forced to accept that what she had seen in his eyes must only have been the reflecting flash of her own anger. She left him in her smoke.

The hard clap of her boot soles announced her down the wharf.

"Say, pig! This isn't the auction block, I say!"

The two slavers looked up, faces filled with amazement, and they stopped in their tracks. The one with his arm looped backward poised in midstrike, about to draw the lash down again.

Before the man could collect his wits, Abbey had closed in on him, raised her beaded handbag like a buggywhip, and whacked him soundly across the shoulders with it. He stumbled a few steps away from her, staring at her in abject shock.

Abbey stood over him. "You want to score a hide with your lash, take it to supper and beat your steak. But this is free territory, and while you stand upon it you won't raise straps to a human being."

The two slavers glanced at each other as though they were both completely confused. Abbey read in their eyes that action would have been easy if she hadn't been a woman—a decided advantage for her at the moment.

The bearded whipsman licked his lips and said, "Miss, these be escaped slaves, rightfully owned by property owners in the South. I'm executing a lawful recapturin'. These ain't citizens under the law."

"Perhaps," she said, bracing her boots on the wharf timbers and giving no quarter, "but I've fanned many a campfire in the company of Negroes who were hard-working, hard-riding cowboys and did as good a job as could be done. We sipped coffee from the same pot and ate stew from the same ladle, and in my presence you'll treat them humanely."

The scruffy face beneath the beard crumpled in disapproval, and the man pushed past her in a dismissing way, then raised the lash again, aiming for the young Negro, who was once again cringing. Abbey felt her lips set. So much for putting on a polite Nantucket lady's facade.

She lunged for the slaver's whip and snatched it out of his hand just as he started his downstroke. The man stumbled, thrown off balance when he suddenly had no whip to swing with all those readied muscles. He staggered, recovered, and whirled around, enraged.

"Miss! Gimme back m'lash!"

Abbey stood her ground. "Not likely."

The man scowled and reached out to snatch his whip back, but Abbey sidled over and let the lash fly. The knotted ends of six leather straps hit the man's forearm. He yelped and recoiled, but rage rose on his face. "Lookit here!" he bellowed, and reached for her again. Again Abbey let the lash sing, harder this time.

"How does it feel?" she demanded. *Whack.* "Have you tested this lash for strength and balance?" *Whack.* "It's nicely weighted. It flows rather well!"

"Lady! Back off! Lady!"

She struck again and again, harder each time, driving him across the wharf into a stand of pilings. He stumbled backward, his arms raised about his head to fend off her lashings, and Abbey read in his eyes that he had no idea where a proper eastern lady got that kind of power in her arms. She snickered past her fury, remembering all the lassoing and branding and calving and riding she'd done in her life, and she continued to whack away. The other slaver offered no help at all, but only folded his arms and laughed. The people on Straight Wharf also paused to look, amazed at her thoroughly untoward behavior, too stunned to do anything about it. It was clear that the men among them really didn't know *what* to do about it. Instead, they kept watching and she kept whacking.

The slaver ducked behind a stack of shipping crates. When he reappeared he was carrying a thick piece of planking, brandishing it like a club. "Ma'am, I don't wanna hurt ya, I don't wanna hurt ya—"

Abbey ignored him and took another whack, but the slaver deflected the blow with his board and came after her. He fended off another blow and took a swipe at her knees, but she sidestepped it more nimbly than she thought she could after so many days of traveling.

"Better you strike me than them, you animal," she gasped at him as they exchanged blows. Her lash landed upon his shoulder, and his board on her thigh.

The blow knocked her down. Her skirt bunched up around her thighs to reveal her calf-high riding boots, and there went the last of her prim facade. Oh well, it was better gone, she realized. Even though the slaver was probably used to the delicate white belles of the Deep South, he had no problem readjusting his behavior to handle a harridan of the West. He thundered down upon her from the edge of the dock, his board raised high and ready to pummel her while she was down.

Just as he reached her though, Abbey saw that a blockade was thrown up before him—a mass of moss green wool and a shock of blond hair beneath a sailor's cap.

The two men came together like mountain rams, and Abbey wondered if she imagined the *thwack* as the slaver's leather coat and the wool sailing jacket slapped together. Before her, a pair of sturdy legs flexed, muscles pressing from within the dark trousers, hard boots scratching for a foothold on the dock.

"Mind your manners!" the sailor growled. "The lady's a guest on the island."

The grappling abated when the lash rang against both men's legs. The men spun toward Abbey, shock patterning each face. Before them, she was getting to her feet. An instant later, she swung the lash again, and swiped both men with one blow. If the slaver was angry about it, the handsome young sailor was thoroughly dumbfounded. His brown eyes widened and his arms came up to defend himself.

"I need no help from you, coward," Abbey said with a wild lilt in her voice. She advanced on the slaver again, and when the blond sailor stepped between them, she whacked him again without a second's pause. "You stand aside. I can handle hogs by myself."

"Lady!" He took one more blow, then something in his face said he'd had enough. His hand caught hers in midswipe and his other arm went around her. He pulled her against him, waist to waist, keeping her off balance, and somehow tolerated an unexpected blow from the beaded handbag as it landed across his cheek. The broad wooden buttons of his double-breasted sea coat strained as she twisted, but he kept his grip tight.

Abbey struggled, but it had been a long, *long* time since she'd felt the firm body of a young, strong man moving against hers. The sensation caught her by surprise, and it disarmed her. The lash clattered to the dock. Just as she was caught in his arms, she was caught in his eyes.

He glared at her, strapped to her with a bond of mutual fury, and she once again saw that poignant flash she'd recognized before. As those eyes gripped her, her struggling flagged for an instant. He took that instant to breathe a stern whisper.

"*Stop it!*" he said through gritted teeth.

His order shook her out of her surprise and gave her back the rage she'd lost for that one mysterious moment. She leaned back against his forearm and swatted him again with the handbag. "No!" Her voice bubbled with defiance.

Then another hand closed around her wrist, and there was another face beside her. Someone was wedging her away from the young sailor, squeezing between them as a pry bar gets between a rivet and its wood.

"Madam! Madam, *please!*"

The voice belonged to a burly, square-faced, red-haired, stoic, proud, and dangerously handsome man. Older by perhaps a decade than the engaging young sailor, the newcomer wore the clothes of a man of business—a stiff blue suit and waistcoat. "Madam, if you will—"

Abbey let him press her away from the young sailor, in spite of an unexpected twinge of regret at losing that embrace. Across the dock, the slaver stumbled to his feet and wiped his mouth with the back of his hand.

The burly newcomer frowned at her, then glanced at the sailor. He brandished a walking stick with a gleaming, ornate goose-head handle made of ivory and sparkling with diamond-shaped inlaid wood. "Mind yourself," he told the sailor. "We don't manhandle ladies on Nantucket, and you know it."

"I do know. Tell me when you find a lady," the sailor responded with just a lick of defiance—or was it warning? "Take care of her. She's rowing with one oar, I think."

"And no water!" the slaver added from behind.

The blond man nailed him in the shoulder with a long forefinger. "*You* shut your hatch."

"That's enough!" The big man towered over both of them, under the curious eyes of a crowd on the wharf that had somehow grown quite large.

Abbey glanced around quickly; she would have given away her discomfort by actually turning and looking. Where had all these people come from? She hadn't really done anything. . . . What were they all staring at?

"Back to your business," the big man said to the slaver. "And act in a more civilized manner. The jail is ready for your charges. Get moving." He turned to the sailor again. "And you—you stay away from here from now on."

The two men's eyes locked for an instant in mutual challenge, and for a moment Abbey thought there might be yet another fight for the crowd to gawk at. A twinge of disappointment struck her when the sailor relaxed, nodded, and turned on his heel without affording her even a glance. In a moment he had disappeared into the crowd.

"All of you!" the big man called, addressing the island folk. "Back to your own affairs."

The ladies in the crowd buzzed with gossip and the gentlemen and seafarers tipped their hats, but the crowd began to dissipate almost immediately at the man's command.

Then, he turned to her, disapproval cutting brackets beside his red moustache.

Abbey straightened her jacket, cleared her throat, smiled sweetly, and extended her hand. "Hello," she said, trying to make her voice sound musical. "My name is Abbey Sutton."

The man's eyes widened, and his lips disappeared beneath a heavy auburn moustache as he frowned at her. "You . . . are Miss Sutton? *You* are?"

Abbey realized what she'd done. "Oh," she said. "You must be Magistrate Nash."

He uttered a little huff, and Abbey got a sharp impression of herself being soundly stuffed on the next boat back to Boston. Then he said, "I am Dominic Nash, yes. I'm . . . pleased to meet you finally, Miss Sutton."

Abbey tilted her head. "*Mrs.* Sutton, sir. The judge is dead, not forgotten."

His ruddy face flushed. "Of course. Pardon me about that, Mrs. Sutton."

He took her arm, partially to escort her to the carriage that waited at the end of the dock, and partially—she was sure—to keep her from pursuing the slavers as they herded their charges, iron hobbles clacking, down the wharf in the other direction.

"Your actions were hopeless, Mrs. Sutton," Dominic Nash told her. "Some things are facts of life in this day and age."

Abbey brushed back a lock of her long tawny hair that had fallen from the oblong knot at the back of her head. "You don't find such hostility distasteful on this pleasant wharf, Mr. Nash?"

"I do," he said.

"The laws should be changed, I think."

"But on Nantucket we cannot afford to change them," he told her with a tone both placating and stern. "We depend on the Continent for far too much, and we are too far out at sea to take chances."

"Why? Nantucket is part of the United States."

"Of course."

"I assure you, sir, my ranch was much farther away from the law, and we had no trouble obeying it. You might be thirty miles from the mainland here, but in Wyoming, thirty miles is often a single ranch."

"As magistrate of the island, I concern myself only with keeping the peace. That means accepting laws of the Continent as laws of the island. We have many more people coming and going from this port than you ever did from your ranch."

Abbey shrugged lightly. "That's true," she admitted.

"My children are awaiting your arrival at the house," Nash told her, moving her quite deliberately through the crowd toward the carriage. "They're excited about the prospect of having a governess. They've been quite without guidance since the death of my wife twenty-five months ago."

Abbey looked at him as they strode down the dock. His water-blue eyes were gazing outward toward the town, not looking at her. She was suddenly warmed by a man who still counted his wife's death in months.

"And I'm happy to have found a reasonable manner of repaying my husband's debts to you, Mr. Nash," Abbey said.

"The judge was a good man, Mrs. Sutton. I think, however, he must have been a bad rancher."

"But a very generous neighbor," Abbey added. "He could never turn down the local Indians who needed food for their children. Instead of money, our ranch house was overflowing with blankets, beads, pipes, feathers—beautiful, but worthless. I suppose that was what you might call his undoing."

"I would," the big gentleman said with a nod that told her he meant it. "The carriage—" He gestured, and she stepped past him and climbed aboard the small, delicate-looking carriage without thinking until afterward that she should have let him help her aboard. As she settled into the seat, he gave her a quizzical look—one that showed the same disapproval as before—and climbed aboard to sit beside her and take up the reins.

As he arranged the leather straps in his hand, evidently particular about how they fit in his palms, Abbey stole one last look at Straight Wharf.

And she did see what she hoped to see—the blond sailor moving among the people. Did she imagine it? Was he glancing her way too? Had he turned away just as she spied him? Imagination?

He was watching me, she thought. *I know he was. I'm sure of it.*

She placed her hand on Nash's sleeve and cocked her head toward the wharf. "Mr. Nash, who is that man?"

Nash made a great show of turning and looking at the man she referred to, as though he didn't already know. He seemed to be trying to dismiss the fellow from his memory—or get *her* to dismiss him. Then he turned back.

"Since you'll be in my employ and residing in my home," he said firmly, "I prefer you not associate with that man in any way."

The reins snapped. The horse flinched and stepped out onto the cobblestones.

Chapter Two

By THE TIME the carriage turned down Ash Street toward the magistrate's home, the sky over Nantucket had changed to an unerring beryl blue over the cobalt sea. The sounds of snapping halyards and creaking timbers had been left behind at the wharf, but the stiff winds and crisp ocean air followed the carriage through town.

Nantucket. A simple workaday settlement of weathered faces and thick-willed people who spent days by the hundreds waiting for sons and brothers and husbands to return from sea voyages. A place of little imagination, but great constitution. A place where folk worked hard and somehow thrived against nature's back jaw—the harsh, unpredictable northeastern bite of wind, sea, rain, and winter chill, not to mention summer heat. Like the pioneers who went west and were determined to survive, these people's parents and grandparents had ventured farther east than any other place, so far east that the ocean surrounded them. No less a frontier than any valley or range in Wyoming, this little island had been whipped into shape and made functional by those who settled it and meant to keep it. A good place. Abbey's kind of place. She could deal with folk who knew what they wanted.

Whalemen. Whalemen's wives. Whalemen's children. That was Nantucket. It was a place where children knew their fathers more by telling than seeing, a place where whalemen came home to find their infants suddenly toddlers, their toddlers suddenly schoolgoers, and their wives older by years than the last time they had bedded together. A place where the men coming down the whaleship's planks were etched in leathered skin and dampened spirits, no longer the soft-skinned boys who'd set out to sea to sight the elusive whale spout and ride the Nantucket sleigh behind a harpooned giant.

There was prosperity here, much more than Abbey expected. Dominic Nash took her through town slowly, the long way, to let her see the place where she would be living. It was a promising little place, this island, this town. He took the time to introduce her to the streets—Main to Federal Street, Broad Street to North Water Street to Ash Street—and Abbey was surprised by the strikingly civilized Quaker neatness of the town. Tight, too. Everything was very close together. Houses and stores were all very near each other. And quite a variety, too. Businesses of every sort, much more diverse than she had ever seen in a western town—not that she had been to so many towns. But here it seemed that everything a person could want was right within reach: optician, watchmaker, barber shop, auction house, grocer—several markets, in fact, and several tailors—boot and shoemaker, glazier, post office, boarding-houses and inns, an insurance company, cooper, block shop, and a particularly pretty bank. Nantucket Pacific Bank, with its Federal architecture—a style of building Abbey could see she'd better get used to—was decorated with big arching windows and Gothic iron railings on its rectangular vestibule, railings that swept out in graceful curves.

The people she saw on the streets of Nantucket seemed to have a cosmopolitan lacing over their Quaker foundation. While many of the buildings and houses were blocky, tall, and flat-faced clapboards with many plain rectangular windows, some of the bigger houses had pillars on their porches, parapeted cupolas, stone fences, and elaborate cornices to decorate them. Some of the stores had shelters over the sidewalks—definitely a sign of civilization, Abbey noted as the carriage bumped along over the cobblestone streets.

"There's much more here than I expected," she mentioned to the magistrate, careful of her tone. She wanted to appear impressed, but not sound like a bumpkin. Carefully she read the signs on the shops as Nash snapped the horse into a steady pace. "I'll have to remember all this. Whittemore Furs . . . Simon Parkhurst Dry Goods . . . Gardener and Hallet Dry Goods, Easton and Sanford Watchmakers and Jewelers . . . Thomas Coleman Sail Loft—well, I suppose I shouldn't be too surprised to see a sail loft, should I, Mr. Nash?"

"Not at all, Mrs. Sutton. That is Nantucket's stock in trade, after all—good morning, Mrs. Nichols, Mrs. Bates . . ."

Abbey looked in time to see two women leading several children along the street as they waved back at the magistrate. She noted that all the children waved also. Charming!

Nash went on after tipping his hat to the women. "Once upon a time, Nantucket's biggest industry was sheep and sheepshearing. But I think we've found our destiny in the shipping business. We are quite an amalgam of sensibilities here, you'll find. Nantucket sits on the edge of the outside world. All ships come home to Nantucket."

A broad statement, Abbey thought, as she caught sight of a huge building at the corner of Federal and Pearl streets. Vast! It had Greek columns all the way to the sky, and pointed stained-glass windows. "Is that a church? Grief, it's big!"

"Pardon? Oh, no, that's no longer a church. That's the Atheneum. It's now a museum and meeting place for the arts. We have readings there and showings and various gatherings. It was deeded to the town by Charles Coffin and David Joy because they wanted to promote literature, the arts, and the sciences. A grand gift, all in all."

"Well, I should say!" Abbey agreed, craning her neck as the carriage toddled past the massive structure. "My! I should like to go in there some time."

"You would be most welcome to do so."

"Mr. Nash?"

"Yes, Mrs. Sutton?"

"Why are there porches on top of some of these houses?"

"Hmmm? Oh, of course. Those are roofwalks, Mrs. Sutton," he explained, looking up at a rectangular porch with a little railed fence right on the tip-top of a house they were passing. "From there you can see the ocean horizon. When a ship is expected—and I daresay sometimes when they're not—wives like to stride about up there and watch the horizon for the appearance of a masthead."

Abbey smiled and squinted up at the roofwalk. "In Wyoming Territory, all we have to do is stand outside our front doors and we can see everything from here to heaven and back."

"You must tell my children all about it, Mrs. Sutton."

"I certainly shall, Mr. Nash."

She settled back on the leather carriage seat and watched the town go by. All at once she sat up straight again and said, "Now that *must* be a church!" She pointed accusingly at a big spired belfry on a stone building with tall Gothic windows and pinnacles on the buttresses.

Nash chuckled at her insistence. "Yes, that's Trinity Church."

"And where are we now?"

"Broad Street."

Abbey sat back again and sighed, shaking her head at herself. "Mr. Nash, I think I'll buzz in the head before I learn all these streets and all these buildings. Where I come from, there's just one road, and it leads to everywhere else. And do you actually know all these people you've been greeting as we ride?"

"I know every person we've seen so far, Mrs. Sutton," Nash said, turning to look at her for the first time since they had left the wharf. Crinkles appeared around his blue eyes as he grinned with sheltered pride. "That is the nature of this island."

Abbey pressed her lips together. "There weren't this many people in my whole county, Mr. Nash," she said finally.

"You, too, will know them soon enough. At the moment, I'm only concerned with your being acquainted with my children—good day, Captain Fields! How did your voyage go?" he called spontaneously to a surly-looking bearded seaman.

"We took six right whales out of a single pod at Christmas, Mr. Nash," the seaman called back, "and glad I am to be out of those Greenland waters. It was a profitable voyage, but a cold one."

"Welcome back, Captain," Nash said as they rode by.

Prosperity was here, Abbey decided, but a hardworking prosperity. Evidently, while the whaleman's life was one of long and arduous voyages, each man would find profit in his trade if he could but find and take a few whales.

"Seems a bit brutal, Mr. Nash," Abbey mentioned as the carriage turned down Ash Street. "Thrusting a barbed steel rod into a whale's back."

"Does it?" he asked, squinting as the sun cleared the clouds. "If a whale ship is very lucky, it might sight a pod once a month or once in two months, and it might take one whale from each pod. They go out in little boats and face the giant man-to-beast, deep inside swells as high as these buildings. The harpoons are flung by hand, if and when the beast surfaces near enough to the whaleboat. It takes—" He paused to tip his hat politely at three townswomen, who nodded a greeting back to him, eyeing Abbey curiously. "It takes many harpoons to do a whale in, and right glad I am that it's not me in the water with such a monster so close by. Mind you," he added, unintentionally nudging her shoulder as he leaned to make his point, "that's if they're lucky. I've known whale ships to go out for three years and come back with the oil and bone of no more than five whales. Three whole years, I say. The sea is a slim hunting ground, cold and wide and unforgiving. Many men never come home."

"My," she said. "The whales' bones are used, too?"

"Oh, indeed. There's hardly a part of the beast we don't put to use. But the odds are with the whales, Mrs. Sutton."

"I suppose," she murmured, grasping the edge of the seat as the carriage bumbled over the hoof-sized rocks that paved the street beneath them. "These rocks make a bad road, don't they?"

"Cobblestones," he said. "Ballast."

"I beg your pardon?"

Nash swept his hand, taking in the whole street. "Every stone you see served as ballast in a ship. Once here, the ballast is removed and replaced with whale products for the Continent."

"Ah . . . very practical."

Nash smiled, and his crusty image dissolved. "Yes, we're practical on Nantucket."

Practicality, though, didn't fully describe the magistrate's home. Yes, everything was useful, Abbey noted as Dominic Nash opened the ostentatious mahoghany door for her and motioned her into a charming brick Victorian home wedged tightly between cedar houses. Whitewashed latticework across the window glass provided, yes, practical decoration on the squarish Quaker architecture. As she had seen, the town was primarily made up of cedar houses and dock buildings, the cedar now turned mouse-colored by years of battering by northeastern weather. It made a strange beauty, this dominance of gray, especially where the doors and window panes were painted and the little gardens came into bloom, as they were now in late spring. There were roses everywhere—rambling roses, white, red, pink, climbing over trellises and up wooden poles, charming and surprising against the gray cedar.

But Abbey's mind went back to the practicality—where was it? Where was the workaday feeling of rough little Nantucket? It dissolved the moment Abbey stepped inside the magistrate's house. She found her boots incongruous against a lovely tufted rug with a colorful picture of a castle, something like drawings she'd seen of Europe. And that was only the beginning. There was nothing here like the bold buffalo-checked couch and tatter-backed chairs of her ranch house. Nothing like the homestead simplicity of the West, even if that simplicity had gathered decoration over the years. Spread neatly on these dark wooden floors were floorcloths, including a particularly beautiful one with crew-eled edges that led to the "good room"—a place where company was received. As the magistrate closed the door and fastidiously arranged his walking stick in a brass holder near the door, Abbey peeked into that parlor.

She clamped her lips against a gasp. If not a place of splendor, this was at least a place of worldliness. The first thing that caught her eye was a dollhouse, made with great detail in an exact miniature of the magistrate's home. Three small tavern tables, polished to a gloss, reflected a black velvet couch and two heart-backed blue chairs with broad madeira arms. Elaborate lamps sat on every table, and a wall-long brick fireplace offered a heavy warmth. Through an archway she caught a glimpse of an eight-board cabinet that held a collection of New England redware—gleaming honeypots, mugs, bowls, and cups.

Abbey touched her finger to her lip, holding in a giggle as she thought of her ranch house again. As she gazed, she remembered her own kitchen with its beehive oven and the big wooden preparing table, the hand-thrown stoneware she'd used to serve dinner. Why, this house even had an aroma! What was it—ginger-glazed ham, yes . . . and warm marmalade—

As her mouth watered she remembered, rather fondly, the vaqueros who had guarded her husband's cattle, Mexican cowboys so dedicated that they would go without food for days rather than slaughter even one of their employer's stock. And when they did eat, it would never be ham and marmalade, but rather hardtack and corn meal, red bean pie and sourdough bread.

"Mrs. Sutton, wait here, if you will," Nash said, drawing her back into the whitewashed foyer. He plucked up a tiny brass bell and rang it.

Abbey grinned. Such a silly wee sound! Hardly a birdcall.

But it was enough. Three whirlwinds appeared at the top of the polished stairs and pounded their way down. When the smoke cleared, there were three round faces looking sternly up at Abbey. Three faces, carrot-topped and strikingly alike. The two eldest—both boys of about nine years old—had barely stopped moving when Abbey discerned they were twins, identical down to their dimples.

"Mrs. Sutton, my children," the magistrate said. Abbey couldn't quite tell if he said it with pride or with reluctance. He placed one hand on the shoulder of the nearest boy. "This is Adam. There is David, and down there, hiding, is—"

A smallish girl of about five stepped forward boldly and announced, "I'm Luella. I'm the one that's not twins."

"She can *see* that," David complained.

Abbey bent down to look the little girl straight in her blue eyes. "You mean there's only one of you?"

"Only one."

"That makes you a rare diamond."

"Oooooh!" Luella howled. "I'm the diamond! Papa, I'm a diamond!"

The magistrate nodded patiently, but without a smile.

"Are you going to be our nanny?" Adam demanded. "Because we like to fish and you have to know how."

"And we climb trees."

"And nobody can tell us apart. Just try."

"What do you think of us?"

Abbey laughed at the last question—David's, if she'd attached the right name to the right boy. "What do I think of you? I think you're precocious."

"Watch this," Adam yelped, and as if they were well practiced both boys suddenly disappeared into the good room, out of sight. They scuffled for a moment, then reappeared, side by side.

"Which is which?" they demanded in a chorus.

"Oh, simple," Abbey said. "You're Adam, and you're David."

"Lucky guess!"

"Try it again."

Once again they disappeared, and once again scuffled. Dominic Nash folded his arms and frowned.

The boys reappeared a second time and made the same demand.

"I told you it was simple," Abbey said and pointed at each one. "David . . . Adam."

The twins' mouths fell open.

"That's amazing," Nash said, narrowing his own striking blue eyes. "Can you actually tell them apart?"

"They seem quite different to me," Abbey said, playing it up a bit for two boys who probably had never had the privilege of being different.

"Excellent! Perhaps you'll be able to avoid their—"

"Papa!" Adam whined.

"—trickery," the magistrate finished sternly. "Children, this is Mrs. Sutton. She is in charge of you. Never forget it, lest you answer to me."

"Yes, Papa," the boys chimed.

"—Papa." Luella's little voice came in like an echo, just a beat behind her brothers.

"Up to your rooms," Nash said immediately, barely waiting for the children's answer. "Mrs. Sutton and I have business to attend to."

"About us?"

"Of course about you. What did I just say? Your rooms, now."

The children took one more long, expert glance at Abbey, then hammered up the polished staircase—racing, of course.

"Mrs. Sutton, this way, please." He gestured her into the good room and onto one of the plush velvet chairs. When she was settled, he stood over her for a moment—could it be indecision? she wondered—then said, "About your actions on Straight Wharf—"

"Yes, Mr. Nash. I apologize." She heard herself say it, and knew perfectly well that although she was apologizing, her tone said she wasn't sorry.

He knew that, too. She saw it in his eyes.

"Regardless," he began again. "I prefer you to understand. We don't care for slavery, of course. But we must keep the peace with the southern states and the federal government. Once runaways are discovered, there's no alternative but to expedite their return to the South. If Nantucket doesn't cooperate, there'll be pressure to search and forestall ships, which would slow the whaling trade to a crawl. It's federal law, Mrs. Sutton. An island so far at sea must show its willingness to work within the law if it hopes to be protected by it. I am the magistrate of this island, after all. I must represent lawfulness at its height."

Abbey nodded, this time genuinely sorry for embarrassing him on the wharf. "I understand, Mr. Nash. It was just the whipping for no reason that disturbed me."

"The lashing was uncalled for," he admitted. "And I plan to speak to the slaver myself. However, as the primary visible law on this island, I must ask for a certain decorous behavior from members of my household. You must curb your . . . Bohemian ways."

Abbey let her lip curl in question. "Bohemian ways?"

"You can't beat up men in public."

"Oh. Those ways."

He sighed with relief. "Yes. Meanwhile, we must define your duties."

As he lowered into the other chair, his glossy red hair and ruddy complexion took on a glow from a shaft of sunlight that struck his face. He drew a pair of spectacles from his waistcoat and arranged them on his face, then drew out a folded piece of paper that Abbey recognized as the letter she'd sent to him three months ago.

"My duties?" she asked, trying to recapture the prim attitude she'd so thoroughly tossed away on the wharf.

His blue eyes flicked up over the spectacles to catch her. "Of course. Why do you ask it that way?"

"I thought I knew my duties. Take care of the children."

The hand holding the letter fell to rest on his knee. "And you think this is a simple thing? Have you ever taken care of children before?"

She fidgeted, then broke into a broad smile and lightly claimed, "Well, I've taken care of cattle, sheep, and cowboys. Can it be very different?"

But her bunkhouse humor clattered to the floor under Nash's cold glare.

Abbey dropped her grin and shrugged openly. "Truly, Mr. Nash, can there be? I'll see that they're cleaned and fed—"

"And properly dressed and schooled and exercised and taught good manners and—"

"Mr. Nash, they're children, not parade horses."

"Madam, you are the one who compared them to animals," he pointed out without losing a breath.

"I stand corrected," she admitted.

"And there will come a time when Luella will have to be taught the . . . facts about womanhood."

"Mr. Nash, she's five years old!"

"She's nearly six, Mrs. Sutton."

"Oh, *six*, I see . . ."

"Mrs. Sutton . . ." Nash put the letter down on a nearby table and took his spectacles off, holding them thoughtfully for several seconds. He gazed down at them and didn't look up as he spoke. "Mrs. Sutton, I am a man. I don't know these things. I don't know when . . . women . . . I don't know when they should be taught . . . these things. If I had only Adam and David to raise," he said, and now he did look up, "I may never have considered the prospect of hiring a governess. My housekeeper could easily handle the getting up and getting dressed and getting to school and getting home. But your offer to come here in my service . . . I confess relieved me greatly. Not only can you suffuse the judge's debts to me about the ranch loan, but you will fill a great emptiness in this home."

Abbey watched him, her heart warm with a sudden understanding of Dominic Nash. He couldn't say it, she knew—indeed he was having difficulty even saying this much—yet she saw him forcing himself to be open with her from the beginning, and she felt the endearing nature of that effort.

He stood up slowly, disturbed by his own words, and went to stare out over the curving cobblestone street and the neat little houses. His back was to her now.

"Since Mrs. Nash passed away, there has been a terrible gouge in our lives here—mine, my children's . . . we need a woman about the house who can make decisions and listen to the troubles of the boys and little Luella. Even boys need a woman nearby. They need to see how a woman walks and thinks and feels and speaks. There are things a woman . . . knows."

Suddenly he stiffened, as though hearing himself say things he had never meant to say, things that embarrassed him, damaged his image.

Abbey sat quietly. Something had told her not to interrupt him, and she followed that instinct. Now, though, as she saw and sensed his embarrassment, she wished she'd spoken up—anything at all to make him feel better, to cut off the thread of guilt she heard. Somehow he felt responsible for his wife's death, or at least responsible for not providing his children with a mother. Yes—that was it. The last part—he couldn't bring himself to be with another woman, and he felt guilty about it.

"Yes, well . . ." Nash brought himself back from a sad reverie. "I want you to go shopping. Purchase yourself an appropriate wardrobe and charge it to my household account. I'm not afraid of color, but would prefer that you avoid the gaudy. Do this as soon as you're rested. Stand by. I'll summon Mrs. Goodes."

He escaped through the house. Unlike the longish ranch houses of Wyoming Territory, this house was piled on top of itself and Abbey could hear every footfall. She could easily tell where Nash was, how many rooms away, and knew that he was bringing another person with him as she heard him return. Sure enough, he reappeared with a dark-haired woman about thirty-five years old, rather petite and plain-faced. Her hair was parted in the middle and pulled severely back into a tight bun, but her eyes were dancing with welcome.

"Mrs. Sutton, may I present Mrs. Cordelia Goodes, our housekeeper and cook."

Cordelia Goodes rubbed her palms on her apron, then stepped forward and offered a hand to Abbey somewhat awkwardly. "Mrs. Sutton, good day."

"Mrs. Goodes, my pleasure."

Nash shifted uneasily. "I have business at the town hall. Mrs.

Goodes, if you would please see Mrs. Sutton to her room and see that she's settled—"

"Yes, sir, I'll do that smartly."

"And after so long a journey she'd probably be glad of a helping of tea and johnnycake."

"I'll do that, too, sir, yes, I will."

"Very well." He couldn't help giving a last glance at Abbey, and turned it into a nod of farewell. He then crossed the parlor, stiff-lipped, snatched his walking stick from the holder in the foyer, and wrenched the door open. The door slammed, and he was gone.

Cordelia Goodes sighed. "The mistress came up, did she?"

Abbey tipped her head. "Did you know Mrs. Nash?"

"Sure did not. I came here three months ago, is all. The lady died a while back. Wish I had known her, the way he acts about her. Your room's upstairs, missus."

"Please, call me Abbey."

"I'm Cordelia. It's a mouthful, but my mama liked it," the house-keeper added as she grasped one of Abbey's travel cases and hauled it up the stairs, gesturing Abbey to follow.

The house's tight upstairs corridor was long, but a loomed carpet runner muffled their steps.

"This is yours," Cordelia said, wrestling Abbey's travel case through a narrow doorway.

Abbey stepped in, and fell in love.

A massive canopied bed, built of dark Jacobean beveled wood, was the first thing she saw. Chunky and dark, it was nothing like the pine pencil-post bed she'd shared with her husband in Wyoming. This bed was draped with a wispy lace canopy and covered with a fat quilted coverlet. Nearby were a pair of comb-backed Windsor chairs and one lovely old rocker, sitting in the same shaft of sunlight that had fallen on Dominic Nash when he needed it most.

Opposite the bed, near an open window, was a big crawly dresser of what looked like mahogany.

"It's lovely! Oh . . . *this* is magnificent," she said, approaching a gently sloped fainting couch tucked against the wall, where she hadn't seen it right away. It was somewhat worn, made of soft-grained leather in a beautiful shade of burgundy, and the stuffing seemed to have shifted a little. But it still looked very comfortable. Its high, sloping, wing-shaped back looked inviting.

Cordelia hoisted the travel bag onto the top of a walnut dresser, careful not to bump a very large and ornate beveled mirror. "Don't touch the recamier," she said.

Abbey glanced at her. Since Cordelia was nodding toward the fainting couch, Abbey figured that was what the funny word meant. "This?" she asked. "Why?"

"It belonged to the wife. He's particular about it. That's why it's in here instead of in the master's room. If you want to unpack, I'll see about the tea and cake."

"Yes, I do. Thank you. Oh, Mrs. Goodes—"

"Cordelia."

"Cordelia . . . may I ask a question?"

The housekeeper clasped her hands and appeared accommodating. "Go right ahead."

Now came Abbey's turn to be uneasy. Her spine tingled, recalling a certain touch. She turned toward the thick-silled window and gazed out, down over the street. From here she could see a corner of the wharf through the nearby trees. She saw—or maybe imagined?—the people milling around there, the sailors and their wives and families gathered for hellos or good-byes, the business dealings, the . . . yes, everything.

"There was a gentleman I saw at the docks. He made me curious. I wonder if you know who he is."

From behind her, Cordelia said, "Describe him."

Those two simple words opened a floodgate of impressions in Abbey's mind. She remembered not only his appearance now, but everything about him. The strength in his arms, the flash in his eyes, the faint aroma clinging to his sea coat—

"He was a little taller than Mr. Nash, but less husky. He wore a sailor's wool jacket, dark green, and plain britches, and—"

"His face. His hair."

"His hair was . . . blond."

"Like yours?"

"Mine? Oh, no, mine's almost brown. His was very light. Like wheat. Like sunshine on the sand."

"Hmmm . . . that's light, I'll agree."

26

Abbey felt the sun work its warmth on her face through the delicate lace curtain, drawing her into the memory until she thought she would fall completely in. "His face . . . it was pale around the eyes . . . rather startling brown eyes. Eyes like pools of molasses. You could fall into them and be caught. His cheeks had a peach color about them that turned flowery when he got angry at me. Flowers—yes! He smelled of wildflowers. But that's impossible. I'm sure he was a sailing man. His clothes, his arms, his hands . . ." Her voice trailed off. She looked down at her own hands, saw her stubby nails and roughened knuckles, and felt once again the iron pressure of his arm around her and the hardness of his body against hers.

A sudden flush of self-consciousness overcame her then, and she turned. Sure enough, Cordelia was staring at her.

"You took some note of him, I reckon," Cordelia said, making Abbey blush.

God! How long had it been since she'd blushed?

Cordelia's lips curled into a smirk. "That would be Jacob Ross. And he's not a sailor."

Abbey had to clear her throat. "No?"

"No. He keeps the lighthouse at Great Point. He's part owner of a pub in town as well. His two cousins run it. He's been on the island but a year now. Not much for keeping company. Mighty unusual that you saw him. He has no reason to be on the wharf." She busied herself fluffing the pillow on the bed that would be Abbey's from now on, then straightened up and headed for the door. "Come down when you're ready for cake. I'll set about brewing some tea. Welcome, again."

"Thank you," Abbey said, but the housekeeper was already down the hall.

Jacob Ross . . . Jacob Ross . . .

Abbey let Cordelia Goodes slip out of her mind almost immediately, once again turning to the window and searching out a glimpse of the wharf. Over the housetops she saw the mastheads of half a hundred ships, Nantucket's links to the outside world. Those were the harbingers of survival for the island settlement, the angels whose spread wings carried Nantucket's whale products to a waiting world, and made for a lonely life for whaling men and the women they left behind. How magical the reunions must be, she thought, when the ships return after so long.

Ships. Daily they skimmed the ocean surface that hung like a ceiling over the remains of their forebears, the countless sunken vessels whose bones lay on the sea floor. None rested far from the mouth of the angry ocean that had swallowed them, sails and all, crew and all, into the unmatched blackness. Today ships laced the seas over that silent fleet, hoping never to join it, never quite forgetting. Yet, too much of remembering losses only makes martyrs, she reminded herself vowing not to be swallowed up by the past.

A light sea wind carried the sounds of the wharf through the treetops and into her window. Voices calling, timbers creaking, carriage wheels rolling, horses clopping. She smelled the fresh aromatic breeze coming in the open window, and suddenly wished she were still on the wharf.

Jacob Ross . . .

For many long minutes her travel bag remained on the top of the dresser, longing to be unpacked, but she did nothing about it. Even the scent of spiced tea drifting up from the kitchen did nothing to shake her from her thoughts and imaginings. She continued gazing out the window, looking over little Nantucket.

And she knew he was out there.

Nantucket was a welcoming place, Abbey discovered as she strode through town. Several times she took wrong turns on the little streets, and folk were anxious to set her on the right track to the shops where she might buy a dress or two and some hats, and certainly some warm stockings for the chilly New England nights. This town was many things, she was finding out, but poverty had nothing to do with any of them. In fact, it was the opposite. Shop windows were neatly decorated with European lace and ruffled curtains, porches had railings of exotic woods from faraway places or wrought iron in styles she'd never seen before. In fact—yes, that was it—everything on Nantucket smacked of foreign places. Even with the domestic artifacts she'd seen, like the endless array of items made of whalebone and whale tooth ivory, there was a sense of distance—a feeling of connection with cultures very far away from this small island.

As a matter of fact, there seemed to be nothing that couldn't be made out of ivory. Dominic Nash's ivory walking stick, she now discovered, was only the beginning. Just on this one little walk through town she'd already seen laundry hung with whalebone clothespins, men smoking whalebone pipes, a ladle with a whalebone handle, children with whalebone buttons on their jackets, whalebone yarn spools, whalebone sewing boxes and doll's beds in a store window, sitting beside whalebone pickwicks, and whalebone knitting needles beside a whalebone rolling pin.

She paused at one of those shop windows and found herself gazing down at more of this stuff. Ivory mortars and pestles, pie cutters, jagging wheels, and corset stays loaded this particular shop window. The corset stays, in fact, were virtual works of art. Not only were they shaped perfectly and even scalloped sometimes along the edges, but there were elaborate rural scenes, exotic birds, hearts, stars, spirals, and every other manner of design carved into them and colored with ink. The detail was amazing. Even the Indians of her home prairies hadn't been so consumed with perfection.

She sighed.

Poor sailors. How lonely they must be on the high seas. She could tell that they were thinking of home, of the women and children they longed for just by looking at the things they had made. Every kind of household thing and every kind of toy, all made with painful detail from the bones of dead whales. Practical things for the house and kitchen, yes, but not made with practicality in mind. These were artwork more than tools and toys. And the hours upon hours it must have taken to make even one of these things. . . . What kind of place had she come to live in?

She shook her head briefly, realizing she had lapsed from looking into blank staring, and that her thoughts had taken over. With a deep breath she cleared her head. As she regained control of herself and prepared to stride away, a reflection in the window suddenly held her fast where she stood.

Across the street—she saw clearly in the sunlit glass—was an oval sign painted with stark red, blue, and black paint and sharp lettering. The Brotherhood. Food, Bed, and Grog. Good Company.

Was that it?

She whirled around, now staring fully at the sign and the simple slat building with its single door. Was that the pub?

Perhaps after she was settled, she would just have a look inside there. Then again . . . how were such things viewed here? In Wyoming, she came and went as she pleased, wherever she pleased. What were the mores here? Would her new neighbors frown and glower if she were to step inside? And if *he* was there, what excuse would she give?

Jacob Ross.

The name was beginning to echo within in her mind, take over her thoughts. Every time her memory spoke it she remembered his eyes glaring down into hers, and the firm grip of a man she had called a coward.

"You're no coward," she muttered, remembering his eyes and the flash she'd seen in them. "There was something else holding you back . . ."

She pressed her lips together and turned down the street again, resisting the urge to poke her head inside that pub.

Two doors down from the shop with the ivory trinkets in the window was the Geary Hat Store. Several of the ladies she'd asked had pointed her straight here, and here she was, with her hand about to touch the doorknob—

Crash!

She jumped back from the door as it clattered furiously. There was a terrible shriek from inside, and the glass in the door rattled. *Bam! Scrrrrape!*

And a voice now—

"Bloody thievin' flea-rode 'airy brute! Come back 'ere so's I can bash yer! Flamin' vile woodchuck! God 'ad 'is 'ead on wrong whenee made yer kind, wicked rat!"

Bam!

Abbey stared at the doorknob. Stay out, she thought. Probably safer. But then she'd never know what was going on. What if someone was being assaulted?

Safety be damned. She twisted the knob and shoved her way in, past what appeared to be a toppled dress rack. The door was pressed shut behind her by the rack, but that was her last concern. Something was actually *climbing* her!

She let out a yelp of surprise, and a broom came down on her head.

"Don't move! I'll ruddy get the black-hearted pest!" a fierce, high voice rasped from behind her.

The broom came down again, but this time it was beside her, and it chased a whirlwind of brown fur. The bundle of fur dashed around the room like a cyclone on a wheat field, except that this cyclone was scampering up the shelving, across the mantel, through lines of stacked hats, chittering wildly as it ran.

No wonder. It was being chased by a little portion of hell itself—in the shape of a tiny woman.

"Malicious swine! Come back 'ere, y'bugger! I'll 'ave yer stuffed! Bloody man-eatin' porcupine!"

It wasn't a porcupine. Actually, it was a ground squirrel. At the moment, it obviously thought it was a dead squirrel. In its blind panic, it was disemboweling the hat store shelf by shelf, rack by rack, its sharp nails scratching furiously on the wooden framework as it tried desperately to escape from the broom that chased it.

The whirlwind behind the broom—who seemed to be a young woman from the glimpses Abbey got of her—suddenly popped up from behind a pile of fabric bolts and tossed a second broom to Abbey. "Take this an' 'ead 'im off! Little villain's molestin' me 'ats!"

Abbey found the broom in her hands. She dumped her shopping bag and took a dive toward the action. "Open the door!" she cried, shooing the terrified squirrel down the window sill as it chittered its rage at her.

The little woman plunged for the door, but the squirrel took a sudden leap and crashed into the fabric bolts, which collapsed beneath its skittering feet. The bolts collided with a stack of hat boxes, and down came the boxes, all around Abbey. She dropped the broom and grabbed the biggest box.

"This way!" She stumbled over the fallen fabric bolts, her dress catching on the wooden edges of the bolt. Her hair was once again in her eyes—she hadn't had this much trouble keeping it neat even during roundup!

"Goin' yo' way! Keep the oys open!"

"What?" Abbey squinted, trying to see through hanks of tawny hair. She caught a glimpse of a fur bundle dashing past her. She lunged forward, hatbox ready. "Hah!"

She landed full-length across the fabric bolts, and there was a yelp of victory as another body landed beside her. Together the two women held the hat box firmly to the floor, in spite of the frantic hammering from inside.

"'Old 'im! I got 'im! I got 'im!" The small woman made a long, uncomfortable reach for a hatbox lid that looked as if it might fit the box, and sure enough it served the purpose. Carefully she slid the lid under the hatbox, in spite of a black rodent's nose that kept trying to push through the bottom. "Got it! Slow, now!"

Working together, they lifted the box, Abbey carefully holding the lid under the makeshift trap. She felt the weight of the squirrel and its scraping claws on the thin wood of the box lid, but forced herself to keep control as they inched toward the door. The squirrel threw itself against the interior of the hatbox, and twice they almost lost him, but a little muscle and a measure of determination got them to the door.

With her foot Abbey forced the door open, shoving aside the fallen dress rack, and the two women nudged their way outside.

"Roun' this-away," the young woman said, moving toward the side of the building. " 'Ang on! Almost there! 'Ang on—oh, nooo—"

The squirrel, thoroughly panicked, went wild inside the box, and they lost their grip.

"Down! Let it down!" Abbey cried, but the box was already falling. Box, lid, and squirrel hit the cobblestones, and the squirrel streaked off toward a nearby elm tree. In an instant, it was nearer the sky than anything without wings.

Abbey and the young woman jumped up and down, pummeling each other and laughing in victory, then they fell together onto the neat little red bench on the store's porch.

"Goo' riddance, yer rum 'earted 'edge'og!" the girl shouted to the treetop.

Abbey sucked in a breath of relief and tried to make sense of the half words she was hearing. What kind of speech was it? Certainly nothing she'd heard so far in New England.

She took the moment to survey her newfound partner in extermination. The girl was younger than Abbey had thought, hardly more than eighteen. Her eyes were an unadorned green, her hair wispy and red, and her face freckled. Her hair was even more disarrayed than Abbey's, but she huffed her victory and leaned back on the porch bench.

"No' a bad mo'nin's work, eh?" she drawled.

"Uh . . . yes," Abbey said, wondering if she was interpreting the words right.

A narrow hand appeared before her. "Lucy's the name. Lucy Edmonds."

"Abbey Sutton. Do you own this shop?"

"Naw, I work 'ere. Got married t'a sailin' bloke, thought ee'd bring me t'America, but I never got no farther than old Nanny."

"Nanny? Oh, Nantucket, you mean."

"Oh, righto, mum. New 'ere?"

"Just got off the boat today," Abbey said, brushing back her stray locks. "I'm caring for Magistrate Nash's children from now on. Well, for a while, at least. However long it takes to pay off his loan to my husband."

"Married? Where's the 'usband, then?" Lucy's bright eyes crinkled with girlish conspiracy. "Scootin' out on 'im, are yer?"

Abbey laughed. "No, no. Nothing like that. He's dead."

Lucy's whole face suddenly shed its light. Every emotion the girl felt evidenced itself on her face without the slightest restraint. "Oh, sorry awf'ly, mum. I didn't mean nothin'."

"Oh, it's all right. He died honorably."

"Died 'ow?"

"Pardon?"

" 'Ow? 'ow did ee die?"

"Oh, *how*? He was killed by rustlers."

Lucy's narrow eyes grew narrower. "Wot's rufflers?"

Abbey laughed again. This girl had that effect—a chuckle at every turn, even just by her manner of expression. "Those are criminals who would steal a rancher's stock."

"Stock, eh? Best start at the ole beginnin', eh?"

"Hmmm? Oh. All right." Abbey sat back and took several moments to rearrange her hair more securely. "My husband was a county judge in Wyoming Territory, and he also opted to be a rancher of cattle. Stock, we call it there. To begin his ranch, he gathered loans from a few old acquaintances, Mr. Nash being one. However the judge was a poor businessman, love his soul, and the ranch failed. But not before he died defending his herd from rustlers who tried to steal them. I repaid most of the loans, but we have an outstanding debt to the magistrate, and Mr. Nash was kind enough to invite me to work away the debt by serving as governess to his children. It's all as simple as that. So, here I am, and here, evidently, I'll stay for a bit."

Lucy leaned forward suddenly and clapped Abbey's knee. "And a fine story it is, mum. Was a goo' man, this judge?"

"Oh, he was a fine, kind man, yes. Older than I am, though, by quite a few years."

" 'Ow old are yer, then, mum, y'don't mine me askin'?"

Abbey controlled her urge to grin at Lucy's halting dialect, which, she found, she was getting used to. "I'm twenty-seven. The judge was fifty when he died."

"Blimey, that is a jump!"

Nodding sedately, Abbey asked, "What's your story, Lucy?"

"Mine? 'ardly anything, mum. I were workin' the docks in Liverpool when I met me a fine sailor lad. 'I promise t'take yer away from 'ere,' says ee. Take me ee did, an' 'ere I am too, jus' like you. Never got no farver than ole Nanny Bucket. Me goin' west an' you goin' east, and 'ere we be togevver."

"Then I reckon we've got something in common, don't we, Lucy?"

"Does indeed, mum. Friends?"

"Friends," Abbey said with a committing nod, and suddenly she felt in place. "Where's your husband now?" she asked, phrasing the question tenderly, for one never knew.

"Out to sea, mum, whalin'." Lucy's round, pink face buckled into a delightful smile. "Don't worry, mum. Ee loves me, ee does. Name's Billy Edmonds. Ee comes back pretty regular, an' ee brings me things from such places! Spain an' Greece, Bolivia an' Peru—wot names these places got! Oh, aye, mum, ee always comes back. Ee can't stand to be wivvout me." An edge of pride danced across her smile, giving Abbey no doubt of that last claim. Then she leaned forward again in that intimate manner and confided, "Ee don't know it yet, mum, but I've got me a surprise for 'im. I'll show yer, mum—'ang on!"

The girl bounded up from the bench and disappeared into the shop. Abbey heard Lucy clunking around inside, and didn't hear anything for a few moments. Then once again she heard the girl's hard boots on the wooden floor, and Lucy once again appeared on the porch. This time, though, she cuddled a round-faced, wide-eyed baby of four or five months.

Abbey sat straight up. "Lucy! She's beautiful!"

Lucy brought her baby to the bench and sat the child down between them, holding the baby up in a sitting position. "Me wee mate, Wilma."

Wilma craned her short little baby neck to look up at Abbey, her eyes round as bright grapes. She broke into a gummy grin that made both women laugh.

"Wilma, Wilma," Abbey cooed, playing with the infant's moist fingers. "Your husband doesn't know?"

" 'Ow couldee, mum? Been gone now over a year. Wait'll ee sees this little face peepin' up at 'im when ee gets off the whaler! Won't he croak!"

Caught up in the girl's genuine delight of her secret, Abbey felt a burst of happiness—perhaps even envy—within herself. "Oh, Lucy, I'm so happy for you! She's a shining baby, that's plain to see. Did you want a girl?"

"Oh, mum, I wants wha'ever I gets, and a 'aff dozen more." Lucy sighed happily, then got to her feet and smoothed her skirt. She scooped up her baby as though all she'd ever done was scoop up babies. Wilma squealed and widened her silly toothless grin. "Pardon, mum," Lucy said. "Time I got to pickin' up that mess inside."

"I'll help you," Abbey offered, getting up.

"Wouldn't 'ear of it!"

"and I wouldn't hear of having you do it alone."

As the baby rode on her hip, Lucy wobbled her head back and forth comically. "Mum, I'd be a liar and bum-brained at that if I turned yer down," she admitted cheerily.

"What a precocious thing you are," Abbey sighed. "I'm surrounded by precocious people all of a sudden. I never imagined Nantucket would be such a lively place."

Those words, falling as they did from her own mouth, struck up a memory. The docks. Jacob Ross.

Abbey let herself look again across the cobblestoned intersection at the door of The Brotherhood. "Lucy . . ." she began, not sure of what the question would be.

"Aye, mum?"

"Do you know a man named Jacob Ross?"

"Runs the Great Point light, mum. Quiet sort of bloke. Came just after I got 'ere. 'Bout a year past."

"So I've heard."

"Why'dee ask, mum?"

Abbey puzzled over her feelings, and found she couldn't isolate them yet. How could so fleeting an encounter embed itself so solidly in her mind? Perhaps the man . . . something about the man . . .

"Why?" she echoed, barely above a whisper. And she gazed at that pub door. "I don't know. I don't know. . . ."

Chapter Three

SHE WAS BEING followed.

Either that or her imagination was working on her again. No, she didn't believe that. Someone *was* following her. Two someones, in fact. Or could it be mere coincidence that the stout man with the mustache shaped like longhorns and the scrawny man who hunched over happened to appear nearby whenever she stopped walking? It was a very small town. But this much coincidence?

Or . . . perhaps . . .

Just perhaps it had something to do with the man *she* was following.

Yes, she'd found him. Jacob Ross. Guilty as charged, she had been . . . all right, following him. Whether she liked it or not, and truly she didn't, she had generally drifted along his same path once she spied him exiting The Brotherhood at almost the same moment she came out of the hat store. With every step she tried to justify this force that nudged her to follow after him every time he rounded a corner, but no matter how she tried to excuse it, she had to chalk it up to curiosity. Nothing but curiosity. No better reason. Yet, she had exchanged something ephemeral with this man earlier today, and that something drove her, admittedly without reason, to "casually" meander in the same direction. Moses!—was it only today? Still Tuesday, and so much had happened to her already!

And now someone was tracking her just as she was tracking Jacob

Ross. Had she angered the wrong people when she reacted to the slave's capture on the wharf? She'd heard of such things in eastern ports—stories of folk being shanghaied, stuffed into some little rowboat, paddled out to a bigger boat, and never seen again.

But those were only stories. Weren't they?

Abbey shook herself. "Don't be a silly toad," she said aloud, and turned her concentration back to not looking at Jacob Ross. She was making a skill of this not-looking business. Not looking at Ross, not looking at the two men who seemed to be following her, herself keeping up with Ross while always being ready to not look at a moment's notice.

His moss green jacket and black cap over that flicker of blond became as familiar to her as her own reflection. But she saw only the back of him—arranged it that way, in fact.

Goose brain, she thought as she ducked behind a pile of empty apple barrels to avoid his glance. What did she intend to do? Follow him all the way to Great Point for no reason? Suddenly she was glad the Nash children weren't officially in her charge yet, for they would probably have been with her, and then what would she say about her actions? That she liked to follow men around port towns?

She ducked again as Jacob Ross paused at a water pump for a drink, and pressed her hand to her mouth, holding back a giggle. What an odd governess she'd be if she thought that was a good answer to tell children. The boys would grow up wondering why women didn't follow them, and Luella would grow up thinking it was all right to follow strangers.

A moment later she peeked out from behind the tree that hid her. Ross was striding away.

"Moses," she breathed, "what long legs!" She hadn't remembered his being all that tall a man, but he cut an appealing figure as he strode, hands pocketed, around the side of a building.

Taking her chances, Abbey struck out across the street in his direction, bothering to pick up her skirts and skip down the boardwalk at a painfully obvious pace. A few townsfolk glanced at her curiously, but their curiosity couldn't match hers.

It was an alley of sorts, a narrow space between two buildings. With a peek for good measure, she started down it, holding her skirts up as she stepped into the mud.

Then, in shock, she felt someone grab her by the shoulders.

She gasped. A tingle shot down her spine.

"Why are you following me?" a stern voice barked.

She blinked, and there he was, inches away—inches near—with his hands clamped on her upper arms, his eyes making the demand over and over.

"You aren't very good at tracking, are you?" he said, not giving her time to think. His brown eyes frothed with contained anger. His hands tightened on her arms.

Abbey's mouth hung open for several seconds while she overcame her surprise. Then at once she wrenched free of his grip and backed up the whole extra foot allowed by the narrow alley. "Holy Moses, man, turn loose of me!"

He stepped out of the niche he had ducked into and put an extra two steps between them. The double-breasted sea jacket, unbuttoned now, revealed a simple sweater of undyed wool, and it gave off a muted scent of flowers and meadow grasses when he moved. "Why," he began again, "are you following me?"

Abbey gathered herself, clutching her packages close to her ribs. "I . . ."

She needed an excuse, and needed it fast. If only her heart would stop thudding.

"I wanted . . ."

"What?"

She stomped her heel in the mud. "If you'll give me a moment! You startled me."

"I startled *you!*" he huffed. "You're tracking me, and I startled *you?*"

Abbey cleared her throat. "Yes," she began, stalling, "yes, well, I only wanted to . . . apologize. Yes, apologize for the way I treated you on the dock."

Oh, that wasn't too bad! Now, if only she could say it and sound as if she meant it!

"You should," he said flatly. "Is that all?"

He seemed to be stepping away, as though he were about to turn and leave her.

She couldn't let him go. Not yet.

"No," she blurted, closing the space between them with a tentative step. She gripped her packages tighter. "No, it's not all. I also want to apologize for . . . for calling you a coward. It was . . . presumptuous."

Jacob Ross's hardened features turned a little softer, though the anger remained in his eyes. He shifted his feet. "It was that," he agreed.

"Do you accept?"

His brown eyes narrowed and pale brows drew over them. He didn't blink, but gazed at her in a long, unbroken, provocative way—as though he didn't understand . . . but deeply wanted to. Odd . . . he actually bothered to think about it, which worried her. After a moment, though, he gave her an unconvincing nod.

"Suppose so," he said.

She stuck out her gloved hand—not as smooth a motion as she had intended—and said, "I'm Abbey Sutton."

For some unimaginable reason, he hesitated. He stared at her hand for a disturbingly long pause, as though he didn't want the burden of knowing her, of having her know him. Just when she was about to withdraw the hand, though, he took it. His grip was firm and warm in spite of his hesitation.

"Jake Ross."

Abbey bit back the urge to blurt "I know!" and managed to keep him from seeing her relief.

"I just arrived today," she said instead.

His mouth twisted into a grin of irony. "I remember, believe me."

She flushed. "I'm from Wyoming Territory."

"Where's that?"

This caught her by surprise, and she licked her lips while thinking of a way to explain. "You know where California is?"

"Sure do."

"It's . . . before there."

"If you're going westward, I assume."

"Of course. What other way—"

"There's the sea route," he reminded her.

"I thought you weren't a sailor," she said. As soon as she let it slip, she knew it was too late to correct the error.

He stepped ominously nearer. "How'd you know I'm not a sailor?"

Damn! Now what?

She bit her lip and stammered, "Umm . . . I . . . you . . . you smell wrong."

No, no, she didn't say that—not that! Perhaps there was a way to crawl into one of her packages. Certainly she was small enough to fit by now.

Jake Ross peeled his cap off, and his appealing face crumpled in total confusion. "Lady . . . I think you're crazy."

Well, there was no crawling out of this stew, so she might as well swim in it.

"You do," she insisted. "You don't smell like a boat and you *do* smell like land . . . and . . . it was just a guess."

"Mighty too good of a guess, Miss Sutton," he said. His tone told her she'd failed to fool him.

She squared her shoulders. "Mrs. Sutton."

Ross's straight lips parted. A touch of . . . disappointment?

"You're married."

"A widow," she corrected, and looked for the relief in his eyes.

There was none. None whatsoever.

"Why'd you come to the island?" he asked instead.

"I'm in the employ of the magistrate."

Once again, perhaps even more coldly this time, he stepped back away from her. "Are you, now?"

"Yes. Why do you say it that way?"

He flopped his black cap back on and stepped even farther down the alley. "I don't say it any way. Best I say good day to you now . . . missus." He touched the brim of his cap and dipped his head in tense politeness, then tried to make a clean getaway.

"Wait!" Abbey called, unsure why she did it.

Ross never quite completed his turn away. "Yes, missus?"

"I . . . "

"Yes?" he prodded impatiently.

"I'd like to . . . to thank you."

His brows tightened in perplexity. "Thank me now? What for?"

"For coming to my aid when that slaver—"

"When he fought back after you attacked him, you mean?"

"Well . . . yes."

"Pity's sake, missus, we're on the verge of overdoing this, don't you think? The thanks is getting bigger than the deed." He held out his hands to illustrate the empty point, swung around, and headed down the alley again.

"You hated it, didn't you?" Abbey called, following him.

He stopped in his tracks, his back to her.

Somehow she knew—he understood. Something in his posture as he halted there in midstep said that he did indeed know what she was talking about.

Even so, she approached him from behind and hammered at the truth.

"You wanted to act just as much as I did, but something held you back. What? Why didn't you help me? I know you wanted to. I could see it in your eyes just as plainly as if you'd stepped out and said, 'I hate what I'm seeing more than pain itself.' I'm a good reader of eyes, Mr. Ross, and that's what yours said to me on the wharf today." She moved closer to him. And closer again. She spoke to the tense set of his shoulders as he stood with his back to her. She spoke, and he listened. "You wanted to pull that slaver's skin off, didn't you? But you wouldn't admit it. You wouldn't help me. And there's a reason why not. Such a man as you doesn't hold back without a reason."

She might as well have etched the words in his back with a branding iron, so stiffly did he stand there, smoldering. As she waited, hardly daring to move, he took a long breath—then another. Actively keeping control, it seemed, just as he had on the wharf.

He turned slowly, his eyes catching her in their glare even before he was completely around. Two creases formed at the corners of his mouth as he fought to keep from turning loose the rage she saw in his eyes.

Now he was all the way around, facing her again. Two long, measured steps brought him threateningly close.

"Lady," he began, his tone a menace in itself, "you know nothing at all. You don't know what kind of man I am. Turn around and walk back out this alley and don't come around me anymore."

"I can't."

"You can't what?"

"I can't go back out the alley that way."

"Why not?"

"Because I'm being followed."

He froze for a telling instant. She expected him to laugh in her face, but he didn't. His dark eyes widened, then abruptly narrowed with concern, and he pushed past her and stepped to the edge of the building. The manner with which he peeked out told her she wasn't imagining things at all. He believed it could be so.

"What did he look like?" Ross asked, keeping his body pressed up against the building as he peered out.

"They. A chunky fellow with a mustache like longhorns, and a smaller one who's hunched over. Are they still there?"

For a few seconds he didn't answer. Then he came back inside the alley and asked, "Why would anyone be following you?"

"I can't imagine," she said. "Except . . . after what I did on Straight Wharf this morning—"

"That'd be a reason," he acknowledged roughly. "But not enough of one." He clamped his hand around her arm, leading her quickly between the buildings. "We'll come out onto Cambridge Street. You turn left, and you'll get back to Main. Turn right there, and you'll lose them."

Somewhat stunned that she hadn't been wrong, Abbey stared at him as he hustled her along. Ignoring the ache where he gripped her arm, she asked, "What if they keep following me?"

"They won't."

"But what if they do?"

He turned to her. He seemed caught between apathy and gallantry—seemed to notice that she was worried, perhaps even frightened. She wasn't frightened, not yet anyway, but she was worried. Slavery was an unscrupulous business and those who engaged in recapturing escaped slaves were unscrupulous enough to have a woman followed and threatened if she got in their way. She saw the truth of that in Jake Ross's eyes. According to the simplest of courtesies, he certainly couldn't stride away and leave her to her own resources. At the moment, though, she didn't bother to tell him that her resources were in good shape. She could take care of herself, but that wouldn't get her anywhere.

"All right," he sighed. "This way. Let's see if they follow."

With a grip on her elbow he led her across the street and around a corner. He stopped once they'd rounded the side of a dry goods store and looked behind them at the way they'd come.

A few seconds later he spoke. "There they are, for sure. Not very bright fellows, either."

"Why do you say that?" Abbey asked, trying to get a peek around his shoulder at the pursuers.

Ross nudged her back, and she was warmed by the protectiveness in his touch. "It's plain that we're trying to get away from them," he said. "They're making themselves obvious by trying so hard to follow us. Good trackers wouldn't do that. Here they come."

He turned and ushered her down the street. Abbey could tell that he was deliberately keeping his pace slow because he thought she couldn't keep up. She could also tell, by his glances behind them, that he wanted to hurry. So she hiked up her skirts and stepped up her pace, even to a point where Ross had to jog to keep up with her. She caught an accommodating smirk on his lips as they ducked down an alley behind a tailor shop and flattened themselves up against the wall.

"Still coming?" she asked as Jake peeked around the corner.

"Gaining on us," he said. "Come on. This way."

He gestured her along the narrow lane behind the row of shops. Just when she was getting into a good run, he drew up short and said, "Here!" He disappeared between two tightly wedged buildings.

Abbey swung around, panting. "Where?" Doubling back, she ducked between the buildings where she'd seen him go. Just as she pulled the hem of her skirt in behind her, she caught a glimpse of Longhorn Mustache and Hunch coming around the last shop after them.

"They're coming!" she hissed to Jake, staring at him.

Jake was bending over a little herb garden next to a clapboard wall. His hand disappeared into the bundles of plants.

"What are you doing?" she asked. "They're almost here!"

He continued to feel around in the clumps of plants. Just as their pursuers' footfalls could be heard in the mud down the alley, Jake suddenly hauled back and to Abbey's surprise up came a hidden hatchway. The top, like a small cellar door, was hidden completely by the little garden on top of it, but swung away neatly and left a gaping hole in the ground. Abbey's lips fell open and she rushed over to look down the hole. Sure enough, there was a stairway. Well, less a stairway than a ladder, really—very steep and very dark. And Jake was halfway down already, gesturing up at her.

"Step in! Hurry!" he called in an urgent whisper, reaching for her. "This'll confound 'em."

Abbey was jarred by the sound of the trackers' footsteps coming closer and closer—running. She shook herself out of her surprise, twisted her skirts into her left arm, and stepped into the hole. She barely made it down two step rungs before Jake got his arms about her and lifted her bodily down into the tight hatchway beside him. He reached up immediately and closed the false garden over them. Just as he got it down to his shoulder level, keeping it from clapping shut, they heard their trackers' footsteps come round the edge of the shop.

In the dark space Abbey's lungs screamed to take a deep breath but she willed herself not to gasp or pant. Her legs were shaking, but she wedged herself between the moist wall and Jake's side and fought for balance on the steep ladder.

Through a little crack between the foundation and the hatch, light seeped into the darkness. Above, she could make out the ankles of the two men who had followed them. The men had stopped just outside the hatch, confused about where their quarry could have escaped to. Neither could imagine, just as Abbey hadn't, that there might be a secret place under the innocuous little back-door garden.

"What is this—" she started to ask in a whisper.

"Shh!" he ordered, and they both fell silent.

Abbey could only hear muffled snatches of conversation between the two men. Most of their words were lost in the layer of soil and plants between the two trackers and the cellar shaft. But even when the sounds failed to trickle down into the hiding place, the sense of danger certainly did.

A moment later the sounds moved away from the secret hatch.

"They're going," Jake whispered.

"Are they?" Abbey muttered as she caught her breath. Suddenly a surge of anger rose in her. What was she doing? She had no reason to hide! "This is absurd," she said spontaneously. "We've done nothing. They've no business following us. Step aside. I'm going up."

She pushed against him, her foot searching for the next step on the ladder, and she pressed her hand against the bottom of the hatch. It started to creak open.

Jake grabbed her around the waist and pulled her back down. "No!"

"Let go of me," she insisted, trying to squeeze out of his grip. She found it was impossible in this tight space. "No one follows me without a good reason!"

"Lady!" Jake hissed, wrestling with her. "Abbey! Stop it!"

She started wriggling, fighting him in earnest, forcing him to clap a hand over her mouth and wrap the other arm about her rib cage to pull her back down into the hatchway.

She struggled against him, her feet slipping on the mildewed wood of the ladder.

"Stop fighting!" Jake insisted, careful to keep his voice down.

He held her hard against the soil wall of the hatchway and pressed his body tightly against her, trapping her there. Moisture from the wall seeped through the back of her dress and chilled her skin, and Jake's firm body pressed the air from her lungs so that she couldn't have cried out if she had wanted to. His hand still pressed her mouth closed, and she whined through her nose with a sudden gust of anger at what he was doing. If she wanted to confront those men, it was bloody well her own business! Her brows drew together in rage and she glared at him through the dimness.

Again she writhed against him, but the sensation of a strong man's body against hers took her by surprise. A thin shaft of light fell across Jake's eyes, and the universe was suddenly caught in his glare. Darkness above, darkness below, all except for that band of light from the crack at the top of the ladder. And in the band, his eyes. Such eyes—like the full, round, determined eyes of a longhorn bull just at the moment of utmost anger. At that instant, just as he pushed his body against hers and his eyes fell into that shaft of light, Abbey was clutched by a single great throb of submission. It took her—yes—by surprise. Had it been so long?

She felt foolish. And the foolishness made her fight harder.

To no avail, though. This time he was ready for her struggle and countered easily with sheer muscle, for he had the advantage in this narrow passageway. He held her efficiently, if not easily against the wall, but it took the whole length of his body to do it.

From above, boot soles scraped on the ground, growing more and more faint. The two trackers were leaving. Or were they?

Jake twisted around, trying to keep a grip on her while getting a glimpse through the crack. He looked up, listening past her muffled commentary. Finally he let his hand slip away from her mouth.

"You bit me," he muttered, examining his fingers in that rogue shaft of light.

"Why did you do that?" she demanded.

"Because," he said firmly, "it's not wise to face down two men in a blind alley, Mrs. Sutton, that's why."

"I've done nothing wrong that they should be following me, and I don't mean to be haunted during my whole time on this island," she insisted, "and I'll take up the lash against slavery or anything else as I please to!"

She tried to wedge past him again, and again he stopped her. "That had nothing to do with it," he said.

"Then I mean to ask *why* they're following me."

She raised an arm to find the hatchway over her head, but by now Jacob Ross had apparently had enough. He got one arm firmly about her waist again and lifted her right off the ladder. Fighting for balance, he carried her to the bottom of this strange narrow shaft and plunked her down on muddy ground in the darkness.

"They're not following you," he said sharply. Then he paused, as though he regretted giving her that answer, or any answer. When he spoke it was as though his feelings of protectiveness had opened a whole new pathway into his mind. "I . . . don't want you to be afraid."

Abbey waited, letting her silence voice her question.

After a moment, in a different tone of voice, Jake confessed, "They were following me."

Folding her arms, Abbey gazed at the lock of blond hair that shone in a single thready patch of light from high above. "About time you admitted it," she told him.

She felt his glare, even in the near darkness.

"You knew?" he asked.

"Even if they had been following me, Mr. Ross, they only started doing it after I started following you," she pointed out, realizing the logic. "You are the common denominator. What have you done that you should be followed?"

He paced the one step allowed by the tight quarters they shared. "I had some . . . trouble on the mainland before coming to Nantucket. Could be that."

"What kind of trouble?"

He stopped moving, and again Abbey felt that cutting glare through the blackness. "Private trouble,"he said indignantly. "Some business dealings went bad."

"Do these men mean to hurt you, Mr. Ross?"

"Jake," he corrected.

"Jake, then."

"I doubt it. Probably they only mean to find out what I'm involved in these days. And they'll be sorely disappointed."

"Why is that?" she prodded, unable to keep from sounding anxious to get to the bottom of this mystery.

"Because," he told her flatly and firmly, "it's trouble to get involved in other folks' business, and I don't mean to. I just run the lighthouse now, nothing else."

"That's all you do?"

"Yes . . . why?"

"Don't you also help run that pub you came out of?"

His silence this time was heavy and ominous. Perhaps she'd admitted too much. She was letting him see her curiosity, but she had no excuse for it—unless she were to tell him the truth: that he aroused her as wind arouses a meadow.

"How do you know about that?" he asked her, his tone this time laced with suspicion.

She hesitated. "I . . . heard."

"You mean you found out," he said sharply.

Abbey nodded. "All right, I found out. You don't seem like a man who keeps a lighthouse. And if you're at risk because of your past, why don't you leave the island?"

"I would," he began.

"But?"

"But I . . . can't get off."

"You can't? What do you mean, can't?"

"I'd . . . uh . . ."

She let the pause ride, forcing his own hesitation to squeeze an answer out of him, and sure enough it did.

"I'd . . . have to get on a boat," he said. The statement embarrassed him, she could tell.

She actually laughed at him. "Of course you would! How else?"

Sarcastically he said, "I could get killed, that'd be a way off."

"What *are* you talking about?"

But evidently she'd pushed ahead just an inch too far into his privacy. Jake stiffened. "I don't understand your interest in my business, but I don't get involved in yours, so you don't get involved in mine. That's my policy, and I've found it works. No matter how hard I have to hit or shake or twist to make it work."

The threat was clear as a bell's knell in the cramped cellar shaft, but Abbey wasn't so easily intimidated.

"Is that why you didn't get involved with the slaver on the wharf?" she pressed.

Jake Ross heaved a frustrated sigh. "That's why. All right, Mrs. Sutton?"

"Abbey."

He paused. His foot struck the ladder's bottom rung. "I think we'll leave it at Mrs. Sutton."

Without allowing another pause to tempt him, he mounted the steep steps and climbed to the top, pushing open the hatch a crack and looking around until he was sure they were alone once again. Then he quietly opened the false garden all the way and climbed out, stepping aside for Abbey to come out after him. He seemed tempted to reach for her and help her out, yet, as he said he would, he also was forcing himself not to do that, not to touch her again. With some difficulty—which she made sure he saw—she managed to get out on her own.

He closed the hatch, also closing the issue.

They came out into the sunlight, and Jake Ross was a slightly different man than when he and a woman he scarcely knew had huddled together in a damp cellar shaft. As he looked at her now, there was a tinge of regret in his eyes. Even sadness. Perhaps she hadn't been mistaken at all. Perhaps he, too, sensed the fellowship between them, this odd attraction that had dragged her toward him all day.

He paused, his gaze hanging upon her, catching all the hopefulness in her face that she couldn't contain.

For a long moment they gazed at each other, both caught up in a trance that Abbey thought she had only imagined.

Then Jake Ross took a sudden and deliberate step away from her.

"I know you don't understand," he said. Suddenly his voice was soft. "Better that you don't."

She stepped toward him, gain drawn by this unexplained feeling, and there was a question in her eyes that perhaps even she was unsure how to put into words.

But Jake Ross backed away.

"No," he said. As though to shut her out, he wrapped his jacket tightly around his body and buttoned it. He paced backward a step, and before he turned he took the time to say the awful words lurking behind his expression. "Don't come around me anymore," he told her. With a sadness that shone in his eyes, he added, "I'm dangerous."

"The children are in bed, Mr. Nash."

Dominic Nash looked up from the dinner table and his copy of the Nantucket *Inquirer and Mirror* to look at Abbey over the top his spectacles. "As quickly as that?"

Abbey started to answer, then caught her breath at the sight of him there, with the lamplight reflecting in the spectacles. She must have paled a little. He noticed.

"Is something wrong, Mrs. Sutton?"

"No . . . It's just that you look somewhat like my husband with those spectacles on, Mr. Nash. I'm sorry. You took me by surprise."

Nash politely removed the spectacles. In spite of his outer layer of harshness, he was obviously trying to make her comfortable. He gestured toward a chair at the dinner table. "Attacked by a rogue memory, I see. Please, sit down. I'd forgotten the judge wore spectacles for reading. Forgive me."

Abbey nodded and stood by the seat he offered, but didn't sit. "It isn't your fault, Mr. Nash, nor mine either. Many people wear spectacles. I reckon I can't let them disturb me."

"Sit down, please," he offered again.

"I hear Mrs. Goodes doing the dinner dishes," Abbey said. "Perhaps I could help her."

"Mrs. Sutton, I pay Mrs. Goodes to do a particular job. She does hers, and you do yours, not the cross-pattern."

Abbey paused, then saw that he wasn't making a joke. "Oh," she said. "I see."

"I run an orderly household, Mrs. Sutton," he told her as she sat down. "I run an orderly island. Ships come and ships go, men come and go, strangers, friends, more folk passing through than in your usual town. Certainly more than you ever saw in Wyoming Territory, I dare guess."

"Many more even in a single day, Mr. Nash," she told him.

He nodded. "Allow me," he said then, picking up a bottle of wine and filling a goblet for himself and one for her. "Please share an evening drink with me—unless you are a teetotaler . . ."

"Thank you, I will have the wine, Mr. Nash."

"I'm relieved, Mrs. Sutton. I run an orderly household, but not a monastery."

Lanternlight made the room eerie and warm, casting light to parts of the room and leaving the corners dark. It was a notch above candlelight in its effect, of course, with that extra measure of civility.

"I'm glad . . . nay, amazed, really, that you handle my children so well. They haven't been in bed on time for nearly a year," he told her, gently placing the goblet before her on the tatted tablecloth. "How did you do it?"

"I told them a story," she said, and she couldn't help smiling.

"What story?"

"Well . . . not precisely a story. I told them what it's like to ride a cattle drive."

Nash frowned, his red brows tugging together. "Is that not rather a rough story for little children?"

Abbey tipped her head. "Your boys aren't so little, Mr. Nash. Many a lad their age rides roundup. We in the West can't afford to be short a good ranch hand because that hand is only ten years old. At any rate," she said with a fatigued sigh, "I withheld the bitter details."

"I'm gratified for that," Nash said. "I confess to you that the judge never seemed a ranching sort of man, Mrs. Sutton. At least, not when I knew him at law college."

"Alas, he wasn't. Here I am in debt to you, after all," Abbey conceded.

"Yes," he murmured. "Mrs. Sutton, I've been pondering our arrangement."

Abbey leaned forward. "You haven't changed your mind—"

"No, rest assured, no. You have a place here as long as you need it. However, I mean to pay you a wage for your services as governess."

"But, Mr. Nash, that leaves the debt still outstanding. I can't have it that way."

"We will consider the debt relaxed if you remain in my employ for one year, at a salary."

"No, sir, I refuse."

"I beg your pardon?"

"I refuse to accept salary and still be in debt to you."

"But I've said—"

"Yes, sir, I know what you said. I take no charity."

Nash fell silent, staring at her through the golden lamplight. He sipped his wine then, contemplatively, and began again. "Of course, I have no wish to insult you. Charity is not my intent."

"Then what is your intent? I plan to work off my debt to you. We've made that agreement."

He placed his elbow on the burnished wood of the table and looked squarely at her now. His reflection shone clearly in the wood as he spoke. "Yes, of course. But where will that leave you at such a time as we decide the debt is satisfied?"

Abbey bit her lip thoughtfully. "I beg your pardon?"

Nash seemed frustrated at not getting across what he'd hoped to communicate. "Mrs. Sutton . . . you may well work off the debt, that's all well and good. But where will you be then? You'll have no cash on hand, no investment, no ranch, nothing. As a gentleman, I cannot allow you to work off a debt to me, only to be left a pauper. I owe the judge more than that for his widow."

"The judge was my husband, sir, not my keeper," Abbey told him, trying to sound both capable and at ease with her fate. "My parents homesteaded when I was hardly older than Luella. I've worked hard since I was that age and could always take care of myself. I still can.

When he was on the county judicial circuit, I ran the ranch myself. I was foreman, in fact. Be assured, you'll not be leaving me indigent. I shall see to myself."

Nash sat back and gazed at her, apparently impressed with what he saw and heard. For many moments he remained silent. Then finally his cheeks grew round as he grinned solemnly. "Lowell Sutton made a wise choice for his wife."

Her cheeks warmed by a sudden blush, Abbey could only nod and allow herself to grin slightly.

"I remember our long talks over whiskey," Nash said. "He used to speak of migrating westward and founding a town."

"He spoke of that to me also," Abbey said, suddenly finding a common ground with this properly stiff gentleman. "He thought a foundation of cattle and sheep ranching in the area would provide a hub in the county. He bought up land and meant to sell homestead property to those who would work the ranch—vaqueros, Indians, Negroes . . . sadly, he was too kind a man for his own good. There wasn't the ruthlessness in him it takes to roust civilization out of the western plains. He had little head for business, and too much head for giving away things he should have been selling. Unfortunately, that only leaves everybody with a little bit of something, instead of everybody with the potential to have lots of something. The people there were willing to work for their gain. Preferred it, in fact. Even the Indians and homesteaders puzzled over Lowell's tendency to give things away. They wanted to work, Mr. Nash, not to be given things." Careful not to insult him with her tone, she added, "As do I."

Nash sighed, bobbed his brows once in subtle understanding of what she was trying to say, and took another sip. "I understand. I would not wish you to compromise your scruples. However, lest I sacrifice my own . . . I should like to arrange an allowance for your personal expenses."

"Mr. Nash—"

"Mrs. Sutton, please let me do this."

She stopped short in the midst of arguing, and stared at him. In his eyes she saw absolute desire to do what he spoke of doing, to give her something to live on above and beyond satisfying the debt she was here to work off. His eyes spoke not of guilt at all, but rather of generosity. Could she deny him that? Even a strong woman shouldn't count stubbornness among her strengths, to the sacrifice of other folks' feelings.

She sat back, grasped her wine goblet in acceptance both of drink and gallantry, and said, "Lowell may indeed have chosen his wife well enough, but I see he also chose his friends well. Mr. Nash," she said, raising the goblet, "I accept."

He smiled, showing a true smile for the first time, and raised his goblet as well. Together, they drank to the new arrangement.

"Thank you, Mrs. Sutton," Nash said sincerely. He sipped the wine again and swallowed slowly. "I'll sleep better at night knowing I won't be leaving you destitute at the end of your stay."

"I've only just begun here," Abbey pointed out.

"Yes, but a year and a-half goes quickly, you'll discover. You're a young woman, Mrs. Sutton. I don't delude myself that you'll be content to stay here tending my children when a whole world lies out there to be conquered. I've already seen you're not the kind of woman who settles for the mundane."

"Your children are far from mundane, sir," Abbey said, smiling.

He chuckled. "That's exquisitely true. They're very lively. I've had difficulty handling them on my own."

"Are they much like your wife?"

Nash's smile fell away and his eyes lost their focus. The change was startling and sad. "No . . . they're not like either of us. She was . . . she was gentle as a songbird, Mrs. Sutton. Those children were her melodies. I think they understood the joy their mother found in them, for they seemed almost to perform for her . . . to take energy from life because they sensed the pleasure it gave her to see them frolic and play and be . . . what did you call them? Precocious?"

"They are," she said with a smile.

He sighed, this time very deeply, and dropped his eyes to gaze unseeing into his wine. "She took the melody with her, Mrs. Sutton. I have been a silent soul ever since."

A chord of sympathy ran deep within Abbey as she watched Dominic Nash. He was so like her husband—the same age, the same profession, the same background. She felt herself attracted to him—she wanted to touch him, to soothe him.

She shifted her feet, preparing to move, but then he spoke.

"I commend you," he said, unable to meet her eyes yet. "You're very strong to accept the death of your husband so staunchly. I have . . . no such strength."

Abbey reached out with a single hand and cupped her fingers over his arm. "Mr. Nash—"

"Quite true," he said. "She might as well have died yesterday as last year, for all the success I've had in recovering from it."

"Mr. Nash," she said again, more quietly.

Now he looked up. "Dominic. Please call me Dominic. Might you do that for me?"

Abbey nodded, smiling gently. "I shall . . . Dominic."

The aroma of wine drifted between them. Perhaps she was fatigued after so long a week of travel, after the excitement in town with Jacob Ross, after the trying days that lay behind her like a trail of dried leaves. Whatever was playing on her, she was drawn to Dominic Nash in this unexplainable moment during which they both shared a need. So sudden . . . yet they had a common past and seemed to know each other because of that.

As she felt Dominic's lips against hers, felt the tickle of his mustache and the intense loneliness of her husband's old friend, Abbey felt affection rise again within her.

Not for Nash . . . not really. Once again she felt her husband's touch. The flickering memory of dreams they'd followed together on the wild Wyoming plains. The low, drowsy, aching desire for a man's hot touch—

Her mind fell away from sense into sensation—

And the face she was kissing changed. In her foggy mind, the mustache changed to rough stubble. The aroma of wine became the scent of wildflowers clinging to moist wool. The red locks of Dominic Nash paled to wheat blond, blue eyes darkening to the brown of almond shells.

Jake . . .

She gasped and drew back.

Dominic drew back almost as quickly, grasping the arms of his expensive leather chair so tightly that his knuckles went white. "Dear Lord—" he choked. "Forgive me!"

He got to his feet, almost stumbling.

Abbey pressed her cheeks with both hands, forcing her mind back to the present, and bolted from her chair. She managed to catch Dominic at the foot of the stairs.

"Dominic, wait."

He whirled around, backing off to arm's length. "No—please. What you must think of me! It was ungentlemanly—"

"But—"

"I would die a thousand times before I'd have you think I was taking advantage of my position as your employer," he said, speaking so fast he was actually stumbling over his words. "This is *not* the arrangement I was trying to propose, please believe me!"

"I believe you," she said sharply, catching his arm before he escaped up the stairs. "Dominic—"

"That was ill-advised. Improper . . ."

"Nonsense," she assured him. "What the future might bring can't be foretold. But for a moment, we helped each other through a patch of loneliness. Is that a sin?"

"Mrs. Sutton, *please*—I must say good night."

He tugged loose from her grip, and she let him go. A moment later, the door on the master bedroom clapped shut, and Abbey was once again alone.

She stared at an empty stairway. "Poor man," she murmured.

Feeling her failure rather acutely, considering she hadn't seen the whole episode coming at all, she let her hands drop to her sides—and found they were moist with perspiration. She touched her collar—it too was moist, tight.

Her whole body . . . quivering with needs she thought she had forgotten. Or hoped to have forgotten.

She spun around and wrenched open the big front door.

The Nantucket night spread out before her, cool and crisp, scented with rambling roses and sea breeze. She stepped out into it and tugged the door shut.

The town was quiet. Was it so late?

Windows glowed with lanternlight, but there was no one on the street. The night was quiet and comforting, but even that couldn't quell the shuddering breaths that pulled through her body. She brought a hand to her chest and found it pounding. She drew the other hand along her forehead and down her face to her throat, and inhaled deeply, trying to drown out the throb of need that rose in her like a reawakened myth.

And something moved.

Her eyes darted. Over there. Under the trellis.

Abbey pressed her back against the little picket fence, peering through the darkness. The starless sky offered her no help.

"Who is it?" she called boldly. Foolish, probably. But she wasn't about to be under siege in her own place of residence. She'd get to the bottom of this. If Jacob Ross said those men were following him rather than her, then who was lurking around under the trellis? She took a step in that direction, but not too big a step. "Come out of there, coward."

The trellis rustled, sending a bolt of terrible confirmation through her. Now she'd done it. She couldn't retreat back into the house like a scared mouse . . . could she? No, of course not. Could she?

Then a voice spoke out, a much bolder voice than that of a person caught in subterfuge.

"You like that word, don't you?"

Abbey gasped. "Jacob!"

Chapter Four

HE REMAINED BEHIND the rose-covered trellis. Crisscross shadow lines patterned his face as the moon broke from behind a cloud and cast its milky light on the trellis and the rambling roses.

For an instant, Abbey was afraid. What was he doing here, skulking in the dark? Then her fear melted. He had come to see her—that much she could sense. But why?

She opted to trust her feelings. That was all right, wasn't it? These feelings . . . they were so strong! So unfamiliar—yet there was something awakening within her that rang as true as a dinner bell sounding across an open meadow.

Meadow . . . yes. Jake. He reminded her of meadows, wildflowers, all the best things about the frontier she'd left behind. In the midst of bonebreaking toil and endless drudgery, there had always been the freshness of open country. She hadn't expected to find it upon coming to New England, so long settled and so tightly populated, but here it was, embodied in a single enigmatic man. And he was here, with her. For no reason.

There had to be is a reason! she insisted to herself, suddenly convinced. She slowly crossed the sidewalk toward the trellis. He felt it, too. It had to be!

"Jacob Ross," she tested, "I see you there. I know it's you. Come out, or I'll call you a coward again."

Faint as bird's breath, she heard a sigh of frustration. A moment later, Jake Ross stepped out into the moonlight.

He stepped no farther out than was absolutely necessary. He said nothing. Imagine his saying nothing, as though there was nothing to say! Abbey shook her finger at him. "You told me to stay away from you," she reminded him. "Now you come to my door and pick around in the shadows. Why?"

His lips parted, as though he was about to speak.

Abbey held her breath. Would he be honest? Could she tell if he wasn't? She tried to read his emotions through the silence.

Then his lips closed, and he seemed to be biting the lower one to keep himself from saying anything. He stared at her, then waved his hand dismissively and started to turn away.

Abbey read anger in that gesture, in the set of his shoulders and the solidness of his stride. The magistrate had told her to stay away from him—and could it be that Jake was, as he had called himself, dangerous? A criminal, perhaps? Had she interrupted him in some illicit act? Or was he here to meet someone else?

There were too many questions to let him slip away without answering.

Abbey bolted forward a step. "Please . . . did you come to see the magistrate?"

Jake drew up in midstride, but he said nothing. He peeled off his hat and pushed his fingers into his hair—a motion of indecision.

She could see the magistrate had nothing to do with it—just by the way Jake paused, half turned to her, fought with himself not to turn all the way, looked curious. Why was he doing this? Why, why, why was he here?

Abbey's heart began to thump within her breast. It was fantasy, this sensation. Insane. Unreal . . . this bond between her and Jake that seemed to be tightening. A bond between two strangers that drew tighter and tighter each time they caught sight of each other. Unbidden and unfamiliar, it wrapped itself around them under the cool moonlight and kept Jake from walking away. Abbey could see it working on him, see that he hated it, that he resisted it, but that it wouldn't break. He could no more break it as he stood poised on the cobblestones than she could have turned and rushed back into the house and slammed the door on this whole spooky episode.

But one thing was certain: She wasn't imagining the uncanny

bond she felt between herself and this man, a bond she'd felt since the first instant their eyes had met that morning on the wharf. [There was a commonality of souls working between them.] He was here because of it. She was certain. Perhaps the idea was crazy, but *she* wasn't.

"Please," she murmured, "don't go."

Silhouetted against the moonlit cobblestones, Jake's body tightened in a kind of anguish. He clutched his cap against his belt, squeezing it, clamped his eyes shut, and tipped his face upward as though some answer lay hidden in the stringy clouds.

Abbey felt his anguish go through her own body.

"Is it me?" she asked. "Have you come to see me?"

Her voice moved through the cool sea air and struck him. He struggled a moment longer, then turned.

An instant later, his arms were around her. His breath dusted her cheek as he let forth another sigh of dissatisfaction with himself, and then the unlikely miracle bared itself between them and his mouth came down upon hers.

Abbey's arms flew outward in that moment of imbalance when he drew her against him. He pulled her up onto her toes, claiming her utterly.

His lips were dry and soft, his passion the heating element. His right arm came around the back of her shoulders and drew her close against him.

Abbey let herself go limp under the curve of his body, wondering what her body would do when confronted with the impetuousness she had dared him to act upon. Sure enough, she felt herself returning the kiss—so natural . . . so *right* . . . not fantasy, but *real*.

Upon that single, clinging rational thought, her mind slipped away into sensation, and she was lost. The world blurred around her, its only solid mass the two melding bodies that were herself and Jake Ross. The moon-dappled cobblestones fell away from her toes and she was standing on nothing, floating against him, as though their bodies were two clinging pieces of driftwood bobbing on the infinite sea.

A small moan came up through her, a meaningless syllable that evidenced the womanliness stirring in her once again for this stranger whose touch seemed so right. The moan broke from her lips as his

his mouth slid aside and lay for a moment against her cheek. Suddenly Jake seemed to reawaken from a dangerous dream.

His arm slid along her shoulders, drawing away. He grasped her arms and placed her flat on the ground as though to hammer her down from the peculiar passion and reinstill reality as abruptly as possible. He uttered a single unintelligible curse as he pushed himself away from her.

"Jake . . ." she gasped.

But he had broken away. For the first few steps he tried to walk away, but that wasn't enough to keep the bond from twining itself around them again, and he broke into a run. His footsteps echoed against the uneven cobblestones in the open night. Abbey reached out with a single desperate hand, but he was far down the street now, running through the grainy moonlight. Then a cloud slid over the moon and stole the light from Nantucket. In a wink, he was gone.

Her bed was a dry, cold place now. Against the sheets she felt the clammy impatience of her own body, the sudden tenderness of her thighs, the clutching hunger in the core of her being, the clatter of her heart rapping against her soul's back door. Over and over, she heard his footsteps echoing on the cobblestones as he ran away from the passion he himself had aroused. Her heart wanted company, but it was alone. Her fingers were cool as she pressed them under her chin; they wanted a man's warm body to stroke. Her shoulders wanted to be held again. They drew inward, tormenting her. Her body shuddered—a deep, heavy torture.

She bit her pillow, trying to drive away the hunger. Her lips still tingled. As the torture burgeoned and refused to go away, she clenched her fist into a ball and rammed it hard into the bedclothes, and damned herself for a lust she couldn't explain.

Great Point. As far from Nantucket Town as one could get and still be on the island. A two-hour ride down a bad road, past swamps and cranberry bogs and scrub oaks and straight up the northeast coast of the elbow-shaped island. Well, two hours more or less, probably less, considering that she had saddled the magistrate's pony and was riding on its back rather than driving a wagon out here, which would have been considerably slower. Riding the horse had allowed her to skirt across open country in some places rather than always following the roads, as long as she was careful not to get lost. Luckily, Abbey had two hours' worth of determination in her favor.

And there were enough surprises to keep her busy as she steered the narrow-boned filly along. It certainly was a colorful little place she'd come to—colorful in history if not in landscape. She passed signs with funny Indian words like Shawkemo, Masquetuck, and Podpis, and a little settlement called Wauwinet just before leaving all signs of civilization behind for that long ride straight up the coastline on a thin ribbon of land. The open sea spread to the horizon on either side of her—disconcerting to someone who was used to land being surrounded by more land. With every clop of the pony's hooves, Abbey felt the warm pool inside her simmer a little hotter.

Stupid, she scolded herself as she gazed down the flat finger of land to the Great Point lighthouse, still several minutes away. The white stone shaft tapered some seventy feet into the gray sky, topped by the turret that held the all-important guiding light. Ominous and enduring, the lighthouse symbolized both a warrant of safety and the enduring danger of seafaring. Strange . . . this stone shaft with its single light was a hallmark of mankind's link with the sea and the forces of nature. Had man not managed to broach the sea, if not conquer it, such a monument would never have been invented. But here it was, towering before her over the bosky, sandy strand, reminding her and everyone that there was both danger and safety to be had at sea, depending upon how the game was played.

What if he's not even there?

When she heard herself wondering that thought, she fought with herself to avoid asking the one resounding question that had hammered at her since Nantucket Town had disappeared behind her. What did she hope to accomplish at Great Point?

Instinct alone had brought her here this morning, a driving force so strong that an impetuous person could not resist it. And Abbey knew she was impetuous, a woman of feelings, of curiosity, of sensation. Her instincts seemed to have taken over, and she was only along for the ride.

Anticipation struck a chord within her. What was this force that dragged her here? Curiosity again? Certainly plenty of that. But she knew passion when she felt it, and she felt it now. Silly to deny it. And the wraith lurking outside her door last night, whose lips she still felt melting against her own, had known it, too, though he hadn't found a single word of explanation to speak into the darkness. Would it happen again?

Or might he try to deny it ever happened? The moon was her only witness. If Jake wanted to call her mad and accuse her of harassing him . . .

"I'll make you admit it," she murmured to the big, white stone lighthouse.

The lighthouse stood silent and imposing against the open sea, out here where there wasn't so much as a tree to challenge its sovereignty. It looked so solitary and alone out there . . . so strong, so determined to do what it was ordained to do.

Was Jake Ross the kind of man, she wondered, who would see the poetry of his work? Or would the job just be lighting and dousing to him? Abbey knew lighthouse keeping was a lonely business, and she wondered if he was the kind of man who chose that life because he wanted to remain alone.

In her deepest heart, she didn't want him to be alone.

"Absurd!" she blurted into the rising wind. "I must be possessed!" She huffed in self-deprecation at her lack of control. But she was here, and she might as well get to it. If only she could figure out what "it" was.

The flat silver sea was becoming less flat with every gust of wind. A chop was rising out there, and there was a corresponding gray cloud haunting the northwest horizon. She hadn't, by chance, picked a very good day to do this. She had to be back in town by three o'clock to get David, Adam, and Luella from school, and she certainly didn't want to be remiss in her duties on her first full day of caring for them. Three o'clock . . . a two-hour ride to Great Point, two back, and it had been nearly eighty-thirty when she left . . . yes, she could make it, and with a few hours to spare in between. Weather permitting. Jake permitting.

"He's weather," she muttered aloud to herself, trying to gain reassurance from the sound of her voice. "He's a storm. A very sudden storm."

She snapped the reins impatiently, and the filly jolted into a trot.

And he was there. She saw a faint glow of light inside the keeper's cottage window. A lantern, golden and warm on this ashen, seaswept day, its faint light glowing behind simple muslin curtains.

She turned the filly off the road and steered toward the keeper's cottage, through pure white sand haired with shoregrass, then around the concentric barrier of stones that surrounded the lighthouse itself. Great Point's tower of white masonry loomed above her, straight up into the darkening sky. She willed herself to ignore it, despite the dizziness it gave her when she made the mistake of looking up. At this close proximity, the huge white tower seemed to waver against the sky.

She had to ride around to the other side of the cottage before she found the seaward door. Steadying herself—not easily—she forced her trembling legs to get her off the pony and move her across the sand to the door. She was used to riding horses and couldn't blame the numbness of her knees on the long trip out here. That wasn't the problem at all.

With a final sigh, she rapped on the weathered wood door.

She waited. Nothing happened. No one came.

Her shoulders tingled as she rapped again, harder. Still nothing. Was he asleep? Did lighthouse keepers sleep all day? She should have thought of it. No man wanted to be caught half asleep, least of all by a woman who . . .

Her thought paused. To that sentence there was no ending yet. She wondered if there ever would be.

She shivered again, suddenly cold. Even the warm woollen shawl couldn't brace her against the wind skimming in over the flat ocean, bringing with it the ocean's very cold. She glanced over her shoulder and saw that the ocean wasn't flat at all anymore. The chop was rising now, bashing against the bluffs, for there was very little actual beach here. Sandy bluffs with beards of shoregrass had to brave the wind and waves on this narrow strand, upon which she could see the ocean's dominance in every direction.

He wasn't here. Good.

She started to turn away, almost making it back to the sturdy pony waiting patiently with reins dangling.

Then she stopped and huffed, "Damn me for indecision itself. I *will* knock again."

She turned on her heels, and a shout of surprise choked itself from her throat.

Hard brown eyes glared through her from under a wave of pale blond hair.

Abbey stumbled back a step and clasped her hands against her chest, gasping. "Lord, but you've got a silence about you!"

He was astonishing as he stood against the backdrop of his lighthouse. His dark green coat was gone; in its place now was a coarse-grained sheep's wool sweater the same color as the pebbles that skirted the lighthouse. Abbey recognized the hairs and neps in the sweater as the chaff from the sheepshearing room. It looked very practical against the rising sea wind, and it caught both the paleness of his hair and the stark whiteness of the stone tower behind him. Not as large a man as the magistrate, there was something none-theless stately about Jacob Ross. It had less to do with size than with presence—that intangible poise he seemed to have even when he was unsure of what he was doing. This wasn't one of those times, though—he knew exactly what he was doing. He was crushing her under that stubborn glare.

"What are you doing here, Abbey?" he demanded. He spoke the words softly, but still they carried clearly over the crash of the waves, rather like thunder in the distance.

It was her turn to glare, because they both knew why she was there. That much was obvious.

"What were you doing outside my door last night?" she counter-attacked. Though she hadn't meant to, the question set bells ringing inside her head—and his, from the look on his face—bells warning that those two questions had the same answer.

He pressed his lips tight, as though remembering the sensation she was out here chasing. "Making a mistake," he said hoarsely. "Go home."

He moved away.

"That is no answer, Mr. Ross," she insisted, following him toward the cottage door.

"It'll have to do," he said. The wind caught his voice and carried it away, but she got the meaning well enough.

Abbey hiked up her skirt and dodged past him, rounding on him before he could reach the door and escape inside. "Why did you kiss me?" she began, suddenly breathless.

His eyes widened and he held himself in place.

Abbey took a step toward him, doubling the pressure. "You owe me an answer." She softened her tone and added, "Or another kiss."

Then, tormented, Jake closed his eyes for an instant and moaned, "God be hanged . . ."

His fists clenched against his thighs, as though he were holding something in.

The breeze tugged at her words. "Did you think you could get away from me on a little burp of land like Nantucket? Whillikers, man, I rode this far just to get water before our well was dug."

He squinted at her, but remained silent.

"Are you afraid of something?" she asked, sympathy rising in her voice. "Have you done something wrong?"

"Yes," he said, "last night."

"I don't mean that." She followed him as he tried to escape her a second time by turning back toward the lighthouse. The pebbles crunched under their feet as he reluctantly led her around toward the lighthouse door. "Have you done something criminal? Something on the mainland that you're hiding from? You shouldn't have to keep paying for your past. How terrible can it be? Jake, turn and speak to me."

"I can't," he snapped, tossing her a glance.

"Why not?"

"Because I *want* to, that's why!" he blurted. His struggle crystallized before her, and he paused with his hand gripping the frame of the lighthouse door. His back was to her.

Abbey halted a step behind him. Her heart skipped a beat.

"Then I'm right . . ." she murmured. "You feel it, too. We're kindred spirits, you and I."

"I don't believe it's possible," he insisted, more to himself than to her.

Abbey moved closer, pressing the tenuous bond. "I believe it's rare . . . but possible. We understand each other. We look at the world through the same eyes. You . . . me . . ."

Mutual attraction kindled once again between them. She could feel it. Within moments, it burned.

"I'm not imagining it," Abbey whispered, relief entwined with her words.

"I don't know what you're imagining," he said harshly, turning back toward her—but not all the way. "I only know it must stop."

"Why must it? Tell me."

Jake pushed on the lighthouse door and slid it open. Abbey could tell he meant to get inside and close the door between them, so she stepped up to it and placed her hands on the cool, rough wood.

"Please don't," she begged, her own torment rising. "I need to know."

Jake stopped short, the door half shut between them, holding it halfway open and gazing at her. His eyes tightened in distress, and for a heartbeat Abbey thought he might come out again.

"This is madness," he said. "We have something in common, but I don't recognize it. I'd like you to go away."

"No." She pressed upon the door and was surprised when he let it slide open another few inches before he stopped it with his foot. Those few inches made her heart jump again, and she became desperate to speak to him candidly, before the tenuous filaments snapped. "We must address it now, or we'll always wonder. I'm bound to stay on this island. Unless you mean to leave, we can't possibly avoid each other. This conjury between us . . . I can't let it lie in the mud. It'll surely get up and haunt us."

"It has already," he grumbled.

A breakthrough! She pressed harder against the door, but not too hard. She wanted him to know she was driven by this enchantment that pulled like a tightening thread, but that she also meant to give him his choice—ultimately. But first she would know what he truly believed, what he felt.

A gust of wind struck her in the back like a blow. She huddled against the door, suddenly shivering, and glanced back at the sea as though accusing it of assault.

"Storm," Jake said in a low tone. He squinted into the western sky at a glowering black thunderhead. "Best get inside."

"My pony . . ." Abbey pushed herself off the door and headed across sand, but she wasn't used to the sandy ground, and the next

67

gust of wind, strong and sudden as a whipping, drove her to her knees.

Strong hands folded around her arms and pulled her to her feet. She tried not to lean against Jake as he guided her back to the shelter of the lighthouse and pushed her inside.

"Stay put," he said, wind tearing at his hair. A sheet of rain came down with the next gust, and Jake raised his arm to shield his eyes from the sting as he headed across the sand toward the pony. The horse was accustomed to rough weather, but not out on the open strand. The reins dragged on the ground as the filly danced about in front of the keeper's cottage, trying to decide which way to run. Jake chased her and finally caught the end of one rein as the wind lifted it. He hauled hard on the bridle, and the pony was glad to follow. Man and horse disappeared around the lighthouse.

Abbey thought about following, and she even stepped beyond the doorway's protection, only to be swatted back in by the rain's sharp hand. This oceanfront rain didn't just come down. It slapped and sideswiped and punished everything in its path. And it was cold rain, too, coming in off the open sea as it did. Just that one stroke had left Abbey numb. She huddled inside, wishing she could close the door, but Jake was out there somewhere and she wanted desperately to know that he would come back here and not hide from her.

A roar of thunder made her jump. She looked up at the sky over the strand and caught her breath. Where a moment ago there had been solid gray sky, there now was a churning caldron of black clouds just a few hundred feet over her head. So monstrous that it stole the air from her lungs, the squall roiled and boiled over the lighthouse as though it meant to swallow the strand. She'd never seen a storm cloud dip so low, nor sweep in so suddenly.

She'd been in two cyclones in her life, and though those were terrifying examples of nature's rage, they at least gave some signal that they were on the way. The air grew hot, heavy, and ominously still before the black cloud formed itself close to the ground and began to twist. This storm, though, gave no warning. It simply hit.

Where was he?

He could have fallen down. He may be confused or injured. The black arms of rain coming down they could knock a man off his feet. . . .

She almost stepped out, looking in the direction he'd gone, and a form loomed at her shoulder. She spun, and then was dragged back inside the lighthouse. The door slammed shut just as the wind started to howl.

"Must you always come at me from behind?" she demanded.

Jake pressed the rainwater from his hair. "It's a good skill," he commented. For the first time, he smiled.

The smile awakened the dim lighthouse interior. Like the lightning, though, it was gone almost instantly, and only the memory of its flash remained. He dashed to a nearby window and surveyed the northeastern sky. His lips went flat and he grimaced at what he saw. "Holy Judas . . ."

He ran a hand down each sleeve of his sweater, and the natural wool shed water like a good shake from a wet ram. Then he grabbed a rag, dried his face, and ran the rag through his hair in a hasty manner. Drying his hands, he glanced up the narrow, winding staircase that led seventy feet into the sky, to the giant guiding light of Great Point. "Got to get her lit or there'll be wrecks."

"Even in the middle of the day?"

His brown eyes struck her like a blow. "Fog doesn't care where it comes down. Gray fog, gray day, gray seas—for a ship, that's more dangerous than night. 'Scuse me," he added, pushing urgently by her.

"Might I help?" Abbey called as Jake mounted the first few steps.

Pausing, he looked at her. "It's not very glamorous."

"Glamor is in the eye of the beholder."

As she gazed unflaggingly at him, he made a guarded decision. He handed her the rag and said, "If you like. Be careful. These old steps can kill you, too." He started up the staircase, almost at a run.

Outside, the howling wind and slashing rain drummed against the hollow shaft of the lighthouse, creating a tunnel effect inside. Abbey hunched her shoulders and felt her way along the damp stone wall. She hadn't been prepared for so ominous a place. Yet this lighthouse, so much bigger up close than it had seemed when she first saw it, was dark and forbidding inside, and it seemed to stretch upward into the very clouds that blew down to engulf it. The narrow winding steps twisted up and up, growing smaller and narrower. Like cellar steps leading down and down into a pit of hell, these slippery wooden steps led up and up, into a kind of celestial hell that was twice as bad. Going down into the bosom of the earth was easier for the human spirit to understand. This, though . . .

She followed Jake up through a hole and onto a circular platform around the actual light itself, at the very top of the stone edifice. Her face tightened when she caught the thick scent of oil.

Once up there though, standing in the open space, she felt an odd relief as she watched Jake go about the business of lighting the lantern that would feed light through the giant lamps and out over the open sea. She counted twelve—no, fourteen—lamps with reflectors that were more than a foot in diameter, arranged in two circles parallel to the horizon. The lantern itself was more than two and a half feet taller than Jake, and about nine inches wide. An odd-looking contraption, all told.

"What's it run on?" she asked.

He glanced at her. "Whale oil."

"No, I mean what burns?"

"It's a wick, like any lantern," he said. "I have to keep it up and trimmed so the blaze burns at its full height. Well, I don't *have* to, but I prefer to. Some keepers let their lamps go down too often."

Abbey nodded as though she understood, which she didn't. "How bright is it? How far will it shine?"

"Twelve thousand candlepower. They'll see it some fourteen miles out."

Faster than she would have expected, Jake set the Great Point beacon alight. She wasn't even entirely sure just what he did—but soon there was a blaze running up that big lantern, reflected through the polished lamps. The scent of oil grew stronger as the wick burned, and a crackling noise hummed around them.

"That'll do it," Jake said. "We'll see what the storm does now."

He gestured to her to join him. From where they stood together, Abbey saw the wide brightness of Great Point's light spreading over the darkened sea, cutting through the squall without a falter, and she suddenly realized what value that light would be to an approaching ship.

"Rain's so thick, it's almost dark as night out there," she said. "Wouldn't it be horrifying to be on a boat in this storm! I can't imagine it."

Jake shook his head and blurted, "I can." His tone was one of irony, and Abbey figured that meant he had been through such an experience.

She coiled her arms about herself, feeling the coldness of the tower's masonry inches from her. Even so, she moved closer to the window and watched the rain slash downward. "Wonderful . . . storms. I love them."

His eyes touched her. "You love a storm?"

"Mmmm," she uttered with a nod. "I used to go into the cutting corral and stand there while the rain crashed down all around me, and I'd smell the grass of the range and the wet scent of our herd, and feel the rain on my face and shoulders. Then, by the time I went back inside, I would well appreciate the warmth of our fireplace."

"Bet so," he muttered.

"I can't wait to go up onto one of those little roof things and watch a storm cut across Nantucket Harbor."

"The widow's walk?"

She looked at him. "The what?"

"The roofwalk," he said.

Leaning one shoulder against the cold glass of the window, Abbey pivoted toward him. "No, you didn't say that. You said something else."

His brows came together for a moment, and then he said, "Oh . . . widow's walk. You haven't heard the term yet, then."

"No," she murmured. "No, I haven't. What a sad term. Does it mean what I think it does?"

Jake ran his hand through his drying hair and said, "It does. Wives in Nantucket stand aboard them and watch out to sea for a sign of a mast on the horizon. Though, it's . . ."

"What?"

"Well, it's sometimes as foreboding to see one as not to."

"Why's that?"

Jake sighed, both in hesitation and in an effort to find the right words for a subject he clearly didn't like describing. "A ship comes back. Not all its crew does, sometimes. It's a scurvious life, seafaring is. If the boredom doesn't kill you, then it'll be disease, the sea, the whales, the heat, the cold, the slippery deck . . . something. And there's no way to send word home when a man dies. No way to find out, and when that mast shows itself, the woman on the walk knows she might be a widow. And she still has a while to wait before she can find out. Makes me glad I'm not a woman."

Abbey clutched herself tighter in empathy. So awful. There was such a terrible mingling of conflicting feelings within her— elation . . . fear . . . hope . . . and that flimsy kind of strength that comes up inside a woman when she realizes she might be alone again.

"I was fortunate," she whispered, turning once again to the black- ened horizon and the kicking sea. "I knew right away."

Jake fell silent for a beat, watching her, and when he spoke he seemed to know exactly what she was talking about, though he couldn't possibly know. He *sensed*.

His face bunched up and he let out a gust of regret. "Pardon what I said . . . I'd no mind to hurt you."

"You've not hurt me," Abbey said forthrightly. "You see, I'm glad I'm not a man. I'd hate going to sea and wondering which of my children had died of pneumonia or fever while I was gone, and not being there to comfort and hold them. Or to be sailing some cold foreign ocean and be eaten alive by wondering if my bride's affections had been stolen by some other man. Or to have little else to do but carve decorations in whalebone and mourn my loneliness for months and years on end."

His eyes moved through hers. "You sound as though you've been there."

A tiny smile tugged at her mouth. "No . . . but I imagine well, and I pay attention to what I see about me. Everything in Nantucket whispers of those feelings." Not without some calculation, she let a short silence fall in order that he might absorb her words. She gave it time, then spoke again. "Have you been seafaring?"

"Me?" he blurted. Then he chuckled and shook his head. "Not *me*. Die first."

Abbey's brows tightened in question. "First?"

He leaned his elbow on the windowsill and nodded. "Me and the sea don't mix, ma'am."

"Why did you come here, then?" she puzzled.

"I was drifting through the South and, uh . . . I told you I got into some bad dealings." A shrug illustrated his efforts to remain vague. "I signed on a ship headed northward, but as soon as that ship hit Nantucket, I got bloody off it."

Abbey stifled a giggle, sensing what was coming. "Why did you?"

Jake huffed at himself. "Never been colder, greener, or sicker. Ten times worse than the South, sailing is. Only time I was that sick was when I tried my first cigar. And I *don't* smoke cigars, you'll notice." He paused for illustration, then wryly added, "Hell's not made of fire. It's made of seawater."

Now Abbey did allow herself a little smile and said, "I bet you take some ribbing on an island full of sailors."

"That I do," he admitted.

"Why don't you leave Nantucket?"

"Leave? I'd leave in a minute. But I can't figure out a way to get off!"

He laughed self-consciously, and Abbey laughed, too, openly now.

That ethereal feeling they both had now moved again between them. Jake Ross took an unbidden, unthinking step that drew him closer to her as the rain roared outside and the great lantern buzzed behind them. "I'm glad you're not a man . . . also."

Abbey's gaze shifted to him and was caught there, willingly. She said nothing, sensing a power in her silence.

When he spoke again, his warm breath wreathed her face. "Is there no loneliness in Wyoming Territory?"

The golden-white light from the lantern shined on half his face, setting ablaze one dark eye and a cheekbone and lighting his thatch of blond hair until it was aflame.

Abbey lost herself in the nearness of him, sharing her soul willingly, and in time she whispered, "More than you know, Mr. Ross."

The rain slashed. The great light burned its beacon over the darkened sea beneath the black squall's clouds. Wind whined and bellowed, whipping itself into knots around the white masonry tower of the Great Point lighthouse. The world had forgotten that it was still the middle of the day. The sun was cloaked, forgotten. Time was forgotten.

Giving in to the threads that pulled at her, Abbey leaned closer to Jacob Ross, until her own breath mingled with his. Her heart boomed against her breast now, pulled upward from its daily business to begin that rare percussion that was the heart's duty at times of poetry.

Was he caught in it, too? Was that why he looked at her now with that long, unbroken gaze? Perhaps he could finally admit they were cut from the same stone. Perhaps he, too, felt the need to draw into one again, as nature meant.

She felt his breath, his warmth—

He blinked suddenly and drew away as though something had pinched him. Some inner reality had struck as surely and cleanly as the lightning outside.

Abbey's lips fell apart, both in question and in disappointment. They tingled from want.

"Are you warm enough?" he asked, breaking away and putting several steps between them.

She was, but she knew an opportunity when one presented itself. All she could hope to do now was somehow to draw him back. "Not very," she fibbed, rubbing her arms to illustrate the lie.

Nervously he grasped his candlestick and headed toward the staircase. "I'll build a fire." He started down the skinny twisting stairway, paused, turned, and offered her his hand. Poised there, he waited for her to decide to come down, as though there was a choice.

Plain enough. Abbey sighed her disappointment, her perplexity at his behavior. She *knew* what he felt. He could never convince her otherwise. It had been there. It was still there. Somehow, she would bring it back.

She would certainly have been lying to pretend she didn't need his help getting down those creaking steps. Each plank seemed smaller by half than when she'd been coming up them. The stairway was harrowing in mere candlelight, its haunting danger redoubled by the storm's rumble against the hollow stone walls. She felt each roar of thunder against the stone wall and then move through her as she felt her way down, one step at a time. This time Jake was patient about it, letting her take the stairway slowly. The light was lit, the seas were . . . well, not exactly safe, but all that could be done had been done. The urgency was gone; all that remained were the cannons of thunder reverberating through the lighthouse. By the time they reached the bottom, her shivering was real.

And so was her sigh of relief. "Do you climb those stairs every night?"

"Nearly every night," Jake confirmed as he put the candle on a small table and approached a stone hearth. He rubbed the warmth back into his hands, then started arranging small logs in the fireplace. "There are a few nights that are as clear as daylight, but those are rare."

"So you must be here every night without fail."

He glanced at her. "I live here."

"But what if you can't be here? What if you have reason to be in town and can't get away? What would happen then?"

He chuckled. "You mean if someone decided to toss me in jail or some misfortune of the like?"

"I didn't mean—"

"There's a boy in Wauwinet. He apprentices the light. If the light's not lit by dusk, he comes and lights it. But that's only happened twice," Jake added. "You are a pile of questions, Mrs. Sutton."

"Abbey," she corrected.

He crouched at the fireplace and paused. "Abbey."

"I like the way you say my name."

Self-consciously he involved himself with getting the kindling to light up under the firewood. "How many ways are there to say it?" he asked, avoiding saying her name a second time.

As the fire's glow began to burgeon and spread, Abbey arranged herself on the heavy rug near the hearth and hugged her knees. "Perhaps it's just you then. I like you, you know."

"You haven't had time to like me," he reminded, forcing himself to be stern about it. "You do remember that you've only been on the island a couple of days . . . you *do* remember that."

"I do."

Knowing what was coming, knowing that she had given him an answer that would strengthen his argument about the attraction between them, Abbey used those words as catalysts to enchantment. She spoke them heavily, with more breath than sound, and as they weighed in the air, she reached up and drew out the single hairpin that was keeping her braided hair in place.

She waited until he looked.

Drawing the long amber braid over her shoulder, she played her fingers through it, loosening it, then ran them through it a second time, more slowly. Her eyes invited him to take over.

Lightning glared through the window in its instant way, clashing with the soft golden luster of the hearth flame. Abbey felt it lay its stark light against her left shoulder, even as the fire's gloss lay against her right.

He watched her, entranced. Waxy firelight spread across his features.

Abbey drew her fingers through her hair a third time, shaking it out completely until it lay over her breast in a wavy carpet.

Jake suddenly turned toward the fire, dutifully breaking his stare. "Please don't do that . . ."

Leaving her hair to flow down her front, Abbey moved her fingers to the small cloth buttons on the bodice of her blouse. One by one she began to undo them. There were ten cloth buttons on the high-necked bodice of her dress, with ten little braided loops. She slipped off the first one. And the second.

"I want you, Jake," she heard a stranger whisper, the stranger that had been pushing her toward him from the first moment she'd seen him. That first moment—when they'd looked down the wharf at the slaves and exchanged a sameness of self.

She'd never really believed in such things before. Life on the plains had always been far too harsh and real to indulge in things so ethereal. But then . . . nothing had ever been this strong.

Jake refused to look at her, but her words had an obvious and immediate effect on him. "I know you do," he said, struggling.

"Look at me."

"I can't. I don't dare." He was fighting to keep the steadiness in his voice, and the passion out of it.

"Why not?"

"Because we're strangers. Strangers don't have love."

"I never claimed love for you," Abbey said logically. Another button fell from its loop, and another.

Now he did turn, rather abruptly, and held a hand out to her in entreaty. "And that's enough for you? The call of the flesh?"

She stopped unbuttoning, her fingers pausing on the button that would open her cleavage to his view. "I've never been ashamed of it."

In an explosion of tension and rage, Jake dragged her to her feet and shook her once, hard. "Did you love your husband? Or is this enough?"

His mouth rammed down on hers again—echoes of last night, of moonlight and rambling roses—except that now there was anger where last night there had been passion, now there was thunder and the slash of rain where last night there had been moonlight and a sea breeze. Somehow it just wasn't the same. . . .

Abbey tore herself away from him, scoring her lip on his unshaven chin. She stumbled back, breathing hard. "You're insane!"

Tormented, Jake wailed, "*I'm* insane?" He slapped his hands against his thighs and stalked around her in a half-circle. "Christamighty. *I'm* insane . . ." He paused then, staring at her through the dim candlelight and the flicker of the growing fire. "Why did you have to come here?"

"What difference does it make?" she shot back. "Fate would have drawn us together somewhere, some time."

"You believe that?"

"I feel it."

He drew backward, away from her. The fire crackled and threw sparks at his boots. His brown boots, his gray trousers, his pebble-colored sweater, his pale hair—all were alight and shimmering with firelight. He was a human taper glowing in the darkness, his blond hair catching the yellow luster of the fire like a candle's wick. "You don't know what you want," he rasped.

Amazed, Abbey parted her moist lips and watched him. He was pulling away from her. How many men would do that? She asked him to sacrifice nothing—she was laying herself before him like a whore because of this undefined bond she felt, and he was drawing away. Any other man would take what she offered without a glimmer of conscience getting in his way. Not Jake Ross.

This was a man who had a sooty past? This was a man who called himself dangerous?

Add two and two—the answer wasn't Jake Ross.

Then what was he? Most men wouldn't turn her down. How dishonorable could he be?

Burning curiosity rose within her, rivaling both lightning and firelight. His resistance alone was a driving factor for her; the more he resisted, the more her desire grew. Thunder continued to boom against the stone column.

She raised her hand to her bodice again, and slowly undid another button. Now another. Firelight touched the crease between her breasts. She ran her middle finger up the crease, to her throat, then back down again, and watched him breathe deeply—in, then out—as though he were somehow joined with that finger.

Jake's eyes held her hand as she worked her magic.

One more button would do it. She saw that in his face, heard it in the ragged breath he drew as her fingers played over the button loop. True . . . she didn't know what she wanted. She had no real idea what had brought her here. In the West she'd learned that life is too short to worry about propriety. Her forefinger skimmed the soft skin between her throat and her breast, skin that was warm now with a sheen of perspiration.

Jake trembled and bit his lip.

"You don't regret the things you do," Abbey spoke softly. "You regret the things you *don't* do."

One more button. Her fingers rotated over the cloth-covered bead. That one button would force him. So incongruous—that in some ways a woman could force a man . . .

Chapter Five

HOW WOULD SHE feel if she were being forced?

Her fingers hesitated over that one button and did not squeeze it through its loop.

"No," she murmured, nearly whispering, "I don't know what I want. I know what I sense, but . . . at this moment you are only a sensation to me. Strong sensation . . . without substance."

With that she gave him the gift of time; her fingers fell away from the button. Outside, whistling wind swirled around the lighthouse, caressing it, and carried away the obligation she would have pressed upon him with that one button.

Jake pressed his hand over his mouth as though to wipe away the desire she'd aroused in him. Then he folded his arms as if to keep holding himself back, and said, "I'm no poet, but I know a bad rhyme when I hear one."

"What's that pretending to mean?"

"It means this sensation you talk about . . . it's—"

"Dangerous?" She stepped nearer, almost destroying the gift. "Like you're dangerous? You said you were."

"I wish I hadn't," he breathed. "Seems you like it."

Abbey smiled, and then she even laughed. "I suppose I do. Fools are like that, Jake. It takes a fool to make pioneer stock, and those are the people I come from. Please . . . don't hate me."

This moved him, if nothing else had. He caught her hand as she raised it to push back a stray curl. "I don't hate you," he insisted. It seemed important to him that she believe that. "But I don't care to be confused, and you confuse me."

She tipped her head, knowing the firelight would catch the line of her chin. "Abbey," she said softly.

His hand grew suddenly moist around hers. "Abbey . . ."

A smile was her reward to him, and his to her was an expression of regret. For the moment, at least. Yet again—how many times now?—he drew away from her very deliberately. "I'll make some coffee."

She gave him a simple nod. "I'll drink it."

He swung his arms again, quaking with frustration and arousal, perhaps even buried anger. No, not perhaps. Definitely.

He was right, she knew. Very right and wise to resist the magnetism between them. She knew that. In fact, she realized that until this moment she'd been fighting the sting of common sense. Impulse had gripped her and she had let it take hold. What if he'd been an ordinary man and not as strong as he apparently was? What if he'd given in to her seduction, and what if nature made itself known upon them in the form of a child? Jake was a man of passions—that much was plain. Would the prospect of fathering a child stop him from being with a woman he didn't know, a woman who put herself before him this way? That wasn't nature's habit; the male of the species didn't bear that burden. Then what was it she had seen in his eyes?

Jake was slamming around on the other side of the bottom stairs. Pots clattered, venting anger and the sexual frustration that still buzzed between them. No . . . it hadn't gone away.

After a moment he emerged from the hidden side of the tower's inner shaft, carrying a battered coffeepot. He hung it on the hearth hook and swung it in over the fire, trying to stay busy.

"I have to leave here by one o'clock," Abbey said, making conversation.

"You're not leaving anywhere until that blow dies down. Then, be assured," he warned, "I'll pitch you out."

His eyes flared with the promise, but there was also curl of a grin on his lips. Sheets of rain slashed against the window, making his point for him, and a roll of thunder pressed the point home.

The coffee filled the air with aroma before they spoke again, and even then Abbey had to force her words to come out. Perhaps he found it hard to trust her as much as she trusted her own feelings. Yes, that was it. . . . she would have to earn his regard.

Licking her lips, she tried a new approach. "Why are you on Nantucket?"

"It's none of your business, Abbey," he said from where he huddled on a stool near the fire.

She bobbed her eyebrows scoffingly. "I mean, where are you from?"

He tugged at his collar, then sighed, deciding the question was harmless enough. "Ohio, originally," he said. "Then Georgia. Then Kansas . . . then New York . . . then here."

"And did you run lighthouses in Texas?" she asked, her tone making it clear that she was prying again, even though she had said she wouldn't.

"Very funny," he muttered.

"I mean only to ask what your real trade is. Do you have a skill?"

His hair flickered in the firelight as he shook his head. "Nothing specific. I do jobs as they come along. This one . . . came along."

"Tell me about the pub. You said your cousins run it. Do you help there also?"

"I'm part owner. But I don't often work the pub. I've got the light to keep me busy."

"What were you doing on the docks?"

He struck her with an impatient glare, apparently tired of her questions. "Getting a fresh stock of whale oil to run this jack-o'-lantern, that's what."

"I'm just asking, Jake."

"You're interfering."

"Abbey," she encouraged. "Say my name again."

"No. Don't play games. They're—"

He stopped himself, but he was too late. They both already knew what he had almost said.

She rose from her chair and crossed the dim floor of the lighthouse, through the golden firelight to his side. As he gazed up at her, she murmured, "Dangerous. Like you."

Jake Ross stared up at her, and slowly—so slowly—drew himself up from the fireside stool. His height matched hers, then passed hers, giving him those few inches that made her tilt her face up slightly to keep the gaze from breaking. Once again he became a tallow-haired taper burning in the dimness.

His fingers moved upward to find her hair. Gradually his hand lost itself in the long twist of amber that hung over her shoulder.

"Soft," he murmured. The fire crackled in punctuation. His eyes caught its orange glow.

Together, as a single bell struck by two hammers, their hearts chimed. The simmering Abbey had felt within her rose to effervescence. His head slowly dropped, tilting gently, until their mouths met once again, but this time with a tenderness that resonated through them both. There was no force, no surprise, no anger. Only the triumphant flutter of something awakening that had been asleep for too long, waiting for the two of them to arouse it.

The intrigue still moved between them—Abbey was dully aware of it as she lost herself in the movement of his lips, the moisture of his mouth, the soft fleshy involvement that quickened their pulses.

He drew her closer, and she sagged against him. Her eyes drifted closed until only a slit of firelight blurred to remind her that this wasn't a dream. He was right . . . this was insane.

Strangers, yes. Two strangers, so physically attuned as to reduce each other to bare passion. Abbey had never heard of such a thing, neither in fairy tale or myth, but she had felt very much the lioness as she encroached upon his domain, looking for the hot-blooded victory she now felt.

His arms slipped farther and farther around her until she was drowning in him, her spine bent back like a reed into the wind.

Incendiary. Fire. Everywhere. There, in the stone hearth, and here, between lonely hearts.

There are some things a man and woman can't stop. A match, once struck, must flare and burn. Where love was, there could be no knowing. Passion had no answers.

Jake clutched Abbey's upper arms until the pain made her gasp, and he gasped, too, but in a different kind of pain. With all his strength of being, he pushed her away and threw himself across the narrow curved space toward the other side of the hearth. He caught himself on the mantel and gripped it with both hands, his fingers going white as he squeezed and squeezed.

Rain and wind slashed at the stone obelisk of Great Point. Some things a man and woman can't stop—

And some they must.

"God's oath," Jake moaned. "God's oath . . ."

"Jake," Abbey murmured, taking a fatal step toward him.

He flung himself away from her, going around the long way, under the spiral staircase to the lighthouse door. He yanked it open and dragged it shut behind him, and was gone in a howl of wind.

Chapter Six

SHE RODE OUT the storm alone. She saw him no more that day.

The storm went away, as storms will, and so apparently had Jake. Somehow, even on this barren strip of land, he had disappeared. His turbulence, though, remained. Finally, time had driven her to leave Great Point. Responsibilities called her back to Nantucket Town, and she was compelled to go.

He watched her leave.

From his hiding place, huddled under a grassy shelf cut into a sandbar, Jake coiled his arms around his knees. His legs were numb, crossed at the ankles, his boots and trousers soaked. Over his shoulder and out to sea, he heard the sizzling sound of the rain as it finally passed them by, leaving only a shroud of fog that would pass within the hour.

His chest tightened when Abbey came out of the lighthouse. His throat throbbed with desire to call out to her as he saw her looking around, wondering where on this formless sandbar he could possibly be hiding. He saw her go to the door of the keeper's cottage and his whole constitution twisted when she didn't knock, but walked right in to look for him there. She was so bold . . . how long could he resist that? Of course, a few moments later she came out, dejected, her shoulders slumped.

He coiled his arms tighter around his legs, forcing himself to stay where he was, no matter how much moisture was seeping up through his trousers, no matter the bone-deep chill that had long ago set into his shoulders and pelvis, no matter the screaming soul inside him that wanted to unfold and stand up and call out.

When he saw Abbey's hand lingering on the doorknob to his house, saw her caress it with regret, he thought surely he would be crushed by it. He pressed his mouth into the coarse sleeve of his sweater and bit into the wool.

And when Abbey disappeared around the lighthouse and reappeared with the filly trailing her, he knew she had made her decision to go away.

That's what he wanted, his mind told him in its private shell. He wanted her to go away. To go, and take his need away.

Since she hadn't given herself time to stop at the magistrate's home and drop off the horse, Abbey rode the nimble roan through town toward the schoolhouse. She realized she wouldn't exactly be the model governess waiting for the children in her mud-splashed, sand-caked riding skirt. Until this moment, she hadn't given it a thought. The skirt was split in the middle for riding, a rugged device of the West. Eastern women rode sidesaddle, but to Abbey that had always resembled suicide. Still, she'd hoped to avoid appearing grotesquely uneastern, but so far she had ruined that hope at nearly every stride. Nantucket women didn't give her quite the disapproving glances she'd gotten in Boston when she'd stepped off the train with her split skirt and cowboy boots, for these women were pioneers in their own way, too, but she did get the occasional questioning blink or two as she approached the schoolhouse.

These blinks, though, didn't command her attention quite as much as the sensation that raised the tiny hairs at the base of her neck. It was back: the sensation of being followed. It had been with her long before she had entered the town, while she had been out near the cranberry bogs, on the road from Great Point. And it was still with her. She had looked around several times, and indeed had caught glimpses of fleeting shadows here and there, or a hand just disappearing behind a tree as she turned, or the corner of a heel drawing in behind a building. Jake?

Could it be?

She wanted desperately to slip around and surprise him from

behind, even thought about how she would do it. But soon the schoolhouse doors would open and the Nash children would be back in her care. Wouldn't it be a nice spectacle for them to come out of the schoolhouse doors in time to see her ramming about between the stores chasing the lighthouse keeper?

On that very thought, a shadow slipped from one side of the nearest alley to the other. She peered in that direction—without completely turning her head—and tried to appear unconcerned or unnoticing. How intriguing that he would follow her, how endearing in its . . . *odd* way. She'd never have pegged him for the following kind. She straightened her shoulders and made a point of not looking while she made a great business of sliding off the pony's back and leading the animal up to the schoolhouse's short picket fence.

She waited for the shadow to move again, but nothing happened. Had she seen it, or was her imagination exercising itself? It was still a gray day, despite the storm's passing. She might be seeing anything down those dim alleys . . .

But she knew those were lies. Somebody was following her again, gray day or not, dim alley or not. It was him and they both knew it.

A charming game, even if Jake didn't entirely realize it was a lover's game he was playing.

Abbey's lips turned upward in a smile she could barely control. She glanced around. Was there time? She fought to keep her lips together and her cheeks from dimpling.

Yes, she decided, there was time—barely enough before the children would come piling from that schoolhouse door.

As casually as possible, she remounted the roan and steered past the place where she'd glimpsed her follower's disappearing boot heel, heading placidly toward Main Street. She tried not to make it appear too deliberate; it would be better to surprise him.

But the surprise was Abbey's.

When she caught another glimpse of her pursuer trailing her pointless lope down the cobbled street, her mischievous joy snapped and turned to rage. Not Jake at all, her pursuer—or rather, *pursuers* were the two men she and Jake had evaded once before. They were back! And this time they were definitely following her.

"We'll see about this," she growled privately, and steered the pony between two stores, each of which had long railed balconies above the alley between them. Her plan formed itself immediately when she glanced up. She picked one balcony, looped the filly's reins around the saddle horn, shook her feet free of the stirrups, and climbed up onto the saddle with her feet side by side on the seat. Managing her balance carefully, she got her balance over the filly's slow walk, and stretched to full height just as the filly passed by the nearest balcony. Up on her toes, and Abbey was able to get a good grip on the floor of the balcony.

The filly turned one large eye backward with lazy curiosity as the weight left her back. Without a rider, the pony paced along for a few more lengths, then came to a stop at the end of the alley to wait for directions.

Abbey struggled up onto the balcony, trying to keep from grunting as she hauled herself over the rail. She crouched immediately behind a rain barrel, and waited.

She couldn't see below, but she could hear. Crunching footsteps, and a muttering of low voices that she recognized from before. Hang them, how dare they follow her!

She allowed herself a grunt as she pressed her shoulder against the rain barrel, heaving it over toward the railing. The barrel didn't argue. Rainwater sloshed within it, lapped over the rim, then crashed out in a great gray tongue as the barrel rolled onto its side. Water cascaded through the spokes of the balcony rail and splashed onto the heads of her trackers, driving them to their knees in the gravel.

Two distinct roars of disgust and shock blasted up toward her after the initial slosh of water. A trail of curses followed, satisfying her utterly.

From above, Abbey leaned over and watched in satisfaction.

When the great splash ended and water continued to dribble onto the two gawking, sputtering, cursing men below, Abbey huffed her victory, strode to the end of the balcony, climbed over, and deftly dropped onto the filly's back. She scooped up the reins and parted her legs, dropping into the saddle once again, tightening her thighs at just the right moment to avoid being jarred to the core. With a click of her tongue she turned the filly around and plodded right by the amazed faces of the Longhorn Mustache and Hunch.

They were soaked to the skin and obviously embarrassed as she passed by them. Longhorn's mustache now looked more like soggy grass after the rain.

For an instant as she passed them, Abbey drew up the reins. "Pleased to meet you, gentlemen. I'll be shopping for fabric later today, if you care to continue following me. I'll be informing the magistrate about you, and that'll be the last of this." Indignation and anger both were evident in her voice.

The two men could do nothing but watch her leave them behind.

Abbey, cloaked in satisfaction, rode the pony back to the schoolhouse. Except for chiding herself for not demanding why those two had been following her—was she so afraid of the answer?—she felt quite pleased with herself.

When she slid off the pony again, she noticed that the two men were gone from the alley's mouth. Good enough.

"Miss Sutton! Miss Sutton! I'm here!"

She turned in time to see little, scrawny Luella plummet toward her from the schoolhouse steps, followed by several other children who promptly dispersed, and eventually by her two brothers.

"Oh, there you are!" Abbey spread her arms, and sure enough Luella leaped into them. Such a unique child—most little girls were shy with unfamiliar people. Not Luella.

"I spelled 'cradle' and 'elephant' today," Luella announced.

Abbey widened her eyes accordingly. "Did you really? Are you sure you did?"

"Oh, yes, I did. And tomorrow I'm going to spell 'lighthouse.'"

Abbey twisted her mouth into a grimace and muttered, "How appropriate." She forced herself to turn the grimace into a smile for Luella's sake. "I couldn't be prouder. Wait until your father hears."

"Why do you have Maribelle with you?" Luella pointed to the filly.

"Maribelle needed some fresh air."

Luella craned her scrawny little neck. "Can I ride her?"

"Well, I don't know. Can you?"

"If you teach me." The child's bright eyes widened and she squirmed out of Abbey's grip.

"All right," Abbey said, leading her to the filly. "Always mount on the left side."

"Why?"

With a shrug, Abbey admitted, "I don't rightly know. But we'd better keep it that way, just in case there's a good reason."

The boys appeared beside her, then. "It's because of soldiers," one of them sedately informed her.

Abbey paused just before lifting Luella into the saddle. "Pardon?"

"Soldiers wear their swords on the left side. Most of 'em, leastways. Can't get on a horse if there's a sword in your way. So they get on from the left. Ever since olden times."

Abbey straightened and patted his shoulder. "That's well said, Adam. I'm impressed."

"How'd you know I was Adam?"

"You really *can* tell us apart," the second twin interrupted. "Nobody else can. Not even Papa, sometimes."

"Mama always could," Adam pointed out.

Self-conscious now, Abbey gazed sympathetically at the two handsome boys. She didn't want to broach the subject of their mother—not this early in their relationship with her. If their mother hadn't died, Abbey wouldn't have to be here tending them, and she knew they were aware of that.

She'd seen children enduring hardship before. The sight was never easy to bear. "Thank you for teaching me, Adam," Abbey said carefully. "I'm glad to know that. I've been getting on horses from the left side all my life and I never knew why. Come on, Luella." She scooped up the little girl and maneuvered her into Maribelle's saddle.

David patted the filly's shoulder and said, "Papa won't like that."

Abbey looked down at him. "Won't like this? Luella riding?"

"Any of us riding. We're not to get on horses."

A glance at Adam confirmed the order, then Luella's saddened face drew Abbey's attention. "I'm sure your papa meant you shouldn't ride when you were alone. But you're not alone. I'm here, and I'll be holding the bridle. And Luella will hold on to the saddle. Won't you?"

Luella wedged her little fingers between the saddle and the horse and nodded vigorously.

"Do you know a lot about horses?" Adam asked.

Abbey nodded as she led the filly—and the children—down the cobbled street. "My husband and I ran a cattle ranch. I rode horses all the time."

David bounced along sideways, suddenly enthralled. "Were there cowboys?"

"There certainly were, plenty of them."

"And bandits?"

"And Indians?" Adam added.

"Yes, all that. But most of the Indians I knew were cowboys."

Adam's freckles competed with each other as he screwed up his face in disbelief. "*Indian* cowboys? That isn't right, is it?"

Nodding, Abbey smiled at his disappointment. "And Mexicans, and Negroes, too. All hardworking."

"Bet they don't work as hard as Nantucket sailors."

"Bet they do," Abbey countered huskily. She gave him one of those looks that said she knew what she was talking about. She smiled at his doubtful expression, and she would have kept on smiling had they not rounded the corner onto Ash Street and looked up.

On the proud porch of his stately home, Dominic Nash stood like an obelisk, staring down at her, more forbidding than the storm that had just passed.

The magistrate continued to glare in silence as Abbey strode toward the house with the boys on either side of her and Luella on the filly. Sternly he watched them approach, without as much as a flicker of welcome. His blue eyes had grown cold, his face stark as the whitewashed trim on his brick home.

"Mr. Nash," Abbey began with a nod that she hoped was disarming. She partially smiled at him, but controlled it. A whole smile would make her appear self-conscious about—about what? He'd managed to make her feel guilty, and she didn't even know why. So far there was no reason whatsoever for his dark mood.

Nash pursed his lips in an effort toward self-control. "Mrs. Sutton, remove my daughter from that animal."

Abbey dropped her half-smile, seeing that it was futile, and lifted Luella down from the saddle.

"Boys, Luella," Nash ordered stiffly, "in for supper, promptly."

The children immediately dashed for the front door, noticeably silent under the pall of their father's presence. Dominic Nash was utterly changed from the man Abbey had shared a glass of wine with the night before. But she knew that gentle man was still underneath somewhere.

"Wash up," Nash added, chasing the children inside with his glare.

Abbey grasped the reins. "I'll stable the pony and be in directly—"

"You'll come now. Turn the filly loose and she'll go round by herself. The boys can remove her saddle and curry her down after supper."

She gazed at him for a few seconds, her lips staunchly set. Her pause was meant to let him know she didn't think she'd done anything to deserve this cold hello. Without a flinch, she looped the reins up over the saddle and gave the filly a light slap on the rump. Sure enough, Maribelle loped purposefully around the side of the house and disappeared toward the little stable in back.

"Step inside now, Mrs. Sutton," Nash said.

His tone set off her indignation. Neither a servant nor a menial, she didn't intend to spend any portion of her life being treated like one. She approached the porch, mounted the steps, and drew up to his level. She didn't go inside before turning to him squarely. "Mr. Nash, is something amiss that I'm not catching wind of?"

The big man clasped his hands behind his back, standing stiffly with seeming effort. She sensed he wanted to speak candidly, but something was stopping him. After a moment he freed one hand to gesture toward the doorway. "Please," he darkly invited.

She sighed, matching his stiffness. "Very well," she said, "but it'll be the same question inside as out."

Her boots rang out on the polished wood of the front hall. As she turned to ask the question again, Nash fluidly guided her into the good room, where the question was choked down before it could surface.

Abbey sucked in her breath. "Them!"

Her eyes opened so wide they started to sting.

Before her stood Longhorn Mustache and Hunch, wrung out but still soaked through, their grimy clothing stuck to their shapeless bodies like cloth dragged in oatmeal.

Her finger jabbed through the air at them. "These two—"

"Were trailing you," Nash finished. He appeared contrite about it, but supremely in charge of the situation. So it was him. . . .

Abbey spun on him. "How dare you!"

"Mrs. Sutton . . . Abbey, please allow me to—" Nash cleared his throat. "Sit down, won't you?"

"No, I won't!" She proved it by stalking halfway around the two bumbling trackers, hands on hips, studying them vengefully. "I've been tracked better by drunken sheepherders. And you, Mr. Nash— what's your explanation for having me followed?"

"I am trying to explain." He calmed her with his tone. Through it all, the two trackers remained resolutely silent. Nash closed the gap between them with another gentlemanly gesture that didn't seem appropriate for the men to whom he referred. "May I introduce Samuel Buck and Jeb Uram. Yes, I hired them. But not to follow you."

"Then they've got bad eyesight, Mr. Nash, because they were indeed following me."

"I know they were. Mr. Buck, will you tell Mrs. Sutton what you told me?"

The man called Buck—the one with the longhorn mustache— shifted uncomfortably where he stood, and his thick lips pulled on his mustache for a few seconds before he spoke. "Uh, yessir. We wuz follerin' the yella-haired fella, like you said, when this lady starts goin' about after him. So we starts follerin' her, too. She bin keepin' his company, is all."

Abbey's arms turned to columns of stone and she whirled on Nash again, shrieking, "How *dare* you!"

"Mrs. Sutton, will you *please* . . . sit . . . down." Nash turned sideways, placed his hand on one of the big velvet-covered chairs, and made it plain by his stance that nothing would progress until she put herself in that chair and was quiet at least for a few seconds.

Enraged—but curious—Abbey glared at him for an extra moment, then stalked to the chair, spun, and threw herself down into the chair. "All right. I'm listening."

Nash looked down at her disapprovingly. "Well, you're hearing, at least. Perhaps you'll be listening soon." He turned to Longhorn and Hunch and said, "You gentlemen are dismissed."

The two awkward hirelings glanced at each other, then made a quick and unceremonious exit out the front way.

Nash watched them leave, waiting until the front door made a satisfying click. Silence fell as he paced to the center of the parlor, his fingers hooked in his waistcoat pockets. He gazed thoughtfully at the floor, searching for words. Several times his lips parted, then closed again. Evidently he didn't know where to begin.

Abbey sat with the patience of butter on a hot skillet.

Finally Nash looked up at her. "You've been seen with Jacob Ross."

"Thank you, I know that," she snapped back.

"Jacob Ross is suspected of smuggling."

Indignation fell away. Abbey felt her features soften from fury to astonishment. She wanted to blurt her disbelief, but common sense forbade her. She simply didn't know Jake Ross well enough to let her feelings be the only judge. In fact, Dominic Nash knew him much better than she did.

Her heart moaned its disillusion. Bile rose in her throat. "Smuggling . . ." she murmured.

Nash rubbed his hands together in discomfort. "As in any seaport, there is a level of contraband coming and going here in Nantucket. There's no way to stop it entirely. It comes and goes with the strangers who populate the various packets docking here. The best way to keep it to a minimum is to arrest those local individuals who participate. In so small a town, they make targets of themselves. Jacob Ross is under suspicion."

"Then why haven't you arrested him?" Abbey asked, her voice suddenly hoarse.

"We are gathering evidence. His associations are suspect. He appears in town at odd times. He is seen at the docks, where he shouldn't be, at least not frequently."

"As keeper of Great Point," Abbey began, trying not to reveal too much, "doesn't he have to pick up whale oil for the light?"

"He does, but not as frequently as he's seen in that vicinity. And he should have only one wharf to go to, if he has an arrangement for oil for the light. Rather, he appeared at Straight Wharf, then Old North Wharf, then at the Town Dock . . . aboveboard business needs consistency, and Mr. Ross is very erratic."

"Is that all your evidence, Mr. Nash?"

Impatiently, Nash raised his voice whether he meant to or not. "He's been seen in the company of known smugglers, Mrs. Sutton." He drew a deep breath. "Mrs. Sutton, this is my business, my duty as magistrate. As your employer, I could blindly order you. But I would prefer that you understand and make a sensible choice. We must contend with these suspicions. Please cease to complicate the matter for us. I wouldn't want you caught in the crossfire."

His words were ominous, but delivered gently. She sensed that Nash felt he had no moral right to demand this of her, though every legal right as magistrate of the island. She sensed his discomfort with the situation, and the part of her that had loved her husband now respected Dominic Nash for his strength of character and purpose.

Abbey's hands grew cold in her lap. Nash's words held an imperative direction that she wasn't sure she could yet abide. Her undefined bond with Jake Ross was without fulfillment yet—even without clarity. It demanded more of her, more daring, more effort, more curiosity . . . more, not less, as Nash was requiring with his firmness. She made no mistake about that; he was indeed ordering her to subdue her attraction to Jake before he had to step in legally.

Nash stood over her now, his bearing one of ultimate responsibility and purpose. He would do what the situation required of him, whatever he was forced to do in order that sanctity would reign on Nantucket.

She looked up at him, her face presenting a question that needed no words. And with the honesty that adults deserve from other adults, despite the gentility of sparing feelings, Dominic Nash spelled out his demand.

"Keep away from Jacob Ross."

Chapter Seven

"WHAT DO YOU know about Jake Ross, Cordelia?"

"What do I know, or what is generally known?" Cordelia didn't miss a beat as she turned down Abbey's bed that evening, rolling the big coverlet onto the blanket chest at the bed's foot and fussing with the pillows.

Ordinarily Abbey would have stopped her from this service, preferring to turn down her own bed just as she'd done all her life. Sometimes there hadn't even been a proper bed to turn down. Blankets and bedrolls with no pillow were the best to be had on the open range. Having done this since she was a child, Abbey could sleep hanging from an andiron if necessary. But tonight she wanted—needed—someone to talk to . . . a rare commodity where she came from.

Abbey hiked herself up onto the bed on one folded leg. "You yourself."

Cordelia paused in her work. "Not much to be known," she said. "Not by me, leastways. Folk on this island come and go, those without families. Mostly the permanent folk are the business owners, the captains, and the owners of the ships. Sailors and men like Jacob Ross are often the drifters, in one year, out the next."

"Have you ever been inside The Brotherhood?"

"Me? Lord, no." Cordelia brushed back a strand of her dark hair and smiled. "Been curious about it, though. Mostly that's for the men, whalers usually, and dockers."

"Is that the rule of the place?" Abbey asked. "No women?"

Cordelia pursed her lips for a thoughtful moment, then shook her head. "I don't suppose so. Never heard that it was. Just how things evolved there. Women don't care to go in. Got our own things to do to keep busy." She surveyed the pillows and decided they were sufficiently fluffed, then helped herself to a seat on a needlepoint vanity bench. "You like to quilt?"

"I'm not very good at it," Abbey admitted, "but I've pushed a needle about from time to time. We had a quilting bee two winters ago, myself and the ladies of four surrounding ranges." Her mind traveled back to the memory. "Miles Crawford's wife had four daughters herself, so there was a fair number of us. We got together and all winter we made quilts of patch squares and stitched in the names of every one of the cowpunchers on our ranches. If they worked our stock even one day, they deserved a square. We made a quilt for every ranch that way. Someday, folks will know the names of our cowhands, our cooks, our branders, and our foremen. Even the driver who came by with the chuck wagon that one January got his name on a square. Hubbards. I stitched that one myself."

"You rode the ranges yourself, I hear tell from the boys," Cordelia mentioned, curiosity flashing in her eyes.

Abbey laughed. "I see news travels fast in Nantucket. Yes, I've done my share of bull-whacking. Of necessity, I would say. My husband and I started with nearly nothing and built a ranch. It didn't succeed in the long run, but I'd say we did our part in building that corner of Wyoming. We fed a few cowhands and trained a few more and set up some decent relations with the Indians that I daresay won't fall away too soon. When there's no one else to do the work, the women just pick up and do it."

"Most women do that out west?" Cordelia looked surprised.

Abbey chuckled. "Not most. Most women—what few there are— serve as laundresses and cooks and teachers. Lots of them teach. In fact, if it weren't for the women, we'd have a mighty ignorant frontier. One woman I knew took half a summer and handwrote three copies of a geography book so the children of her settlement could have them. She even copied maps. She'd carried the book tucked in her bodice, all the way from Indiana on a wagon train."

"My," Cordelia breathed.

Abbey nodded nostalgically. "All that, and still some women manage to keep a fluting iron warm to put ruffles in their skirt hems. But I admit to you," she said, "I've never seen as many women in my whole life as I saw just on that one dock when I stepped off the boat. Where I'm from there's just one woman for every twenty men."

"That'll narrow as the years pass," Cordelia predicted.

"Oh, it narrows with every wagon train that migrates. There's land to be homesteaded and profit to be made, cattle barons and sheep barons coming every new day, building and investing, and with them come more and more folk to do the jobs that need doing. It's for the stout of heart, but women are stouthearted when they need to be. I knew one rancher who'd gotten old and crippled and had naught but his five daughters. Those girls shoveled irrigation ditches, branded steers, hunted wolf, and drove stock with the best of them."

"And so did you?"

Abbey laughed again and said, "Well, I'm not one to be left behind!"

Cordelia clapped her hands together once in delight and nodded with her lips approvingly pursed.

"What about you, Cordelia," Abbey asked. "Where are you from?"

The housekeeper abruptly got to her feet and said, "Oh, me. I'm hardly as interesting as all that. Sounds like you've got good stories to tell the children."

"And they've got good stories to tell me," Abbey said. "I'd never seen an ocean before a few days ago, or a ship, or even a big town. I never imagined so many people could cram into so small a space as Boston."

"Grass is always greener," Cordelia said. She appeared to be leaving, then paused and lowered her voice. "You got the eye for the Great Point keeper, don't you?"

Reluctantly, Abbey grinned a self-conscious grin and nodded. "He's got my eye. But for some reason, I don't think he's flattered." She inched herself forward a little on the brushed woolen blanket. "Do you know anything about him?" Why he might be so reclusive?"

She held her breath. Could Cordelia know about Jake's being

under suspicion for smuggling? Was that common knowledge on the island, or was Dominic Nash—as Abbey suspected—too gallant a man to allow a rumor to spread, even an official one?

Cordelia glanced out into the corridor, then lowered her voice even more. "Hear tell he's done some crime, when on the Continent, but there's no proof. So far he's done nothing here, but the magistrate's having him watched."

With more than a hint of irritation in her voice, Abbey burst out, "Yes, I know. And so does Jacob Ross. I wonder what good it does to watch a man who knows he's being watched."

"Fair little, probably. But if he's a criminal, it'll surface in time."

"If he is," Abbey repeated, hope rising even as her voice slid away to a whisper. "The magistrate has ordered me to keep away from Jake Ross."

Cordelia took a step back into the room. "And will you?"

For several seconds, even Abbey didn't know the answer. But as she parted her lips to speak, the words formed themselves without hesitation. "If I do," she said, "it will be for my own reasons, not the magistrate's."

Dominic Nash's warning, if that indeed was what it was, hadn't fallen entirely on the hard part of Abbey's common sense. Prudence told her to give herself time and Jake room to move. For days she neither saw nor heard about him. Yet that absence only intensified the plaguing thoughts that came between waking and sleeping, the errant gazes down the long, curving northwestern coast of Nantucket Island toward Great Point. Her only real distractions were lunches with Lucy Edmonds in the back of the Geary Hat Store, listening to Lucy's disarranged point of view on all issues and events. If somewhat ill-bred, Lucy provided the liveliest entertainment on Nantucket, for Abbey at least. She'd found herself a steadfast—if unorthodox—friend. And Lucy Edmonds had a ringing talent with language, despite her mutilation of it. When she spoke of her husband's duties out on the whaling grounds in distant seas, Lucy imbibed those stories with an eagerness that engrossed Abbey. If only the cowboys could have heard such tales around the campfires on those long cattle drives.

"Ee's aboard the *Nancy Ames*, a sweet little bark wot whales the grounds of Greenland for the North Atlantic right whales." Lucy spoke past a mouthful of yesterday's cranberry pie. She eyed her infant daughter, who was rolling about on the floor on a patchwork quilt. "It's a fine crew of blubber hunters that Billy's been sailin' wi' for nigh onto foive years now. Ee's got two skills, so's ee's valuable to 'em."

"And what are those?" Abbey prodded, as it had become her habit to keep Lucy talking—not much work to that, though.

"Ee's a cooper, for one, an' a blacksmith for the other. Ee's the mug wot tends an' mends the casks they pour the oil in. After the whale's all sectioned an' the blubber's minced an' tried out into oil, they pours it into these great casks—"

"Oh, barrels!" Abbey interrupted, realizing the look on her face had caused Lucy to try to explain.

"Barrels, right enough," the scrawny girl yelped, licking off a piece of cranberry that had slipped down her lip. Her enthusiasm alone was catching. "An' ee's apprenticin' to tend the whale irons wot they use to kill and strip them beasties. It's a better payin' job than cooper."

"How many barrels come off a . . . what did you call it?"

"A right whale, mum. Because it's the 'right' whale t'catch. Yer get like a hundred casks of oil off a usual one o' them, that be why they call him that. You also get baleen off 'im."

"I'm afraid to ask."

"Toothy stuff. They strains wee fishes through it fer food. Ain't got no teeth, that kind of whale don't."

Abbey held her tongue at Lucy's terse expression as the girl tried to appear an expert on such an odd subject. But at this she leaned over the small, round table and asked, "No teeth? But whales do have teeth. I've seen them in store windows here. Carved and inked with some kind of drawings."

"Right you 'ave, but thems the teeth of sparm whales."

"Sp . . . arm?"

"They got long bottom jaws an' fine poky-up teeth that's good for carvin' when things get slow combin' the sea for whale pods. They got oil, too, better stuff than the right whales, but not as much."

Abbey had to force down her next swallow of pie, and put down her fork. "Sounds like a grimy business."

"Oh, twice that, Abbey. Dirty, stinky, greasy. Oh, Wilma, love—"

Lucy jumped up and dashed to the quilt in time to rescue her baby from rolling under a rack of dresses. She expertly replaced the child in the center of the quilt and rattled a toy over the baby's smooth, round face. Wilma's eyes widened, her arms straight up and flailing, spindly fingers trying to find the right muscles to grab the rattle. After a period of enticement, Lucy folded Wilma's fingers around the rattle's shaft and came back to lunch. She sat down, still gazing at her daughter. "Wot a dumplin' I got there, Abbey. Ain't she somethin'? I dunno 'ow Billy an' me ever put out this beau'ifful baby. Me bein' plain as potatoes and 'im bein' ugly as the captain's dog."

"Oh, Lucy, shame on you!" Abbey derided, smiling.

"True enough, mum, ee's a mug. Wee round eyes an' a patch of mushy 'air, and a scruffa fuzz on his chin . . . but I loves 'im pretty good, anyway. I keep on tellin' 'im some day that beard is gonna grow and cover up most of that face. Then I'll let 'im leave the lamp burnin' at night!" She leaned conspiratorially toward Abbey, and they laughed out loud.

The town clock rang three times then, alerting Abbey to her duties. She took a moment to lick her fork before maneuvering out of her chair and putting an end to their late tea. "Oh, that's my call. I've opened a kettle, Lucy. I told the Nash children and their friends that I'd finish telling them about life on the range. They nearly climbed down my throat when I stopped the story last night and made them go to bed."

"I don't wonder, Abbey. Kids in Nantucket don't 'ear such stories much."

"And it's all they want," Abbey said. "Strange, isn't it? All I want is to hear about life out east, and all they want is to hear about life out west. Like Cordelia says, grass is always greener. Lunch again tomorrow?"

"'Morrow's Saturday, Abbey," Lucy pointed out.

"Already? Saints . . . Monday, then."

"Monday like clockwork," Lucy beamed.

By Saturday, when there was no school, Abbey had acquired an audience of at least a dozen town children, besides David, Adam, and Luella, who crowded at her feet on the Nash front porch, eyes bulging at her stories as though she was making them up from her wildest imagination. Which she wasn't.

"The wolves needed our cattle as much as we did. Every winter was an endless wolf hunt. We had to keep watch in the blizzards, because the wolves would come upon our cows from behind and bite their hamstrings to cripple them, so the pack could bring them down. In a good Wyoming blizzard, you could be five paces from a wolf and not see him."

"How big are they?" Adam asked. "As big as horses?"

"No, but they're as big as big dogs," Abbey told the smooth young faces that peered up at her. "And twice as fierce, being wild and all."

"Couldn't the cows run away from them?" one of the town girls asked.

Abbey rolled her eyes, making the children laugh. "Well, let me tell you something about cows," she said. "You can go far and wide and not find creatures as stupid as cattle. They're tasty and they make fine milk, but they're not brainy. They'll shiver in the blizzard, starving and thirsty, and die where they stand rather than move along in search of food. We had to find places where the wind had blown the snow off the grass, then drive the cattle there to graze— and that's only if we could find the grass at all. We had to chop through iced ponds so they could drink. Cattle won't break the ice themselves like wild horses and deer will. Many's the time my gloves were frozen to my lariat while I lassoed one after the other and dragged them to water."

"What's a larry-hat?" Luella demanded, coming up onto her knees.

"It's a long rope with an eye tied in one end and a loop pulled through the eye. . . . " She tried to demonstrate with her empty hands, but saw complete noncomprehension in the wide, round eyes of her audience. So she clapped her hands on her knees and said. "I'll just show you. Come on!"

She felt a bit like Pied Piper as all the children bounced to their feet and followed her around the house. "Adam, bring out Maribelle," she called out. David, find me a length of rope. You other children, you'll all be the cows!"

Even the older children, those right on the verge of sophistication itself, dropped their propriety and began milling about the yard, mooing. Adam appeared, hauling Maribelle from her shed by her bridle, and a moment later David appeared with a length of hemp rope and handed it to Abbey before he, too, began mooing merrily.

"David, I need a roundup dog," Abbey announced as she gathered her skirts between her legs.

David immediately stopped mooing and started barking. For someone who'd never seen a roundup or a roundup dog, he figured out the logical necessities of the job almost immediately and began yipping the "cows" into a smaller and smaller bunch. The cows, of course, began to delight in trying to evade him.

She smiled at them as she hauled herself up onto Maribelle's bare back, then took a few moments to tie a honda in the rope and pull a lariat loop through it. "Cork the mooing and pay attention for a moment." When she'd gotten their attention she held up the rope, loop in one hand and coils in the other. "This is the loop. These are the coils. The eye down there is called a honda, and the loop is called the main line. This rope is pretty short, though. Usually they're about sixty feet long. And not this loose—rawhide or braided grass tend to be stiffer. This doesn't want to loop quite as well, but I'll make do."

"Why does it have to be stiff?" David asked.

"It has to be stiff enough for the loop to stay flat and open while the rope pays out. And even more, it has to be strong, much stronger than this, if it's going to rope a thousand-pound steer and yank taut without snapping. Then it has to hold while the steer plunges and wrenches. I never found a steer yet who liked being roped. We call this contraption a catch rope, because we catch with it. I'm going to do a head catch. Go on and moo now."

The yard was so small that Abbey couldn't even get Maribelle into a decent trot, much less the grueling gallop Abbey was accustomed to on the range during branding time. The children giggled between moos and did everything they could to outrun David as he pinched and yipped them into a bunch.

"H'yah, yearlings! Branding time!" Abbey whooped as she narrowed in on the herd, the lariat loop singing above her head. Roundup was never this easy. She cast an overhand throw. The loop sailed through the air, tilting toward Luella, and dropped neatly around the child's red curls. Luella grabbed for the rope and dropped into a huddle in the middle of the grass.

"Creepers . . ." Adam gushed in respectful amazement.

"Now, if I had a saddle," Abbey explained without a pause, "I'd throw a few dallies around the horn and yank the rope tight. But since Luella is a sweethearted calf and doesn't fight, I can just walk right over there and brand her smartly. I do that about fifty more times, and my day's work is done. Till morning, of course, when I start again right after breakfast."

"What's for breakfast?" one of the girls wanted to know.

Abbey laughed. "Same as yesterday. Sowbelly, sourdough biscuits, coffee, and grits. It'll be the same tomorrow, too. For dinner, we get liver-and-heart stew, red bean pie, and more sourdough. Lots of sourdough. Sourdough up to here and out the ears."

The children laughed, and for the first time Abbey discovered herself feeling almost at home on Nantucket.

"Can I try it?" David asked tentatively.

"Well, of course you can try it." She retrieved her coil as Luella shook off the catch loop. The children, tall and small alike, watched with fascination as Abbey drew the lariat in and it snaked back across the yard toward her.

Abbey slipped off Maribelle, then shook the coil free of her skirts. "Might just try that on the charming Mr. Ross one of these days," she muttered to herself. "All right, David, up you go. You be the cowpuncher. I'll be the cattle baron and supervise the roundup. You over there—"

"Zeke."

"Zeke, you'll have to take over as the roundup dog."

She arranged the coil and main line in David's hands, showing him how to hold the reins and steer his mount even as he roped a calf. He wasted no time, of course, going after his twin brother. The other children fell into the pattern of mooing and milling, trying to confound the cowpuncher in his task. Lanky Zeke made an odd dog indeed.

This roundup soaked up the entire morning, until every child had been roped at least once, and several had tried their hands at the lariat. Maribelle was unflagging in her tolerance of having child after child up on her back, her reins pulled and twisted, and her flanks kicked without purpose. Lariat after lariat flew across the small yard, and more than once a fence picket, a tree branch, or the pump handle was caught instead of one of the herd.

It was a silly business, but Abbey found herself having genuine fun for a change. Until this moment, her only enjoyment had been those lunches with Lucy, and even those had been plagued with glances out the window toward The Brotherhood. The roundup might have gone on all day.

Might have—had it not been for one of fate's nasty twists.

It was Adam's turn to master the lariat. He sent it looping across the yard with more power in his arm than Abbey would have guessed—unfortunately. The loop flew majestically into the air, then dropped in a perfect circle . . . right onto magistrate's Nash's red head.

Abbey and the children froze solid in their tracks. Mooing died away as the rope settled nicely on the big man's shoulders.

Abbey held her breath, her lips tucked inward, her eyes stinging from the stare. This could hardly be considered teaching Luella about being a lady. . . .

Magistrate Nash stood on the other side of the picket fence, stock still, glaring.

She might have been incinerated by that stare, had she not been saved by the sudden knell of the church bell ringing in the clear spring air.

Dominic Nash took his harsh eyes off her and turned toward the sound, something entirely new crossing his squarish features. The children spun about also, their heads all turning toward the open sea—or at least in that direction through the town.

"Ship!" David cried.

He led the dash for the street, and Abbey found herself standing alone on the open range.

"What is it?" she called, drawn into a run simply by the children's enthusiasm.

"Somebody sighted a ship!" Adam tossed back as he tilted into a faster pace toward the warfside of town.

"A whale ship?" Abbey called back, but the children were swept away by the bell's frantic chiming. Of course it must be a whale ship. They wouldn't be so excited if it was just another transport vessel from the mainland, would they? Or would they? She hadn't been there long enough to know for sure. But she could see it in their faces . . . all those children were hoping it was their father coming home.

Nash grasped the rope at his shoulders and threw it off. His eyes widened at the flurry of children flying by. Then he reached for Abbey's elbow. "Come on. There's a whaler coming in."

Abbey didn't have time to respond—they were already running. And so was half the town. Well, perhaps the *whole* town. There didn't seem to be a door left unopened as the church bell rang furiously. The only people not running toward the wharf were those clutching the rails of the hundreds of roofwalks throughout Nantucket Town. A chill ran down Abbey's spine as she glanced up at them and remembered Jake's description of the widow's walks.

They ran down Ash Street to North Water Street, came to Broad Street and swung along the jog to South Water Street toward Old North Wharf, never once slackening their pace. Townspeople flocked around them, all heading in the same direction. Abbey caught the flame of excitement and realized what this meant to these people. Not only were the ships their staple source of income and their link to the outside world, but these were their husbands and sons and brothers returning, perhaps for the first time in months upon months. If nothing else—and there was much else—the ship brought with it stories of its adventures and songs of its toils.

"Abbeeeeeeeee! Abbeeeeeeeee!"

She twisted around, breaking her stride, and saw Lucy wobbling toward her at an awkward run, arms wrapped around little Wilma. The baby bobbed in her mother's arms, and Lucy was gasping by the time she got to Abbey and Nash.

"Abbey! It's the *Nancy Ames*! It's the *Nancy Ames*! It's Billy's ship! Ee's comin' back! Oh, ee's comin' back!"

"How do you know?" Abbey grabbed Lucy's hands while Dominic chivalrously scooped Wilma from her mother's arms and carried her the rest of the way to the open docks.

"They told me! They told me!" Lucy babbled.

"That's wonderful news!" Abbey laughed, realizing it was pointless to ask the frantic girl just who had told her. "Lucy Edmonds, you know Magistrate Nash—"

"Mrs. Edmonds, good day," Dominic said to Lucy in midstride, nodding past the curls of Wilma's tousled head.

"Yes, sir, righto, sir," Lucy gasped, craning her neck at the horizon, anxious to show Billy Edmonds the baby he hadn't known was coming and had never seen.

They came up to the edge of the dock amidst a crowd of onlookers, and Abbey had to hold Lucy back from the edge. She seemed to be thinking about swimming out to meet the ship.

On the blue-gray sea to their upper right, there was indeed a ship. Bluff-bowed, clunky, without a hint of comfort or speedworthiness, the whaler carried heavy masts built straight up, without the graceful angle of schooners' and clippers' masts. Even at this distance she could see the great bulbous hull bobbing in the sea, lumbering home with its cargo. Then, confused, Abbey realized it was sailing crossways to the island instead of toward it.

"Why doesn't it turn in?" she asked.

Dominic sighed. "There's a shoal. The scourge of Nantucket. It's a great task to get deep-draft barks and brigs like that one over the sandbar. We have to use the camels."

"Camels?"

He nodded once, shifted Wilma in his arms, and pointed.

Abbey sucked in a quick breath. Far out at the mouth of the harbor were two great rectangular chunks of . . . well, they looked for all the world like docks on the tops of two hulls. Even from here she could tell they both were huge, each almost as big as a whole pier. "What are those?" she blurted, her voice rising almost to a squeal.

"Camels," Dominic repeated matter-of-factly. "Steam-driven drydocks. They'll meet the bark and fasten to her, then lift her up over the shoal and escort her in."

"Amazing!" She squinted at the chugging camels.

"Yes, it is. Someday that sandbar will be the death of Nantucket. New Bedford's already surpassed us as a whaling port simply because our harbor has that bedamned shoal blocking it. We've petitioned the federal government time and again to build a breakwater, but so far they've not done it." He squinted at the incoming ship. "The spouter looks heavy-laden, too."

She leaned toward Dominic. "Will it have whale meat on board?"

she asked, not too loud lest she look foolish in front of the other onlookers. It was a stupid question, she knew. She realized then that she'd only half listened to Lucy's cockney explanations of duty on board a whale ship. Among a crowd of people to whom this was commonplace, she wished she had paid heed.

"Oil," he told her. "Fully processed."

"Processed on board," she attempted, forcing her memory to work. If Billy Edmonds was a cooper . . .

Dominic's red brows lifted. "Yes, of course. You're looking at a floating factory out there. The whale meat is stripped from the carcass, sectioned, tried out, and casked within hours of the whale's capture, right on board the ship."

"Wouldn't I like to see that," Abbey murmured.

"We also make use of the parmaceti here in Nantucket at the candle factory, if they've caught a sperm or two, that is. This ship's a Greenland packet for now. She hunted Atlantic rights this voyage. May not've seen sperm at all."

Abbey battled with her memory to absorb which whale had which kind of oil for which purpose, but it was eluding her. "It's *right* to catch 'right' whales, but it's *better* to catch sperm whales. . . ."

Falling into a pose of endless patience, Dominic leaned toward her and explained in simple terms. "Essentially, yes. The Atlantic right gives much more oil than a sperm, but a sperm's oil is purer and fetches two or three times the price of right oil. Even more valuable, they supply white parmaceti wax, which is mixed with the junk fat—head matter. It results in the brightest burning candles available. We make the candles right here on the island and turn a good profit. Occasionally, if the whale is ill, we'll get ambergris for perfume—"

Dominic stopped speaking.

At nearly the same moment, a disturbing hush had come over the crowd. Some of the women clasped their palms to their lips. Others simply fell silent. The men murmured quietly among themselves. They all continued to stare out at the *Nancy Ames* as she lumbered heavily down the coastline toward them, but the mood had decidedly changed.

"What is it?" Abbey was driven to ask.

Dominic remained silent for another few seconds. Then he cleared his throat and spoke slowly.

"She's bearing a black flag."

The hulking whale ship lolled through the briny waters off Nantucket Harbor with a slowness that now was agonizing. The ship nodded through the water with determination, a few sails raised to carry her through the last leg of her long journey to the camels, which would bring her in. The camels steamed resolutely toward the ship and finally overtook her, but the process was damnably long. Ever since Dominic had mentioned it, Abbey saw the little flicker of black fabric more clearly than she saw the huge sails themselves. For many long minutes no one spoke; then Abbey had to.

"What does it mean?" she asked, still keeping her voice down.

Beside her, Lucy had grown quiet.

"Usually," Dominic said carefully, "it means that the captain has died during the voyage."

"Did you know him?" she asked, looking up at Dominic's blue eyes to find the sky reflected in them.

Dominic held his breath for a moment before responding. "Yes," he softly said, "very well." He stepped around behind her to hand Wilma to Lucy, and said, "If you'll excuse me . . . I must speak to Mrs. Whiteside." As Abbey watched, he moved through the crowd. Finally he came to a stop beside a woman in her midforties who was gazing painfully at the approaching ship. Two teenaged girls hugged the woman, and a boy of about eighteen stood staunchly beside her. Abbey realized the woman must be the captain's wife. How sad for her, she thought, knowing how she must have felt.

As she watched Dominic speak to the captain's family, the tall boy put his arm around his mother's shoulders and the other around one of his sisters, already prepared to take his place as head of their family.

Abbey wondered if the flag flew only if the captain died. Could it also mean the first mate, or any of the crew?

She opened her mouth to ask Lucy, then clamped her lips shut. This wouldn't be the right time nor the right question to ask her friend. That was confirmed in the way Lucy clutched little Wilma against her.

All this scurrying around we do in life, Abbey thought, *makes us forget what's really of value. There's Dominic, who can't be with his wife . . . the captain's wife who hasn't seen her husband in more than a year . . . and Lucy. Poor girl's still on her honeymoon, considering the little time she's been with her Billy. And I can't be with the man I'm attracted to. . . .*

She let the thought drift away. But something did strike her as she watched the crowd's sad anticipation ripple across the wharf. She'd been burying her head in the sand, ignoring her own nature. This hiding behind Dominic's orders was getting her nowhere. She would have to confront Jake, if for no other reason than her own peace of mind. They wanted each other. That was right. But something held them apart that wasn't right. She should at least be told what it was. This vague business of smuggling . . . what did it really mean?

A tingle of awareness ran up her arms then. Thoughts of Jake had set her nervous system on alert, and she found herself looking around the dock area for no reason. While everyone else was watching the incoming ship, Abbey was scanning the water below the docks and the many workaday vessels moored along the wharf and throughout the harbor. Masts short and tall speared the sky all around her, rigging like the tangled webs of drunken spiders confused her glimpses from boat to boat. The dockside sky was a mess of yardarms and halyards and rigging and timbers, the water broken by the decks of a hundred ships and boats of every size. Eerie, in its way. Exciting in another.

All they could do was wait. Wait the long, interminable minutes as the *Nancy Ames* crawled through the waters, over wave after wave, one at a time, toward the camels.

Abbey continued glancing around the dockyard, her arms still tingling with that strange sense of . . . what? Presence? Yes!

And there he was!

She pushed past a stout woman and craned her head for a better view of one dirty little sandbagger with its extra-long boom poking out over its stern. On its deck, Jake Ross crouched. He was peering down into the hold. He was talking, but glancing about in a manner that seemed self-conscious and wary to Abbey.

She couldn't see who he was talking to. Someone was in that

hold, though. From time to time, Jake handed down one of a stack of smallish crates that crowded the port side of the sandbagger. He continued talking as a pair of hands came up for each crate and was time after time swallowed back into the hold. Abbey got the unfounded but definite impression that Jake was doing more than helping someone load his cargo. The brim of Jake's cap was drawn low over his eyes—as though anyone wouldn't know who he was from that mop of blond hair and that perfectly recognizable sea coat!

Abbey huffed through her nose. She decided to go over there right then and ask what he was up to. Right there in front of everyone.

Across the port, Jake glanced to his right, then straight ahead. That forward glance, a skillful one that said he did this often, put his eyes right on Abbey's. The formless magnet pulling at them had worked yet again. Jake stopped talking, frozen where he knelt. He stared at her through the network of rigging and masts and yard-arms, and slowly came to his feet.

She would have excused herself, but one glance at Lucy told her the girl had no interest in politeness at the moment. Nearer now on the harbor seas, the *Nancy Ames* was brought slowly toward them, nestling between the hulking camels.

With a shrug, Abbey squeezed through the crowd on the wharf in the direction that would take her to that sandbagger. People moved between her and the open port, and she lost sight of Jake for those few moments.

She broke out of the crowd and raced down the wharf, rounding the pilings toward the sandbagger, then she stopped short.

He was gone!

But how?

She hovered for a moment, then hurried down the dock to the sandbagger, which bobbed placidly in the water, straining its ropes and creaking against the pilings.

"Excuse me!" she called, hammering her foot on the dock. "Excuse me. Are you in there? Excuse me!"

Moments passed. Finally a black tuft of coiled hair appeared from the hold. Then a brown forehead, and two white-ringed eyes.

The Negro was afraid of her, that was plain. Certainly no northern Negro would give her that look. She knelt down on the dock. "Are you a slave?"

"Uh, no, ma'am, ah's free," the skinny dark fellow said, keeping low in the hold.

"Good. What happened to the man you were talking to?"

"What man was I tawkin' to, ma'am?"

"The blond man—you know exactly who I mean. You were just talking to him. Where is he?"

"Uh, ma'am, I sho' don' know nothin' about no man. Sorry, ma'am . . . I gots t'get below and stack these here crates. Sorry, ma'am."

"You come back up here," Abbey ordered as the Negro disappeared into the hold.

But he refused and wouldn't come back up. Evidently he was more afraid of someone else than he was of her.

She put her fists on her hips and thought about climbing down onto the sandbagger and looking into the hold for herself, but that might not be wise. She'd heard enough lately about how rude it was to set foot on someone's vessel without permission—it just wasn't done. All right, for now. She'd catch up with him soon enough. She'd be sure of that.

Fuming, she made her way back along the wharf to Lucy's side, but she never fully stopped looking for Jake's face through the long wait for the *Nancy Ames*.

Nearly three quarters of an hour passed before the camels and the whale ship came abreast of Old North Wharf. Despite the black flag, several sailors aboard her were waving frantically at their families on the docks before they all had to settle down to the business of docking the massive vessel. Lucy kept scanning for Billy Edmonds's face among the men, but there were too many sailors and too much rigging and too much work to do to get the big ship up to the dock and tied up.

Abbey watched silently, wrinkling her nose at the smell that accompanied the ship into the harbor. It was an oily, rank, smoky odor—whale oil had soaked through every plank and rope on the ship, along with the cloying scent of hundreds of barrels of oil in her hold.

Terrible long minutes plodded by before the gangplank finally dropped with a clunk to the wharf. Squeals of relief and delight began to spread through the crowd as, one by one, sailors raced down the plank into the arms of their families. Even men without families were welcomed like old friends. Some people were weeping; Abbey wondered if it was the joy of homecoming or the sadness at the sight of the black flag.

Only a handful of men had come off the ship when Dominic Nash suddenly left the captain's family and dashed up the plank to meet a tall, bearded man in a heavy coat. At the same moment, the captain's three children gasped and broke away from their mother to run up the plank and into the arms of the tall man—Captain Whiteside, apparently. As he held his tall son and young daughter, the captain spoke solemnly to Dominic.

On the wharf, the captain's wife stood among her friends, tears of silent joy streaming down her face.

Group after group of sailors came down the gangplank—Abbey lost count after twenty-four—while other crew members continued to furl the sails and do finish work aboard the ship. Cargo crates were even being taken off the vessel already. Lucy stood beside Abbey and watched each face that appeared from the whale ship, bouncing Wilma in her arms. Abbey noticed again, as she had before, that the baby looked nothing like Lucy. The baby's round face, oval eyes, and dark brown hair must belong to Billy Edmonds. He couldn't be all that ugly to have such a pretty baby. Abbey found herself watching for a young man with those features among all those who filed from the whale ship with their sea bags over their shoulders.

There was none. No young man came off the plank and headed for Lucy. But finally, after the last man had walked down the plank, someone did head for Lucy Edmonds.

Dominic Nash and Captain Whiteside.

Abbey had stopped watching the gangplank and now watched Lucy. The girl's delicate face looked grief-stricken as Dominic and the captain approached. Lucy buried her mouth against her baby's lacy dress, and small sobs began to gush out. She never took her eyes from Dominic and the captain as they drew nearer. Tears dropped onto the lace of her baby daughter's sleeve.

Abbey touched the girl's hair. "Oh, Lucy . . ."

Chapter Eight

"How is she?"

Dominic stood up from the velvet wingback chair in which he had been sitting and drew himself up to his full height.

Abbey approached him slowly from the hallway, keeping her footsteps from sounding on the bare wood floor. She bit her lip sympathetically, then murmured, "She's young, Dominic. She's very young."

Settling onto the other wingback, Abbey shook her head in disbelief and fell silent.

Dominic hovered nearby, plainly discomfited. "Hardly seems fair, I know," he said, forcing strength into his tone. In a single gesture he pulled off his spectacles and dropped them on the polished mahogany of one of the side tables. "Losing a spouse seems to be the badge of courage for this day and age."

Abbey stared into the knobby woven rug beneath her feet. "And there is always more than one casualty when children are involved."

"The Whitesides will be holding a funeral luncheon for Seaman Edmonds come Sunday," Dominic said, making sure the room didn't fall prey to any more sudden silence than he could avoid. "He saved the lives of eight of his shipmates in that whaleboat. It's not the same as a man dying from sickness—which, by the way, is the unglamorous fate of most who die at sea."

Abbey squeezed her hands into a ball. "Why do you feel it's necessary for me to know that fact at this particular moment?" She got to her feet and paced over to the window, only to find herself staring at her own reflection against the darkening sky.

When Dominic spoke, it was plain her attack had hit home in his sense of responsibility, even his sense of guilt at not knowing what would comfort her. "Only because . . . you should know that Edmonds did not die for nothing . . . but for the lives of eight men who also came home to young families." He paused, then turned away. "I'm sorry."

He was honestly apologizing, not merely expressing sympathy.

Abbey stopped him as he moved through the archway to the dining room. "No . . . I'm sorry. I shouldn't have barked at you. You've been kind beyond call, letting me bring Lucy here tonight. I simply couldn't leave her all alone tonight to look at that sweet little baby's face."

"Of course you couldn't," Dominic said, sadness softening his square face. "Neither could I." Once again his fingers hooked into his waistcoat, an affectation that Abbey sensed denoted his discomfort. "I must . . . I must thank you for banking my shortsightedness."

Her brow furrowing, Abbey thought over the past few days and tried to think of what he was talking about. Unable to put a picture to those words, she finally had to ask, "Pardon?"

Dominic sighed. Plainly he'd hoped she would understand and spare him explaining. "This afternoon, in the backyard. The children."

"Oh." Abbey blurted. "Yes . . . I never thought it would upset you. I didn't realize you might disapprove until I saw your face. I'm sorry if—"

"It did upset me," he said firmly, "with myself." He paced around one of his wingback chairs and placed his hands on its back, caressing the velvet. "Since their mother died," he said, "I haven't seen them so happy. I'd forgotten the look of it. What you saw on my face," he said, pausing at the memory, "wasn't disapproval. It was astonishment. And it was disgust. . . . With myself. I was on the verge of making them spend their childhood in a mausoleum of tribute to their dead mother. I had forgotten how to laugh, and because children are wonderful they were willing to forget how to laugh, also, just so I wouldn't be alone in my misery. A man loses his perception sometimes. The dead can make us forget life. Had you not come along with your . . . your . . ."

"Bohemian ways?" she supplied affably.

He rolled his eyes in amused embarrassment and admitted, "Yes. You caught us just at the precipice. Or shall I say, you caught me. I've been dangling there for a year, and only the children were holding the rope. Children shouldn't have to hold their parents' lifelines, Mrs. Sutton . . . I mean, Abbey. The children have changed utterly for the better since you came, just these few short days. They speak of little else than you—your fire, your cheer, your spontaneity, your ostentatious approach to life. You attack life, Abbey. I'd forgotten how to do that, if indeed a somber law student from Philadelphia could ever have known. You are a tonic for my family."

Abbey felt a rush of warmth. By telling her what the children thought of her, she realized, he was telling her what *he* thought of her. In his gallant way, he was really quite shy. The man could be so endearing!

Then why were her thoughts turning even now to Jake Ross?

With a hard squeeze of thought, she drove the tough brown eyes and thatch of blond hair from her mind and tried to concentrate on Dominic. He deserved her first consideration, for he had been nothing but considerate to her.

"When my wife died," Dominic went on, glancing up the stairs. "I didn't know what to tell Luella. She's so small . . . to be told she could never be with her mother again. I find myself—am I being cruel? I find myself glad Mrs. Edmonds's daughter is so very little. In many ways it's a blessing that she never knew her papa. And yet, Mrs. Edmonds must bear the sorrow alone." He shook his head, as if trying to free it of a confounding burden. "There is no equation of ease, is there?"

A pang of empathy went through Abbey—for Dominic as much as for Lucy. "Lucy's a strong young woman," she told him. "She's already accepted her husband's death completely. You should have heard her. Her odd, silly accent sounded so incongruous compared to the words she spoke. She said she still had her baby, and a better life than what she had before she met Billy. She's glad she still has her job at the hat store and already speaks of the future. Even though my husband was older and we had no children, I know I wasn't as strong as that. Sweet Lucy. I find myself fortified by her."

Dominic gazed at the floor, eluding her eyes. "You . . . didn't tell me you'd made a friend."

Abbey folded her hands and said, "Because you've been avoiding me, Mr. Nash."

He looked up now, his lower lip pursing beneath the red mustache. "My dear, I never avoid people," he announced indignantly. "I simply allow fate to misplace them."

His eyebrows bobbed in punctuation, and Abbey laughed lightly.

"You're a kind man, Dominic," she said simply.

He cleared his throat and tried to appear stern. "Please keep that rumor from spreading." He smiled in a reserved fashion. "She's young, and so are you. These things pass, in time."

Abbey folded her arms and without thinking said, "The voice of ancient wisdom."

She was instantly sorry for what she had said. As she watched, she could all but see images of Dominic's dead wife passing before his eyes once again. He seemed embarrassed by his own concern for her and for Lucy. Why was it that in the East people's own feelings embarrassed them? His concern for her was ingratiating, but it shouldn't come at his own expense.

He recovered almost at once and said, "May I never be such a liar as to claim that. I'm sorry . . . I never meant to appear callous."

She smiled. "You don't appear callous. You appear strong. In fact, you're much like Lowell was."

Dominic's blue eyes sparkled. "Am I?"

"I hope it sounds like the compliment I mean it to be."

"Of course. He was a sensitive, intelligent fellow, and I'm deeply complimented, but—" He stopped himself and didn't seem obliged to finish.

Not to be dashed by his hesitation, Abbey said, "But what?"

Dominic turned away and fiddled with a doily on the end table. "Perhaps it's only the difference in our ages," he said, and he appeared to drop his guard. "To be with a man the age of a father . . ." He deliberately let his words trail off, and Abbey was there to catch them.

"Dominic, I loved Lowell," she said. "I was also *in* love with him. And I would never think to do with my father the things I . . . well

. . . I like men your age," she boldly claimed. "They've lived life. They know life as a friend. Youth is such a frivolous thing to covet."

His eyes followed her now, rather full of awe. "It's true," Abbey went on. "Don't you find that it is? We all wish to be young again, but always with the proviso of knowing what we know now. When we were young we hadn't the brains to appreciate our own vitality. Innocence is ignorance, I always say, and who wants ignorance back?"

Dominic laughed heartily now. The sound of it filled the house, pushing back the aura of mourning that had pervaded—if barely noticed—until now. "Abbey, you speak like an old gypsy. One would never guess you were so young yourself."

"I have lived with a man twice my age and twice my wisdom," she said. "Are you so surprised that I appreciate it?"

"A bit," he conceded. He glanced toward the stairway. "I shouldn't be so loud. It wouldn't do for Mrs. Edmonds to hear me laughing."

Abbey strode toward him, poking a finger. "That's just what I mean. What younger fellow would be so sensitive to a woman's feelings?"

And instantly they both thought of Jake Ross. In a flash of cognizance, Abbey was sure of it. She knew what she was thinking, of course, and something made her certain the same face had forced itself into Dominic's thoughts. A man—a young man. A man to whom they both knew she was drawn. And after all her trumpeting about older men and their appeal to young women . . . She looked at Dominic and knew that if it weren't for Jake . . .

If *what* weren't for Jake? What? So far there was nothing. Attraction, rejection, denial, question—was there any kind of unity there? It was a bad adventure so far and nothing more. Or was it merely the suspense that had somehow been spun around Jake Ross that pulled at her?

Here stood Dominic Nash, subdued and ready to accede to her comforts.

She didn't have the courage to tell him just how romantic he seemed—standing there so restrained and so chivalrous, waiting for her to decide what she wanted. If only she knew what that was. But Abbey knew one thing; To find out, she must disobey his orders.

• • •

As if by calculation, fate fell into her hands and waited for her to shape it.

For a man who kept a lighthouse on such a far shore, Jacob Ross seemed to find plenty of reasons to be in Nantucket Town.

The next morning, while almost everyone else was still in church, Abbey was just closing and locking up the door to the Geary Hat Store where she'd gone to gather a few things for Lucy, when who but the wraith himself came striding across the street. He was headed for the door of The Brotherhood, and he was accompanied by two other men. They strode across the cobblestones, self-concerned and speaking only to each other. They were almost at the door of the pub before Jake saw Abbey.

She was headed right toward him, her arms tight around a bundle of baby things.

His boot soles scraped on the cobblestones as he skidded to a quick halt, glaring at her. He stopped so suddenly that his two companions had to double back. Then Jake did an about-face and started walking away.

"Oh, no you don't . . ." Abbey gritted her teeth and bolted forward, right between the two other fellows, to catch Jake's arm by the sleeve. "Broad daylight, no storm, and no excuse."

"What are you doing here?" he demanded.

"I live here."

"You know what I mean."

"I do, but I'm not giving you any straight answers until I get the same from you."

Jake hovered self-consciously before her, glancing at the two men he'd been walking with. When he decided there was no way out of the situation, he took her elbow and pivoted her toward them. "Mrs. Abbey Sutton," he said with unexpected formality, "my cousins, Elias and Matthew Colbert."

Abbey took the time, in the midst of her now-silent quarrel with Jake, to give the cousins a good looking over. They both were handsome young men and were quite clearly brothers. They bore a strong resemblance to each other, as well as to Jake. Their blond hair, though a few shades darker than Jake's and perhaps a shade redder, joined their brown eyes and bespoke a common relative—probably on his mother's side, judging from their last name. Matthew had a neat red-blond beard, and seemed to be older—somewhere in his midthirties. If not for the crinkles around Matthew's eyes and his beard, the Colberts could have been twins. Elias's youth also showed in a certain wildness in his eyes and a funny crookedness to his mouth that became almost noble as he pulled his cap from his head and nodded at her, muttering, "Ma'am."

Abbey nodded at him, then looked at Matthew, waiting for him to greet her, too. But he simply glared impatiently at her, making it quite clear that she'd interrupted the business he had with Jake.

She matched his arrogance measure for measure, though, and stood there stoically, waiting for her greeting. After a moment, she dared to raise her brows as though she were asking him what was taking so long.

Jake looked from one to the other, then muscled Matthew aside with rough familiarity and sternly said, "'Nough of that."

Matthew shifted his glare to Jake, and the two men faced off for an uncomfortable moment.

Enjoying the turmoil she brought to Jake's clandestine life, Abbey raised her chin a fraction and refused to budge, while the men stared at each other. She was disappointed—albeit slightly—when Matthew's mouth turned up at the corners within his neat whiskers and the crinkles around his eyes deepened. He was visibly keeping down a chuckle.

Jake's pale cheeks pinked, and his eyes steamed. "Off with you," he said to his cousin tersely. "I won't be late."

"Don't get into trouble," Matthew mentioned, with a kind of intimate undercurrent. He bounced an amused glance off Abbey, then warned Jake with his glare again.

Abbey followed him with her own suspicious gaze as Matthew stepped back away from them. Had they been talking about her? Had she been the subject of pub gossip?

While she was trying to decide if she wanted to be offended or not, the younger cousin, Elias, clapped Jake's shoulder and said, "Stay sharp, landlubber."

Jake responded with a swat on Elias's arm that was a little less than friendly. The rosiness in his cheeks deepened.

Elias arranged his cap on his head again, paced backward a few steps, then wheeled around and followed his brother into the sanctity of the pub, leaving Jake at Abbey's mercy.

Well, perhaps mercy wasn't the word for it.

Jake gazed after them, plainly wishing he was with them instead of standing here blocked off from the world by a stubborn woman who probably could bite. He pressed his lips together and sighed.

"They don't seem like tavern keepers," Abbey said flatly.

"Abbey, stay away from me," Jake said with clear resolve. "It's better for you."

Ready with her response, Abbey shot back, "I keep hearing that and never the why of it. Here. Be a gentleman. Walk me home. Carry these."

She shoved her bundle against his chest with such force that his reflexes made him grab it. Then she immediately stepped too far away for him to shove it back at her.

Frustration colored his peach cheeks. His wide lips tightened, and he worked to shore up his resistance to her. "You are a madwoman," he said, in almost a conspiratorial whisper.

"With luck I'll never find sanity. Why did you run away from me at Great Point? Did you burrow into the sand like a clam? I couldn't find you anywhere."

"I didn't mean to get found. Don't you understand plain English? You're in danger."

"Why? Are you a crook?"

He dropped his head and shook it. Like a miracle a little light of insulted honesty popped up on his face. "No, I'm not a crook. I wander in bad company that's not suitable for you. So stay out of it."

Abbey cast a look toward the pub. Your cousins don't seem like such bad company."

"It's not them I mean," he said defensively. "I'd die for them and they for me."

"That won't be necessary," Abbey tossed back fluidly.

He drew in a breath and stepped past her, but she caught his sleeve.

"Come here—I have something to tell you!" She crooked her finger at him, then pointed to a secluded corner at the side of an ivy-covered trellis. She glanced around the street, then tiptoed rapidly toward the wall of ivy and hid in its bend. Peeking out at him, she whispered, "In here," and waved him toward her.

Her game of intrigue got the better of him. From where he was standing all he could see was the latticework trellis and the layers of dark green ivy draping from it. Knowing she was back there, waiting, baiting, had to be more than he could stand.

She could hear him coming toward the secluded corner and forced herself not to look. At the first glimpse of his jacket as he appeared beside the trellis, Abbey grasped the lapel and drew him under the trellis, pulling him off balance so abruptly that he dropped the bundle of Wilma's things and stood empty-armed before her.

The ivy created a sun-dappled arbor over them. Abbey made a great ado of peeking about to make "sure" they weren't being watched or followed—how rare!—and continued this until her playfulness brought out a reluctant smile on Jake's wide lips.

Seeing that, Abbey flattened back against the ivy and grinned in satisfaction. "I knew I could make you curious."

Jake shook his head. "Judas," he muttered. "You're something strange. What do you have to tell me?"

Saying nothing, Abbey let the tension between them take over. She spoke with only her eyes for many long seconds, and soon, as she suspected it would, the enchantment began to take hold.

Of him, too. That was how she knew it was real.

She saw, as surely as dawn coming up from nowhere in the morning, his senses spiraling toward her. Her indiscreet ribaldry had brought amusement into his prismatic eyes, and that served as a bridge for a simple confession of souls: they *liked* each other. They felt a common appreciation for each other. At least she thought so.

Abbey reached out and caught his hand between hers. "I don't know why," she began, "but there's something between us—not just of the body. Some . . . power. I don't know what it is yet . . . but I intend to find out."

His grin widened even more, but his brows came together. "I thought . . . you were going to say something else," he confessed.

"What?" she pressed. "That I love you? No, I don't love you. Not yet. Nor you me. But something is going on between us. Don't you feel it?"

"I never thought it was love," he said. His confession was a little disappointing.

"What, then?" she asked.

He returned the grasp she had on his hand, and for the first time, instead of her doing all the holding, they were holding onto each other. With a slow, steady pull, he drew her against his chest and breathed the word.

"Want."

Triumph surged through her as he said it, wrapping its coils around them with a heavy, humming energy. Still, he didn't bend down to kiss her. They gazed into each other's eyes, scanning for confusion, deception, all those odd things that this sort of magnetism could blur until it was too late. But there were none of those things, nothing that might signal the downfall of whatever was cultivating itself between the drapes of ivy. There was a texture of discovery in the sunlight that patched their faces, and in the awareness of their clothed bodies pressing slightly tighter with every breath.

She smiled. "And?"

His lips pursed quizzically. "And . . ." He shook his head, confusion descending over his thickly lashed eyes.

Abbey laughed aloud, her eyes twinkling with pleasure—and suddenly a wagon came by, clattering on the cobblestones.

They pulled apart. Abbey folded her arms nonchalantly. Jake pulled his cap down over his eyes and turned his back to the street until the wagon had wobbled past.

"I wonder what we're hiding from," Abbey mentioned.

She reached for him, got her fingers under his sea coat's lapels, and pulled him back across the little arbor's width until his body trapped her against the ivy. "You're not an evil man, Jake," she said softly. "I can't explain how I know that. But I know it as surely as my name. I'm going to make you say it. Tell me what you like about me."

Jake sighed. "You mean, *besides* your having the humility of a barn cat?"

"Yes," she murmured, giving voice to the sensations running between them. "Besides that."

His hands clenched at his sides, and when he spoke there was a tinge of bitterness to his tone. "I think we're put on this earth so destiny can laugh at us."

Terrible regret—or some kind of undefined sadness—layered his words so heavily that Abbey pulled back enough to look clearly into his eyes. "What does that mean?"

"It means," he began, hesitating, "that you're right. I can't resist you. My arms hurt to be around you."

Victory. Abbey drew his arms up around herself, and still she felt the tremors of denial in him. "I wouldn't want you to hurt, Jake . . ."

"I'm asking you once more," he said, rasping. "For your own good . . . resist me."

Their hearts beat in percussion as though they were trying to hammer through their chests and merge into a single beat.

The playful smile fell from Abbey's lips. If there was any mischief left in this moment, it now had simmered away.

She touched his face with her fingertips and murmured, "Would you light your lamp, then ask it not to burn?"

As though some unknown hand had finally pulled that string tying them together, their lips met. Blood-heat rose, and bubbled.

The sparks hadn't been imaginary. They hadn't been wishful thinking or idle musing or the effects of a storm on a man and a woman alone together. They hadn't been, because they came flooding back now, brighter than before and more stinging. One by one they peeled back the layers of Jake's resistance just as she hoped they would. For an instant, the kiss was only a tool, a test, but as her fingers dug into the fabric of his coat and she pulled harder, pressing her mouth tighter against his, her mind began to fog. Purpose blurred. A wonderful, salacious yearning exploded between them—she pulled harder, pressed tighter. Its potency grew until kissing alone couldn't assuage it.

Her hands found their way inside his coat, and his hands painted her back with strokes that burned through the fabric of her dress. She bent against him with sudden pliancy. They rocked against each other, hearts racing. The knot of need twisted tighter.

Her hands slipped under his sweater, experiencing the thrill of finally touching his skin—so much silkier than she expected. Abandon caught them, like two children indulging in a first curious grope, knowing that somehow they were committing a sin that nature demanded they try. Breaking a rule that was made to be broken. Defying that which begged defiance. A rascal and a scamp, that's all the two of them were, and that's all they wanted to be as they allowed the floodgates to slip open a crack.

Until Abbey heard voices—women's voices.

Jake dragged his lips away from Abbey's in a moist gasp. With volcanic effort he pushed himself away, so abruptly that his shoulder knocked the edge of the trellis and shook the whole arbor.

A clutch of town ladies strolled by and noticed them hiding in the arbor, particularly noticing Jake's back turned to them. But Abbey gave them a nod of greeting and they nodded back. They passed by, their conversation falling off only for a moment as they looked into the arbor, but then picking up again in a manner that seemed fairly harmless.

Harmless, from Abbey's point of view, but apparently not from Jake's.

He tugged his cap down even farther over his eyes, as though everybody in town didn't know who he was already anyway.

"Judas—" he muttered, glancing about again. "We can't talk this way, not now and certainly not here."

"Why not?" Abbey asked, trying not to sound accusatory.

"You have to trust me," he said. "Though if you had any sense, you wouldn't."

"I have no sense at all."

"I can tell that. You shouldn't be seen with me around town for a while."

This time Abbey was ready for his reaction. She ducked deeper into the pin-neat little garden and crouched behind the heavy veil of English ivy. On one side of them there was nothing but the side wall of a house, with nothing but a little window way up in the attic. On the opposite side, a tangled garden, poorly kept but somehow reflective of their senses at this moment. To Abbey's right as she sat with her back against the wall of ivy, there was a tall wooden fence, solid and weathered, starkly different from the dainty picket fence on which the ivy grew. They couldn't possibly be seen here.

Pulling her skirts under her as a cushion, she sat down against the leafy fence and motioned to him to join her. "Seclusion," she whispered.

Jake hung his head, closed his eyes, and chuckled. Muttering, "Aren't you something . . ." he wandered toward her and lowered himself onto the grass. The way he sat down betrayed a kind of exhaustion—not physical, but mental. A stressful weariness that begged for relief. And that, it seemed, was the real power that pressed him to sit beside her behind the ivy.

"If I'm going to trust you—even though you say I shouldn't—we should know more about each other. You said you're from Ohio. Which part?" Abbey asked gently, careful of her tone.

He contemplated his answer, obviously judging whether or not there was any risk in telling her. That contemplation, that signal of something hanging over his head, Abbey saw clearly now, dominated his every word, every move, every mood.

"My home town is Williamston, Ohio," he said, still being careful. "Grew up there."

"With those two?" She cocked her head in the direction Matthew and Elias had gone.

Jake actually looked in that direction as though he'd forgotten the two other men existed. "Oh . . . yes. We were raised together. In the same house. My mother and theirs were sisters. French immigrants. Our fathers shared a business. A saloon. Matt and Elias and I always talked about running our own place. We took over our fathers' business eventually, but . . ." He trailed off, listless about the whole conversation, making it necessary for Abbey to prod him on.

Softly she asked, "And why did you leave it?"

He gave her a quirky grin, knowing what she was up to. "Starting at the beginning, eh?"

She shrugged, wrapping her arms about her knees. "Good as any place."

Jake sighed. "If you insist. I wanted to . . . travel. See the United States."

"Why?" she asked. "Travel is a hard way of life. I've grown to know it intimately of late, and I wouldn't wish it on a dead sow."

His eyes widened illustratively. "I discovered that. The hardship I saw was disillusioning for a while. But then I discovered something rather special."

"Which was . . ."

"Which was," he picked up, "the independence of it."

Abbey felt her eyes narrowing. "I don't follow."

Jake crossed his legs and picked at the grass. "I found out how much I love the United States. And I found out why I love it. Independence, self-possession . . . that's what we live by, even if that means the hardest life on earth. You know, my father—my father himself—was there in 1789 when James Madison presented the Bill of Rights to the House of Representatives. He used to tell me all about the fight to make this country a real place. How the process took year after year of war and revolution and proposals and ratifications. Even that had a certain victory in it—no king to say what and when. So . . . I went out to see what we'd made." Jake gazed silently at the grass for several moments. "I found hardship, pain, people dying on the frontier trail, in the mines, on the wagon trains, nothing very pretty. And it was everywhere, from folks fighting drought and heat in Texas, to here, where we fight the wrath of the sea on a daily basis." Now he gripped a handful of grass. His hand closed around it and he pulled. As he raised his tightened fist, the grass came up with it, making a soft ripping noise. "But it was *theirs*. Their fight, their hardship. The hardship of choice."

Abbey said nothing, but merely smiled gently at his discovery. She'd never thought of the West that way; never thought of anything that way. This new perspective intrigued her, and her wish to listen to him went far deeper than just trying to pull him out of his shell.

Sensing her interest, Jake looked up now, his brown eyes filled with respect for the people who had made the country what it was, and something in his gaze said he knew that her life in Wyoming had been part of what he was talking about.

"No one cared about how hard life got," he went on. "They just kept on hammering through it to forge the life they'd chosen for themselves. It was *their* hardship to have as they pleased. No one ordered them to be there. No one decreed that they should carve out an existence from the prairies and the mountainsides and the canyons. They weren't subject to the whims of the elite, and anything they earned was their own. So the tough life was a kind of reward, too. I was amazed. Still am. Amazed at how alive this country is!" He shook his fist in front of her again, tendrils of grass vibrating from his knuckles, as though that grass were his testimonial. "The spark of life in America caught ahold of me. There are huge varieties of pain here, but all by choice. What happens to a person is up to him. You know, Europe is still waiting for this country to fall apart," he said with an arrogant grin. "Instead, aristocracies the world over are being kicked out by people following the American example. I *love* the United States. I love it. . . ."

". . . and my mother never let us forget those stories about her childhood and what happened in France. We grew up with the history her family had brought with them from Europe when they emigrated. When you look at the long history of the world, it's mind-boggling that a nation like this finally emerged. There's no precedent for it. We're a piece of art in the making, shaping ourselves out of the clay of this earth, and we have the chance to be more beautiful than any other work of art in all of history."

Abbey hadn't spoken a word in—how long? Her chin rested on her knees, and she was listening with an exquisite attention, mesmerized by Jacob Ross. She knew his stories intimately. She had dug in that soil he spoke of with her bare hands, had helped carve the civilized nation he adored, and all without really appreciating her own participation. For her, Wyoming's hardships had been just that—a way of life. She had had a hazy awareness of the East, but nothing substantial. She only vaguely remembered the wagon train her parents had joined when she was still a toddler. As Jake spoke these words, described his rapturous love affair with a concept for a country, Abbey gained unbidden respect for her parents and, no matter the agonies of pioneering, for the freedom that allowed them the hardship of their choice.

She was utterly caught up by his story. Jake had lost himself in his soliloquy as though his words had been waiting for years and finally had been able to say them all at once.

At length Abbey raised her chin from her knee. "All this talk of independence," she said, "and you fail to allow yourself any."

For an instant, Jake seemed not to know what she meant, but then a comprehending look passed across his features. "Everything can't be as we might like it."

She inched closer to him on the grass and touched his hand—a deliberately subdued gesture. "We deserve our own choices, you and I," she murmured. "Would you deny them?"

"That's plain wisdom right now, Abbey," he said. "I can't tell you why."

"Won't tell," she corrected. "Burdens are easier to bear if they're shared. Share yours with me, Jake." Her voice dropped to a whisper and she added, "Perhaps I can even help."

Jake's lips were pressed into a line of indecision, as though an explanation lurked behind them, pushing to get out. He returned the touch of her hand, wrapping her fingers in his and gazing at the entwined hands with a look of wishfulness. "This isn't . . ."

"Don't say it," Abbey breathed quickly. Lifting her other hand to his face and caressing his cheek, making him look into her eyes. "I don't believe it. You're not the kind of man who speaks of choice and then denies yourself your own. There's a way. We'll find it. We'll think of it. I'll fit into your life somehow. Fate brought us together—I do believe that. This is a perfect time in my life for change. You may find it's perfect for you, too. Believe, Jake . . . believe."

Warmth rose in her cheeks as she lost herself in his almond-shell brown eyes, and the moment felt endless.

Growing upon itself like memories piling upon one another to make a mosaic of possibilities, the moment bent its endlessness into a kind of seclusion and told them it was all right to be alone, here, together, apart from both past and future, separated from all eyes but each other's. As Jake clung to her whispered words, the strings that bound them together softly began to tighten. Closer, closer, swallowed by need. His lips pressed on her open mouth, engulfing it with his gentle touch.

Abbey slid into his arms with alarming naturalness—even she was surprised by the ease of it, by the quiver of her skin and her instant forgetfulness. She felt as thin as paper as he lay her down on the place where the grass and ivy met, paper made of silk threads, its edges curling under the heat of his fingers. She brought her hands up—no, they came up of their own will—to become lost in his hair. His cap toppled to the grass. She kneaded the back of his neck, where the skin turned soft and his hair invited her to stroke it, grasp it, tangle her fingers in it.

She felt his lips slip off her mouth and graze the side of her face, then her ear, then the wild spots on her throat. She bent backward against the unyielding earth, pushing herself up into him. Her body screamed invitations to his as she pulled her hands down and dove deep beneath his sea coat and under the sweater to his bare skin. He was hot—searing hot. Moist. Soft, so demonically soft . . . Her legs began to throb, to tighten.

Every thread of her being stiffened and shivered like tips of shore grass in a breeze. She was a thousand separate bits of sensation, all trembling and acute, reaching up in that breeze, reaching toward the top of the sky, pushing off the earth to fly with him. Jake was kissing her face, her temple, the side of her cheek, the bridge of her nose, making his way slowly back to her quivering lips.

She sucked in a breath of surprise, of victory, and of approval when his hand escaped to her leg, pushing her dress out of the way with possessive little gestures until he found her bare calf and kneaded it, tugging it against his own leg until it bent and caressed his buttocks. Abbey was lost in folds of clothing—the cotton of her dress, the woven yarn of her shawl, the wool of his coat, and deep inside all that fabric was their skin, screaming for freedom. Every one of her pores wanted a taste of Jake's sweat, just as his body pressed and dug at hers for a quenching it had so recently been denied.

"I can't fight you anymore," Jake rasped. The sound of his voice was so startling, it seemed like thunder, the words drumming through their bones as though they didn't need ears to hear the confession. "I can't do it, I don't want to do it—"

His voice caught fast in his throat and destroyed itself in a wet, crushing kiss.

Abbey answered by returning that kiss, by pushing upward into him as he lay across her possessively. Each response cued another. Her, then him, then her again, then him—a symphony of echoes riding each other like waves. His tips of his shoes dug into the grass as he pushed harder and harder. The ivy reached out for them and cloaked their indiscretions with a soft rustling.

On a gasp Abbey forced herself to ask, "Are you afraid?"

"Terrified," he choked back without a hint of pause. His hands burned across her back, damning the fabric of her dress with every stroke. "I know you'll devour me and that scares me. But I want it, I want it . . ."

Desire ate at them, teasing and tormenting them. Abbey knew that no matter how they hungered, no matter how they pawed and pressed and probed here in the ivy, there would be no fulfillment here and now, for this was someone's backyard in a town where everyone knew about everything, where people could read a face as clearly as reading a newspaper, where anyone strolling by on the other side of that fence could hear their soft, sucking kisses and their frayed breaths. And somehow Abbey also knew that such a thing would be far worse for Jake than for her—somehow his life dangled on the tenuous threat of his reclusiveness, on his not getting involved with other people . . . with *her*.

But to let go of him now? To become stupid and socially proper just when he—

Oh, God, was that his hand?

Her buttocks flinched under a glorious pressure that caught her thigh and pushed upward, all strokes moving toward her heart. An insane plan sprung up in her mind. If she could take him just far enough—just to the point where passion and panic blended and made a man insane—then perhaps she could guarantee reawakening the spell, leaving him at the mercy of a thought or a word, a magic word that would draw him back to her at the right time, in the right place.

So she pulled him down deeper against her, plunging into his kisses.

As though to echo the strong pulse of their hearts, the clock in the town hall rang its slow, relentless announcement of the hour.

It rang and rang. Lost in each other, they chose to ignore it. But the old clock had no intention of being ignored. It plied their ears until they heard it, and something inside Jake made him add up all its gongs.

Jake blinked, as though he were coming out of a trance, as though someone had pinched him.

Only in that moment did Abbey realize he hadn't let himself become so drunk on her that he couldn't think anymore. She felt his whole body tighten, felt his soul retreat and his hands grow cool.

He raised his head, squeezed his eyes shut, then opened them as if to shake away the visions that had been flying in his head. "God, Abbey . . . let go of me. Let me go." He pushed her hands away, stiffly got to his feet, and stumbled as his legs almost buckled under him. "Noon . . . Judas—two whole hours . . ."

Her legs tingling, Abbey struggled to get up. "Jake, don't do this."

He spun back toward her, catching her hand, but this time with a clear regret. "Shhh . . . I have to go. I can't stay. Don't ask me to."

Abbey felt the noon hour tugging at her, too—she had obligations to a girl freshly widowed—yet the urge to stay was nearly too strong to resist. Had Jake not been the one to resist it, she might have sat there all day. "We've spent a while together," she said, her tone begging for more. "It's not a crime."

"It hasn't been a while," he corrected. "It's been two hours. I'm late for a . . . I've got to go," he stammered, his face flushing with color that might have been embarrassment at having rattled on for so long. His brows furrowed with concern, or regret—Abbey couldn't tell.

He didn't want to leave, that much was plain. Yet something pulled at him, some kind of obligation that he had to fulfill.

Abbey caught his arm as he slipped through the arbor. The sunlight fell on his face differently as he turned to her. During their time together, the sun had shifted, and now its light advertised the time that had gone by. "When can I see you again?"

Still breathing heavily, Jake glanced down the street. "Certainly not in broad daylight," he said, as though being cautious was a given.

"Then when and where?"

He clamped his mouth tightly shut, obviously having a last-ditch wrestle with himself. "Tonight, he finally relented. "Behind The Brotherhood. After dark." He scooped up the forgotten bundle of Lucy's possessions and shoved them at her, took her wrist, and folded her arm around the bundle in a firm good-bye.

"Then will you tell me what it is you're afraid of?" she pursued.

His hand lingered on her arm for one last second, and a testy smile pulled up one side of his mouth. "No . . . but we may find other answers. We'll . . . talk."

He had other plans besides talking. That much was plain in his expression, in the set of his shoulders as he held himself back from embracing her, which would have been so natural after these moments of secretive touches. He meant he couldn't resist anymore either. He was plainly giving in—but he regretted it. Or was it that he thought *she* would regret it?

Without wasting another word he spun on the ball of his foot and strode away, not too fast, but apparently with a clear mission in mind. To Abbey's eyes, he seemed to be holding himself back from running—as if running would draw attention. What was he so frightened of?

As soon as he could without being too obvious, he vanished between two dockside buildings and was gone. Abbey was left alone beside the trellis as a breeze rippled the shinglelike layers of ivy. Only then did she realize her face was hot and her heart was racing.

"Drat him," Abbey grumbled. "All right then, Jake. Tonight. Outside The Brotherhood."

"This girl," Elias Colbert mentioned, trying to be casual about a forbiddingly personal subject as he wiped a grog mug dry and handed it to his cousin. "You, uh . . ."

Jake took the mug and stacked it with the others in a cabinet behind the dark wooden bar. "Not yet," he said, avoiding clearing his throat.

"Better make it never," Matthew told him, turning to him with fatherly sternness.

Elias looked across the pub at his brother and said, "Don't tell him his business."

Flashing the younger cousin a thankful glance, Jake said nothing, but continued stacking mugs. This was a place that was, for Jake, the safest haven the island could offer. The only spot he felt sheltered. Even remote Great Point couldn't present the security of The Brotherhood. The small pub was an L-shaped room made partially of wood and partially of the redbrick foundation of the building above it. Long shiphatch tables of dark polished planking butted up against the brick all the way down the narrow room, each cozy with four captain's chairs and bearing a round-globed lamp. Each lamp cast a golden light across its respective table, and there were already a few sailors bent over wooden bowls of steaming soup. An hour from now the place would be packed wall-to-wall with seafarers enjoying the comfort of a warm room and a floor that didn't move under them. There would be chanty singing and the drum of old work songs, the music of a seafaring heritage and the scratchy baritone yowl of a crowd of sailors. They would be singing both of the grandeur and the toil of a life none would wish on his little brother.

Jake involved himself with stacking the mugs and whiskey glasses, very aware of the glances coming his way from Matthew, who was pretending to be interested only in rubbing a glow into the battered plank tables. Any minute now. Any—

"Don't forget what we heard last month."

Not quite able to stifle a grin at Matthew, who had stewed until he predictably burst, Jake was ready with his response. "I'm not forgetting. We don't get a warning from the mainland every day, you know." Against his will an edge of defensiveness wrecked his tone. "What are the chances it has anything to do with Abbey?"

Matthew straightened to face Jake over the bar. "What are the chances it doesn't? How many newcomers come to Nantucket these days, Jacob? They don't come here. They leave here. We don't even get a handful of strangers coming to live on Nantucket anymore."

"And she's one of the handful," Elias defended. "You could leave, then we'd be even."

His reward was the light smack of a cleaning cloth in his face. In spite of the playful gesture, Matthew didn't drop the cloak of doom he held across the subject. "Damn this, Jake," he said, grabbing on to the solid wooden bar and shaking it as though he could make it move. "She's suddenly appearing right after we get word there's a federal investigator on the island, looking to break our operation. Think, man!"

Jake dropped his head and sighed. "Please, Matt, I'm struggling enough, thanks."

"That's yet to come," his cousin foretold.

Matthew started to say something else, but a knock on the back door distracted him. With a scolding glare to punctuate his meaning, he broke off and disappeared into the kitchen.

Jake held his breath as he listened to the back door opening to a mutter of voices, then the back door clapping closed again. A moment later Matthew reappeared, tearing open an envelope and pulling out a folded sheet of paper. He read it, then immediately spoke up. "He's here."

"Who?" Jake and Elias chimed at the same time.

"Thomas Pollock. A broker from the Continent."

Jake stepped out from behind the bar. "A *what?* You didn't tell us anything about this!"

"Because I wasn't sure it was genuine," his cousin said. Shaking the paper, he said, "But he came through. He promises he can expedite our transportation process, maybe double what it is now. More direct routes, bigger ships."

"Matt! Are you blinkers, trusting somebody we don't know?"

"Then you meet him. Judge for yourself. He's coming in tonight. Be outside after dark."

Jake caught himself in midbreath. "Tonight?"

"Right after dark," Matthew said. Then he looked suspiciously into his cousin's now-blank eyes. "Why?"

Elias Colbert had been watching all of this in silence, and now he read Jake's expression as clearly as if it were a page in a newspaper. "Uh-oh," he muttered.

"Aw, Jake," Matthew groaned. "You're meeting her, aren't you?"

There was no need to answer. Silence did the job.

"This is more important," Matthew insisted, slapping his fingers against the piece of paper and making it snap.

Jake rubbed his palms together, suddenly feeling nervous and overtaxed and embarrassed. "I have to know, Matt." He glanced from Matthew to Elias and back again. "I have to find out why she makes me feel . . . so hollow. Like an empty glass waiting to be filled up." Words failed him utterly. He twisted away, unable to face the other men with this wholly poetic affectation. He could feel the burning stares of his cousins following him around the bar as he tried to hide behind it.

Careful silence passed, then Matthew turned on his controlled diplomacy and said, "All right. I'm a man, too. I know what's after you. So let's say she's not the investigator. Say she's what she appears to be. A girl who likes the looks of you." He reached his brawny arm over the bar and grasped Jake's arm, forcing him to look up. "Do you pull her into the pit with us?"

Truth made his question penetrate. It was nothing Jake hadn't heard ringing inside his own head already.

Matthew sighed. "While you're jawboning about whether yes or whether no with this gal, you're getting closer to a yes. I see it in your face. This is the kind of business that kills people, Jake. I'm telling you . . . shake her," he urged, "before it's too late."

Jake felt suddenly queasy. He glared unblinkingly at Matthew, who wore the very face of sense.

After a moment, unable to contain the misery it brought him, he nodded.

"I will."

Abbey looked out the parlor window at the darkening sky. Why wouldn't the dratted sun set faster? The afternoon had been torture for her, since she knew what was coming. No matter how she tried to distract herself, the knot of sexual tension at her very core continued to tighten in anticipation. No amount of activity with the Nash children, no gentle conversation with poor Lucy, no cooing and cuddling with little Wilma, no level of attentiveness from Dominic could assuage it even for a few moments. It continued to pile need upon need until she thought it would twist her apart. This would be the night when she would know, when she would find out. No matter the circumstances, no matter the inconvenience. At The Brotherhood, in the hat store's back room, on the ground behind the buildings, somehow . . . somewhere. This would be the night, or she would know why not.

And if passion died in its being spent, if the binding fabric tore when it was tested, at least the ache would go away and take all questions with it. Then, these terrible cutting threads would cease their hungry pull on her and, yes, on Jake.

No matter how he tried to escape her, his eyes betrayed him every time. The desire had shone itself plainly in them whenever he looked at her. She and Dominic had spoken of the advantages— even the sweetness—of experience, and Abbey knew she wasn't misinterpreting what she saw and heard.

Jake Ross was no criminal. In spite of all his clandestine sneaking about and all his talk of danger and such, the clearest image she had of him was the most recent one: the picture of him sitting there behind the ivy, telling her all about the wonderful new concepts that had forged the United States and how much it all meant to him. This simply wasn't the kind of man who was a criminal. As she thought of it, she smiled. How adorable it was, really. He was probably involved in something as harmless as smuggling European liquor onto the island to skirt around tariffs. And he thought that was so unconscionable as to be ashamed about it. What a sense of conscience!

Luella was already in bed. The boys were playing checkers in their room, Cordelia was off mending socks, and Dominic was generously spending his evening hours in the parlor with Lucy, doing his duty as her host and, no doubt, twisting himself inside out to keep her distracted, no matter how improbable that seemed on the day of her husband's funeral luncheon. Today Abbey had seen what Nantucket was really about. Half the island—at least that—had turned up at Trinity Church at one o'clock for a memorial to the young man they hardly knew. The church's Gothic windows had reverberated with the bell chiming from its spired tower, and the congregation had spilled out onto the street and all the way across it. Sailors came and went, lived and died, that was true, but this particular young man had done more than just that—he had *given* his life in an act of heroism. A snagged line on a toggle iron had nearly taken down eight men in a whaleboat. Billy Edmonds had been the ninth man in that boat. He'd plunged overboard and cut that line, only to be buried beneath the descending flukes of a Greenland right. In those churning waters, his body had never turned up.

That had been the end of music on board the *Nancy Ames*. Billy Edmonds's penny whistle, hurdy-gurdy and little wrist bells had come home silent.

And as immediate as the grief felt to Lucy, to Abbey, to everyone on the island of Nantucket, all that had happened over three months ago.

As the preacher spoke of Billy Edmonds, Abbey had thought it strange to be mourning a man three months dead as though he had died that day. In Wyoming they always knew where their men were . . . except for the mountain men, who disappeared for years at a time, but they never wanted families anyway. Those women who had husbands always knew where they were.

So the day slowly ended—luckily for Lucy, it had taken its time.

The townsfolk didn't hurry through their memorial. After the memorial service, after the tears and the sympathy and the tender gazing at baby Wilma asleep in the arms of all those people who wanted to hold her today, the town ladies had set out a fine luncheon to ease the pain. These people gathered up all their strength and sympathy to spread out Lucy Edmonds's grief. She might be widowed, the attention said, but she would never be alone. Not here, not on Nantucket. Home was still home.

And the sun finally set.

Abbey tugged the big wooden door shut with a click. The last thing she heard from inside the house was the gentle voice of Dominic Nash speaking to Lucy. Such a kind man, to bother spending time with a girl like Lucy. Yes, Lucy was sweetness itself and vivacious to a fault, but she was out of Dominic's league entirely. There wasn't really much for them to talk about—Dominic was forcing the conversation to keep Lucy from falling into a mood. And so generous. He wasn't avoiding the subject of Billy Edmonds; he was pursuing it. Abbey had heard him as she retrieved her shawl from her room and threw it around her shoulders. Dominic was asking Lucy how she had met Billy, what she liked about him . . . anything to keep her talking, never mind that he probably couldn't understand a third of her shredded sentences.

A pang of guilt stripped away a portion of Abbey's enthusiasm as her feet hit the cobblestones. Dominic was clearly attracted to her, and here she was sneaking off to rendezvous with a man who had done his best to avoid her.

Still, she set her mind forward as the Nash house fell away behind her and faded into the darkness.

Nantucket Town at night. All fell quiet, although there were unending signs of life. The warm golden glow of lanterns shone through countless lace curtains in tiny rectangular windows. Occasionally the soft sounds of a horse's hooves and the creak of carriage wheels would creep along the cobblestones from some other street. Distant voices in some evening conversation would trickle across the shipyard docks from the deck of a sleeping vessel. The twitter of a penny whistle and the scratchy lilt of a fiddle played badly rolled across the water from a ship moored in the harbor.

To Abbey's ears, these were pleasant, peaceful sounds. The streets were milk-bathed with moonlight on these clear seaside nights—no matter how gray the days, nights always seemed to be clear. At least so far. As she walked through the blue evening, Abbey thought about the Nantucket nights and knew that fog would come eventually. She'd heard much about it from travelers, people who'd been east or came from the East. One of these nights, there would be fog. She looked forward to it. The steam of the sea.

Now there was a new sound, very sudden, like the opening of a door—voices, men's voices. More music, louder, clearer . . . fiddle, hurdy-gurdy, banjo, concertina, penny whistle . . . voices both singing and talking, and there was laughter, too.

Then the door abruptly closed with a hush.

The Brotherhood.

Abbey hauled up short. *Am I ready?*

She hovered there in midstep, one of her shoes wedged at an angle between two cobblestones. She didn't breathe for a few moments after the door closed. If only the walk between the Nash home and The Brotherhood could have been a bit longer. . . .

"Yes," she spoke aloud, forcing the word out. "I'm ready." She leaned forward, ready to move, although for a second or two her feet didn't go with her. Soon they had no choice and she was striding with deliberate resolve toward the wide intersection across which lay The Brotherhood.

The intersection opened before her. She could almost read the sign. THE BROTHERHOOD FOOD, BED AND GROG. GOOD COMPANY. She remembered all that from before, though tonight darkness obscured the lettering. The simple brick and wood building was attached to all the other buildings from here to the brink of Old North Wharf, and the tavern door was nothing but a portal of planking cut into a wall of gray cedar, displaying the same Quaker reserve that most of the other buildings on Nantucket did. Like a plain woman on the outside, but gurgling with activity within.

She forced herself to keep walking, and with every step there was less force involved. The magnetism was at work again, that line leading her to Jake Ross, drawing her unerringly and without pause toward The Brotherhood and finally around the corner to the back of the pub.

But she did slow down now . . . she did stop to hide behind a cluster of tree trunks. Just to look first, just to get the upper hand, or at least to pause and think of what she would say to him first.

And he was there. He hadn't noticed her yet.

He paced aimlessly, then paused and put his foot up on a food crate. He leaned one elbow on his knee and sighed deeply.

Abbey wasn't close enough to hear the sigh, but she saw it, and wondered what it meant, what he was feeling, what he was thinking.

A thread of moonlight came between the housetops and touched Jake's head, leaving a gray spot where his cap was and a shimmer of silvery fringe where his hair fell below the cap. It cast a shadow on his face from the cap's brim. His coat hung open around his body, its broad lapels parted to show a wedge of oatmeal sweater. More of the sweater showed when he pushed back the coat on one side and stuffed his hand into his trouser pocket—a gesture of comfort in a moment of unease.

Was she imagining all this? Was she forcing him to react to his own loneliness out there on Great Point? No—she wouldn't believe it. There was something between them. But because it wasn't a concrete something, neither of them knew whether or not it was real.

Finally, she resolved to make it real. She straightened her shoulders and stepped out from the clutch of trees.

Boot soles crunched on the cobblestones—not hers.

She ducked back into the trees, admittedly a silly and unnecessary action. Part of the sensation of making all this a game, probably, as she thought about it. She was sneaking around, and she enjoyed it. It was fun.

But then the fun abruptly ended.

The footsteps grew louder. A man came up from the other side of the street. Abbey saw Jake look up, saw him suddenly straighten and stare. He glanced about, then looked back at the man who approached.

The man strode by Abbey's hiding place in the tree trunks without as much as a glance her way; he didn't see her at all and strode resolutely toward Jake.

Abbey felt as though her chest were caving in when she saw the man's face in the glare of moonlight. A big round face, framed with a pair of broad broom-shaped sideburns, gray-shot black, very bushy.

Above the sideburns were cheekbones like broad cliffs, and above those his crescent-shaped eyes were hardly more than dark wedges in this evening light.

Her heart slammed against her breastbone. She'd know that face, no matter the darkness, no matter the crowd, no matter the impossibility that this particular man would be in this particular place, or that Abbey Sutton would happen to be in the same place at the same time.

It was a long way from Wyoming.

She parted her lips, and whispered into the night, her breath warm against her face.

"What are you doing here . . . murderer?"

Chapter Nine

ABBEY CLUNG TO the tree in the darkness, mostly to keep from falling over, all the while experiencing a hatred deeper and blacker than the blackest pit on earth. Pollock. Thomas Pollock. What was he doing here?

A cold hand wiped away the hot-blooded need that had been simmering expectantly inside her. A shudder of protectiveness replaced it, and wracked her. Pollock was heading straight for Jake. A moment more . . . and they were talking.

No greeting had been exchanged. She was sure of that. There was no sign of friendliness, but no sign of rejection, either. Jake accepted the man's presence with only a slight tightening of his posture.

She heard snatches of conversation, but only pieces.

"—watching you—"

"Before it's too late—"

"—part of the bargain—"

"—by morning—"

"All right."

"—in Baltimore?"

"—dependable transportation—"

"—don't like the sound of it—"

"—Proof? Your proof's in the—"

"—try it—"

"But don't . . . my way—"

In between the cogent words, the rest was muttering. Abbey dug her fingernails into the tree's bark, her teeth pressing together in frustration until her jaws ached. If only she were closer. If only the breeze would change direction. Pollock! Astonishing! He *couldn't* be here!

Her mind screamed its anguish and rage. *Murderer!*

Deeper into the bark her fingernails dug. Her heart was begging her to step out and shout the accusation. But then she'd get no further here than she had back home—and she'd never find out why he was there and why he was talking to Jake. To Jake, damn it all!

Jake . . . Pollock. Mystery . . . murder. Oh, God . . .

Did Jake know who that man was. If he didn't, he was in awesome danger. If he did . . . then she was a fool.

"—have to be now?"

"Don't argue with me."

"—not arguing."

Abbey stiffened, holding her breath, straining to hear. Peering between the trees, she watched as Pollock strode away from Jake. Jake didn't follow—at least, not immediately. Instead he passed his eyes over the street, sweeping from one end to the other, pausing in the direction Abbey would be taking to meet him. Her legs tingled when she thought—for an instant—that he saw her.

Then Pollock, now halfway down the street, turned and barked, "Right now."

Jake closed his jacket and buttoned it—somehow Abbey knew that was a gesture of fortification. He glanced one more time toward Ash Street. Then he made a decision and jogged down Candle Street after Pollock.

May hell burn you Thomas Pollock. It was her Jake was waiting for, Abbey raged in the privacy of her mind. How many times did the man think he could interfere in her life . . . before she struck back?

Pollock had given Jake orders, firmly and with the same pompous authority in his voice that Abbey remembered him using in Wyoming. Wyoming. That far! Yes, Pollock had disappeared, cleanly and utterly, but to show up here?

"Is he following me?" Abbey whispered aloud, battling to sort out the possibilities. Almost instantly she knew that made no sense. The ranch was dissolved, sold to pay its debts. She had just about had it with being followed.

It was her turn to do the following.

She stepped out from behind her stand of trees and took her shoes off, tucking them under one arm. Ignoring the punishment of hard, misshapen cobblestones on her stocking feet, she started down Candle Street.

Where Candle Street merged into Washington, she lost them. Not until she was to Fayette Street did she realize they must have turned off down Coffin Street while she was busy sneaking up behind them. Desperate to catch up to them, she turned up Fayette, gathered up her skirts, and tilted into a run toward Union Street, hoping they turned left and she would encounter them here.

Bad luck . . . they were nowhere to be seen. Only moonlight occupied the silent street. Either she was too late and they had already passed, or they hadn't come this way at all. Such a small, tight town . . . two skulking men could disappear without really meaning to.

Pollock . . . Pollock . . . Pollock, of all the humans on earth!

Coincidence? No. Fate! Providence!

Yes, fate. It had brought her there to give him what he deserved.

"But first," she rasped, "answers."

And she knew where those answers lay.

Though she knew exactly where she was heading, she took the long way through town. She went up and down the short streets with their blocky Quaker houses and their tight, neat gardens and their lamplit window curtains, but she had plainly lost the two men she was following. Twice she pulled herself to a stop as dark forms strode out of the night, but neither time was it Jake and Pollock. Once it was a man and a woman, and the second time it was three men hobbling down the street toward the docks, profoundly drunk, still howling the sea song she'd heard threading into the night air from The Brotherhood.

Finally there was nothing to do but admit the obvious and dash for the one place where she could unshackle herself from this cloying question.

Abbey stormed into the Nash house, rattling the door nearly off its frame. Even without her shoes, she made a terrible noise on the foyer floor. She flew into the parlor and tossed off her shawl—

And found herself staring at a roomful of men, shrouded in cigar smoke. All were standing, none in a relaxed manner. Something was happening—happening now.

At the center of them, Dominic glared at her, openmouthed and seemingly profoundly embarrassed.

Then one of the men, an older fellow with a bright yellow beard, gestured toward Abbey and said, "Retired, had she?"

Dominic's cheeks grew pink. He stepped past the bearded man.

"Mrs. Sutton, I thought you had gone to bed," he exclaimed.

Abbey glanced self-consciously around the smoky room at the pack of men. "What is all this?"

"Where've you been just now, miss?" another man demanded.

With a slicing motion, Dominic cut the man off.

"Mrs. Sutton," he began, "I must ask where you've been for the last hour."

Abbey pressed her lips together, not exactly in defiance, but she didn't really have a very savory story to tell. That she'd been dashing about in her stocking feet with her skirts all hiked up, chasing two men, one of whom she hated and the other she desired?

Unable to force herself to say that, she fell back on indignation. "Who's business is it?" she demanded.

Uncomfortable but determined to do his duty, Dominic peered at her. "It is the official business of the island, I'm afraid." He paused then, making Abbey supremely aware of the hard glares of all these men, almost a dozen of them. "The town jail has been broken into."

Abbey blinked, her brows lowering. "The jail? What's that to do with me?"

"Runaway slaves were being held in it. The very slaves you defended on the wharf the morning you arrived. All these men saw what happened that day. Suspicion, naturally—"

"Naturally falls on me," she supplied fiercely. Folding her arms, she admitted, "That makes sense. I overpowered the guard and ripped the door off the jail. You can look at me and easily imagine the sight."

The men in the small parlor muttered at each other. Her narrow, feminine body made the point for her as she stood with her hands on her hips before them.

"I didn't do it," she said flatly, without blinking. "Though I wish I had."

The men shuffled uneasily, caught up by her honesty.

She didn't give them time to think. Instead she glared straight at Nash. "Dominic, I must talk to you."

Dominic clenched his fists in contemplation, then swung around and addressed the men. "All right, I'll handle this. You men organize a search of the harbor front.

Muttering among themselves, the men filed out of the parlor and out the front door, one or two of them giving order to the others about who was to search where and how thoroughly.

They were barely out the door before Dominic asked, "What is it? You seem agitated."

"That I am. I want to know what's going on."

"With the jail?"

"With Jacob Ross."

Dominic tensed. "We discussed that subject, Abbey."

"We skimmed that subject, Dominic," she corrected.

Dominic gazed at her perplexedly, but he seemed to get the idea that there was no escape. If she didn't get her answers here, she would go out and get them somewhere else, very probably somewhere much more dangerous.

"Did you think you could deflate my curiosity with an order?" she demanded.

He tilted his head. "I thought I could. Evidently I was mistaken."

"I want to know what's going on." She gestured toward the big front door, indicating the men who had just passed through it. "Obviously there's more to Nantucket than meets the eye. I assumed Jacob was suspected of petty smuggling. Liquor, perhaps, to avoid tariffs, and that sort of thing. Small things. A few dollars here and there. But I saw something tonight that makes me believe otherwise. I want to know specifically what kind of smuggling he's being suspected of.

Dominic cleared his throat and clasped his hands behind his back. "It isn't very honorable."

"I don't care what adjective it carries. I'm interested in the man, and I want to know."

"All right, but please calm yourself." He maneuvered himself into the center of the room as though that might insulate them from each other. When he spoke, it was slowly and with contemplation. "You realize that, as a government official, there's a limit to what I can tell you."

"I'll take what I can get," Abbey bit back.

His jaw stiffened. "I want you to stay away from Jacob Ross because . . . Ross is a special danger. He's not just smuggling a few spirits in under the docks to avoid tariffs. We suspect that he's aiding in the transportation of valuable stolen property from the Continent. There's piracy involved. There've been deaths. We think he's part of a ring that uses Nantucket as a funnel. They're thieves, Abbey, pure and simple. Organized and dangerous."

A terrible chord chimed inside Abbey. Thieves. Rustlers. The kind of people who stole the fruits of other people's labor. It turned her stomach. She'd spent her life working cattle and sheep ranches only to watch in near-helplessness while rustlers cut away portions of whole herds. Abhorrent. Smuggling the stolen property of others!

Her perception of Jake shriveled. And of herself—she wasn't usually that bad a judge of character. But perhaps this was why he never quite seemed like the kind of man who keeps a lighthouse. Boiling with conflict within, Abbey shut her mouth tightly on her own anger, anger at Jake for even the tiniest possibility that he could be one of these men Dominic had described to her. She wanted to defend him, counter Dominic by describing the Jake she knew, the Jake she *felt*. Yet there was that nagging doubt—and the roaring testimonial that Jake himself had been trying to keep her away from him all along, as though—as though he were too dangerous to touch. Dangerous . . .

Abbey clenched her hands into a lump. She stared at the rug, knowing Dominic was watching her.

"They are the kind of men," Dominic went on for effect, "who killed your husband. My friend."

This snapped Abbey out of her thoughts. She felt a blade of cold hatred jab from her eyes. "More than *like* them. It *was them*."

Dominic's gaze narrowed as he interpreted her. "What was it you saw tonight?"

"Not an it," she snapped back. "A him. Someone who shouldn't be here. Someone whom deceit follows wherever he goes. Someone who makes me not surprised that there's untoward activity in the town tonight."

Now Dominic's hands flared out at his side to punctuate his question. "Who?"

Abbey's throat burned as she spoke the name. "Thomas Pollock," she said. "The man who killed my husband."

"Here?" Dominic's voice lifted beyond its normal firm baritone. "On Nantucket?"

Abbey's arm shot out, and her finger extended accusatorily out the appropriate window. "Not five blocks from here!"

Dominic looked at the floor, frowning, and he paced thoughtfully. "That's . . . very strange."

Abbey's eyes narrowed, and she slammed her fist against her thighs. "I suppose one might suggest a strangeness about it!" she fumed impatiently.

"What was he doing?" Dominic asked her.

"He was talking to Jake!" she blurted, anger making her speak right out.

"Was he, now?" Dominic drawled, his red brows lifting.

Abbey looked at him, holding herself in place as she realized she had just betrayed Jake, giving Dominic good reason to widen his suspicions that Jake was involved in illegal dealings. She shouldn't have done that—she wasn't that sure of what she'd seen tonight. Damn Pollock and the confusion he set upon her!

A criminal was setting her alight. A criminal. She didn't even know Jake well enough to know that about him, yet she quivered for his touch and the taste of his skin. The hunger was bitter, but it wouldn't go away.

"I go out for an evening sojourn, end up seeing my husband's murderer, and come home to discover I'm accused of conspiracy. I've had more ideal evenings, Dominic."

He nodded. "However, you must admit the logic of the accusation. You did attempt to pulverize the slaver."

"And would again."

"Yes, I know that, and I wish you'd cease saying it in public, Abbey," he sputtered in frustration. "It does not help."

"Well, what *would* help? Dishonesty?" she wailed.

"Of course not . . . restraint. Ross is using you."

Abbey blew a huff of anger out her nose and said, "I assure you, he hasn't."

Dominic's ruddy face flushed berry red. "Please, I didn't mean—"

"I know what you meant. He hasn't used me in any sense. Not yet, and nothing I haven't suggested myself. In fact, he's been beating the brush down trying to avoid me. Tell the truth, I can't believe we're speaking about the same man."

"You intend to see him again, even after this?"

"I'll wring the truth out of him somehow," she said. "Something is gravely amiss. It's not in his nature to take the possessions earned by others."

"Abbey," Dominic began in a subduing tone, "you hardly know him well enough to make that kind of judgment. We've been watching the man for some time. And now this breakout at the jail— activity on Nantucket seems to be coming to a head. I don't want you caught in this maelstrom when you hardly even know your way around the island yet, much less around its folk."

"You think Jake has something to do with the breakout?" she asked him directly.

"That wouldn't make sense," he admitted, "but one can never be sure. Slaves are valuable commodities, especially young ones like the group we corralled the day you arrived. A man who . . . well, a man involved in nefarious dealings could easily be swayed toward dealing in recycling slaves to new owners in the South. There's a considerable market, and it's much more profitable than the honest business of rounding them up in Africa and dragging them halfway across the world. For one thing, they're healthy if they're already here. And they're trained if they've already belonged to someone else."

"Dominic," Abbey interrupted, turning sharply. "I'll admit your argument makes sense. But I'm telling you here and now that I'm a better judge of character than to be taken in by a good actor. Jacob Ross is simply not the kind of man you're describing."

"Can you prove that?"

"Of course not. You know I can't. He went with Pollock, and that confuses me. They're not like each other, and not the kind of men who get along."

"And you're certain it was this Pollock fellow and not someone else that Ross walked off with?"

"That Pollock rattlesnake, yes—" Anger boiled into panic as she clapped her hand to her lips and drew a quick breath. "Oh, God—what if Jake doesn't know about Pollock? What if he's been lassoed into something more dangerous than he thinks?"

"Now, Abbey—"

"Dominic, I must follow my feelings. There are times when a woman must simply follow her feelings—"

He caught her by the shoulders and forced her around to face him. "Abbey, what if you're wrong? Think clearly. What if you're mistaken about him?" His blue eyes burned into hers with that ugly truth. He lowered his voice. "Could you ever accept it?"

Abbey stared up at him, at the common sense he represented, and felt her turmoil deepen. When she tried to speak, it came out as a whisper. "Please don't stop me . . . I've got to find him. I've got to tell him."

She pushed away from Dominic, suddenly realizing she was escaping as much as pursuing.

"Don't be ridiculous." Dominic stepped in front of her, cutting off her dash for the front door. He clasped her arms again, more firmly and somehow more gently this time, and prevented her from pushing past him.

"Abbey . . ." Whatever he planned to say suddenly fell away. "I understand," he began with some effort, "what you're feeling, these confusing sensations . . . the island and its folk are strangers, the East is new to you, you're a widow hardly a year now. . . . Jacob Ross is an attractive young fellow . . . I know. . . ."

He looked down at her with something else pulling at him. It was as though the power of speech had been pulled right out of his mind, leaving only the intensity she saw behind his eyes. The depth of his loneliness showed itself in his desperation to help her, to try to stop the wheels of suspicion from rolling over her.

Before he could take another breath he drew her up against his big frame and was dipping his head to meet her lips.

The power and gentleness of Dominic Nash caught Abbey off guard. Everything about him was recognizable to her senses. He was so like her husband, in so many disconcerting ways—enough ways that she reacted to his kiss almost out of habit alone. Memory took over, flooding her with the comforts of familiarity, burying the hot streak of concern for Jake that sizzled in her now. Dominic was comfortable, sensible. Friendly, nice, gentlemanly, recognizable, easy—

Much too easy.

She broke away, even though the breaking off wasn't easy at all. "Please, Dominic, don't confuse me now. Let me sort things out." She squeezed past him and dragged her shawl over her shoulders again.

Dominic collected himself quickly from this embarrassing moment and clasped his hands together as though to keep them from reaching for her.

"You mustn't go, Abbey," he said, clearly working at not being too stern with her. "Not if you hope to see Pollock pay for his crimes. You do want that. . . ."

"Want it?" She swung around. "I'll burn in hell for eternity if it'll get Thomas Pollock down there, too, once and for all."

"Then you mustn't mention anything to Ross yet."

Her fingernails cut into her palms. "Why not?"

"Because," Dominic said, pausing to slow down his words to a deliberate, placating pace. "Because if he's in league with Pollock, Pollock will be tipped off and he'll get clean away. So far he's done nothing on the island to incriminate himself. All I have is your word. Is there any legal writ against him in Wyoming Territory?"

Abbey's shoulders slumped. "No. He was the ringleader, but he always sent others to do his dirty work. We couldn't prove anything outright. But he engineered the bushwhacking of my husband and two other cattlemen who wouldn't sell out to him. Our county was convinced enough of his guilt that Pollock was run out of the territory, but we couldn't get the skunk behind bars where he rightfully belonged." She clasped her hands to the sides of her head. "I can't believe what's happening. That he's here, of all places!"

"But he is. And if what you say is true, and"—he paused, clasping his hands behind his back—"I *do* believe you, then we have a potentially explosive situation on our hands that is much larger in scope than I ever guessed. It's plain we're not dealing with a petty smuggling operation. Now I'm sure of that."

"A landgrabber like Pollock doesn't involve himself with petty

150

thievery," Abbey said fiercely. "He does it on a grand scale. The risk is bigger, but when you're unscrupulous to begin with—"

"The job is rewarding, yes." Dominic's red eyebrows drew inward. "I will not allow you to wander through town alone tonight. If you insist on continuing to see Jacob Ross, I shall be forced to keep tighter watch on you," he promised, summoning up that facade of cold resolve, "for your own safety."

Even in this moment of supreme ferocity, Abbey felt a grin rise on her cheeks. "Is that a threat?"

"Of course," he admitted. "What else would work on such a woman as yourself?"

She nodded then and huffed a small sigh. "Little. But I'll heed your words. I want Pollock. Dangling, if possible. If I have to coil the noose myself."

The face that haunted her as she tried to sleep that night was not Pollock's, but Jacob's. What was Ross doing with him? Did he have any idea what kind of man he was?

Well, enough thinking about it. Enough tossing, enough pitching.

The drawer of her dresser rattled in its socket as she pulled it out too far in her anxiety. She grabbed at it; the noise sounded as though it had shook the whole sleeping household. The pounding of her heart was enough to do that on its own as she pulled out her split buckskin skirt, a collarless shirt of thick flannel—ugly, but functional—a leather vest that would break the cold ocean breeze before it chilled her skin, and her wide-brimmed plainsman hat. Just to remind herself she wasn't an eastern lady—tonight she needed not to be—she pulled out her stiff leather belt with the buckle of heavy Spanish silver. Laternlight glinted on the design etched into the silver, and she paused over it. A gift, from Lowell. For their third . . . no, fourth anniversary.

She buckled it around her waist, though it didn't quite fall right over the buckskin skirt. What matter? Some part of Lowell would go with her as she tracked down his killer.

And do what when she caught him?

Burying her thoughts in action, Abbey threw herself down on the floor and dug her boots out from under the bed, swiveled about, and pulled them on with impatience pecking away at her.

Halfway down the narrow hallway, she flinched at the click of a door opening. "Abbey?"

"Oh, Lucy!" she gasped, spinning. "Shhh!"

Lucy was pulling on her dressing gown. She stepped out into the hallway, leaving her door open in case the baby cried. "Well, wh'ever are you off to, eh? An' wot yer dressed in?"

"These are my everyday clothes. I'm going out. And what are you doing up so late?" Even as she asked, Abbey sensed the reason, and she added, "Couldn't sleep?"

Lucy's youthful face glowed in the light of the single tiny lamp that lit the hallway during the nights. "Not too good, mum. I were downstairs, wanderin' about, an' Mr. Nash, ee found me an' talked me inter 'avin' a cuppa tea wiv 'im."

Abbey frowned. "Dominic's down there?"

"Sure 'nuff. Ain't ee sweet, though? Takin' such goo' care of 'nuther feller's widda like ee do . . ."

"Yes. Lucy, can you—"

Another door popped open down the hall, and Abbey thought she'd end up putting the boys back to bed, but it wasn't the boys' room that had spawned more unwanted company. It was Cordelia's.

"Something amiss?" the housekeeper asked as she belted her night robe. In spite of the late hour, she looked as neat and unruffled as ever, and wide awake.

"Oh, Cordelia . . . nothing. Well, yes, something." Abbey motioned the two women close and lowered her voice. "I'm going out."

"Seems you are," Cordelia said, scanning the unusual clothes Abbey was wearing. "Why, at this hour of night?"

"Unfinished business." She bandied about the idea of not telling, then decided the situation couldn't be stranger if she did. "The man who killed my husband is on the island. I mean to find out why."

"The man oo—" Lucy's round eyes bulged. "No jokin'?"

Cordelia's eyes also widened. "What's this man's name?"

"Thomas Pollock," Abbey blurted hatefully. "If you see or hear anything about it, I'd be obliged if you'd tell me. Cover for me, won't you both? If the children need anything—"

"Not to worry," Cordelia said. "But you shouldn't be going alone. Let me get dressed—"

"No, no," Abbey interrupted. "I'm much happier by myself, and much faster. I've been by myself for a long time, Cordelia, so don't fret over me. Just don't let Dominic know I've left the house."

Lucy nodded and offered her crimped little smile. "I'll keep the mister busy, mum. Ee's tryin' ter teach me ter talk proper. I'll jus' let 'im!"

"Thanks to both of you. You're gems."

"Oh, we know that," Cordelia whispered. "But don't you be too late. No telling what I'll have to do then."

"Where yer going?" Lucy asked as Abbey doubled back toward her room.

Abbey swung about. "I can't go downstairs if Dominic's there. I'll have to climb down the trellis outside my window."

"Oh, 'shaw, mum! I'll get yer out. Foller me." Lucy clutched the too-long skirt of Cordelia's borrowed dressing gown and pulled it up as she started down the stairs, motioning Abbey to follow after.

Abbey stole a comforting glance from Cordelia, then sneaked downstairs after Lucy. It made sense; Dominic was expecting Lucy to come back down. When Lucy reached the bottom she swiftly tugged open the big front door and shooed Abbey out.

As the door shushed closed behind her, Abbey heard Dominic call from the kitchen, "Is that the front door opening?"

"Aw, naw, sir, jus' me chasin' out a mouse. Not t'worry—'ere I cum—"

Lucy's voice was muffled as the door clicked shut.

Night air folded around Abbey's shoulders. She immediately forgot the house and Dominic and the children and set herself forward toward her undefined task: to find out what business Thomas Pollock was weaving on the island and how best to hang him with it.

It was after midnight. The town of Nantucket was snoozing beneath a cloud-threaded sky. The sound of her boot soles on the cobblestones, soft slaps like leather striking a horse's hide, jarred her over and over with a terrible ambivalence. Jake's face swarmed in and out of her mind, swimming between the pulling sensuality of the lighthouse—a place to be alone—and the unexpected incursion of Pollock's eyes, long ago turned bitter and greedy by his way of life. Abbey's memories clogged up with the feeling of victory when the law forced Pollock to leave Wyoming. It had seemed so final, such a ringing defeat for him. Now she knew a man like him was never completely defeated as long as there were other fields left open for him to sow, and Nantucket was providing that open space. Remote, bustling with trade, needful of connections to the mainland, and far from anyone who knew his background. Until now. Now, she was here.

This victory was a cold lump that wouldn't melt until she played it out, until she pushed through the ice and found out what involvement Jake Ross had with this awful man. And she wondered, as the lump grew frostier, what she would have to do.

Or even what she intended to do in the next few minutes. She hardly had time to decide. She could already hear the steady thump of muffled sea songs from inside The Brotherhood. Tell Jake . . . not tell him . . . tell him and make him save his own skin somehow, risk losing her chance to slap Pollock with a good club of revenge. She had to look in Jake's eyes. If she could do that, she would know what to do. That mystical connection between them would tell her the truth. Certainly a man like Jake couldn't look at her and lie with his eyes.

She almost turned away as her hand touched the gnarled iron handle of The Brotherhood's door. But her hand wouldn't come away from that latch until she had already pulled the door open. By then she was already inside.

Very dark. Very loud. Smoky. Voices—howling sailors lost in an off-key song.

The clink of glasses, the stewy smell of rum and coffee and moist wool. Not altogether unpleasant once she got used to it.

From the low-ceilinged foyer in which she stood, Abbey spied an inner doorway through which all the noise and smell was coming. She was still hidden from that inner sanctum and had a second chance, no matter how unwanted, to change her mind. She almost wished that she hadn't been given this chance, rather than having to stand here with the opportunity to leave clean and quick.

She stood there, prey to the vacillation that worked at her. If she waited until the song ended, she'd be making too obvious an entrance. Better to slip in while the men were still involved in their howling.

Too late. The sea song climbed to a drawn chorus and ended in a round of laughter, applause, and mug-pounding. Then, without a beat of hesitation, another song picked up in its place, but this song wasn't as rat-eaten as the one before, and its singer's voice was deep and enticing.

She had to go in. There was no choice. Be there, Jake, she prayed silently.

She stepped inside, straightening her posture. She wanted no mistakes about her intent to be in this place at this time, nor her intent to stay until she got what she wanted.

The Brotherhood's inner room was crowded with men in dark sea coats, most of them still wearing hats and caps. There was a slight scent of oil clinging to them like the glow cast on them from a dozen globed candles on long wooden tables. Redbrick walls caressed blurry shadows and softly wedged yellow light from hanging lanterns like those she'd seen on the ship that had brought her to the island. In the crook of the elbow-shaped pub, the man with the nice voice was playing a concertina and leading the song. Beside him was a man with a fiddle and a young boy playing a whistle. The crowd of men beat their grog mugs on the worn wooden tables and indulged in the chorus. Warm and low-slung and cozy, the pub epitomized its name.

Suddenly, the music died away, voice by voice, fiddle by concertina, until only the whistle twittered a few extra notes and finally stopped, too. One by one, heads turned toward Abbey as notice of her presence spread through the pub. From the far end of the elbow-shaped room, faces craned at her as layers of men tried to see what the interruption was.

A self-conscious smile tickled her lips, but she tried not to let it take over her face.

Soon there was nothing but an uncomfortable shuffle, where a moment ago there had been singing and pounding.

The silence was deafening. Finally, after what felt to Abbey like forever, a seaman stepped forward, dragging his cap from his head and holding it in both hands as he approached her. "'Scuse me, ma'am," he began, "this is a tavern."

Abbey didn't blink, but opened her eyes a bit wider and said, "Yes. Thank you."

A relay of nudging moved through the pub, and caps started coming off as though someone had just dropped a church on top of these men.

Abbey's lip stiffened, holding in a giggle. Their discomfort would work in her favor. They'd seen women before, but certainly not any dressed as she was dressed tonight. They didn't know quite what to do with her.

Finally one of the men stepped forward and offered her his hand. Abbey took it and was escorted down the short ramp into the pub itself. Two other men actually picked up a table and moved it out of her way, while another pulled off his coat and lay it across a chair for her to sit on. Her hand was passed from man to man as she was drawn into the pious fold toward that chair. She arranged herself in it, not knowing what she had done to encourage their gallant behavior. When she was seated, she scanned their candlelit faces and asked, "Has anyone see Jacob Ross?"

The men glanced at each other. Then somebody said, "He's probably down at the beach, hoping there's a low enough tide so he can walk to the mainland."

A ripple of chuckles moved through the crowd, but it was self-conscious and short-lived. When it faded, one of the men near her gave a nod toward the back of the pub, and a younger man shouldered his way through the crowd in that direction. Going to get, Jake, perhaps, she hoped.

A heavy gray beard with a face lost inside came close to her, and she found herself looking down at a mug of steaming rum drink.

"Like a grog, miss?" the voice from the beard asked.

"Not grog, you mule-eared sea cat!" someone else hissed. "Tea!"

The mug was snatched away and a search launched for the nearest available cup of tea for the visiting lady. At one point someone let out a mild curse, which Abbey could barely hear in all the shuffle, and he was attacked by the men around him and bodily hauled away, as though the lady were going to dissolve from hearing it. As she watched the offender being swallowed up by his mates, she rather wished she had.

Sermon-silence was soon restored, and another man hunkered

156

before her, kneading his poor cap. "Would ye . . . would ye care for calf's head stew, miss? We got plenty."

"Or chowder?"

"Or Spanish hash?"

"Or potato pudding?"

Abbey found herself staring down at wooden bowls and hand-thrown stone plates full of various concoctions, most of them half-eaten.

"Oh, no, thank you," she declined.

But they were relentless in trying to make up for the fact that they'd been having such a good time.

A bony, clean-shaven sailor pushed through the crowd and begged, "Muffins?"

Abbey forced herself not to smile, but she nodded. "Well, perhaps a muff-"

"Muffins!"

"Muffins!"

"Muffins!"

The order rang from a half dozen voices and ricocheted through the pub on its way to the kitchen. Several men stumbled away, only to be replaced by several others. They'd probably kill each other if she asked for butter.

Ah! At last, a recognizable face. Jake's cousin—had he said Matthew? Yes, the one with the beard. His sleeves were rolled up and he wore a yellowed apron. The other cousin was close behind, nudging his way through the crowd toward her. She couldn't remember his name, but it mattered little now. They were in turn followed by four other men carrying, respectively, a muffin, a butter knife, a plate, and a small stone crock, presumably with butter in it.

They reached her, and Matthew immediately slid into a chair across the table from her. He wasn't able to say anything until the muffin, knife, butter, and plate had been arranged before her with supreme care.

She nodded at the sailors who had provided her spare repast. "That you all very much. It looks delicious."

That triggered a congratulatory round of back patting and hesitant little grins.

Finally Matthew waved the men into silence. "Mrs. Sutton," he greeted, if a bit sternly, "what could we do for you?"

Abbey parted her lips to speak, but the goggling eyes stopped her. It only took Matthew a moment to realize what the problem was, and he branded the crowd with a chiding glare. "The lady's business isn't any of yours. Back to your grog, every one of you. James! Sing a song, curse you!"

James shifted on his stool and asked, "Uh . . . which one?"

Matthew threw his hands up. "What do I care? Any one! Sing "New York Girls" or something."

James shifted again, thought about the songs, then shifted yet again. "Uh . . . I can't sing that one." Clearly he *could* sing it, but because of Abbey's presence, he didn't *want* to sing it.

Matthew leaned forward, glaring again. "Anything!"

The men gradually moved back to their tables, well-behaved as schoolboys during a spelling test. Several of them whispered suggestions to James, who could only shake his head at them. After several failures, James and his fellow musicians struck up a half-hearted tune that had no lyrics at all, but only music. The lilt was gone from the beat, and most of the sailors now huddled over their mugs and stew and engaged in properly quiet conversation. Occasionally one would glance toward Abbey, probably wondering when she would leave and rescue them from church services.

"Now," Matthew urged as his brother hauled over a third chair and sat near Abbey.

"I suppose this means Jake isn't here," Abbey said. "Do you know where he is?"

Matthew and his brother glanced at each other. Then Matthew said, "He's got business tonight, ma'am. He's not available."

"He's in town then, not out at Great Point?"

"Can't say, ma'am.

"Maybe you can't say, but that's what you're implying," she told him. "He could be in danger."

The two cousins exchanged another look, this one of a different dimension than the previous.

"Danger of what sort?" the younger man asked, leaning forward.

Abbey lifted her eyebrows. "I can't say." she retaliated. "I'm not altogether sure of my facts. If I could simply speak to him for a few moments, I'm sure things would clarify themselves. Please . . . I don't want him to be hurt or get into any more trouble than he might already be in. After all, it's his decision. If he doesn't want to talk to me, he can make up his own mind, can't he?"

If there was any honor among cousins, she had played on it well enough. She saw in their eyes that neither of them wanted to make any secondhand decisions regarding her relationship with Jake.

They shifted uncomfortably. Then the younger man said, "He's out on Old South Wharf. Or he *was*. Whether he's still there or not—"

Matthew shot him a scolding glare, but said nothing to keep him from telling her more, so Abbey asked, "Some specific boat?"

"Not sure, ma'am. Ma'am . . . the wharf is no place for a lady at night.

"Neither is a pub," she tossed back, "but I've been treated gallantly here. One never knows where good or evil hide. Thank you for your hospitality." She slid out of her chair and headed for the door, relieved to be on her way again, then doubled back long enough to pluck up the muffin that had been presented to her with such ceremony. After all the trouble she'd caused, it wouldn't be polite to leave the muffin behind. She nodded at Matthew and his brother and spun toward the exit again, leaving behind her only a mutter of curious voices.

Chapter Ten

THE NIGHT WAS treed with mastheads. Cool spring wind off the Atlantic left an extra measure of chill in its salty wake. Old South Wharf was its own kind of hinterland—separated, surrounded by an expanse of water, reaching its long wooden arms out into that vastness as though to embrace the sea that nourished it. In the obliqueness of night, every ship docked looked derelict. Rigging buzzed and whistled as the breeze twisted through the ropes, hulls creaked and moaned, rails bumped the pilings, bowsprits swayed slowly back and forth, deckhouses were overshadowed by the bases of big mainmasts, and not a living soul walked on any deck.

There didn't seem to be anyone there at all, not at all. If there had been just the slightest glow of a lamp inside a wheelhouse, a shuffle of footsteps inside a fo'c'sle, a whiff of beans cooking in a galley—anything would have been comforting. But tonight the wharf was a graveyard. The only sound was that of waves lapping at the pilings. There was no Jake, there was no Pollock. There was no one.

Abbey scrutinized every ship and boat that looked even remotely familiar, toying with the idea that the boat where she'd seen Jake lurking about might have been moved here for some reason. But to someone who could tell cows apart at a glance, boats all look pretty much the same.

All this would have been disappointing but acceptable had Abbey not also been awash with the feeling that someone was following her, watching her. The wharf appeared completely abandoned, yet there were ghosts. These sleeping ships had eyes. The sensation prevented her from calling out to Jake, though she started to several times, only to swallow her words without uttering a sound. It made her tread lightly on the dock planks, not letting her boot heels clack, and she flinched every time the wood groaned under her weight.

She walked, slowly, all the way to the end of Old South Wharf, scrutinizing every ship as much as was possible without boarding any of them. Some were large barks and brigs, and she couldn't see over the rails. Others were small schooners and even smaller sloops and sandbaggers, all dark, all uninhabited.

A sense of futility struck her about what she was really doing out here. What had she hoped to accomplish? In the hours that had passed since Pollock and Jake had disappeared on Nantucket's quiet Colonial streets, they could have gone anywhere on the island, even have left Nantucket entirely. And then there was the question of what she would even say to him about all this.

A terrible aching began in the pit of her stomach and moved outward to her limbs. Her arms quaked to hold him as they had expected to, her legs throbbed with the want. They'd been promised something, and they still craved it. Somehow she had been foolish enough to convince herself—if shallowly—that if she could just find him, all would fall into place. She would discover that he knew nothing of Pollock's past and had been swindled into dealing with the man. She would find herself in Jake's arms, their hearts beating in unison with the melody she was sure they both knew, her lips toying with his.

Hopeless. None of that would happen tonight; she had just reached the end of Old South Wharf. There was nowhere left to search, at least not here. She turned and shivered in the ominous quiet of the wharf. The walk back down the dock to town appeared much longer and eerier from this vantage point halfway at sea. Old South Wharf was a long wooden centipede, leggy with extensions and hairy with masts jutting up into the blue-black night sky, twisting its thin body this way and that.

The wharf extended off Whale Street and from here it seemed to merge with Straight Wharf to her right and another wharf, whose name she couldn't remember, to her left. Town Dock was beyond that one. A mess of masts. What minutes ago had looked like a forest of possibilities now just looked like a breezy, damp walk all the way back to town.

A moment later, that damp walk became even more ominous. As she turned along one of the dock's bends, her feeling of being watched realized itself in the forms of three men, not ten feet away. Their faces darkened to shadows by cap brims, and they came at her. Now toward her—*at* her.

Abbey had seen the threatening set of human forms before; there was no mistaking it. She knew it instantly—by the determination in their shoulders, the slight bend to their legs, their lack of conversation. And they knew she knew. With a scream she scrambled backward in her tracks. But they had her.

Or they *thought* they had her. Abbey bellowed a single howl for help. One of the men tried to cover her mouth, but she clamped down on his hand with a healthy set of teeth. His yowl was even louder than hers had been as he tried to get his forefinger back.

"She's biting me!" he bellowed, moving his hand out of the way and digging his stubby fingertips into her chin.

The taste of blood drove Abbey through fear and into rage, and she growled her response to him around his finger until he managed to wrench it out. A second shout for help ran across the water, obscuring her location even if anyone had heard it. She would have cried out a third time, but like the rest of her body her lungs were gathering for a fight. She was alone, and that meant she had to do her own work. They might win, but it would be a hard victory for them.

She twisted a hand free from the two men who now shackled her arms, and she let swing. Her fist rang against an ear, and her left side fell free of its captor. The man staggered away, clutching the side of his head and cursing. His cohorts were yelling at each other, but the roaring of her own breath in Abbey's ears muddled their words. It was clear they hadn't expected her to fight them, but years of life on the ruthless frontier had taught Abbey to move on her instincts and let the facts surface at more convenient times.

But these men learned quickly. After her feet and fists landed a few impolite blows, Abbey found her arms forced behind her back and a length of ship's rope wound around her ankles.

"Got her," snapped the man who was tying her legs. "Go get him."

One of the other men disappeared down the dock, his feet rapping little staccato echoes as he ran.

She started to demand who they were and what they wanted of her, but the two who remained must have assumed she was about to scream. In an instant, there was a gritty cloth in her mouth, and any chance of shouting had been snuffed. A touch of panic made her writhe in the arms of her captors as her feet left the ground. She was being carried. For a wild, terrifying moment as the water passed beneath her, she thought they meant to fling her over the dock's edge, arms and legs tied, to die at the bottom of the harbor without ever knowing why. Then shoes scraped against wood, and she realized that they were lowering her not into the water, but onto a ship's deck.

Enraged, Abbey continued twisting and flexing and even managed to bloody one of the men's noses before they stuffed her into a wheelhouse and slammed the door gratefully.

Her buckskin skirt came in handy against the splintery wooden floor that grated under her hips. She had been dropped in the middle of the small area with nothing to lean on, and she had to raise her feet up into the air before she could force herself into a sitting position. Eyes wide with fury, she sucked a deep breath through her nose and bellowed a whiny nasal shriek, just to vent her anger and clear her head. That done, she began the business of using her tongue and her lips to push the rotten rag out of her mouth. By the time it flopped into her lap, the rag had made her lips raw and dried her mouth completely. That was all right; it just made her madder.

For the first time since coming east, she found herself wishing for the soft eastern shoes she'd been trying to get used to. Her favorite old boots were stiff-soled and made of thick leather, which only made it easy for the rope to keep a purchase around her ankles and feet. No matter how she scuffed and rubbed, her ankles stayed bound. And so they would remain until she could get her hands free.

She stopped struggling for a moment and looked about the dim wheelhouse. The only light came from the moon shining through the clouds as they parted over the harbor, and that little milky glow was muddied by grime on the wheelhouse windows. She would never see very clearly in here, but she could tell well enough there was nothing to cut a rope with. In fact, there was less than nothing. Only the ship's big wheel kept her company here.

Breathing heavily, Abbey suddenly stopped moving and began to listen. Voices. Men. Her captors. She wriggled to one side of the wheelhouse and put her ear against the wall.

They were out on the dock, speaking softly to each other. She couldn't make out a single word, which only piled frustration on top of her curiosity and . . .

And her fear. Now that she realized she was at their whim, now that she had no fingers to bite or noses to kick, that reality sank in. She was still angry, but now the fear came slinking in. Even an oak tree can be cut down and reduced to planks by the right number of men. She couldn't fight forever.

All she could do was not be here when they came for her. Yes! Of course! There had to be a good answer, and that was it.

"I can swim," she growled, convincing herself. As she dragged her feet under her and used the wheelhouse corner to lever herself to her feet—an annoyingly long process—she fought against trying to remember when she had last tried swimming. Better that she not start counting years just now.

All she could do was hop about the wheelhouse, looking out each window for perspective. Her captors were obviously waiting for their compatriot to return with "him," and on the other side was the open water of the harbor.

"Windows," she murmured, scooting back a few hops. "Glass breaks." . . .

Yes, the glass would break, but it would also make noise. And right now all she had to hit it with was her face. Not the best option.

If she took a good leap . . . and twisted just right . . . and got her feet up into the air . . . of course, she'd land on her head, but . . .

Some inner sense made her hold her breath and listen. Something had changed out on the dock. She held still, her hair falling into her face, the jute string that held her hat against her shoulder blades now pressing on her gullet as though to remind her of the pulse in her throat.

The voices had stopped. Replacing them were footsteps. Quick, sharp footsteps.

Forcing her aching body to hop across the wheelhouse again, she fell against the window pane and peered through the crusted salt streaks.

Figures came down the dock—the third attacker, and "him."

"Jake!" she shouted, driven by that inner trigger; if her mind hadn't been sure, her body recognized his silhouette instantly. The cry was out of her mouth before she even had a chance to think.

He stopped in midstep. His face, a pale blue smudge of moonlight reflecting off the water, turned her way. At his sides his arms were poised, and he hovered there like a cat.

Two of the attackers strode toward him, but stopped short of getting too close.

If Abbey had a chance to wonder where the third man was, she didn't wonder long. The deck vibrated beneath her feet, and a moment later the wheelhouse door creaked open and she was being dragged out. Her escort untied the rope from her ankles, but didn't untie her hands. A moment later, protesting less than before, though still not especially cooperating with this ruffian, she was back up on the dock and being paraded before Jake.

"Abbey," he said, then restrained himself with difficulty. His voice was hoarse, knotted with anger. "I thought they were bluffing."

"We don't bluff," one of the men said. "Tell us what we want to know. Where's the valuables?"

"You've been talking to Pollock, haven't you?" Jake returned without allowing the man's demand to sink in. "I told him I want time."

"Break his ribs."

Only now, as the second man moved toward Jake with two quick steps, did Abbey notice the size of him. He was the biggest among them, the brawn held in check until they needed him. Not taller than Jake, but much wider, with shoulders like ox yokes. Jake anticipated the man's move, but although he tensed and tried to block the blow, the bigger man simply had too much extra power on his side. Jake made the mistake of blocking a fist punch. Anticipating the defense, the man drew his arms inward, gathered himself, and swung a hard kick upward into Jake's rib cage. From the ship's cramped bridge, Abbey could hear the gush of breath Jake made as he folded over and went down on one knee.

"Jake!" she shrieked. She struggled against the grip the third man had on her arms, but the grip got tighter. Enraged, she lifted her right foot, twisted half way around, and slammed her foot down on the man's toe.

Her captor let out a shriek. His hands fell away. Abbey rammed her shoulder into him, knocking him off balance, then ran to the ship's rail. She held her breath, climbed up—awkward because her hands were still tied—and jumped from there to the dock.

"Maynard, you idiot—" the leader barked, and immediately took possession of Abbey before she could regain her balance. "Get up here."

The third man limped to the rail and climbed up onto the dock.

"Over there," the leader told him, nodding sharply toward Jake.

Jake was gasping, fighting for control over his battered lungs. With one hand he supported himself on the dock, the other arm was tucked tightly against his ribs. Only his defiant glare at his aggressors showed that he remained unmoved. The harder they hit him, the less he would tell whatever it was they wanted to know.

But these men didn't sense his resolve. Maynard and the big man moved in on Jake a second time. Maynard wrenched Jake's arms behind him, and the big man hit him again.

"Damn you all," Abbey growled, trying to kick the leader as he held her from behind.

They let Jake fall to his knees, holding onto him only as long as it took to strike him. He had nothing to brace upon as the pain worked its way through his body, not even the firmness of his attackers. No wall to lean upon, nothing to push against, except the waves of pain.

"Jake," she begged, "tell them what they want to know. How important can it be? Tell them!"

Jake shuddered, managing only a glance at her, a glance as clear as the defiance still rising in his face. *No.*

"Don't be stubborn!" she insisted. "It's not worth this."

"She's right," the leader calmly told him. "Better tell us, Ross. Your goods'll rot where they sit if you don't. Just as easy as we can get them off the island for you, we can make sure they never get off. Don't fool with us. You asked for the contract, and now you're pulling out on us."

166

"I didn't ask you to come here," Jake choked. "I just asked you to leave."

"Stupid jar-head, am I gonna have to cram your legs through a lanyard? Cobb, tell him."

The big man moved in again, and once again his large foot swung, this time catching Jake hard in the side.

Jake managed to stay upright on his knees, but the blow screwed his face into a knot of pain and twisted him sideways.

Abbey reached against the man who held her. "Jake—" she gasped. Then she gritted her teeth, driven by both instinct and impulse. "If you won't tell them," she called, "then I will."

As she hoped, Cobb and Maynard turned to look at her, suddenly willing to ignore Jake. If she could only give him a few moments to catch his breath . . .

Behind her, the leader grabbed a handful of her hair and turned her head toward him. "Tell."

Across the dock, Jake gripped a piling and dragged himself to his feet. "She doesn't know, Sumner," he rasped. "She's bluffing."

But Abbey was ready for that. "Don't try to protect me," she snapped.

"Then you better do the talking!" Sumner said with a snarl, yanking on Abbey's hair and making her wince to impress Jake with his anger.

Struggling to appear less battered than he was, Jake tried to straighten up, holding onto a piling for support. He had to clear his throat before he could speak. "Let Abbey leave the dock, and we'll discuss it," he said.

Sumner pushed Abbey forward to the middle of the dock. "Maynard, come here. We'll show him how we discuss things."

Abbey caught the reek of fish and smoke as Maynard came up close to her. He gripped the front of her flannel shirt and yanked hard. The buttons strained, then popped off one by one, exposing her cotton camisole.

"Sumner!" Jake shouted, and bolted forward.

But Cobb was there before Jake could reach them. He grappled Jake's arms and wrenched them behind his back, forcing him to watch.

"Get her puppies out," Sumner said, pressing his mouth against the side of Abbey's throat, still keeping his eyes on Jake.

Abbey hunched her shoulders, hoping to break his grip, but Sumner's hold on her hair prevented any movement.

And Maynard was a professional. He came even closer, until his smelly body was pressed against her. He coiled his leg around one of hers, forcing her knees apart.

She started to struggle, just as a few paces away Jake also pulled against Cobb's hold on him in a terrible echo of her desperation.

Abbey flinched, and then sucked in her breath as a flash of silver appeared before her eyes—an inch away . . . a blade. She recognized it in an instant. A Bowie knife. Bone-handled, shiny, thick and broad, with a point so mean and so unforgiving that moonlight glinted upon its tip, the hunting knife appeared brand new. Abbey's mind flapped with wild ways to avoid being the one to break it in.

She began to tremble as though she were in convulsions. Maynard turned the knife before her, scratching her nose with its tip, making sure she saw it in all its draconic beauty. Abbey tried to close her eyes, but they were caught by the cachet of death by steel.

Maynard's facial muscles quivered. His breathing got heavy. Rape or murder—he seemed to throb at the prospect of either. Maybe today would be lucky and he would get both. With a snide flick, he dropped his arm and held the bowie knife against her.

Abbey nearly choked on her own saliva. Her whole body crawled as expected to feel the blade sink into her.

"Maynard!" Jake thundered. He yanked against Cobb's grip.

Abbey felt the cool metal brush against her skin, felt the camisole rip neatly away as Maynard poked the blade through the fabric and drew it upward, cleanly opening the garment and exposing her breasts. The tip of the blade left a scratch all the way up her chest, and tiny beads of blood began to form along the thin red line.

Feeling her nipples harden in the chilly air, Abbey recoiled. But that movement only pressed her buttocks against Sumner and doubled her disgust.

Jake wrenched against Cobb. "Don't touch her! Maynard!" Suddenly he stopped struggling, though he still pulled against Cobb's grip. "Sumner, you let him hurt her and I'll feed you your legs."

It was a cold threat. Even Abbey was chilled by the conviction in his tone.

Sumner was unimpressed. His rough hand came around Abbey from the right, and mashed her left breast, getting a smug, rolling grip, stroking her boldly so Jake could see every move.

Abbey tried not to react, but bile rose in her throat and she couldn't stop the gush of revulsion that came up through her. The cloying force of Sumner around her and the loathsome stink of Maynard beside her made her nauseous. She tried to sink downward out of their grasp, but they had her pinned. More than anything she wanted to tell Jake not to fight them for her sake, that she could stand it, but the sickening sensation of Sumner's hand kept her teeth gritted and her throat closed.

But Jake was gone, and there was an uncontrollable creature in his place. Sumner's ploy had worked. Jake sank into rage and emerged on fire. He roared against Cobb, driven to viciousness. His elbow came up into Cobb's throat and knocked the big man away, then Jake plunged for Maynard. Cobb stumbled backward down the dock, and Jake had time to lunge into Maynard before the bowie knife could come up between them. Jake pinned Maynard's knife hand down against his leg and butted the heel of his hand into Maynard's left eye. Maynard cried out like a clubbed dog.

Jake's rage was contagious. Abbey gritted her teeth, mentally found her hands where they were tied behind her and aimed them like a weapon. Sumner's legs were spread for balance. Abbey bent her fingers into claws, shoved them outward from her back with a scooping motion, and clamped down hard on the inevitable location of Sumner's crotch. Once she knew she had him, she squeezed hard.

Sumner's reaction began as a yelp and stretched out across the water into a high-pitched howl. He squirmed and fell back away from her staggering. "Damn crazy bitch!" he gasped, bent over double. His face twisted in fury, and he forced himself toward her.

She tried to step away, but anger and pain carried Sumner across the dock with a threatening swagger.

Out of nowhere Jake shot past her and headed Sumner off with a roundhouse smash of his fist into Sumner's jaw. Abbey thought she heard a terrible crack—Sumner's jaw, or Jake's hand?

The two men went down hard on the dock, twisted in battle.

Abbey dropped to the dock, as well, going after the bowie knife, which lay where Maynard had let it clatter to the planks as he grabbed his wounded eye. With considerable difficulty she found it with her tied hands, turned it upward, and began sawing at the ropes around her wrists. She wished she could see what she was doing, but only the brush of steel against her back guided the blade. Finally, the ropes strained, then snapped. She shook them away from her raw wrists.

Before she could roll over and get to her feet, Cobb had taken hold of her and was yanking her up. For a moment she lost track of Jake and Sumner as they grappled and rolled down the dock toward its blunt edge. Maynard was stumbling toward them, still holding his eye but very much on his way to joining the fight. If anything was going to end Jake's chances, it was Maynard.

Their gasps and grunts distracted Abbey for a fateful second, long enough for Cobb to grasp her wrist and wrest the knife from her hand. He held it before her eyes for an instant, then shouted, "Maynard!" and flung the knife, handle-first, down the dock.

It clattered to the wood, and Maynard scooped it up, then turned toward the tangled forms of Jake and Sumner.

Damn! Foolish! Abbey derided herself. She would have enjoyed pressing that steel into Cobb's fat girth. Instead, she had to be satisfied with sinking her teeth into the back of his hand.

"Goddang!" Cobb blurted, and hit her.

She went sprawling, her cheek throbbing from the blow. Cobb lumbered toward her, but she was already on her feet. She stumbled backward, helpless for a moment, until she saw a coil of ship's docking rope a pace away. She lunged for it. The rope was heavy, and splintery as broken wood. It lacerated her hands and forearms as she picked up the entire coil and heaved it at Cobb's face.

Struck in the face, Cobb let out a satisfying groan and toppled backward. Abbey ran toward him now, butting her shoulder into his chest, completing his backward tumble—right off the edge of the dock into the water. His yell of surprise was cut short by the splash as his bulk hit the water and set it to churning.

"Abbey, run! Ru—"

Jake's warning cry was cut off in a gush of breath as someone punched him. He and Sumner and Maynard were a solid blur against the dark wharfside shapes.

She ran. Clutching her ripped shirt closed over cold breasts, she ran, stumbling, toward the dark island town. Behind her echoed the sounds of fists against flesh.

Chapter Eleven

HARD DECK WOOD spread beneath him. The smell of fish and salt-soaked ropes surrounded him, making him nauseous. The night was silent.

His heartbeat was the only sound, droning in his ears. He tried to count seconds, to keep aware of the minutes passing, to keep his senses close to him, but that ability was rapidly failing him. The deck was flat, rough against the side of his head. His right shoulder was crushed up against his ear as he lay there, both arms coiled around his battered body. The reflex to hold tight against his wounds caused him even more pain.

He couldn't remember. Had she gotten away?

Had he been fighting with two men, or three? He only remembered two. He begged his memory to recall the other man, to tell him Abbey hadn't had to grapple with Cobb.

But there were only two faces hating him there in his memory, and only four fists hammering him.

His legs were a mile away. He tried to move them. Moans rolled across the deck, like wounds. On his fingers, moisture. He knew the feeling of seawater, but this was sticky. Warm. It flowed down the side of his hand to his wrist, then sneaked into the cuff of his coat and was absorbed by the sleeve of his sweater. Blood.

He clung to a vision of Abbey. It was torture to see her again and again struggling against Maynard and that knife, to see her lips screwed up in anger and defiance. Torture, but it also gave him strength. If she could fight, so could he. So *would* he.

He raised his head from the deck. A flush of dizziness destroyed both his thoughts and his vision, and only now as he stared out at the blurry night did he realize his eyes had been open all this time. He thought they'd been closed; in fact, he thought he'd been unconscious.

Not so, it seemed. Some part of him had clung to wakefulness, and now his senses were gathering themselves. He refused to let his head sink to the deck again. His neck began to ache, but he resisted. A terrible trembling gripped his shoulders and thighs, but clinging to the effort itself, he pulled up one arm and heaved himself up on that elbow.

Pain cut through his midsection. All kinds of pain—a bite, a stab, a throb, a rip, all at once, in several places.

A loud gasp bolted from his throat. On its heel he rasped her name and clung to the sound. A whisper, a whimper, a shout—he had no idea how loudly or softly it came out of him.

If only he could be sure of one thing, anything, to hold onto.

Revenge drove him up onto his knees. He didn't like to be hit. He hadn't liked watching Sumner paw Abbey. As Sumner's hand had palmed Abbey's bared breast, Jake knew his anger was partly from wishing it was him, wishing he'd done it when he had had the chance, when she wanted it from him. Sumner had taken from him that first moment of seeing each other naked in the soft light of the evening. That moment would never be recaptured. Jake raged within himself as he thought of it, feeling that somehow this pain was his punishment for failing to give Abbey what they both needed and wanted. If he'd only given in to her, she would never have been on the dock tonight.

So everything was his fault. Her humiliation. His pain. Their loss.

And he hadn't told her yet. He should've told her.

He pressed his hand into his wounds, and the other hand on the fo'c'sle hatch of the ship he'd been dumped on, and struggled for balance. These were humiliating feelings. Humiliating for Abbey, and for himself. What disservice he'd done her, denying his hunger to touch her and feel her, stalling too long.

"I'm sorry," he whispered to the amber-haired image flooding his muddled mind. *I should've told you . . . Abbey . . . I'm in love with you. . . .*

She hadn't gotten away. He knew she hadn't. Sumner, Maynard, and the knife. It was all he remembered. Cobb . . . Cobb . . . Abbey . . .

His legs shook like a newborn's as he forced himself to his feet. Each puff of breath tore a new hole in his effort. Pain roared through him relentlessly. He crushed his arms into his middle and folded over them, his lips quivering, his eyes blinking in the closing darkness. There was no fighting the weight of his feet. He stumbled to the edge of nightmare.

Two steps, possibly only one.

He slammed to the deck. Blood flowed over his arm and dripped onto the thirsty wood.

She never imagined she could run so fast. Fury gave her good wind.

Her boots clattered back onto the dock planks not five minutes later, and she brought the cavalry with her.

More than a dozen men clattered after her. At her side were Jake's cousins. As they ran down the wharf, her mind was full of the thudding memory of fists against flesh.

But the dock was completely dark, and there wasn't a soul in sight.

"Jake!" she called, panting. Had they killed him? Pitched his body over the side?

"Jacob!" Matthew called as he and the other men dispersed to search the dock and the ships. His booming voice spread out across Old South Wharf. "Jacob!"

"That one!" Abbey gasped, pointing at the boat where she'd been held captive. Immediately four men dropped onto its deck and swarmed it. Abbey watched from the dock, clutching the lapel of the sea coat one of the men had chivalrously lent her when he'd seen the condition of her clothes.

Where was Jake? Her skin crawled with worry.

The intensity of her fear surprised her. Attraction, yes. Hunger, Desire, passion, curiosity, a bond neither of them understood—all that had been present before. But this feeling was none of those. This was a feeling of excision. Something was being cut out of her as though Maynard had used his blade on her heart. She knew, within the deepest part of herself, that if they never found Jake, or they found him dead, part of her would die as well. Part of her. Jake . . .

How had he become part of her?

Several men were running down toward the end of the dock, searching. Elias Colbert was with them, leading.

Matthew Colbert appeared beside Abbey, his thick body strung with tension. "Might they have taken him with them"

Abbey swung around. "I've no idea," she gasped. "They might do anything, those kinds of men. Anything. I shouldn't have left him—"

"No, ma'am, you did right to come for us," Matthew told her. "Ladies can't face down mariners and win."

"What if they threw him in the water?" Her voice cracked on the question. "Can he swim?"

"Uh, no, ma'am," Matthew told her solemnly. He bracketed his mouth with his hands and called, "Elias! Search the boats! Ma'am, you know the names of those men?"

"Yes!" she blurted back, caught in the chance to say something constructive. "Cobb, Maynard, and the leader was called Sumner."

Matthew made a surly sound in his throat. "Yeah, that figures. . . .

"Figures with what?"

Matthew glanced at her, then squinted evasively down the dock, pressing his lips together. "That's for Jacob to tell you, missus, not me."

She stepped closer to him. "It's Pollock, isn't it? Those were his men, weren't they?" she demanded.

Matthew's eyes focused on her, wide now. "How do you know about Pollock?"

"Matthew!" Elias's voice trailed across the water from one of the boats tied at the end of the dock. "Here!"

"Oh, God—" Abbey choked.

Matthew Colbert took her arm and they broke into a run.

The dock planking had an unsettling give, not like land, not like sand, not like a sidewalk, and it made an awful rattling announcement of their fears, its terrible clatter echoing *he's dead he's dead he's dead* in Abbey's mind. But that spark . . . it still lay in her soul, glowing softly, a tiny amber light against the blackness of her fear. Like the beacon of Great Point seen from an impossible distance, the tiny glow signaled a quiver of life. Life, hope, the unrelenting token that Jake wouldn't allow himself to die before the nexus between them had been fulfilled. They couldn't have beaten it out of her, she knew, and she clung to the belief that they hadn't been able to beat it out of Jake either.

The boat was a sandbagger, a low-slung single-master with a transom stern and a ridiculously enormous sail plan for its size. A bunch of sandbags sat idle on its afterdeck, to be heaved port or starboard as deadweight ballast when the ship tacked. Abbey and Matthew and half a dozen men clamored to the dock's edge to peer inside the boat.

Elias and two other men were crouching on the deck, blocking the view. All Abbey could see was a pair of familiar legs lying on the deck at Elias's left, one leg sedately crossed over the other, neither moving.

"Jake!" Her cry battered the solemn silence that had fallen over the wharf. She jumped down onto the deck without waiting for help, with Matthew following, dropping at her side with an ominous thud.

Jake's head and shoulders lay in the crook of Elias's arm. His face was oyster-gray against his cousin's sleeve.

Before Abbey could make a move, Matthew had stepped over Jake's legs, knelt down and tenderly turned Jake's face toward him with his big hand. "Jacob, look at me."

Abbey dropped to her knees beside Elias as the other men got up to give her room. She wanted to speak, to call his name out, to sob her apologies for getting him into this situation, but her voice caught in her throat and wouldn't come out.

Matthew brushed the damp blond bangs out of Jake's face. "Jake, look this way. Open the eyes, mate."

His cousin's voice sank through Jake's unconsciousness and took hold. He moaned. Then he followed in discomfort and turned his head toward Matthew. After a moment he looked at him.

"That's the way," Matthew said. "Hold on. Let me see you."

Carefully Matthew slipped his hand into Jake's open coat, palming his ribs for breaks. Judging from the look on his face and Jake's wincing, he found some.

Abbey held her breath, still afraid to speak. Elias was silent, too, his youthful face stiff as he watched Matthew hopefully probing Jake's battered form.

"Christ Almighty," Matthew whispered. His eyes clamped shut for an instant, and he pulled his hand out.

Abbey covered her mouth, stifling a moan of horror. Matthew's hand was a canvas of blood. Shaking, Abbey pressed her tongue to the roof of her mouth to keep it silent, unbuttoned the coat she was wearing, and found the edge of her sliced camisole. Without thinking, she ripped along the cut fabric, then forced the rip to change to the bias, and finally half the camisole came away in her hands. Gently she pushed Jake's coat aside and found the bloody place. *Maynard's knife. That knife . . . meant for her.* She stuffed the swatch of cotton into the wound. It would hurt him, but the bleeding had to be stopped. The pain might as well have been her own.

Jake's face crumpled and he arched against Elias. His hand came up out of nowhere and clamped around Abbey's wrist.

"Godameracy—" he ground out.

Matthew wrapped an arm around Jake's shoulders and helped him sit up, which closed the wound somewhat, though it probably did little to ease the pain. His head fell forward, his eyes clamped shut, and his breath came in chunks.

"Jake, I'm sorry," Matthew said. "I should've listened to you."

Jake found a pause in his panting to offer his cousin a tight grin, partly of reassurance, partly of forgiveness, and as he glanced up, he saw Abbey. His glance bounced off Matthew, catching Abbey in his periphery, and he suddenly realized whose wrist he was holding onto.

"Abbey!" he choked. Then in a different way, "Abbey . . . I think . . ."

"Not a word," she said, touching her palm to the side of his face. "I'm here. So are you."

He tilted his head into her hand, relief flowing over both of them.

"He's cold," Abbey said, gathering her self-control. "We've got to get him out of the night air."

Matthew craned to look past Elias at the crowd of sailors waiting tensely on the dock. "Louis, find a stretcher!"

"Got one on board," one of the men said, wagging a finger toward a big old schooner tied up nearby. He grabbed another man's sleeve, and the two of them dashed across the wharf and disappeared into the other ship.

Elias shifted Jake to Matthew, then stripped out of his own jacket and wrapped it gently around Jake's shoulders. "Only landlubbers freeze to death within sight of shore," he said.

Jake smiled thinly and put a great deal of commitment into his response. "Elias . . . you're . . . stuffed with . . . seaweed."

Though Abbey shuddered at the weakness of his voice, Matthew and Elias smiled and shared a glance that contained more than amusement. They knew him well. Well enough to know when he was going to be all right and when he wasn't.

As if to reassure her, Jake's hand slipped down her wrist and found her fingers. Her hand, like a thing with its own mind, fell into his as naturally as a bird into its nest.

The stretcher came and was handed down into the boat. After that things moved very quickly, too quickly to sort out. The only anchor Abbey remembered from those minutes was Jake's unremitting grip on her hand. He clung to her now, and no amount of prying could rive him from her. The sailors had to maneuver Jake onto the stretcher with Abbey still holding his hand. They had to squeeze the stretcher through the door of The Brotherhood with Abbey at its side. They had to lift him onto the bed in back of the pub with his trembling hand gripping her fingers in something akin to desperation. They had to undress and stanch his wounds and bind his ribs with Abbey alternating which hand she was holding with which sleeve they had to get off or which rib had to be examined. He refused to let go of her, no matter what limits of consciousness engulfed him or failed him. Lucidity came and went with the sensation of losing that precious grip. He would slip into sleep for a few moments, only to drag himself back to wakefulness if her hand fell away from his even for an instant. His eyes would open in a kind of surprise, he would search for her face, find it, find her hand, and sigh back against the pillows again.

The Brotherhood's back room was warm, and Jake's chilled body soon began to accept the warmth as Matthew stanched the flow of blood from a wide gash Maynard's blade had left under Jake's right rib. Once his body no longer had to fight the loss, color came back into Jake's cheeks, and his fingers grew warm around Abbey's.

There had been a doctor waiting at The Brotherhood who had tended Jake swiftly and stoically and had finally left, leaving Jake in his cousins' care, and now the only people there were Abbey, Matthew, and Elias. Abbey didn't have to guess where the other men had disappeared to.

They were combing the wharves for the criminals who had done this.

The hours passed slowly. Darkness on Nantucket seemed unending tonight. Daylight wouldn't come until it knew Jake was going to get better, so it waited just offshore and let the candles do its job.

Jake had no sense of time when he started to realize what he was seeing and feeling. The smell of The Brotherhood swarmed around him—food stewing in the kitchen, warm grog, the faint smoky scent of lanterns and candles. The familiarity of it pushed him deeper into the bedcovers. He finally managed to open his eyes and keep them open.

For many minutes he watched, unseen, while Matthew and Elias shuttled in and out of the room. He had the vague awareness of a pillow beneath his head, bunched up around his ears, a charming and comforting feeling after the hard chipped wood he had been lying on before. How long ago? A day? An hour . . . he couldn't tell. His hands felt warm; a good sign.

Before him his body lay stretched out under the blanket. A brown wool blanket, tattered and worn, just the blanket he had dreamed of as he lay chilled and bleeding on the deck of the sandbagger. Wooden panels and the brick above it surrounded him in the small room, glowing with the warm gold of lanternlight. He felt that warmth on his cheeks. Yet none of that could assuage the hole in his soul, nor brush aside the memory of Maynard's hunting knife sinking into the right side of his stomach, the grate of it upon the underside of his rib, mutilating any chance of his helping Abbey.

He blinked. His eyes were dry. They focused on Elias's familiar blue shirt and brown vest.

Jake stiffened for a moment, to test his muscles, and tried to move his hands. His left hand wouldn't move, but his right palm slid up his thigh to his midsection, to the place where the knife had sunk in. He pressed it down.

Dull pain suddenly turned sharp and burned through him under his hand. His eyes tightened, and he sucked in a short breath, wincing.

Elias turned and instantly snatched Jake's right hand from the wound, clasped it and patted it. "Oh, not a good idea there, landlubber," he said, holding on to Jake's hand as it naturally tried to pull back to the pain. "Don't touch. You'll scotch all our handiwork."

Hearing that, Matthew reappeared from the pub kitchen. When he saw Jake, his face broke into a grin. "Rosebush! Wide awake." He strode into the room, wiping his hands dry on his pub apron, and sat down gingerly at Jake's side. "The mates'll be glad about that."

Jake cleared his throat and murmured, "Sumner?"

"No sign of any of 'em. Wouldn't bet they'd stay on the island. Couldn't show their faces if they did. They'd find themselves staring at their feet from a tops'l spar." He wobbled Jake's knee and grinned reassuringly. Even past the grin there was a haze of defined threat for those who had done this to his cousin.

Strengthened by Matthew's private anger, Jake forced out a single, terrible question. "Where's Abbey?"

"Where do you think?"

Matthew's mouth hadn't moved, and it wasn't Matthew's voice he heard. This voice was soft as meadow wind, strong as the scrub oaks, and sounded amused that he would even have to ask. It came from his left side, and the sound of it gave him the strength to turn his head.

There she was. There she was.

Beside him, still holding his hand, there was Abbey. Her hair was a delirious wreck. It was longer than he remembered from that hazy time in the lighthouse, and in this lamplight the color was darker, the shade of buttered toast. She wore one of Elias's shirts, this one gray flannel, and it hung on the round bulbs of her shoulders like a napkin draped over the back of a carved chair. Its big buttons gave weight to the soft fabric, holding it down between her breasts—safe. The gentle territory was safe. . . .

Her long fingers were coiled around his left hand—that was why it was so warm, and why he couldn't move it.

Her presence shocked him, fortified him. His mind, fogged with guilt and anguish about what happened on the wharf, hadn't let him remember that she'd been here all the time. Those had been only dreams and wishes—no, they'd been real. She was here.

"Abbey!" he gasped, raising his head and his right shoulder as he tried to turn to her, tried to sit up, tried to reach for her. *Abbey, I think I . . .*

Elias and Matthew both grabbed him and pressed him down before all the stitches broke.

"Whoa, rosebush," Matthew soothed. "Stick to, now. No roving tonight for you. Not for a while."

"He just wants me, that's all," Abbey murmured, drawing his hand to rest between her breasts, where she knew it wanted to be. She pulled her chair right up to the bedside until her knees pressed into the slats and leaned right down against him, her face impossibly close to his, her eyes right where he could stare into them. "I'm here, Jake, here with you."

"But Cobb . . ."

Abbey smiled at him, stroking the side of his face. "Oh, it takes more than an overstuffed porkhead like him to get the better of me. Don't you know that by now?"

His head dropped back onto the pillow, and his eyes, quite suddenly, cleared. "Guess I do now. . . ." he murmured. "Don't leave me, Abbey."

She brushed at his hairline with just enough playfulness to reassure him. "In the morning, I'll go just long enough to get Dominic's children up and fed and off to school. Then I'll be back with you." She smiled at him and whispered, "And even when I'm gone, you know we'll be together. That's the way it seems to be between us . . . you know."

"I know," he whispered back.

Abbey leaned even closer, until her cheek lay against his and her lips brushed his ear. She kissed the soft flesh in front of his ear and whispered even more softly. "I want you . . . I get what I want. No one can take you away. Sleep now, and I'll be there with you in your dreams. You may not see me, but I'll be there, somewhere near you. Don't forget. Go to sleep, now. Close your eyes . . . that's right . . . shhh."

Again she kissed his neck, his ear, his temple, until his eyes drifted closed and a small groan of comfort fell out of him on a sigh.

"Sleep . . . dream . . . and I'll be there with you. . . ."

Chapter Twelve

SHE WAS A ghost of herself when she pulled the Nash's back door shut and leaned upon it, exhausted. Sunlight was threading through the rooftops at a strange angle. Thin arms of budded trees made it ripple, and it already carried the reflection of the sea. A twinge of resentment burned through her. It was the first time she'd seen an eastern dawn.

What would the wharf look like in the dawn light? How would the sun, which had abandoned her last night, strike the big block and tackles, the battered wooden decks, the sea-stressed planks of the docks that had become so intimate with her in the darkness? She suddenly wished to see the yellow-white shimmer skittering among the halyards and rigging, to see if the wharf could be anything pleasant, anything less ugly than it was last night when it helped Sumner and his men do Pollock's work for him.

Her resentment burned hotter. This was supposed to be her dawn. Hers and Jake's. They were supposed to be awakening now, just in time to see the soft sunlight glow across the fine hairs of their naked skin. There was supposed to be the faint scent of sweat, rising like incense, hers and his mingling together. There was supposed to be lovers' laughter about which of their limbs had to be raised first in order to untangle their bodies from the luscious, ridiculous, impossible position they'd fallen asleep in. Their dawn. Ruined.

A year ago she thought Pollock had stolen everything from her.

But somehow he had found a way to steal even more.

She leaned back on the door, her head touching it with a faint thud. It hurt enough that she closed her eyes for a moment, then realized she had a headache. Her hand fell limp against her thigh.

She almost screamed. Almost. She almost tilted her head back and screwed her eyes shut and shrieked a scream so loud it could have broken glass. The hot core of her womanhood made her moan deep in her throat. Though she stopped the scream, she couldn't hold back the moan.

You promised me. And I'm still empty.

Abbey pressed the heel of her hand between her thighs and summoned up the last of her power to control it.

Her body was a bag of aches. Her back, her thighs, her arms, nothing but aches. She looked down at her clothes.

"Oh, lovely," she muttered. Elias's gray flannel shirt was hanging over her breasts, and a pair of Matthew's trousers was tied around her waist, about two times bigger than she needed. Only her boots were her own. Her shirt, skirt, bolero, and vest had stayed at The Brotherhood, too gritty to be comfortable until they were cleaned. So here she was, wearing this. All she wanted was to be seen by Nantucket society while she wasn't wearing a corset. Her usual dresses were stiff enough to hide the fact that she didn't wear one, hated them in fact, but this flannel garment hung on her like a wet rag and showed everything.

"Abbey!"

She jumped so hard that the door rattled behind her. Her eyes flew open and she was staring right at Lucy. The girl still wore Cordelia's night robe, and though she looked tired, she was still ten times more presentable than Abbey was.

"Gawd, miss, where'd yer disappear to!" Lucy wailed. "I bin muddlin' awl noight over yer! Coo! Yer never said yer'd be gone awl noight. Gawd knew wot 'appened. An' yer look a wreck as well. Wot 'appened?"

Abbey's foggy mind struggled, and finally she pulled enough sense out of what Lucy had said to mutter one phrase of response. "Plenty happened. I'll tell you later."

"You well?" Lucy approached swiftly and wrapped her arm around

Abbey, steering her into the warm kitchen. "Yer don't look well a'all."

"I'm fine. I have to get the children up and ready for school."

"Oh, 'shaw, I'll do that, Abbey, no trouble!"

"No," Abbey said, pulling herself away enough to look at Lucy squarely. "I'll do it. I don't want to shirk my duties, Lucy. That's important to me. But if you could just start their breakfast—"

"No sooner said," Lucy told her, waving her hands. "Eggs an' ginger biscuits, specialty of the 'ouse."

Abbey gazed at the fortified girl for a moment and gushed, "By God, I don't know how you do it, Lucy."

Lucy's little mouth drew up into a bow and she nodded humbly. "Aw, mum, I bin on my own a long time. Yer gets used to it."

Footsteps coming toward the kitchen roused her and made her stand straighter. If it was Dominic—

Cordelia's severe dark hair and plain face appeared over her customary dark dress. Upon seeing Abbey, her eyes shot open wide and her brows drew tightly together. "Mrs. Sutton! How can you—when did you come in?"

The housekeeper closed the distance between herself and the other women very quickly with her tickety-tackety little steps.

"Just now. It's been a very long night, Cordelia," Abbey told her wearily.

"Where were you all night? And what are you wearing?"

"Oh . . . never mind, please. I need a favor from both of you, even more than I needed one last night. Will you help me?"

After glancing at each other, both women nodded. They were friends—that much was clear from the help they'd given her last night, and their willingness to do even more now. Perhaps Nantucket wasn't such a hopeless place to put her future.

Abbey licked her lips. "I need information. Discreetly collected information. I want to know anything I can find out about Thomas Pollock."

"That man oo kill't yer 'usband?" Lucy asked.

"Yes. He's on the island. I want to know where he's staying. I want to know who he sees and where he goes. It's very important. Lives are at stake. You two can both move about the town much more freely than I can. You already know everyone. Will you do this for me?"

Lucy hesitated, twisting her mouth to one side in contemplation, then quickly made her decision. "No problem, mum! I got me connections, y'know. I keep me little ears open. Didn't spend two years on the Liverpool docks wivvout learnin' a fing er two. Bet on it!"

Abbey reached out and clasped Lucy's shoulders, warmth running between them. She was ashamed of herself to realize what she was demanding of her friend so soon after the death of Lucy's own husband. "Oh, Lucy . . . I shouldn't ask. I'm so sorry. This is rude of me, rude and crass."

Lucy patted Abbey's hands as they fell into hers, and said, "Nonsense. Best fing for me, get up and get movin'. No good lumpin' about, pinin' for somebody oo ain't nivver gonna come back." She shook her head sagely and tucked her chin. "I loved him, Abbey, but I ain't stupid. I got a little girl t'raise an' a life t'live. Now I got somethin' t'do wivvit. At least, for a coupla days. I'll see wot I kin discover about yer man."

"Yes, so will I," Cordelia said. "Especially if lives are at stake. Are you sure about that part of it?"

"Very sure," Abbey told her ruefully. "Very sure. And please don't tell Dominic. He has enough to think about, and this is something I want to work out for myself."

Cordelia gave her a quick, impatient nod. "Where were you all night?"

"Oh, Cordelia . . . so many places . . . I don't care to explain just now, all right? I'm sorry. I didn't mean to cause so much worry, but things took a turn. I just want to get the children up and off to school. Oh, and I have to change first. . . . Thank you both so much, for everything. I never thought I'd have such good friends when I came here." She held up a finger and added, "But you be careful, you hear me? All I need is information. Nothing else."

"Thinks she's dealin' wiv amatoors," Lucy crowed to Cordelia.

Cordelia ignored her and told Abbey, "I think you should get some sleep."

"I can't. Not yet," Abbey said. "I'm fine, really. Don't worry about me."

"I wish you'd tell me where you were," Cordelia said with a frown that said the curiosity was eating away at her.

"Enough," Lucy scolded. "Get out wiv you. I'm makin' breakfast."

"*You* are?" Cordelia blurted.

"That's roight. And jus' try ter stop me."

Relieved, Abbey left the two women behind. She'd liked to have been more cordial about making her way upstairs, but she heard Dominic moving about in the master bedroom over the kitchen and she wanted to get into clothes that didn't need an explanation before he came out and saw her. Her mind projected anxiously forward to the next couple of hours. The children would be gotten up, cleaned, dressed, and delivered to school, and she could get back to The Brotherhood, to a promise she'd made deep in the night.

His own moan awakened him. It was a little gusting breath that fell from his lips and carried a sound with it, telling him at the same time both that he was weak and that he was alive. He blinked his eyes and this time they opened easily. Judging from the angle of weak sunlight coming in the one tiny window, it was early morning. The lantern on the table beside him was still lit, but its golden glow was diffused and paled by the coming light of day. Above him, the wooden rafters still held the warm shadows from last night. The panels that went halfway up the wall and the brick that went the rest of the way had a particular depth and texture to his concentrated senses. They were deep golden brown—the color of buttered toast. . . .

He turned his head from one side to the other on the pillow. Alone. She promised she wouldn't leave. And she had anyway. Nothing could measure the depth of his hurt as he realized he was alone again.

He had dreamed about her. They'd been in the flowers together. Vines made their bed, rambling roses their rooftop. The front of her dress had been torn open, but she made no effort to close it as he gazed through the dream at her. Her hair was loose on her shoulders, draping down her back, with tiny threads floating around her face like a thousand whispers. He held her so close in the dream that his arms sank into her flesh, melted into it and fused in place. The taste of her still lingered in his mouth. His wet lips opened against the coolness of her throat and took in great mouthfuls of sensation. With a single motion his body and hers had crushed up against each other in the dream, moving together until the pressure had become too much and his head had dropped backward, his lips hanging open to the sky beyond the roses, utter ecstasy running through his body instead of blood. There was nothing in the universe but Abbey. Strong, determined, unshakable Abbey, whose faith in their bond refused to untwine itself from his heart.

But he failed her because the pain came back then, the ice-hot cut of Maynard's blade in his gut. Because of the pain, tears had welled in his eyes. The pain kept him from being the strong one in the lovemaking, as a man should be. Because he couldn't be strong, couldn't get his arms around her anymore, she began to slip away. Once again, as it had on the sandbagger, the knife sliced through him and kept him from finding her. Where was she? Only a moment ago she'd been there. . . . Abbey. . . . he failed her, and now she was gone.

Jake lifted his head from the pillow, a movement deliberately sudden. The dream fell away, taking most of its memories with it.

"Judas," he muttered. His lips pressed flat and he blinked a few times. Despite the effort he wouldn't let his head drop back again. A deep breath, then—

"Matt!"

Not even a whole second went by. Matthew shot into the room, bringing with him a scent of eggnog.

"Whoa! Whoa, whoa, Jake. We didn't leave you," Matthew assured, holding his hands out in a placating gesture. He sat down carefully on the edge of the bed—a position Jake found somehow familiar—pointed at Jake's head and said, "Back on the pillow."

Jake dropped back. "How long?"

"Just overnight, is all," Matthew told him with a shrug.

Letting the scent of rummed and brandied eggnog bring him back to consciousness, Jake forced himself to think clearly. In his mind he saw the small, round, red clay pots with the spoons sticking up from them, from which sailors would eat their morning custard and plum flan before heading down to the docks, either to set sail or to scrub down their ships, stitch their sails, reweave their sheet ends, douse the wooden decks with salt water, or a thousand other duties that went with docking. Mostly he thought of the little clay pots. A touch of hunger growled in his stomach.

He brought his hand up along his body and felt the stiffness of a bandage beneath the blanket. "I thought they killed me."

"Nah," Matthew smacked. "In order to die on board a boat, you gotta go to sea once in a while. That's maritime law, you know. You don't qualify."

"What happened to Sumner and the other two?"

Matthew's brows furrowed. "Don't you get tired of asking me that question?"

"Did I ask you before?"

"Sure did. Coupla times."

"I don't remember."

"That don't surprise me, given what shape you were in last night. We, uh, haven't caught up to 'em yet. Likely won't."

Jake breathed deeply and nodded. Then he frowned and wondered, "Why do you suppose they didn't kill me?"

Matthew laughed, a laugh laced with relief. "Little blessings don't come cheap, rosebush."

"I'm serious," Jake told him. "They could have been sure of it. They could have disemboweled me once and for all. Why d'you suppose they left me alive?"

Matthew fussed with the blanket over Jake's chest. "I dunno. Could be . . . a warning, I reckon."

Jake's voice lowered. "That's what I reckon too."

"Guess Pollock figures if he kills you, we won't deal with him at all. But if he don't kill you, maybe we'll be scared of him and let him do our transporting. 'Course, I don't exactly trust him to do a good job for us anymore. . . ."

Seeing something in Matthew's face, in the way Matthew was avoiding looking right at him, Jake stuffed his hand into his cousin's elbow and said, "Matt, forget it."

Disgust pursed Matthew's lips. "Can't forget it," he snapped back. "I should have listened to you. You were right and I should have listened. Pollock's not our kind of partner. He fooled me all along, and you figured him out in no time. I blundered, and you took the punishment for it. Jake, I'm mighty sorry. Mighty ashamed and sorry."

Matthew almost choked on those words. All night they'd been sitting on his gullet, keeping him from swallowing so much as a steadying gulp of whiskey. Jake noticed his cousin's wan complexion where usually there were two ruddy cheeks, as well as circles under eyes that usually were glistening, and he saw what the long night had done.

"Matt," Jake grumbled sympathetically, and that was all he said.

A moment later Matthew folded his hands in his lap, rubbed his thumbs together, and stared at them. "We're gonna get them, Jake. We're gonna see those bastards hang."

"For what?" Jake chuckled. "For *almost* killing me? For *almost* meddling Abbey?"

"Why'd you go out there, Jacob?" Matthew asked him. "Why didn't you come for us before you went out there alone?"

Jake held out a hand. "I'd no choice. I was on my way back to the pub, trying to think of how I was going to tell you I'd cancelled Pollock's deal, when Maynard showed up and told me they had Abbey out on the wharf. I didn't believe him at first. I couldn't figure how Pollock could've done it all that fast. Somehow he got word to those three, and somehow they got Abbey and dragged her out there before I even had time to get back to you. How in perdition they could move so fast—" He cut himself off wearily and shook his head.

Matthew licked his lips guiltily. "I think I know how, Jake. I mean I know how they got her. She came here, looking for you. We . . . we sent her on out to South Wharf."

"You did what? How could you send her out there alone?"

"Didn't figure there was risk in that . . . not in *that*. But how they was ready for her beats me all over. There's something going on with those three weasels. They got connections on the island somehow that we can't follow. I can't cipher it, Jake, but something's fishier than Louis's schooner. Them three scared me last night, moving on you so fast. Last thing I expected was that gal of yours come thundering into The Brotherhood and saying what she said. When she said it was Sumner, I damned near peed in my trousers."

Matthew brought a big hand to his eyes and rubbed them too hard, and his shoulders shook as he chuckled at himself, a mixture of relief and awe that somehow the night was over.

The sight of him brought a smile to Jake's drained face, and he pushed his hand deeper into the bend of Matthew's arm and squeezed it.

"Forget about them," he said. "Pollock's the one to worry about. Now that he knows for sure we're doing business off the island and that we won't work with him, he might try to shut us down."

"Or head off our sources," Matthew agreed. "I thought of that."

"We can't let that happen," Jake told him firmly. "Even if we cut off our own suppliers, we can't let him shoehorn our sources. Have Elias put messages on the next ships out to all our suppliers on the Continent. Tell them to reroute through Albany quick as they can, and don't let anybody know about it."

"Sure you want to do that?"

"We got no choice. We'll clear what we've got on the island, then shut down for a while. There's too much at stake. Pollock's out for no good, Matt, I can feel it."

Matthew looked at him and sighed. "I sure know you felt it. You felt it good and deep."

"Shut that hatch, will you?" Jake scolded. "It's starting to stink up the place. Holy Moses, I'm tired. . . ."

"Don't doubt it," Matthew said, standing up. He tucked the blanket tighter around Jake's sides, but clearly there was little he could do that hadn't already been done, and that seemed to frustrate him. "Sleep's the best medicine for you."

He couldn't tell his cousin he was wrong. That the best medicine for him had gotten up and left. She said she'd stay, but she left. He wasn't good enough. He fell short of her needs. She had expected him to be hardier, to meet her own level of virility and sturdiness. He had failed her. That had to be why she left. . . .

"Don't worry, now," Matthew said as he straightened. "I'm just out the door there. Ain't going nowhere, either."

Jake felt his head grow heavy on the pillow, his eyes drooping, and he forced a weak grin to reassure Matthew that he understood. He let his eyes drift shut, and listened.

There was a faint shuffle of Matthew's footsteps moving toward the doorway, finally stepping out onto the stone floor of the kitchen.

Jake opened his eyes on the silent, empty room. A touch of pain came to his face, but this was not pain of his wounds. He turned his head slightly, just the few inches it took to let him see the top of the chair at his left. The empty chair.

The empty chair.

"Mr. Colbert?"

Matthew answered the quiet call by stepping out of the kitchen into the pub itself. "Mrs. Sutton," he said, keeping his voice down to avoid awakening Jake. "I figured you'd be getting some sleep by now. You ought to, you know."

Abbey approached him with a sudden wave of familiarity. After what they'd been through together last night, they would have to trust each other. "I could say the same to you, Matthew. How is he?"

Matthew shrugged and sighed. "Real weak. Pale. He woke up and talked to me for a while pretty early this morning."

"Sleeping now?"

"Yes'm, he is. I figure that's the best thing for him."

"Yes, I figure you're right," she said, her eyes blinking heavily.

Matthew gazed at her, reading the fatigue. "Ma'am, maybe you could do with a nice taste of warm plum flan. I got a full batch of it back there. Maybe you'd like to taste it."

"Taste it?" she said. "I'm not sure I'm awake enough to pronounce it! Flum . . . plan . . ."

Matthew chuckled. "Yes'm, it took me two years to teach Elias to say it right."

Abbey allowed herself a smile. "Thank you, but I just had breakfast at Magistrate Nash's house. Part of my duties of caring for his children is to set the example of a good breakfast. It feels as if I swallowed a bag of rocks."

He nodded. He'd heard that same complaint often enough from the sailing men who dragged in like whipped cats, having worked too hard and slept too little, then ate too much when they finally got the chance. He took her elbow in a no-arguments grip. "I got some nice rooms upstairs, Missus. Best you rest."

"I want to sit with Jake. I promised him I'd be back." She tried to resist Matthew's grip, but her muscles were thready.

"You can sit with him later, Mrs. Sutton," Matthew told her reasonably. "He's fast asleep now and wouldn't even know if you was there or not. No point sitting there staring at him just so's you can say you did."

Before she knew it he was leading her up a narrow staircase cut into the brick structure of the house above The Brotherhood. The hem of her dress licked at the doorway to the back room where Jake slept, as though trying to pull her in that direction.

Something roused him. A movement, a voice—he couldn't tell. It pulled him back from his dreams like a tide being sucked back out to sea. Reluctant. Clinging.

He listened, but all he heard was Matthew putting some drunken mariner to bed upstairs.

To his right, suffused daylight came through the thin curtains. Its angle said noon, or after.

He turned his head to the left. The chair was still empty. His hand lay cool and untouched against the covers.

Noon. Noon, and she hadn't come back. How could she have been so stalwart and unrelenting for so long, only to give up on him now? Her faith in him had buckled, crumbled. He'd failed her once too often for her to go on forgiving and go on trying to convince him of something that, deep down, he already knew better than his name.

Even the tide could only fight so long.

He stared at the empty chair beside his bed and tried to glean from it the tiniest warmth that might still be left from her body.

Nantucket's scrub oaks were low-growing and scruffy, more like bushes than trees, so tightly knotted and thorny that they were almost impossible to cut through. Somehow deer lived among them, but how long-legged creatures could move about in such entanglement was one of those elusive mysteries of nature.

So it was also a mystery how Abbey could have gotten inside a wide thicket of scrub oaks, a thicket that surrounded her like a ring, with no opening, no tunnel, no bridge. All she had was a chair. A chair, and nothing more, to keep her company.

She wasn't even sitting in it. She was just looking at it, while around her the thick scrub oaks began to rustle.

She rolled over and discovered her arms and legs were almost numb from lack of movement. She woke up in the same position she'd gone to sleep in when Matthew steered her onto the bed and dropped a blanket over her. She flopped down on her side, and now her left arm was numb.

The room was dark. Too dark.

Abbey sat upright, instantly forgetting the dream, the scrub oaks, the chair. Dark!

Stumbling from the bed to the doorway, she focused on the golden lamplight coming from the bottom of the stairs, creating a wedge of light up the staircase. Forcing her sleepy limbs to keep control of themselves, she somehow got down those narrow steps and grasped the doorframe to Jake's room off the kitchen. Hanging there as though there were no floor under her and nothing to cling to but the frame, she pressed back her tousled hair and blinked her eyes clear.

Jake lay asleep, his head turned casually to the left, away from the small window. Perhaps the light had bothered him. Or perhaps he hadn't awakened at all today.

Seeing he was safe, Abbey turned and stumbled into the kitchen.

Burning wood crackled inside a big black iron stove, and large pots of chowder gurgled on top of it, but otherwise the room was empty. Abbey went straight through to the pub without a pause, registering the sounds she heard from its direction. There was no music yet—too early for that, apparently—but a dozen men or so were involved in various stages of their evening meals. Quiet conversations between masculine voices rippled through the pub. They seemed to be acutely aware of Jake asleep in the back room. As she gazed through the light of the little globed candles on the tables, still trying to force her eyes to wake up, Abbey thought she recognized several of these men from that harrowing search on Old South Wharf. She turned to the bar and saw Matthew and Elias with their backs to her, stacking glasses.

"Matthew," she called softly.

Several glasses clattered, and the two men swung around, startled.

"Oh, awake, finally," Matthew said, moving toward her.

"How could you let me sleep so late! It's after dark!" she hissed at him.

He put out his hands in a comforting signal and said, "There's no problem, missus. Everything's taken care of. That little girl from the hat store came by with the Nash children this afternoon and she said you wasn't to worry about them."

Abbey drew back her indignation. "Lucy came here?"

"Yep, and she said you shouldn't worry. Said she was going to take the magistrate and his kids to her house and cook them what she called a Liverpool potlicker supper, and they wouldn't be none the wiser about where you are." He shrugged his thick shoulders and said. "So I figured I'd let you sleep."

Stripped of any reason to be angry, Abbey felt suddenly light-headed. She heaved a sigh of relief and sat down in a wooden booth behind an empty table. "Ye gods, ask Lucy Edmonds to cover for you, and you're good and covered." She stared into the layers of depth in the table's wood and broke her stare only when a steaming clay mug full of coffee was set before her. Matthew was standing over her.

"Thank you," she said simply. "What about Jake? How is he?"

"The doctor came by about four-thirty," Matthew said. "took a look at him, and redressed the wound. Seems he's on the road to recovery, all right."

Elias appeared behind Matthew's shoulder and added. "He lost a bucket of blood, Mrs. Sutton, that's the biggest danger. Doc says he'll be weak for a couple of days, then he should get stronger pretty fast after his wound seals and his body picks up the pace of recovery. Good thing he wasn't lying in that sandbagger any longer, though."

Abbey shuddered at the thought. "Did he wake up?"

"Jake? Oh, sure, for a while."

"Did you tell him I was here?"

Elias looked at Matthew. "Did you?"

Matthew blinked back. "I didn't . . . didn't you?"

"I thought you did."

"Naw, I didn't."

Abbey gazed up at them, and discomfort settled over the booth. Her voice cracked slightly as she spoke. "He didn't ask for me?"

Matthew pulled out one of the chairs, which squeaked on the stone floor and creaked as he sat down in it. "I wouldn't worry abut that. We tried to get him not to waste his energy talking, and the doctor kept him busy, what with changing the dressing and all. We just gave him a cup of soup broth and sent him right back to sleep in no time. Rest is what he needs."

She pressed her lips tight. "It seems that's what he needs," she murmured.

Matthew leaned toward her. "Pardon?"

When she didn't answer right away, Elias sat down on the bench beside her. Though he wasn't quite sure what to do with his hands, he tried to make his words the right ones. "Mrs. Sutton, Jake knows you were here. You told him you'd come back. He was plenty awake then to understand. I could wake him up now, if you like—"

"Oh, no, please don't," Abbey said quickly, looking up. "That wouldn't do at all, would it?" She forced a smile and added, "Don't say anything at all about me. It may remind him of what happened on the dock."

Matthew snickered. "Ma'am, I doubt he'll be forgetting that any time soon. Oh—speaking of forgetting . . ." He rummaged in the pockets of his apron and pulled out a sealed envelope. "Your friend left this for you."

"Lucy?" Abbey took the envelope, tore it open rather anxiously, and pulled out a note.

Clapping his brother on the shoulder as a none-too-subtle hint, Matthew got up from his chair and said, "C'mon, 'Lias. We got a pub to run." When Elias was up and heading back to the bar, Matthew added, "You're welcome to stay, missus."

Invigorated by what she'd just read, Abbey jumped up from the booth and asked, "Do you have my clothes from last night—my skirt, particularly?"

"Oh, yes, ma'am, we cleaned it all and put a new seam in your shirt, too. Figured we owed you that."

"You don't owe me anything, Matthew."

"Yes'm, we do. You saved Jake's life."

Abbey flattened her mouth and said, "And provided Sumner with a way to lure Jake out there."

Brows lowering, Matthew told her something that, until this moment, she hadn't completely realized. "Mrs. Sutton, they were out to get Jake. If they'd done it when he was alone, he'd have been helpless. Just as well it worked out this way. It's a pity you had to get wrapped up in it at all, though."

"Don't pity me, Matthew, she said. "I eat pity for breakfast and spit it right out. Where can I change?"

He started to point toward the staircase, then stopped. "Ma'am, you're not planning to go roving the island by yourself again in the dark of night. . . ."

"Of course not. I'm simply more comfortable in my old clothes."

He nodded, though he seemed not to believe her entirely.

Matthew Colbert was an intuitive man.

Abbey waited until he had stepped into the kitchen to retrieve her clothes. She looked down at Lucy's note, a hastily scrawled message full of Lucy's kind of enthusiasm.

Abbey,
  No sooner I got out movin then I herd tell of a bote belongin to Tomas Poolok. Its mored way out on Brant Pointe. Dont know wy it wood be out there awl by its lonely self. Goode luk.

Your friend, Lucy E.

"Bless you, Lucy. You're a fast worker." Abbey smiled, wondering how Lucy had managed to spell "lonely" right. She folded the note and held it to her bosom.

"Brant Point," she whispered. "Brant Point."

Brant Point on a very foggy night.

An ugly stretch of beach and shoreline with very little going for it, so little that only the fog could improve its aura. It was a lonely place, Abbey noted, probably the most unpopulated spot on this side of the island. There was a single empty lifesaving station, very small, hardly more than a shed, a small dock going out onto the ocean. She could barely make out the end of the little pier. And—sure enough—at the edge of the fog she saw the pointed bow of a small ship. From amidships back, there was only the cottony fog.

The pier was narrow, hardly more than a foot bridge. It quivered as Abbey stepped onto it, violating its loneliness. It swayed under her weight, making her glad she'd worn her boots again tonight; they had the surest grip of any shoes she owned. The warped wood was soaked through and low to the incoming waves. This little dock wasn't likely to last much longer, for it apparently hadn't seen repair in quite a while. Abbey wouldn't have been surprised if it chose this night to moan its last moan and topple over into the sea under her weight.

The sloop seemed small until Abbey got out to it, moving carefully and quietly along the small dock, on the lookout for any light on board the fog-shrouded vessel.

There were no lanterns burning on the sloop. There was no sign of life at all.

Somehow that made her nervous. She would rather have faced Pollock outright.

Well . . . perhaps not outright.

But sitting around doing nothing was worse than riding drag on a drive, she told herself, trying to fortify her courage. If you eat dust, you breathe dust and you look through dust, well, you can't get ahead of the herd that way.

The narrow dock swayed beneath her, and her arms flew out for balance. There was nothing to hold on to. The pilings were short, stubby things, jutting only high enough over the edge of the dock to let a rope get a purchase, nothing like the thigh-high pilings on the big wharf in town.

She glanced back toward the end of Brant Point to make sure she was alone, finding it disconcerting that she could no longer see the shoreline. The thin pier stretched off into a milky gray emptiness back the way she had come and stopped with a blunt drop-off just a few feet from where she stood. Only the dock itself and the vessel beside her proved to her there was land nearby at all.

Shivering, Abbey forced herself to move. She stepped onto the rail of the sloop, then down onto the deck.

There were shadows everywhere. Where there wasn't fog, there were shadows—undefinable shapes that made up the deck.

Her legs quivered beneath her, forcing her to wait several moments before she could move about on the dark deck. She was more afraid than she had realized, now that she was actually aboard this mysterious, hidden vessel, a vessel that belonged to a man who would be her bitterest enemy in the world if he knew she were here on Nantucket. In Wyoming, she'd failed to bring enough evidence against Pollock to give him just punishment for his sly dealings. She would not make that error again.

Jake would hate her when he found out she had come here. But she was doing this for him. She wouldn't let Pollock take another love from her life. She didn't know why he was dealing with him, and he might hate her for interfering, but he was on a slippery slope to jail or death, and she meant to stop him before he got there. If she could implicate Pollock . . . perhaps Dominic would listen to her and let Jake go in exchange for the bigger wickedness.

She wondered if Pollock even knew it was Lowell Sutton's wife his men were grabbing. Was it truly coincidence, or were there other forces at work? They wanted information from Jake and used her to try to get it—perhaps Pollock had yet to find out who he was angering with his presence here. Perhaps he thought he was safely anonymous on Nantucket.

Her thoughts began to muddle as she stepped along the squeaky deck toward the aft cabin hatch. Dark, like everything else. She leaned down, listening for the sound of breathing. If someone was asleep down there . . .

She heard nothing. No breathing, no movement. Nothing but the sedate wash of waves against the hull.

She looked around and found a small lantern on the deck. Quickly she glanced down the dock again, one more time, then lit the lantern and stepped toward the aft hatch, letting the lantern lead her way.

Unlike many of the ships in town, this sloop didn't smell like fish. It smelled of lamp oil and old wood, but nothing more. The hatch was narrow and disturbing. She had to force herself to keep calm as it swallowed her up. The lanternlight made a yellow moon before her.

A moment passed, and she was in the after cabin.

Abbey's mouth dropped open at what greeted her. She drew in a long, airy breath.

Before her, on either side of the cabin, were stacked bunks—four where there would ordinarily only be two, twelve in all, with barely enough room for an adult to slide in. Such a vessel as this would never require that many people to crew it.

But these berths weren't for crewmen. No.

No—for each bunk had a rusted set of ankle irons attached to its frame. Leg gyves.

"A slave ship . . ." Abbey gasped, choking on her next breath. What had Dominic said—the unscrupulous business of reselling slaves—

"No, Jake . . . you can't know about this."

Even though she heard the words aloud, she knew she had no choice but to accept what she saw. This ship certainly had nothing to do with transporting goods. Not goods that weren't alive and beaten into submission, at any rate. Each berth whimpered of bondage and humiliation. Like a haunt going on around her, she heard the soft clink of manacles and the whimpering of humanity bethralled. It was unforgivable. People bridled and bartered like common goods.

A huff of anger spilled from her lips, and with a shake she threw off the whispers of the aft cabin.

"No longer. Not with me about," she muttered. Holding the lantern up so that its meager light could show her through the ship, she found her way to the forecabin and found it much the same— more bunks, too many for the space, more ankle irons. Only the fo'c'sle had normal-sized berths with warm blankets—four of them.

"Pollock and his three curs," Abbey guessed.

All at once, the ship rocked. She froze still for an instant, not daring to breathe, listening acutely for footsteps, voices.

There was nothing. Only the waves gently moving the ship against the dock.

Pushing her weak little lantern up before her, she climbed up through the fo'c'sle hatch.

There was no moon tonight to brighten the low-rolling fog. Patchy clouds covered it, but its suffused light made the fog appear pearly and full of motion.

Carefully Abbey made her way to the main ship's hold, yanked back the hatch, and held her lantern down inside. The hold was full of crates and muslin bags, which anyone from a pioneer area would recognize instantly. Hardtack. Rations of dried meat and dried beans, ready to feed transportees on the long sail back to the South where they would be sold again.

She shook her head in fury. Damn this kind of behavior!

She lifted the lantern out of the hold and placed it on the hatch. Using her mind and the filtered moonlight to help her move about in the tiny hold, she jumped down inside and started stuffing crates and bags of food up the hatch onto the deck. When she got about half of the foodstuffs out, she vaulted back onto the deck, took a deep breath, and systematically began shoving the stock overboard. Rage piled strength on top of her determination, and with each heave she gritted her teeth. Each splash of food stock going over the side suffused her with satisfaction. Only once did she pause to catch her breath, and she used that moment to lean forward over the rail and watch with bitter pleasure as the bags of dried beans filled and sank, and the crates of meat and hardtack bobbed off into the fog.

"Welcome aboard."

Her lips fell open and she stiffened in place.

The voice was completely recognizable. Its sound awakened with a click something indelibly branded into her memory.

"Turn around," he said.

Bitter hatred became a cloak against her own fear. She slowly straightened, still not turning.

By the sound of his voice, she judged how much space was between her and him. A pace. Two at the most.

Moving only her hands, she released the Spanish silver buckle on her belt. The belt slackened just enough, leaving her feeling undressed and unprepared during that one second of indecision before the attack.

"Who are you? Turn around!"

The buckle settled into her right palm, and she grasped the leather end with her left—damn. It *would* have to work out that way, and here she was, patently right-handed. She'd have to make do.

"Turn around!" the voice ordered again. The murderer's voice.

So Abbey did.

Fast, hard, swinging.

The big silver buckle swerved outward at the end of her belt, propelled by its own weight and the sheer fury she put behind it. That blow carried a year's hatred, and the grinding determination that if this was her one blow, it would be the greatest, most crippling.

The coarse leather strap caught Pollock across the left ear. The heavy buckle continued around his head, its momentum bringing the belt all the way around, and with a smack the buckle struck him right in the throat.

Pure satisfaction ran through Abbey as Pollock's eyes opened wide, and he instinctively dropped the gun he held and brought his hands up to the buckle at his throat. That motion pinned the buckle against his gullet.

Abbey needed only that instant, for she'd never let go of the belt. Now she hauled down upon it, the effort wrenching a shout from her. Leverage as much as surprise worked in her favor. Pollock was hauled toward her.

She pulled harder, stepping to one side and drawing downward on the belt, pulling Pollock's mass alongside her and finally past her—

Where the rail of the sloop lay waiting to trip him.

Pollock howled a gagged protest, but the cold Atlantic swell closed up around him as he hit it headlong with a crash. He came up blubbering and suffering, still trying to yank the belt from around his neck, finding the task more difficult now that the leather was soaked.

Running on rage, Abbey swung around, grabbed the lantern that had been her only friend tonight, raised it over her head, and with a grunt pitched it down onto the deck of his slave ship. The lantern smashed, strewing oil across the deck, which instantly burst into flames and sizzled into the sail bags on the port side. A moment later, the old wood, fabric, and ropes had greedily sucked up the flames.

"Burn," Abbey whispered.

The ship answered with a soft crackling and a sudden heat.

Pollock managed to save himself from strangling, but there was no quick way back onto the boat. He struggled to tread water, while he caught his breath. There was nothing for him to do but stare up at the ghost of his own crimes.

Abbey glared down at him with eyes of stone. She knew he

couldn't make out her face in this foggy dimness, yet somehow she also knew he recognized her silhouette—the bolero, the split buckskin skirt, the boots, all backdropped by the flames as they grew behind her and began to roar. The yellow-orange fire and the smoke rising above it were a fitting haven for the demon who stood before them. Out of the foggy night a torch arose, burning and smoking, wobbling in the water, its disgusting purpose going up in smoke. She wore her hatred for him like the fiery wings of a phoenix, rising again out of a past he thought he had left behind.

Abbey stood on the ship's rail. She gazed solemnly down on Pollock as he coughed and fanned the water. As though unaware of the growing flames and sparking ropes behind her, she put her hands on her hips and waited until he finished sputtering and she had gotten his full attention.

"You know who I am, don't you?" she said, speaking just over the crackling fire. "I know who you are. Providence brought you to me. I shall not abuse the gift. I'll see you in jail, Thomas Pollock, in jail or dead, and by my own hands. *You,*" she said, pointing right at him, leaving him no doubt of her hatred, "have come to the wrong place."

Chapter Thirteen

THE WAVERING YELLOW glow of the fire remained safely hidden in the fog, and by the time anyone had seen the diffused glow and called out the volunteer fire brigade, Abbey was very sure Pollock's slave ship was no more than a charred hulk.

She walked back toward The Brotherhood with a distinct purpose in her stride and the nagging sense that she hadn't done enough, or at least that she wanted to do more. Around her, the quiet town awakened to the clattering fire bell. Men ran past her, heading for Brant Point, but she knew they were too late. Her steps became deliberately slow, toying with the ground, as she savored thoughts of Pollock clinging to the little pier while his boat burned.

That was how her husband felt. That was how they felt when Pollock stole their stock out from under them. Now he knew how it felt to watch an investment go up in smoke. That was how she felt when they told her Lowell was dead, along with four of the men who went with him when he tried to run Pollock down. Helpless. Now he knew.

She stopped in her tracks, hovering on the uneven cobblestones. Her own perception—or was it a decision?—startled her.

It wasn't enough. No, it wasn't enough. Dead or in jail. Preferably dead—that would be enough. She should have done it when she had the chance.

She spun around on the cobblestones, her arms flaring outward as though to decorate her curse. "I'll do it next time," she swore out loud.

But none of the people running past gave her their attention. A boat was burning. That was their priority.

Abruptly she found herself committed to her own threat. Now that Pollock knew she was on the island, she had given up her advantage and put him on equal footing with her. Yet, there were changes in her favor, too. A year ago she couldn't bring herself to kill him, and because of that he got away. How many had suffered because Pollock lived? Now Abbey knew: to preserve the life of someone like Pollock was simply to assist the suffering of others.

Jake, for one. Jake, who probably had no idea what kind of man he was dealing with. Pollock was like that—easy to trust at first. Lowell had made the mistake of trusting him.

Jake . . ."

Her step quickened. She must get to The Brotherhood. Jake had to be wondering where she was, why she hadn't been with him in so long. She should be there now to help ease his pain and his worries, to stroke him and comfort him as only a woman in love could.

"Mrs. Sutton?"

She stopped abruptly and looked toward the voice. Two familiar forms materialized out of the fog. Longhorn Mustache and Hunch. For the life of her she couldn't remember their names.

No matter.

"Are you two following me again?"

Longhorn raked his hat off his head in some kind of humble gesture and said, "No, ma'am, we wuzn't. Mr. Nash sent us out to haul you in. He wants to talk t'you. We ain't s'pose to come back without you."

"Then don't go back."

She started to step past him, but he caught her arm. For all his contrite behavior, the grip said he wasn't about to let go. "Mr. Nash said you might put up a squabble, but we wuz to make you come."

Abbey glared at him. "Oh, did he now? Did he mention that I've brought down bigger men than you?"

Longhorn glanced at Hunch, then said, "Yes'm, and I got a purty good recollection of that for m'self. Don't make no difference, though, I'm to take you home. Mr. Nash sent a message for me to tell you."

"What is it, then?"

"He says he'll come a-looking hisself if'n you don't come along quiet. And from the way he said it, ma'am, I reckon he'll do it."

Abbey scowled at him, her lips puckering. She sighed. "Yes, I reckon he would. All right, then, keep up."

She started off down the street in a new direction, ignoring the crunch of footsteps behind her as Longhorn and Hunch tried to match her furious pace.

Ash Street unfolded around her in the fog, and a few moments later she was stomping rudely into Dominic's good room with Moustache and Hunch close behind.

Dominic barely had time to turn before Abbey was confronting him.

"What's the meaning of setting these two scholars after me again, Dominic?"

Dominic frowned at her and said, "Mrs. Sutton, please don't take my methods so personally." He waved his hand at the two men and told them, "You gentlemen are dismissed."

"I thought you were at dinner with Lucy," Abbey immediately said as the two men left.

"I was," Dominic said. "I confess surprise at discovering a woman on this island who makes you seem subdued."

"Did you bring me here to insult me?"

He folded his hands behind his back and rocked on his heels, mentioning, "Well, it's hardly an insult. . . . Mrs. Edmonds is an entertaining young—"

"Are the children in bed?"

"They are, yes."

"Then I'm free for the evening. If you'll excuse me—"

"No, I will not excuse you. Come back here and sit down, please."

Abbey glared at him. "Dominic, you employ me. You do not own me."

He gestured toward the nearest chair. "Please."

It was neither a request nor an invitation, but something decidedly more strict.

Stiff-lipped, she turned on her heel and planted herself in the chair, keeping her spine straight. "If this is about my shirking my duties—"

"No," he said. "You've done your duties admirably."

She looked up. "Then what is it?"

Dominic tucked his chin scoldingly. "Get your hackles down, my good woman. You're disrupting my island and I won't have it. I go out for a simple dinner, and before I know it there's a boat burning on Brant Point."

"So?"

"So I smell a branding iron, Mrs. Sutton. Do I not?"

The fleeting idea of denying what she'd done came skittering through Abbey's mind, but she stepped on it and proudly raised her chin. "It's Thomas Pollock's boat. Did you men find him?"

Dominic's brows came together. "Find him where?"

"Where I left him. In the water."

"There was no one in the water."

Abbey huffed, "Damn it all," and banged her heel on the floor.

Pacing past her, Dominic asked, "Am I going to have to take official action to keep you away from Jacob Ross?"

At those words, Abbey vaulted to her feet. "Why should you?"

"Abbey, the whole town knows what happened last night on the wharf. Pure luck it turned out as well as it did."

"It wasn't Jake who tried to hurt me," she blurted, frustration adding a tiny whine to her voice. "It was Pollock's men. They work for him, I'm sure of it!"

"You're *not* sure of it. And whatever is occurring, it's still *because* of Jake Ross," Dominic insisted. "I've avoided arresting Ross on speculation because I haven't enough proof, and it's not really him I want. I want the ringleaders of this operation."

"It's Pollock, I keep telling you!"

"You may be right about Pollock," he placated, "but there's still no proof, Abbey."

"Then extradite him back to Wyoming Territory. He'll be hanged in a minute out there."

"I have nothing but your word on that, and it's not enough to arrest him."

"Then contact the marshal in Wyoming!

"That'll take weeks. And you said yourself, did you not, that there was no hardcore proof of his illicit activities in Wyoming and that's why he got away scot-free. Didn't you say that to me?"

There was a pause.

"Yes," she admitted.

"Then until he makes a move on Nantucket, my hands are tied."

Abbey dropped back into the chair, leaned on her elbow, and stared at the floor. "Then I'm back to killing him," she muttered in a voice too low for Nash to hear.

Flapping his hands in utter frustration, Dominic swirled around the chair once, then turned to her again. "Why did you burn his boat?"

Abbey startled him by leaping to her feet again. "That boat had bunks with leg gyves attached to them, the kind used for transporting slaves, just like you said! He must be reselling slaves! Isn't that illegal?"

"Illegal, but try to prove he's doing that. Such ships aren't uncommon, and we do have people on the island who are legally recapturing escaped slaves, supposedly to return them to their rightful owners. Be realistic. There's no provision on Nantucket for verifying that process. We're simply too far away from any real means of practical application. They have to handle those things on the Continent, at the source. Even if we could deal with such things expeditiously, you've burned the evidence. I hope you're beginning to see how your efforts are only complicating the situation. You're going to have to rein yourself in and above all to keep away from Jacob Ross."

"I've no intention of that."

"Intention or not, you'll do it!" he roared. "If I have to put you into protective custody for your own safety, then so be it.

"You wouldn't dare."

His expression said he would. In fact it said it so clearly that Abbey dared not challenge his determination. The island would be safe and peaceful no matter what methods Dominic Nash had to resort to.

Trying to hide her intentions, Abbey spoke carefully, testing his expression as she went.

"If I do," she began, "if I stay away from him and let things play out your way . . ."

"Yes?"

"I want a promise from you."

"Yes . . ."

"I've virtually given you Thomas Pollock. In return—"

"In return you want a pardon for Ross."

Though she had walked away from him, she turned now to face Nash. "Please, Dominic."

A stiffness came over his features, a hardness of defense as much as duty. The next words came as an effort to his lips, and there was a rasp in his voice. "You actually do care for him, don't you?"

Abbey squeezed her hands into fists. "Oh, Dominic, I scarcely know what I feel yet. I only know that a good man is a good man and sometimes that goodness shows so clearly, no matter what appears to be going on around him. You, for instance."

"You're being unrealistic," he accused, walking apprehensively toward the window as though to escape her compliment.

"That may very well be," she said, yet she stood resolute and waited for his answer.

"Then I hope you understand this," Dominic said, steeling himself. He paused, then turned to her. His eyes were filled with strain, his mouth bracketed by lines of intense control. "It would be frivolous of me to accede to such a treaty. The harmony of this island is my mandate. I would be compromising Nantucket were I to bend to an emotional judgment in these circumstances."

Anger welled up within Abbey, only to shrivel before it even began to show on her face. There he stood, so proud, so committed, before her, and here she stood, having asked him to walk with her to the edge of compromise. These strange turns of events had escorted her unwittingly to the borders where honor and dishonor became muddled, to the threshold of crime, and she had almost stepped over. Had she had a second chance, she might have killed Thomas Pollock when the opportunity presented itself. Fine, but she had no right to ask Dominic to step over that line with her. These were not his conclusions, but hers alone.

Dominic's hands were clenched behind his back. His shoulders were pinned back, his spine straight, his brows slightly furrowed, and there were tiny lines creasing his eyes, almost as though they were frozen in a flinch. He didn't blink. He waited, watching her.

Until this moment Abbey hadn't realized how much her opinion of him mattered to him, but that was what she saw in his eyes. A request that she not loathe him for what he must do.

If he could be honorable, then so could she, she decided then. "That was unfair of me," she said.

Dominic inhaled slowly. "Yes, it was."

"All right," Abbey began. "I understand your predicament. I shall offer you a compromise. I'll visit Jake only one more time, tonight. I feel I owe him an explanation. I want to tell him what I know about Pollock—no, Dominic, please don't say anything. I want to tell him. I feel I must. If he knows what kind of man Pollock is, if he's dealing with him in spite of that . . . then you're right and I must face it. If that is the case, then you fully deserve to take action and Jake Ross belongs behind bars. I won't stand in your way. And . . . I won't see him anymore until justice is played out."

The breath went out of her body with the last of those words, and a terrible fist squeezed her as though keeping her from breathing ever again. The promise crushed her even as she spoke it.

Dominic's eyes narrowed. He rocked on his heels for a thoughtful moment, then said, "I would be an idiot to agree to such a contract."

Abbey waited, neither moving nor speaking, for she felt something else behind his words that had yet to come out.

Sure enough, he sighed and mumbled, "I'm an idiot."

"Oh, Dominic!" She strode to him and planted a kiss on his cheek. "I think you're the world's grandest man."

She made no hesitation about getting to the door, but in that moment of pause it took to pull the door closed behind her, she thought she heard him mutter, "Not grand enough."

He was lying awake, staring at the darkness through the window. Much strengthened by a day of pure rest and Matthew's chowder, he found his senses were stirringly acute and that his thoughts cut through him with a million tiny jabs. Too acute to be real. He had just awakened—or had he just fallen asleep? The lamplight was hazy and gave the room an orange cast, making him drift on its color of warmth. Above him on the low ceiling the blocky rafters made shadows in which his thousand doubts hid. Doubts and questions. Fears, wants. Wishes.

All his senses were mixing as he lay there, ever so slightly out of touch with everything that was going on in the next room. How odd that he should have his eyes on the door separating him from the world just when its hinges creaked and the aroma of brandy and stew slipped through.

He turned his head.

There she was.

She wore clothing from a different place, perhaps even a different time.

Her hips were cloaked in buckskin, her waist accented by the soft creases of the flannel shirt, soft pliant flannel, with a makeshift seam where none had been a night ago. Somehow the danger represented by that seam made her presence here more daring, more enticing. Clothing. He wished he had more protection at this moment than the thin blanket covering him. Wished he wore his nubby sweater and the simple, stately sea jacket that would protect him from her eyes, from the way she was looking at him.

Beneath the covers his legs tightened imperceptibly. Would she sense that?

She said nothing, but merely dropped back to lean against the door and gaze at him, her mouth touched with the tiniest smile, her face wreathed by fine amber hairs that had escaped from the ribbon at the base of her neck. Lamplight turned her complexion to gold, and he felt pale by comparison. He hadn't imagined it to be this way, with him lying injured, so unattractive, so unmanly.

Were her eyes that color, or was it the lamplight? They held him rapt in their hazel orbs, almost golden—he mourned his failing to notice their color before. So much to regret, so little time to make up for it—

Then she licked her lower lip, only the tip of her tongue running from the corner of her mouth to the middle. A small sucking sound fell toward him. He felt as though he'd just been tasted.

He wanted to speak, to warn her off, but he couldn't move, had lost contact with his voice, had become suddenly enchanted beyond speech. Every muscle in his body tightened a little, just enough to prevent him from protesting as she reached up knowingly and pushed the door bolt shut with the side of her hand.

He was spellbound. Caught utterly in her indefatigable intent.

She'd been put off and put off and put off, and nothing, nothing would put her off one more time. His wound might bleed again, his bruises might darken, his voice might be found any moment and cry out a protest not to commit them to a future that was a sheer cliff before them, but nothing would stop her this time.

His ego jumped up and shouted. His maleness swelled, preventing him from resisting as she moved toward the bed. A jagged breath cut through him.

She lifted her hands to her breasts, her thumbs brushing past them with a tantalizing pause. Her fingers pulled at the strings of her newly mended flannel shirt, at the threads which held together the rip made by Maynard's knife, and she began pulling the stitches out, thread by thread, until her white breasts shone like half moons in the light.

Smoldering, the way she moved. Like the last weaving flickers of Great Point's beacon on the water just before he snuffed the light at dawn. She was smoke, slithering out of her buckskin. The cool room had become balmy.

With mind-boggling familiarity, even possession, he watched her take hold of the blankets at the end of his bed and lift them up until she found his feet. He knew she had found them partially because of the cool air washing up over them and partially because of the satisfied glimmer that came into her eyes. They were just feet, weren't they? Nothing to be proud of.

But her eyes reflected a kind of grandeur that made him want to get a second look at his feet, just to be sure they still looked as they always had looked. But then she did something that made him forget his feet.

She pushed the blankets up around his knees, then still farther, to his thighs and past them. With gentle force she began stroking. His body fell into her rhythm almost instantly, as though it were ordained to do so. Her strokes were tender but firm, as though she knew she ran the risk of hurting him if she was too rough.

Because of the blankets he couldn't see what she was doing. Not being able to see made his mind dissolve, because it was so much like a dream—a completely indulgent dream—and with that trick she took away the last of his control.

She slipped up onto the bed on her knees, never breaking the cadence of her strokes up his thighs, his sides, his stomach. From time to time she glanced at him, letting her eyes do the caressing, and she would give him a tiny smile of reassurance. When the time was right, she raised one leg and placed it over his, ignoring his little wince as their combined weight changed the shape of the mattress beneath them.

His hands clutched the edges of the bed, and he moaned a senseless syllable. Flattered and enchanted, his body became a panting bellows to the flame of this extraordinary woman.

Her gliding fingers traced the bandages around his ribs as though they had somehow become erotic, and her kindness toward his wounds blended with the succulent movements as her legs straddled him and she wordlessly asked for his response.

He'd had relations with other women before, professional women who knew what to do at every turn, whom nothing surprised, who would do anything, anywhere, anytime a man wanted it. Wasn't that supposed to be a man's ideal? Anything, anywhere, anytime? He'd had those kinds of passion, the passion of necessity, of frustration, of empty release. Those were fine enough for men to whom that was all. But hadn't it always seemed lonely? No matter that another human being had been present in his bed, stroking his body and calling it out, he had always been alone.

She wasn't like that. Her motions weren't so deliberate, so practiced at the "anything" parts. These were the motions of a woman who had loved a man, one man—loved him, not simply serviced him whenever he barked. She didn't know to do everything. There were some parts of his body that she seemed to avoid, but other parts which she adored as she moved against him.

That was it—the love. Was that the difference? Why she felt so good against him? Why she was such fantasy to him now? Because he loved her—?

His head slipped back onto the pillow, his shoulders pressing deep into the mattress. The pillow bunched up under his neck as he arched his back and gave himself to her movements. Even the pain in his torso became a signal of victory, adding to his heightened sensations.

Suddenly his body expanded and his mind exploded. His hands went off by themselves and cupped her breasts, drawing them toward him as the edges of flannel swabbed against them, a soft envelope protecting his caress. He could do nothing less than participate entirely as, in the golden glow of the single lantern, her movements ushered him on toward the reward. Over and over again knelled the confession: he loved her, he loved her, he loved her. . . .

When she awakened, lying at his side, she somehow knew he was already awake even though his face was turned away from her and she couldn't see his eyes.

Her fist was tucked up under her chin, and her chin was pressed lightly against the tip of his shoulder. She thought of last night. Of how flimsy her efforts had seemed at the beginning, when she'd slipped into this room, not knowing what she was going to do or say to him, and finally not being able to say anything at all. Finally being driven utterly by instinct and a silly feminine fear of rejection. If she'd spoken up, she knew he would've resisted her and she wouldn't have had the courage to touch him.

But he hadn't said anything, and she'd forced herself to stay quiet too, letting her hands do the talking. Were her fingers cold? Was that why he had flinched when she first pulled back the covers to reveal his strong legs? Was that why his calves had tightened as she stroked them? She vaguely remembered trying to give him a smile of confidence, and she wondered if that smile had seemed nervous. Had he been able to tell that she really didn't know all that well what she was doing, that she didn't have the experience of a dozen lovers at her beck and call? Had her simple ways, learned from one simple and generous husband, seemed old-fashioned to him?

He hadn't rejected her, though, and he hadn't seemed anything less than beguiled. So satisfying! To finally touch him and love him completely! Her whole body swelled with the memory of it as she lay beside him in the tincture of predawn light from the window. How gentle his touch had been, and somehow she didn't think it was only because of his injuries or because it hurt him to move at all. She had always imagined he would be gentle, simply because of his outward demeanor—always a thought before a word or a movement, always a contemplation, a worry, a consideration before a commitment—which was really why it was so very satisfying to entice him into being spontaneous. She breathed deeply and remembered the victory of his reactions when she moved her hands upon his body, when he gasped or moaned or bit his lip. Those little moments were medals for her, proving that she'd succeeded in making him forget all those worries that kept him from her before last night.

Although he couldn't possibly have gotten up and walked away from her last night, she knew even one word would have put her off. If he had simply murmured, "Don't." Anything would have shriveled her tenuous determination, because it had taken the whole walk over to convince herself to do this.

She had wondered as she stroked him if he noticed her nervousness at touching another man. There had been only one man in her life, an older gentleman who was strong and patient. She'd often wondered what a young man would be like—more curiosity than desire, because Lowell was everything she needed. But still there had been that curiosity, suddenly reawakened when she followed that irresistible magnetism out to Great Point. Now that youth had a name—Jake. She had wondered all along—would he thrash and grab and rake at her? Would she be able to enjoy frantic lovemaking as much as she had learned to enjoy the slow, methodical, sweet pace of Lowell Sutton?

But Jake hadn't grabbed at her. He hadn't clawed her arms or squeezed her breasts until they hurt, as she suspected a young man might. She smiled, remembering his palms cupping her breasts with only the slightest pressure, as though he wanted to feel the real shape of them rather than crush and mould them in his grip.

Because of his wounds she hadn't been able to lie down upon him as instinct told her to. She hadn't been able to feel his lips on hers. Everything had been done from below, very carefully. And that, in its way, had been tantalizing—the boundary of bandages. It left something for the future.

There was a slight hue in the sky now, though the land beneath it was still as dark as night.

His arm was no longer around her as she had expected it to be. She wondered if she had hurt him, then decided that some things are worth a little pain. His jaw moved slightly as his lips parted, and Abbey simply lay there, not moving, but with a tiny smile tugging at her lips, as she waited to hear what his first words after their first journey into passion would be. These were important little things, things the heart was made of, an embroidery of little moments.

Jake cleared his throat faintly. Abbey continued to wait, watching the silhouette of his face against the lamplight.

Finally, he spoke, softly and with just the kind of assurance she expected, his voice hovering over them like smoke.

"You've made a terrible mistake."

The words cut through her. She vaulted up on an elbow, ignoring how the abrupt movement might have hurt him.

"What?" she rasped. Her voice squeaked. "That's it? That's all you have to say to me?"

He turned to look at her now, gathering all his remaining strength to avoid staring at her breasts as they winked at him over the top of the covers. His head was clear now, not like last night, and it paraded regrets before him as he gazed at her. "You shouldn't have come back here. Certainly not . . ." He waved a hand in a self-conscious gesture. ". . . like you did."

"Well, isn't *that* charming," Abbey fumed, sitting up abruptly. "I expected no poetry, but *something*—"

"Abbey, I don't want you coming around me anymore."

She snapped a glare back upon him. "You men should form a brigade! Am I the only person on this island who knows what I want?"

Jake rubbed his face, a motion of fatigue, and insisted, 'I can't do my work with you about."

"Your work," she snarled, "is keeping a lighthouse. Which, I noted, is burning just fine tonight."

"My apprentice is tending it," he said, as though she had demanded explanation.

"Then what other work is there? I wish you'd say it."

"I've no intention of telling you more," he said flatly. "After what happened on South Wharf, you should see that you've already endangered yourself by coming around me. I don't know if that can be mended."

"Who asked that it be mended?"

He rubbed his face with his whole hand, trying to avoid looking at her because he knew how beautiful she would look to him at this moment. "I've let this go too far. My mind kept telling me to keep you away. Unfortunately . . . my mind isn't the boss." He sighed, drawing the blankets up around his hips, then over his ribs as though to secure the territory from further poaching. "And now this. Now you've given me a taste of what I can't allow myself to have. I can't even think with you around me anymore. And the secret's out that I can't. Now you're in danger, too. I've got friends who can get you safely to the mainland—"

"Is that so? How nice that you have friends." She yanked the covers back and slid off the bed, only to be caught fast by the wrist and pulled back around.

Jake glared at her, and there was an almost tangible chill running off him as he held her wrist with a power that hadn't been present the night before.

"Get it through your head," he said. His dark eyes were hard as nuggets. "You're not stupid. Don't act stupid. I'm a criminal, Abbey. I could end up dead any moment. The closer you are to me, the more danger you're in. You should know that by now. Things are becoming more and more treacherous. You're distracting me. I have to be ready to deal with them without worrying about you flying in to foul up the lines."

"The web, you mean," she spat back. "What are you involved in? I want to hear it from your own lips!"

"Abbey, I'm warning you—"

"Slaves! The reselling of escaped slaves. Despicable!"

She tore the top blanket off the bed and wrapped it around herself, then started circling the bed.

Jake's face paled. "How do you know about that?"

"As you pointed out, I'm not stupid. And I know about Thomas Pollock, too."

His eyes widened and his lips fell open. "How do you know?"

"Because he's the man who arranged for my husband and four other ranchers to be ambushed, that's how. He ran a ring of rustlers. When my husband and the others started fighting back, he had them killed. He killed my husband, Jake. He killed my husband."

Jake fell horribly silent, and she heard the pieces clicking together in his mind. When he spoke again, his voice was low, ominous. "Is that what you're on the island for?"

"No. I'd no idea he was here. It's pure providence. We never proved the rustling was Pollock's work, but all my shouting and accusations caused him to leave Wyoming Territory. I should've done more than accuse, but I didn't. Now providence has given me the chance to destroy him as I should have a year ago."

That statement put a flash of fear in his eyes. then he shut them quickly and pressed a hand over them. "Good lord almighty," he muttered. The bed sighed as he sank back into it.

"Jake, why would you deal with a man like Pollock?"

"I wouldn't. I refused to."

Abbey clutched the blanket around her. Her feet felt cold on the wooden floor. She squinted at him. "You refused? Why?"

"I don't know. I . . . just didn't like him. He offered us things that seemed too good. And he was smug about it, like he knew we couldn't turn him down. So I turned him down. That's why they wanted to get me out on the wharf. To convince me. With their fists."

"And Maynard's blade."

"Exactly my point," he said, sticking up a finger.

"Good thing I was there," she told him.

"If you hadn't been there, neither would I!"

"Wouldn't you?" Abbey let her eyes widen until they stung. "You think they wouldn't have come up with some other bait to get you there? Smarten up, Jake." The blanket swished around her feet as she moved to the bed and crawled up on the edge of it. "Jake, listen to me. We have the beginning of something good between us. This business you're in will put it to ruin. Get out of smuggling. Get out before it's over for us."

He turned his shoulders away from her. "It's already over, Abbey. I can't get out."

"Jake, this life of stealing . . . it's not for you. You're a better man than—"

"I'm a smuggler. I admit it. If I get caught, I'm going to prison for a long time. No sense your going with me."

"Are you afraid to stop?"

"I'm committed. I can't stop. If I tell you what's about, you'll be involved and I don't want you involved. You'll have to trust me."

She sat back on a folded leg and tried to threaten him with her tone. "Then we're finished. Trust isn't enough."

"Good," he clipped. "Then we'll finish what should never have been started. We've had our night of passion and we don't have to wonder anymore. It's time for common sense to take over."

He turned away from her, as far as his wounds would allow, and buried his face deep into the pillow. The gesture had a stinging finality about it.

Abbey saw clearly in the set of his shoulders and the coldness of his face that he meant what he had said. Whatever he was involved in, whatever profit he gleaned from it, and whatever insidious pleasure it gave him, it was more tantalizing to him than she was. That was the only answer she could find, for certainly it wasn't the resplendent life-style that kept him bootlegging. He didn't seem concerned for comforts and grandeur, so it must be the intrigue that held him, the conniving and trickery, the adventure. The art of slipping under the law.

As she gazed at the lamplight that lay on the ridge of his shoulder, she knew she couldn't compete with intrigue. She wasn't mysterious enough. All this time she'd been honest and blatant with him, hoping it would attract him, and that had been all wrong. It had gotten her one night, then rejection. She imagined quite clearly the kind of woman she would have to be in order to hold Jake Ross. She would have to be a shadowy thing, glancing at him from behind red velvet curtains or peeking seductively over a fan just before turning away and disappearing in a crowd. The type of woman a man wants to follow.

She wasn't that. She could never be that.

She'd never be mystery for him. Never be intrigue.

Abbey closed her lips, biting the lower one to keep it from quivering. Pulling her eyes from the buttery lamplight that fell on his shoulder, she gathered her clothing, drew the blanket tightly at her throat, pushed open the latch, and slipped out of the room.

With her she took all the promises.

Chapter Fourteen

RESPECT DIED A quick death. The chance of a future together withered from the blight. Some things live and thrive and some things die. Love is not enough. Passion falls despicably short. Desire lives between the legs. Alone it cannot cement a relationship. When respect died it killed both trust and hope, too.

There was an arm's-length easiness about walking away and never looking back, an ease that made Abbey nervous. A simmering doom settled around her shoulders like a cloak meant to soothe her from the cold, and somehow it did soothe her. Somehow her heart closed itself off from the pain and her mind accepted the death as though she were standing over a coffin, gazing at the sedate sleeping face of a departed friend. Some things, some living things, were indeed better off dead. Sometimes the pain they brought and the tension of their existence was simply harder to bear than the loss when they finally died.

Terrible, to think this way. Terrible for turning away to be so easy.

She found herself moving through her duties with the three Nash children as though she, too, had died and simply gone on moving. She managed to smile and laugh occasionally for the children's sake, to pour herself into them and play with them and lasso with them and actually forget for a few moments at a time, moments which were great relief. Whatever she did with the children and with Dominic or Lucy or Cordelia, those teatimes and dinners at the big table and even a picnic that Thursday under the Nantucket sun, all happened to someone else. A distant person, moving by rote and accepting a death. She recognized the feelings; she'd done it before, a year ago. She knew she would live through it.

Except that he was still walking around this island. No matter where she went or how deeply she poured herself into her activities, he was never more than a matter of minutes away. And that was the single thorn always under her clothing, pricking her. She could only walk so far before the ocean would stop her and gently turn her back, and if she turned back—which she always had to because of her obligations—she would invariably be facing Jake. She wouldn't see him through the streets and brick and cedar walls, but she sensed him there. Shopping in town or taking the children to school was annoying and nerve-racking because Abbey knew all she had to do was turn the wrong corner at the wrong moment and she would run into him.

How long had it been? Five days? Eight? Strange how she had lost track. He would be walking about by now. He wouldn't bother to hide himself away. The whole town knew what had happened, the whole island. It was that kind of place. And by now it was no secret that the new lady from the Continent had participated in this dockside brawl in some improper way.

She avoided going around corners. She often found herself walking right down the middle of the street. The children, of course, thought this was delightful.

Abbey found her frozen state of mind almost to be a relief. For the first time since she stepped off the ship and whipped that slaver, she could be numb. Fine, except that people around her noticed the death. Dominic was even more attentive in his uncomfortable way. Cordelia kept putting hot meals in front of Abbey in hope of thawing her. Lucy dragged her here and there to do this and that as though the roles were reversed and Abbey was the one in mourning.

Abbey conscientiously worked at letting them succeed at their efforts, at least outwardly. She fell into Lucy's clutches willingly and even started learning to mend the hats at the hat store because Lucy was desperate to keep her busy. She allowed Dominic to converse with her about dull island business. Which tax law applied to which element of sheepshearing, the island's first industry. Which ship had to be moved from its berth at the docks in order to build an extension to fit in four smaller ships. Progress on trying to get the federal government to construct a breakwater so that large whale ships could negotiate too-shallow Nantucket Harbor.

The time passed. Nine days? Twelve? Nights were hardest—dusk especially, when the beacon shone from Great Point. Like him, it was almost inescapable. And when she did manage to escape it, she found her loneliness had become a physical pain. Those moments just before falling asleep were pure torture.

And during the days, there was no sign of Pollock either. It was truly strange. As Abbey began to reawaken and think about it, why hadn't she encountered him? Her dramatic threat was good, but not *that* good. Thomas Pollock was a vengeful man, and she half expected him to appear the very next day after she torched his boat, kill her, and stuff her body under the boardwalk. He hadn't. Then again, he was also a practical kind of criminal. He didn't do things if they were too hard. There was always better pickings just over the hill, so why fight? That was why he'd left Wyoming. Leaving was easier than fighting uphill against the judge's raving widow, who wasn't about to let the county forget that he was at the bottom of the ambush.

Odd . . . to be enemies with a man with whom she had never exchanged more than fifty words. She'd never talked to Thomas Pollock at all. In pioneer territory it was always the men who did the trading and the talking. The women did the practical work, the men did the dealing and the buying and selling. She learned about Pollock only in hindsight, after Judge Sutton and the other ranchers were already dead and it was too late to warn them. Oh, she'd heard his name and had half listened, but not enough to bring him down, not enough to knock his knees out from under him and get him in jail or dangling. By the time her accusations began to make sense to the authorities, Pollock had smelled the scent of retribution on the wind and abandoned Wyoming.

By the time she spied him here in Nantucket, he was nothing more to her than a name, a face, and a crime. She had no idea what motivated him, what he wanted from life, or what kind of man it took to do the things he did.

He had tried to coerce Jake Ross into working with him. Coerce, entice, seduce . . . convince . . . Jake had refused. But had he refused because he saw more profit working with the competition? It was unthinkable. . . .

For something unthinkable, she thought about it a lot. A damned lot. Almost constantly. She thought of it from one angle, then again from another angle, then went over the previous angles again, reexamining the facts until her recurring thoughts made her nauseous each time they started up.

Gradually, by the hour, she found herself beginning to accept that she had no future with Jake. Her mind accepted it, her reason discovered it palatable. Her working from day to day became more fluid, and she was more likely to speak back when someone spoke to her instead of having to be called two or three times before she returned to reality. She was learning to survive without the possibility of winning the prize she had so diligently and so unrelentingly fought for, this man who mirrored her own visions.

But with acceptance, the life had gone out of her. She performed necessary duties dispassionately, only summoning up her enthusiasm for the sake of the children and almost only in front of them. Dominic didn't trouble her with questions, though she often felt his concerned gaze and his desire to help her. Cordelia was generally quiet, but tended to fuss about Abbey's comfort more.

Lucy wasn't quiet at all, though. In fact, she had nearly taken over the Nash household. Wilma played with the Nash children and with Dominic's mustache. The Nash children listened in rapture to Lucy's wacky accent telling stories about England—stories Lucy was obviously tapering down to their level. Abbey's sole pleasure came from listening to the stories and translating them into adult terms. What really happened, and how. These stories, properly interpreted, were nursery rhyme versions of events of questionable safety and no propriety at all. For a woman barely out of her teens, Lucy had a life worthy of several people's experience. Somehow even in the midst of her mourning, Lucy provided the greatest light in the house. Abbey would never again refer to her as a girl.

But there was always this clutching sense of loss. Lately Abbey was half the woman she'd been when she stepped off the ship from the mainland. She was less than the person who had taken up the whip, less by half. Less, and still hurting.

Sometimes her hurt was so terrible, it burned. It came to her in the night like a wraith, sat on her, and burned. Jake. Jake . . .

And the humiliation—that he loved her, yes, but not as much as smuggling. Probably that was the only thing that kept her from seeking him out, the true force that kept her away from corners, away from the docks, away from Great Point, and certainly away from The Brotherhood.

Dinnertime was a bit tense every day, but Abbey looked forward to it. Though she conversed somewhat less, usually only when she was asked a direct question, she enjoyed listening to Lucy's yammer and then watching Dominic's mouth turn up in a stern smile when Lucy said something entirely inappropriate. Then Dominic would regain control over his face and scold, "Madam, your language," and Lucy would throw a dinner roll at him. The children would dissolve into guffaws. This went on with alarming regularity, but somehow the regularity itself was a comfort to Abbey.

That was why the pain tripled when she herself had to admit that this couldn't go on, that she had to rupture the artificial peace she had crocheted and had been lying in.

She strode rather stiffly into Dominic's study one evening when he was still working on government documents.

Pausing involuntarily at the archway, Abbey hovered on her toes as though an invisible spiderweb was strung up against her and kept her from going into the room. Dominic was bent studiously over his desk, sitting in the filtered yellow glow from the frosted-glass hurricane lamp beside him. His curly red hair had a cast like polished copper. A pair of reading spectacles were balanced on the tip of his nose, and his brows were raised as he contemplated one of the thousand little problems in running the island. For many moments he didn't realize she was there. He turned a page, turned it back, pursed his lips, then affixed his signature to the document and went on to the next one.

Abbey was entranced. Dominic was such a bastion of common sense. He exuded order from every pore. He would never know the comfort and strength he gave her in these moments.

He blinked then, and his eyes lost their focus on the papers. After a beat, he looked toward her. He didn't glance or flinch, but looked right at her as though he knew she was there.

"Mrs. Sutton," he said, rising to his feet gallantly. "Abbey. Please . . . come in. You're not interrupting."

She pushed through the web. It popped around her, but she made it into the room. "Dominic, may I speak to you?"

"Why, of course." He gestured toward the velvet chair. "Please."

Abbey did sit down this time. By now she knew that standing or sitting, her announcement would be just as sour.

"Dominic," she began, though it sounded indecisive to repeat his name, "you're the kindest man in the world, I think."

A ruddy flush appeared on his cheeks, and his lips disappeared under the mustache. "Oh . . . not at all. But thank you. What brings this to the fore?"

Abbey lowered her eyes and fixed them on the rug beneath her feet. "You've let me come here to live, under conditions that do me nothing but good. You've let Lucy stay here with us just when she needed to have a family. . . . I don't know—you simply are a well of kindness."

"Abbey, please," he said. He strode across the room, hiding his mouth with his knuckles. "I must look like a tomato by now."

She looked up and smiled warmly. "You do. It's endearing."

He placed a hand on his hip and said, "Madam, I'm not supposed to be endearing. I'm conscientiously fostering a reputation for surliness."

Unable to accept his effort at levity, Abbey nodded as though he actually meant that. Solemnly she went on. "Regardless . . . all this only makes it difficult to say that I must leave Nantucket."

Dominic sank into the other chair, facing her. His hands came to a rest between his knees. "Leave?"

If only he wouldn't seem so much the little boy when he looked at her like that.

He spoke too softly to be referring to business when he said, "But our arrangement—"

"Will have to survive with some kind of alteration," Abbey finished smoothly. "I can't endure living on the island, not for as long as I'd planned. It simply isn't working out."

Dominic sat back in his chair. The velvet breathed as he settled against the upholstered heart-shaped back. "That Ross character," he said, almost a snarl.

"Yes," Abbey handed back. She lowered her eyes again, licked her lips, and nodded.

A grim sobriety fell over Dominic, and he was silent for a long time. Then he flatly said, "Abbey, the man is a villain. A highwayman."

"I know that!" she snapped.

"And you could still go with him?"

Gripping the sides of the chair seat, she leaned forward. "Go with him? Hardly. No, it's not that, for pity's sake, Dominic. It's that . . . it's that he's here and I'm here, and we both know it."

He slumped until his shoulder blades pushed back into the velvet. "Oh," he murmured. "Oh. Oh, I see. . . ."

Abbey gazed down, neither embarrassed nor expecting things to get better. "In fact," she said slowly, "I hope never to see him again."

There was a knock at the big front door. "I've got it," Cordelia's voice clipped through from the kitchen. Then, as though rematerializing from a different place altogether, she appeared near the front door through the hallway and opened the door.

Neither Abbey nor Dominic rose, but they both were silent, their conversation holding on through this moment of interruption.

"Thank you," they heard Cordelia say, and the door sighed shut.

She appeared at the parlor doorway and was holding an envelope.

Dominic stood up immediately and went toward her with his hand out, ready to take the message, but Cordelia gave him a pointed chin and said, "Not for you, sir, this time." She strode in and handed the envelope to Abbey.

Abbey glanced at each of them before actually taking the envelope. She couldn't imagine why she would be getting a message here. She murmured something polite at Cordelia and looked at the envelope. It was blank. She looked up as Cordelia was stepping past Dominic toward the dining room. "Cordelia—"

The housekeeper turned around. "Yes?"

"Who delivered this?"

"I didn't know the man, Abbey," she said. "A seaman."

She offered no other description of the messenger, leaving Abbey with nothing to do but look at the envelope.

Dominic hovered nearby until he realized she wasn't opening the letter. Finally he cleared his throat and muttered, "Yes . . . excuse me. We'll talk later." He made a quick gesture toward the note in her hand. "There's no need to be hasty, in any case."

"I'll go to my room," Abbey offered, but Dominic was already at the archway, on his way out.

"Not at all. Be my guest," he offered with a final wave of his hand before slipping out, a gesture that gave her the parlor and its privacy as a gift.

The envelope blurred before her eyes as she tore it open. There was nothing on it. It hadn't been officially mailed, but sent from someone nearby. Didn't take much guessing.

Now what did he want? Hadn't it all been said?

Even though she knew, she still flinched when she saw his name scrawled on the end of the message.

> Meet me. Pacific National Bank.
> By the north meridian stone.
> Nine o'clock.
>
> Jake

Some message. Fewer words than a common polite hello on the street. The instant her eyes touched the words, she considered not going, but she knew a second later that she would.

Dominic's words rang . . . no need to be hasty . . . no need to be hasty—

She had her shawl around her in two seconds. And may she be damned for it.

Outside, it was the first truly warm night of spring. There was no bite in the air at all, but only the cool, moist breath of the sea. The warmth of a sunny day still radiated from the ground. She didn't even need her shawl. It hung on her shoulders and flapped against her arms. She was walking too fast.

The bank was as dark as all of Nantucket, but there was something restless about it. It stood there, a huge brick building, just as stubbornly unintrusive in its own way as the ocean. At its side there was a conical limestone obelisk about the size of a gravestone, which was the marker of the north meridian line. Etched on the conical part was "1840," the year the stone had been erected, and on the main part was etched with typical Nantucket reserve, "Northern extremity of the Town's meridian line."

And he was there, standing right beside the stone. Leaning with one knee against it, in fact.

Abbey crushed her eyes closed for an instant as she rounded the corner and saw him, then forged forward so she didn't look as though she couldn't make up her mind. She couldn't, really, but that was beside the point. Impressions were everything now. She might buckle to her needs, but she would never let him see it. Never again. Appearing miserable would only swell the pain.

"Abbey," Jake breathed as she came up to him, and he reached out for her.

Just before he would have caught her shoulders in a gentle grip, Abbey stopped and backed away.

Jake lost his equilibrium and stumbled forward a step before catching himself. He closed his empty fists—a gesture very human, and very sad. Abbey couldn't resist gloating a little. Now he knew how it felt.

He pulled his hands back and stuffed them into his pockets—for the first time Abbey noticed he wasn't wearing his sea coat, only a loosely knitted sweater.

"How are you?" she asked him. Luckily her voice didn't clog up in her throat.

"Better," he said with a tip of his head.

"All better, or getting better?"

He smiled. "Getting. Matt insists it's the Colbert blood in me making me heal fast so I can get back to work."

Abbey folded her arms. "Work's a sore subject with us right now, Jake. At least yours is."

He closed his lips tightly and nodded, rocking on his heels. "I know." Briefly he studied the meridian stone, then looked up. "You saved my life, Abbey."

"Before or after almost getting you killed?"

Silence squirmed between them. When Jake couldn't bear it any longer—Abbey could see clearly that he couldn't—he stepped close to her, so close that she caught the scent of smoke from the pub clinging to him.

"Abbey, I'm leaving Nantucket."

She drew her shoulders in. "What? When?"

"Soon. I'm not certain of the day or time, but soon. It'll be sudden when it comes, I know that. Abbey—" He moved even closer, a lover's closeness now. "Abbey, I want you to come with me."

She turned her back on him. Perhaps it was overly dramatic, but it was what she had to do in order to keep from looking into his eyes—which would be her undoing.

"Go with you?" she murmured, tasting the prospect.

"Yes," he said, too quickly.

"Are you leaving Nantucket because of me? Does it have something to do with me, with us?"

There was a pause. "Yes," he said again, this time more slowly, his tone completely different. "Yes, it does. It's all about you now. Everything is you now. It's distracting me," he complained, but his complaint had a certain sweetness about it. He pushed his hand through his hair and strode away a few paces, taking a little of the pressure off her. "I can't stand to be without you anymore. Abbey—I love you."

I love you. I love you. I love you. . . .

Were the words echoing in her head from his saying them, or were they her own words hammering at her, trying to get out? For a fleeting moment Abbey wondered if he had really said them or if she simply wished him to say them so much that she was hearing things. But his eyes were still saying it, even in the deep blue night.

Before she could ask him to hear the words again, Abbey's ears caught a noise at the front of the bank. Both of them turned—and glimpsed a retreating form. Someone had obviously been hiding, watching them.

Abbey whirled. "Damn them again! It's *them* again! Those two! How dare he send those buffoons after me again!"

She strode toward the front of the bank, but Jake pulled her back before she had gone more than three steps.

"No, no. Forget them. Come this way." His hand was a tender, irresistible force as it cupped her elbow.

He led her across the street and between two darkened buildings, into a kind of an alcove. Inside the alcove was a door, and inside the door a room that was like a shed or a laundry area.

"Do you know all of Nantucket's holes, or only the best ones?" Abbey saucily commented.

She turned, and found the utter darkness unnerving, entrancing. She knew he was there, but she couldn't see him. In this complete blackness, with only her memory to offer any substance, Abbey rediscovered Jake as the quintessence of mystery. She thought of his tallow-blond hair and his contradictory brown eyes gazing at her through the darkness and seeing her body the same way she was seeing his. In the darkness they might as well both have been naked, for those were the images that popped into Abbey's mind—Jake standing there naked, the long muscles of his legs twitching with an endearing nervousness, the twitch of lust that made all lovers curious and hungry. In the darkness his arms were bare and strong, his chest plush with a few soft yellow curls—not too many. Just enough to finger. His buttocks flicked like his legs did, tightening in and out with little muscle tucks, making promises.

In the utter darkness there was also an utter silence. She almost spoke, almost called his name just to have the reassurance of hearing his voice. Soon there was a small movement, and a match flared. Just as the tiny flame settled down, Jake touched it to a candle, and a globe of gold light hung in the room. The tiny room was all wooden and very appealing. Here they were completely separated from the rest of humanity, perhaps even more than they had been way out at Great Point. At the lighthouse, Jake had many duties to perform. Here, he had only one.

He turned to face her. All expression of contempt slid from her features as she gazed at him, knowing his heart was pumping beneath the soft gold tuft, and that his legs were warm. There was absolutely no malice in his eyes, no risk whatsoever.

He held his hands out to her and he said nothing, made no entreaty at all, but merely let his eyes do his asking, and his hands as he reached out without moving closer. She moved to him.

Their lips, arms, their bellies, their thighs, all came together at the same instant. Abbey's eyes sank shut and she poured herself into him, heat to heat, moisture to moisture. They became lovers again, tugging and pushing at each other's clothing until fabric made way for flesh. Their garments bunched up around their waists and under their arms, and the glow of the candle caught the ivory dunes and beaches of their skin. Slowly Abbey began to rotate against Jake. Power built gradually, hanging on to the promise as much as to the fulfillment, and their velocity rose. Tiny sucking sounds from their own kisses drove them onward, their rapid breathing becoming gasps and moans. As Abbey pressed forward, bending her body deeper into his, Jake wrapped his arm against the small of her back and dipped her to the earthen floor. He came down on top of her, his knee spreading her legs in a single fluid motion.

She lay back, her head against the packed dirt, and despite the intensity of her pleasure as she gazed up at him in the dim candlelight, she couldn't will herself to smile.

She felt him rising against her leg and told herself it was all right, that it couldn't do them any more harm than they had already done to themselves. Jake's face was half in shadow, half in the candleglow. He took hold of her wrists and spread her arms out above her head until he was prone on top of her like a man diving from a cliff. One long study of her features, and he dropped his mouth to her throat.

The world fell away beneath her. Her head rolled back and she pressed up hard against him, her eyes falling shut again, this time squeezing tight at the burning of his mouth beneath her ear. The velocity that had paused now took up again with a raw new fury. The pressure of his weight and the rotation of his body provoked her, and she forgot everything that had led them to this moment. All she could feel or know now was the bubbling that rose in her thighs, the gasps that racked her throat, and the moans that poured from Jake as she writhed beneath him.

They hadn't had this kind of freedom before. The other time they had been ever so careful, so cautious of his wounds. But now his wounds were healed over enough to be forgotten despite the occasional wince. Even Jake, as he felt his body telling him he wasn't quite ready for this, seemed driven on harder every time the pain went through him. Or was he trying to prove something to her?

With each thrust he rocked her back and forth on the dirt floor, her shoulders rubbing the cool, dry earth, rubbing heat into it. The movement increased, driving Abbey backward, deeper into the vortex, and all her rationality fell away, bit by bit, fluttering around her and sparkling.

He stiffened once, twice, and a long breath wheezed from him. He was stargazing, his face tipped up toward the dark ceiling, his eyes closed, his mouth open, held there by the grip of passion.

Beneath him, she was an echo of him, pushing upward against his weight, lost in the achievement.

Another gushing breath, and he collapsed on top of her, his face nestled into her throat again, his lips plucking at her skin, playfully this time. Little nips of accomplishment.

She lay on the cool earth, her arms still sprawled beneath his at their sides, her face turned away from him.

After a moment, he raised his head. "Abbey?"

There was no response. Only a tinge of desolation following their marvelous moment.

Jake rolled over and sat up, gently pulling his sweater down over his bandaged torso. "Abbey? You did want to, didn't you? I didn't push it on you . . . did I?"

His uncertainty crushed her to the floor. She rolled over in the opposite direction and sat up with her back to him. One by one, she pushed the loops over the buttons of her bodice. She hadn't even noticed him undoing them, hadn't noticed her breasts falling free under his touch. There had been only sensation and fire.

"No," she said, meaning it. "You didn't. You're not one of them." She closed her mouth before the rest came out.

"Come with me, Abbey," he murmured into her ear. The words rode on a hot breath. "I can't live without you, but I can't stand making you live with danger, either. We can make a life somewhere else—"

"What's the matter with life here?" she whispered back, spreading her dress down over her legs.

Jake sat back abruptly.

"I'm trying to tell you! You're not much on listening, are you? Nantucket's too much in the center of trouble for me to keep you safe. Loving you puts me in danger and it puts you in danger. Like the other night. Someplace else . . . I can keep the danger away."

She turned to him now, feeling the night air sparkle in her eyes. "While you keep on with your smuggling?"

The truth came forward in his eyes, and he closed his mouth because the answer was so obvious. It embarrassed him, saddened him, Abbey could see that. But it didn't sadden him *enough*.

"What kind of life is that?" she said softly. "What would it be like for us? Whenever you bring me a present, would I have to wonder, did he steal it? Did someone die for this bauble?"

"I've never killed anyone in my life," he said, sounding injured. "I don't intend to start. Certainly not for any petty contraband."

Abbey sighed heavily. "You sing several songs," she told him. "All different."

He struck the ground with the flat of his hand. "You think you know all of it," he fumed.

"I know this," she told him, pushing her prerogative. "I know I despise you."

Perhaps not *him*, but this part of him. Yet she failed to make the distinction as they sat a foot apart on the cool ground. Jake glared at her for many long moments, battling with the emotions that flew around them in a swarm.

He dropped his eyes, reorganized his thoughts, and looked up at her.

"Abbey," Jake said slowly, almost a whisper. He held out his hands to her. "Come with me. I want you. Marry me. Come with me."

Without moving, without blinking, she let the request fall and rest before parting her lips to answer.

"If I go with you," she asked softly, "will you give me your word that you'll give up smuggling and never deal this way again?"

His brows came together slightly, his lips parting as though to speak the vow, but no sound came out. In the empty air before his lips was the soft glimmer of the answer he couldn't choke out.

Abbey caught the slightest spark of hope, but it was instantly smothered in his hesitation.

She gazed at him. "I thought so," she said.

A million troubles ran through her mind. And joy—the tremendous joy of what they had just shared—was scattered by a heavy reality. It was a simple, disastrous reality. The reality of what would happen on the day she became a liability to him again, as she was now. What honor is there in a man who admits he smuggles for a living and won't give it up? She drew her legs under her and got up before finishing what she had to say. Some things had to be said standing up.

She pulled her shawl back around her shoulders and closed it over her heart. Her crumbling heart.

"No," she said.

Chapter Fifteen

THE MAGISTRATE'S HOME was all alight. Lanterns burned in every window.

Abbey knew in her mind that it was too late for the children to be up and that their windows were dark with sleep, but somehow as she stood across the street, stalling, she saw the life light coming from their presence inside that warm family home.

If possible there was too much love in that home, and it had been hurting her. She knew that now. Envy, perhaps. Or perhaps something as simple as the quiet passion she sensed Dominic held for her. How gallant could a man be? To want a woman and keep his mouth shut about it because he wasn't sure if he was wanted back, because he knew she was drawn to another man, even if that other man was a criminal and the worst thing on earth for her to be drawn to.

Her body surged with memory of lying beneath him against the warm ground of evening. She'd lost track how many hours had gone by. She'd walked around the whole town once, and halfway around again before coming to stand across the street and gaze at the Nash house. There had been some comfort in the grind of her heels against the cobblestones and the sandy streets, and the constant tick of her steps falling away beneath her as she ran away from her thoughts. Over and over her own voice gonged in her mind. *No.*

Every possible scenario had gone through her mind. Marry Jake and become a thief; marry Dominic and let Jake slip into the past, grow old dreaming of the man who should have been her lover; follow him, find his contraband, and burn it like she'd burned Pollock's boat; tell him she—

That wasn't bad, that last one. The burning one.

She tilted her head and thought about it. Her lower lip pursed upward. Force him out of business. Force him to see what it would be like to be free of it.

Of course, smugglers weren't notoriously loyal to their associates. Jake's suppliers and "clients" wouldn't take kindly to their merchandise being burned. Jake could end up in bigger trouble than he was already in. Of course, he would be forced out of the business. And probably out of the country.

So what? What difference did it make where they lived as long as they lived together? Was it possible? Could their love be salvaged?

Jake obviously wanted it salvaged. And Abbey knew all her coldness had been a lie.

But there could never be a future until the past was put to rest. She thought about it.

She was still thinking when the front door of the Nash house clicked and wheezed open, and, surprise—Longhorn and Hunch came stumbling out the door with Dominic on their heels.

"I don't care what it takes! I want chains on him!" the magistrate roared, swinging his hands as though to brush the two men from his property.

"But we ain't got no proof," Longhorn contradicted.

"I'll worry about the proof," Dominic blasted. "You worry about doing what I pay you to do! Now where is he?"

"Hear tell he's at the tavern—"

"Get two more men and go after him!"

"We can do it."

"You can't do it by yourselves—you're too stupid!"

The two men took the front steps in a single leap and headed toward town in a hurry. Abbey ducked behind a tree as they came down the center of the street past her, close enough to hear Hunch mutter, "Dang. He *is* mad."

"Mad or not, he can presume trouble when he starts arrestin' folks without proper proof. Wonder what set him off?"

Their voices faded as Hunch simply shrugged. Abbey watched

them go. On the porch, Dominic stomped back inside, leaving the front door hanging open.

A sense of panic skittering across her shoulders, Abbey pushed herself away from the tree she'd been leaning on and headed toward the house. Voices came from the open door—Dominic, Lucy. Shouting.

"I'm putting a stop to this absurdity," Dominic raged. "I'm having him arrested just as I should have at the beginning!"

"I don' bleeve she'd do this," Lucy argued.

"Feel free to believe it. I'm not going to allow it."

"But if it's wot she wants—"

"She's going away with that blight! That bootlegger!"

"But it's 'er business, Nicky. Daresay, I'd run away wiv 'im too, if ee'd 'ave me, a bloke oo looks good as ee do. Does, I mean. If it's wot she wants—"

"Abbey doesn't know what she wants."

"She's a growed-up woman, Nicky. You got no right. No right a' awl."

Dominic's voice faded, then came back, as though he were pacing. "She lied. She *lied*. She lied because she knew I wouldn't approve."

Lucy instantly snapped, "She don't need your approval."

"My point is that she lied! He's already having that effect on her. Despicable . . . despicable!"

They both looked up when Abbey appeared like a ghost within the frame of the big front door. Dominic's cheeks flared with guilty color. Lucy tucked in her chin and bit her lip.

Abbey stood at the door, sternly silent, glaring at them, her eyes boring holes through the tension.

"How dare you," she whispered. Finally her eyes struck Dominic. "How dare you interfere."

The accusation came out as a simple statement, without the slightest tinge of wrath, but the power of it was in its plain truth and the depth of her indignation.

Dominic turned toward her, his shoulders pivoting beneath his red curls, his gaze already welded to her glare. He stepped toward her, but not too close. "It's for your own good, Abbey. This cannot go on. Not on my island. Not to you. You're too fine a woman—"

"What have you done? What are you doing to Jake?"

Dominic clutched the watch fob dangling from his waistcoat—why was he still dressed at this hour?—and tried to appear to be the absolute authority in this situation. "My men are hunting him down. We thought . . . we thought he'd taken you with him."

"You did, did you?" she struck back, her voice coming up out of the pit now. "Did it occur to you that I might make my own decision? Did it strike you that perhaps I could make a judgment?"

"Abbey . . ." Dominic struggled with an expression that was difficult for him. "Women in . . . in . . ."

"Love?" she said roundly.

He shook with frustration, his face flushing again. "It's difficult to make a clear-headed decision—all right! Pardon me, but I do care what happens to you. Pardon that, then. The man is going to end up in my jail, and I am going to extradite him to the Continent as soon as I make the proper connections. He's breaking a dozen federal import laws by doing business on Nantucket, and it's going to stop now. Tonight. If you want to be with him, you'll be a hanged man's wife. I, madam, have had enough of watching you do this to yourself."

His eyebrows went up in punctuation. He strode around Lucy, who was standing in the middle of the rug with her lip still tucked, and in spite of his words he gave the unmistakable impression of trying to hide.

"What about Jake?"

Dominic slashed his hand through the air. "The man is being arrested. That's final."

Abbey ripped her shawl from her shoulders and whipped it to the floor in consummate anger. Incoherent sailor's language fell from her mouth as she flashed one last hammering glare on him and spun from the room toward the front door.

After Abbey was gone, Dominic was about to sigh his relief and somehow endure his guilty feelings. He closed his eyes for a moment, and when he opened them, Lucy was just turning into the room. Her hands came up in tight balls and pressed into her hips. Her eyes flattened to wedges and her mouth was twisted up in anger. She raised a single needlelike finger and opened her mouth, drawing a breath from which would tumble the tongue-lashing of Dominic's life.

She had time. If Longhorn and Hunch obeyed Dominic's orders to gather other strong-arms before they went after Jake, then she had time.

Elias and Matthew Colbert were easy enough to corral in the pub's kitchen, and the pounding chanties from the main tavern room was enough to drown out their conversation to inappropriate ears. The two men actually backed up as Abbey stormed in upon them and demanded, "Where's Jake?"

"He's at the mill," Elias handed, as though the information had just been pressed out of him.

His brother immediately swatted him and said, "Curse your mouth."

Elias held a hand toward Abbey and said, "She's got a right to know."

"That ain't for us to decide."

"No, I'll do the deciding," Abbey told them roughly. She turned to leave, then twisted around. "What in the devil is he doing at the mill?"

"Just picking up some grain—" Elias began, but he drifted off at the look his brother gave him.

"Is he there now? Or on the way, or what?"

Matthew shrugged. "Oh, I'd presume likely that he's right there right now, ma'am."

"If he shows up here before I find him," she said, "tell him the magistrate's ordered his arrest. There are men out hunting for him, so tread carefully."

Matthew crushed his way between his brother and the cupboard to get to her as she reached the door. "You sure, ma'am?"

"As sure as if it were me. Now clear my way."

On the north side of the chandlery, the small grain mill was deceptively peaceful under the night sky.

She found Jake easily, too easily for his own safety. He was loading sacks of grain onto a tip cart that was attached to a sleeping donkey.

238

When Abbey approached out of nowhere, the donkey jolted and brayed.

"Abbey—" Jake blurted. Then he suddenly settled down. "What do you want?"

"Jake," she began, hoping the sound of his name on her lips would draw him to her over the gulf she'd dug between them, "you're in danger."

"As always," he drawled, heaving the grain sack he was carrying into the tip cart and heading back for another. "I presumed we discussed that to its death."

"But Dominic—Jake, please wait, will you?"

"I've no real wish to talk with you at this moment, truth be known."

He turned his back and strode into the granary, moonlight shining on hair that looked almost alabaster under the night sky.

She followed.

"How can you be so unconcerned? Men are tracking you down."

"What men?"

He didn't turn to face her, but kept on with his work, dragging another grain sack from the stack.

"Dominic's men."

"Those two oafs, you mean?"

"Those two oafs and—" She stepped up to him and pushed away the bag he was trying to lift. "This is no time to be hauling food to The Brotherhood. The order has been given for your arrest. Ignore it and you'll be sitting in jail, rotting."

The bag dropped heavily on top of the other bags as Jake gave it up. He stared into the pile of fat sacks, then looked at her. "My *arrest?* Why arrest me now? He's got no more or less reason to arrest me today than he did yesterday."

"It's the no-less part. He's decided to act upon the suspicions he already has about whatever it is you're up to, which, if you would tell me, at least I could help. Will you please stop walking away from me? I'm tired. It's been a terrible night."

"I don't want your help." His voice filtered back at her as he strode toward the granary door, carrying the sack. When he reached the door, though, he hugged the sack to his chest and pressed against the wall, pulling quickly out of the line of sight. "Get down!"

Abbey stooped to the dusty floor. The smell of dry wheat was oppressive. "Is it them?"

There was no answer from Jake, but from outside—a clatter of hooves and footsteps. Then Longhorn's voice. Ordering the granary to be searched.

Jake pressed tighter against the doorframe of the wide loading dock. He let the sack of grain slide down his body to the floor. With a quick motion, he ordered Abbey to get away from the middle of the floor. His face and hair were opalescent in the wedge of moonlight.

Keeping low, Abbey sneaked to the other end of the huge stack of grain bags and wedged herself between them and the side wall.

Several men were gathering outside to begin their manhunt.

She flinched when Jake dropped beside her and pushed her deeper into the tight space. The tall pile of grain bags cast a black shadow upon them.

"How did they know you were here?" she whispered.

"They have their informants, too," he breathed back, adding in accusation, "or maybe they followed you."

"That's a mean thought for you to have when I'm trying to help you."

"I thought you despised me."

"Don't you give me reason to? Oh, God . . . come here. Your hair's like the Great Point light. Here—" She pulled off her shawl, unfolded it, and draped it over both their heads. The shadows around them instantly deepened. They huddled together, damnably close, and the scents and sensations of Jake Ross again began to play upon Abbey. His nearness alone infected her. Close to him like this, she felt the way she had before, when she had been thin as paper in his arms, paper made of silk threads, its edges burned by his fingers. The memory had a cutting wonder.

Now there were footsteps on the loading dock. The searchers were coming into the granary. Her heartbeat quickened.

Longhorn was barking orders, mostly threats with the magistrate's name attached to them for effect. If they let Ross get away . . . if they botched it this time . . . the magistrate would this, the Magistrate would that. . . .

But Abbey only half listened. She was crushed up against Jake, smelling him, feeling him, sensing the connection that ran between them. They had moved through lust and into love without her even noticing the changes, and now the lust was returning to make the circle complete. It resonated within her, this playful, antic passion, this desire to be wholly indiscreet. In her mind she saw his nakedness and felt herself gliding over it, her curves colliding with his, rubbing and skimming with raw acceleration. His gentility, his easy strength hadn't been fabrications of her lusty imagination, and now as she remembered those things she wanted to experience them again. She wanted the forgetfulness and the soft utterances, the untethering of her sensual self as he made the moves only a man can make.

Blood-heat came up and broke out as a thin sweat on her skin. Her heart raced.

Longhorn and his men were spreading out slowly through the granary, a presence close enough to keep her and Jake crushed together in the tiny space between sacks and wall. Jake shifted against her, ever so slightly.

She tried not to breathe hard. Impossible—he was brushing her cheek with his lips. How could he know?

She turned her face toward him—or her face turned itself, she never would know which. Jake kissed her open lips until they quivered.

The shawl draped over their heads became like a private room, like bedcovers under which they suffered their need, awaiting the glorious spasms and the nerve-stirring strain as they obliged each other.

One by one the layers of rationality began to peel back, blinding Abbey to the decision she had made. Jake knew it. He carefully and slyly tampered with the reason she had used to shore herself up against these very feelings.

She pulled away from him, bumping the back wall with a noticeable thud.

"Stop," she breathed. "Stop."

She drew inside herself, holding the shawl over their heads like a tent, pressing her crooked elbows close to her ears and turning her face away from him. With every power of her being she blocked the physical tumult and kept it from getting through.

He stopped moving, and she knew he was gazing at her even through the blackness of their hiding place. His reedy breaths gradually subsided. A moment later, he shifted again.

"Fine," he murmured.

Longhorn was snapping to his men to reassemble now. A clatter of bootsteps on the granary's hollow floor, and the men gathered on the loading dock, empty-handed. Soon they were discussing where else to look. In their hurry, they hadn't even taken note of the donkey and the half-loaded tip cart. A moment later, they were stepping out into the street and dispersing in several directions.

Jake dragged Abbey's shawl off them. His features were pearly and appealing.

"I knew it," he mumbled. "I have to get to Elias and Matt. We've got to move tonight, if this kind of thing is going on."

"I'm going with you."

He looked at her. "No. There's no point to it. I know I'm having an effect on you, and frankly I'm insulted you'd fight it so hard and that you could win out. Makes its own answers for me." He stood up, hovering over her, and dropped the shawl into her arms. "I love you, Abbey. Remember that. Do or die, I love you." He stepped out of the shadow and into the moonlight that was cast on the wide granary floor. "But we've got no chance, things being what they are. I've got work to be done before dawn, and I can't spend time coddling you. By morning I'll be off Nantucket altogether, and you'll have nothing more to fight against. But just remember. Someday you'll be glad you can remember."

She would never know why she walked by The Brotherhood that night. It wasn't on her way home. It wasn't on her way anywhere. The feeling that something was bitterly unfinished clouded her reason and forced her to the far end of Steamboat Wharf. The sense of something unfinished churned in her stomach and bounced against her heart, and The Brotherhood was rattling so from inside that the whole block seemed jumpy. How late was it? What did it matter?

She was hollow. A hollow woman.

With hollow eyes, she watched the door.

Sailors came, sailors went. The movement of humanity. But she was hollow. Her purpose had walked away.

The evening chill became an intimate. It wrapped her inside her shawl and held her tight against the night's breast.

Until a familiar shape came out of that pub door, she was numb and haunting. Jake . . .

No—

Elias.

It was him, wasn't it? And not someone else of the same height? Yes . . . his gait was like Jake's, his build was like Jake's, his deliberate stride, his plain determination to simply walk to his destination without as much as a glance in any other direction. She had seen Jake walk like that. Head tilted down, eyes forward, resolute. And where there was the cousin, there was eventually Jake.

Abbey hung back in the shadows, and as she stood there, her sense of purpose rejoined her. Dominic's men might fail to find Jake, but she was willing to use stealth to get to the bottom of all this.

Half her conscience wanted to let him take his due punishment and put the smuggling into the past. The other half, though, was the one in control.

Elias had come out of The Brotherhood alone. He glanced about to be sure no one was watching him, then immediately turned left and was walking toward Steamboat Wharf. Toward the docks. What business Elias could have at the docks was anyone's guess, and Abbey was quite ready to speculate. Nefarious answers skittered around her ankles, biting.

She stepped off the clapboard sidewalk and headed down the street toward Steamboat Wharf after him.

Elias had fallen into shadow. All she had left was a strange ability to sense he was there.

Her footsteps clattered, and she held back, afraid he would hear and turn to see her following him. There really wasn't anywhere to hide on this street.

A movement in a shadowed doorway, a door out of nowhere and leading to nothing, made her duck back. She waited.

It was Jake. For a man being hunted in the night, he hadn't wandered far.

He came to Elias's side, and Elias didn't even break his pace. Jake fell into a stride beside his cousin. Together, the two men strode toward Steamboat Wharf.

Abbey held back and crept along the moon-bathed cedar storefronts. The bait shop, the cooper, the wheelwright . . . little closed shops whose windows held signs proclaiming their hours of business. She hid in the doorways, peeking out at the forms of Jake and his cousin.

Elias had picked up his pace, gained a purposeful stride. She was losing them.

She hiked her skirt up and dashed to the next doorway. Trying to keep control of her breathing, she peeked out—and the street was empty.

"Damn!" she cried, and stepped out to follow. But there was nothing left to follow.

Well, that was absurd! How could they be *gone?* There simply wasn't anywhere to *go.* All the shops were closed, and as far as Abbey knew Elias had neither keys nor reasons to get into any of them. Of course, any reasons Jake or his cousins had for doing what they did had become unclear to her lately.

What business did she have trying to decipher Jake's reasoning when she couldn't even translate the hammering of her own thoughts? Jake was right the first time—they'd had their night. They'd spent the awful need and set it aside. Yet her heart still thrummed his name again and again, over and over.

The shoreline washed up under the docks with a sedate swish. Damn the sea. It didn't care. For eons past it had caused lovers to love and sailors to sail, yet it tossed their desires into its maw and covered them over with brine just as heartlessly as it drew them to it. There was no justice where the sea was concerned.

Under the docks, soft muck-rimmed waves brushed up against a lace of shore rocks and spiky grasses. Jake and Elias were nowhere. Impossible.

Abbey craned her neck from a hiding place across the square. She scanned the docks as far as she could see out across the ship-crowded harbor. Perhaps they had gone out to a ship. Her shoulders drew in and she shivered as she forced down thoughts about Jake's business aboard ships and boats that slipped in and out with the silent tide. How disgusting, unthinkable, sickening that Jake Ross could be a criminal and like it.

But he didn't like it. She knew him at least that well. He didn't. His voice said he couldn't get out of it—not wouldn't. Couldn't. His eyes said he wanted to be rid of the crime in his life. She believed him when he spoke about the grand idea of the United States. But when he spoke about wanting to stay a smuggler, she knew he lied.

He lies.

"I know all about lies," she heard herself speak aloud to that unapologetic sea. "I know about lies, because I've heard all the truths the world has to offer and I can tell the difference. Where are you, Jake? Where in perdition are you?"

She squinted so hard that her eyes hurt.

The harbor remained silent, motionless.

Something inside told her that if she could just find out what he and the Colberts were up to, specifically what they were smuggling and how, then she could gain a weapon to use in collusion with Jake's conscience. She could talk him out of it, bully him into quitting as he really wanted to do but for some reason couldn't. He wasn't given to indecision. Despite how much he had resisted her in the beginning he had finally succumbed. This wasn't a matter of not being able to decide; something else was holding him to his nefarious commitments. Discover it, and she would have the high hand she needed to speak to him.

A chill took her shoulders. It would be like speaking to a stranger. The past days had driven a wedge between them as surely as a stake through the heart of an immortal demon to make it mortal and kill it. Was their chance of love dead now?

The idea of talking to Jake became as alien and cold as distant ice caps. Abbey folded her arms and shivered at the notion. She had gotten herself on a tightrope and now stood quaking at its center. Going back was as scary as going forward, and just as dangerous. Perhaps more dangerous.

There was only forward. Her feet were like bricks as she crossed the square.

There was a steep, short embankment leading from the street to the actual sea level beneath the dock. The main dock here was tall and massive, big enough to harbor huge sailing vessels, high enough over the water for a rowboat with people inside to easily pass under. Was that how he did it? Funneling his contraband back and forth to ships from the shoreline by going under the docks?

No matter the intrigue of the idea, Abbey knew it was silly. There would be no point to it. Small supply boats came and went all the time, all across the harbor. Dinghs and catboats ran almost constantly from dawn to twilight and no one thought a thing of it. Jake's contraband could be shuttled anywhere on open water without a glance from anyone.

Abbey sighed, staring down the embankment. There seemed to be no alternative.

She lowered herself to the edge, put one leg over, and started to slip down.

The rough, stony bank scraped her skirt up her thigh, and only her laced-up boots offered any protection after her bloomers were tugged up, too. Bare leg touched the cold stones, and she flinched. Her arm was hooked over the top of the embankment, but there was really nothing to hold on to once her feet skidded onto wet rocks and lost their hold. She inhaled sharply, felt herself slipping, then held her breath and tried to keep control over her slide down the short bank. Stony shore junk scraped her shoulder blades as the ocean sucked her down to its edge. Her head bumped once, but other than that she found herself landing hard on her backside at the bottom of the bank without too many bruises. Her skirt immediately soaked up half the ocean.

The underdock was yeasty and green. As she got to her feet and the sea water flowed out of her clothing, her skirt was decorated with a squiggly line of green suds. She looked down at herself and her lips curled back.

"Better be worth this," she mumbled, enjoying her victimless threat.

Her head snapped up. Something—a sound, a breath—had alerted her senses even before she realized it.

She dipped low and huddled against the embankment. There was no time to get to the dock supports, so she had to do her best to hide in spite of the moonlight. The best she could do was be still and hope no one noticed.

No one—yes, there was someone there, moving against the underside of the docks. And she was hearing voices now.

Jake's voice.

She pressed close to the embankment, wishing the moon would go behind a cloud.

Then she saw him, dipping his head and coming out from underneath the docks not twenty-five feet from her. A moment later, Elias came out just as Jake straightened up. Elias was pushing against something. A door.

A door? Into what, a cellar? A door under the docks, in a place where nothing could seal well enough to keep the sea from encroaching at its very edges.

Contraband. Probably stored in crates. So this was his cache.

She had to know.

Jake and Elias were talking, but so low that Abbey couldn't hear their words. Deliberately low, almost whispering. Elias fought to get the wooden hatch to shut over the opening, which was slanted to conform to the embankment. After a few moments of watching him struggle, Jake pulled his hands from his pockets and stooped back under the dock to help press the door shut. Under their combined weight the hatch finally shut, and they came out together, still whispering.

Abbey watched with curiosity as Elias gestured upward and helped Jake climb up the embankment at a point where the dock pilings went into the sand. Only then did Abbey notice Jake was still moving stiffly and favoring his ribs. He tried to keep from leaning on them, but that was almost impossible, and he had to pause for breath while Elias supported him from underneath. Then he spoke a single word to his cousin and Elias shoved him up the rest of the way. He rolled onto his side, paused only a moment, then reached back down for Elias. Elias declined, and Jake immediately barked, "The hand, will you?"

Elias hesitated, then took the proffered grip and let Jake help him up the embankment. The effort took its toll, though, because Elias had to lift Jake to his feet. After a moment, they shared some joke or other that made them chuckle and started off back up the street together.

The family resemblance was even more pronounced in the dark of night than when they were together under the midday sun. At this late hour, under the milky moon, with only their silhouettes showing on the buildings, the two men looked more like one man walking beside a mirror. Their height was almost the same, their stride the same length, their bodies had the same kind of lopsided sway, and coincidence had made them step off on the same foot so their paces were matched. Each had his hands in his pockets, each wore a sea coat, and under the coat, each pair of legs looked particularly lanky tonight. Double vision. For a moment Abbey actually closed her eyes and opened them again, just to make sure.

Abbey waited.

Gradually, the men's voices faded and winked out.

She started toward that slanted hatch. She stumbled twice, a forced reminder of how dark it really was in spite of the moonlight. But soon a flat hatch of very old wood spread itself beneath her hands. It was knotty and roughly hewn and had never seen polish or oil, judging from the planks. They were separating from each other in places and had weathered to oyster gray. The texture was more like uncut bark than woodwork. And it was warped—that must have been why Elias had such a hard time getting it closed.

Abbey rubbed her palms together to bring blood back into her chilled fingers, then felt around for a latch or a handle. Surprisingly, she actually found one. Perhaps things were going to start getting better for her.

Betting on the "perhaps" part, she pressed her left hand onto the stony bank beside the door, flattened her feet in the mushy sand below, and got a good grip on the handle. Two deep breaths, and she tugged.

Nothing.

She tugged harder. Still nothing. She put her foot up on the bank where her hand had been and used both hands to hold the handle and pull—

The door squawked—and rasped open so suddenly that Abbey went flying backward. A short yelp escaped from her throat, just before she landed on her sore backside in a foot and a half of seawater.

"Aaaack!" she howled. Cold seawater seeped up her dress jacket and clung to her skin. She sat there for a terrible moment, unable to move, her knees stuck up over the water and her skirt swirling around her idiotically.

Well, curse it! Elias had had a tough enough time getting it closed; the least it could do was open a little less easily than this!

The hinges creaked; the door wobbled before her, pushed in and out by the moving water. Beyond it there was a tunnel.

Dragging her soaked skirt and petticoat, Abbey struggled to her feet in the water. The smell was dizzying here; scum and foam and brine. And now, wet soil stinking from inside that tunnel. She moved toward it.

Go in, her curiosity told her.

"All right, all right, I'm going. . . ." she muttered aloud. "Don't hurry me."

She put her hand inside the tunnel and felt the wall. She didn't want it caving in on her like some old mine shaft. Her fingers chilled instantly at the sensation of grit. A mixture of sand and soil, mostly sand, and just enough rock to give it support. No, that wasn't rock—it was brick. Part of the buildings above. Substructure, man-made. Foundation. Above her head, there was more brick, chipped and violated by portions of sand. She stepped inside. She went forward.

Blackness closed in. The moonlight refused to follow. It was ghastly. The walls dripped, weeping. Soil and brick, like in a crypt. It was like a mine, but it had a sense of the unfinished, the aban-doned. Even a mine shaft had support rafters. But this was just a hole. Abbey wasn't even sure it was squared off at the top, because she couldn't see anymore—which was the real horror—the open-eyed blindness.

She went about the first twenty feet or so without incident, carried only by her determination. Then the floor began to tilt downward and noticeably to the right. Not a turn—a tilt. When she first felt it slip away beneath her feet, her arms flailed out-ward, and she stopped breathing for an instant, desperately try-ing to tame visions of herself plunging down some sudden abyss. With one foot she toed the ground in front of her. Although soft and disgusting to walk on, it was still solid. She felt her way along the pitch black passage, her steps getting smaller and smaller, along with her courage.

Above, she heard muffled sounds—from living quarters behind and above the shops. Their sounds funneled down at her through vibrations in the brick and wood. Footsteps on wooden floors, voices like ghost voices, the clank of someone dropping a skillet, the thumping music she recognized as coming from The Brotherhood all the way at the end of the street. All that way, and somehow the sound still filtered through, if faintly.

But these sounds—this was horrifying to her. Layered over them was the click of insects and the drip of runoff, and over those was the rank underground smell of moisture and decay. It was like lying in her grave and hearing the realm of the living, just beyond reach, just beyond the layer of soil that bound her to the earth.

Abbey drew a breath, but it came out as a gasp. Something was sitting on her chest, a weight like all that soil. Buried alive—

Wheezing now, she spun around and stumbled back the way she'd come, abominated by the fact that she couldn't see any better going out than going in—something she hadn't counted on.

Was she heading in the right direction? Had she mistakenly gone down a wrong shaft, one she hadn't known was there? Was this a maze? Where was the opening? Had she really come this far into the tunnel already?

The smell of the ocean struck her exactly when she saw the faint gray outline of the shaft door. She heard the sea licking on the stones and let out a cry of relief as she staggered out and fell to her knees on the rocks on shore. She scooped up handfuls of seawater and splashed them on her face.

Behind her, the shaft opening hung wide like the mouth of a serpent, frozen in a hideous gape. A shiver went through her as though someone were actually shaking her. She felt the tunnel breathe on her, its cold wheeze engulfing her lower back as she bent over the water.

Rage took over. She clawed up a soggy handful of shore junk. Spinning around, she hurled the scum into the tunnel's mouth. A choking roar of anger came out of her just before she heard the handful smack the wet inner wall.

"No empty hole beats me," she vowed, gathering her legs under herself and standing up. "I'm going in. You'll tell me your secrets, or I'll choke them out of you. Or out of Jake. One of you. Just wait."

Chapter Sixteen

"ABBEY? WHAT ARE you doing?"

"Go back to bed, Cordelia."

"Why, it's nigh onto two in the morning."

"I know that."

"What are you doing with the garden lantern?"

"Lighting it."

Cordelia closed her night robe around her and drew her shoulders in as she crossed the cold kitchen floor. "I can see that. But why?"

"Where's Dominic?" Abbey pushed a strand of hair out of her face.

"He's retired by now. What happened to your skirt? And your arms are covered with mud—"

"It's sand. Wet sand. Your damned ocean."

Cordelia palmed Abbey's back and said, "You're soaking wet. Where've you been?"

"Prowling the shoreline, under the docks. Where do most ranchers' wives spend their evenings?" For the third time, the lantern refused to take the match. She was doing something wrong, but was too flustered to calm down and correct it.

Taking the matches from Abbey's hand, Cordelia pushed her gently back, cranked up the wick, tipped the lantern to moisten the wick, then successfully lit it and replaced the glass globe. "There. Now are you going to tell me where you're going?"

Abbey sealed her lips. Talking about it would only complicate things.

Cordelia broke every personal habit of her own decorum and gripped Abbey's arm, rather tightly. "What did you find there?"

Only a long breath allowed Abbey to steady herself and realize that Cordelia wasn't to be fooled, that she needn't be alone in this, at least in the knowledge of it.

"A tunnel," she murmured. She looked up into Cordelia's coal-black eyes and said, "Would you believe it? A tunnel! A mine shaft or something."

Ominously the housekeeper told her, "There are no mines on Nantucket."

"Well, there's certainly a good imitation of one! Right under the houses on Steamboat Wharf."

Closing her hand over her mouth, Cordelia tightened her features. "Tell me!" she whispered. "I wonder what it's for. . . ."

"I wonder, too! Excuse me." Dragging the heavy lantern, Abbey nudged the back door open with one foot and stepped past Cordelia.

"Wait—" Cordelia called, diving for her work shoes, which she kept at the kitchen hearth. "You're not going alone this time."

Abbey swung around, loathing the hesitation. "No, Cordelia, please stay here."

"No, no, I'm coming. If you're going, so am I. Two are as good as one, and better." While she talked she pushed her bare feet into the shoes and dragged a cooking smock over her nightclothes.

"You're not even dressed," Abbey pointed out.

"And you're soaking wet. Neither of us is prepared to go out, but here we go."

She buttoned the smock furiously, breathing rapidly, not blinking at all, seeming actually enthusiastic about having an adventure.

Abbey gazed at her quizzically, then cocked her hip. "I declare, Cordelia, at times I hardly know you."

Cordelia smiled her minimal smile and pulled the back door shut. "And you thought Lucy Edmonds was the only one who could manage a surprise. Off we go!"

The tunnel was, if possible, worse by lanternlight than it was in pitch dark. Now, on top of feeling and smelling, Abbey could also see the nauseating saturated walls of muddy brick and see the insects and worms sliding in and out of cracks. And she'd actually been touching it before! It was an awful thought. Crawly awful.

Abbey led the way, holding the lantern out before her with both arms. If she'd had her wits about her, she'd have brought a less utilitarian lantern, one of the small ones meant for carrying. This one cast a broad glow down the tunnel, but it was heavy and its weight made it hard to hold. The glow wobbled every time Abbey took a step.

"This is more gruesome than I ever imagined," she muttered, holding the lantern high and squinting into its glow.

"Aye, it could use a coat of paint and a sweeping," Cordelia said. Her voice had a lilt to it, despite the fact that she pressed up against Abbey's left shoulder rather tightly, so tightly that Abbey was being pushed forward faster than she wanted to go. "Keep on going. Every tunnel with a beginning is a tunnel with an end."

"You're being uncommonly stout about all this, I must say," Abbey said to her. "Not everyone would follow a lunatic down a hellhole."

"True enough," Cordelia told her, "but I suppose there can't be anything more ugly down here than I've seen lurking in some of the corners I've dusted in my time."

Abbey chuckled nervously. "And I wish we'd brought your hearth poker. I've a feeling we'll need something to strike with before this is over."

"Or a good round skillet. Fancy a kitchen cupboard being such an arsenal."

"Shhh—I hear voices," Abbey blurted, halting.

"I hear them, too. From overhead. People walking and talking in the houses up there." Cordelia swiveled her face upward. "Wager they don't know what's under their houses any more than we do. Funny, doesn't it seem?"

"I'll laugh later, if you don't mind," Abbey drawled. Then she turned her head and whispered harshly, "No, listen! That's not what I hear! I hear voices from in front of us. I'm sure of it. Listen. . . ."

They stopped moving, bothered by the swinging lantern. Its disregarding light wobbled on shiny tunnel walls.

"Yes," Cordelia whispered. "Yes, I hear them . . . you're very right."

Abbey's eyes scanned the darkness up ahead. "Cordelia, look! There's a light!" she whispered harshly.

The two women stopped in their mushy tracks. Sure enough, twenty yards or so ahead of them there was indeed a light showing which had nothing to do with their lantern.

Abbey hovered there, not wanting to take another step, unsure about what to do next. Finally Cordelia said, "Are you not going on?"

Abbey bit her lip. "We should've brought a weapon or something. We've no idea what's there. Or who. And I tell you there are people on this island we don't want to confront head-on." She turned her head toward Cordelia, taking care not to make the lantern wobble and attract attention. "I understand if you want to turn back."

Cordelia barely let her get the words out. "No need on account of me. Might as well cook the whole pie, mightn't we?"

Strengthened by her companion's resolve, Abbey set her lips, nodded, and pushed forward through the wet grit. "Let's see what Nantucket hides."

The twenty-some yards went quickly. Too quickly, Abbey thought. She knew it was only her imagination that an inexorable arm was pulling her deeper toward the unknown light while Cordelia's presence close behind her seemed to be pushing her in that direction, but she couldn't gain control over the draw.

As they came close to the opening they saw it was a child-sized doorway. The quavering glow of firelight played at their feet. Within, there was light.

And whispers. Then, silence.

The two women stooped down. Abbey's knees barely held her. She was trembling as she lowered herself and the lantern.

There was a room, and in its center a stout iron stove. The stove's door was open, letting the fire flicker out.

Abbey stopped breathing. Over her head the pounding of grog mugs and the storm of music thudding from The Brotherhood made the tunnel quake. Would the noise protect her, or be her undoing? Taking a deep breath, she looked inside.

The faces that greeted her were as unmoving as if they were painted on the wall. An antediluvian scene. A mural of a foreign place, etched and carved into the wall. Young faces, shiny and out of context, the color of Jake's eyes.

The women's heads were rows of tight braids, ink black. Or wrapped in some kind of turbaned cloth. The men—hardly older than sapling trees—wore tattered shirts whose tails hung from beneath heavy woollen sweaters. The women—they were young, too—clutched tiny children, at least two to each woman. One woman had four children clustered around her. Tiny faces gathered like acorns around a tree stem.

"Oh, dear God!" Abbey gushed, nearly falling through the opening. Her skirt dragged beneath her knees as she crawled in, leaving the lantern behind in the tunnel.

The people clutched each other tighter and pressed closer against the walls, as though trying to push through the sod and get away from her.

"Oh, God," she stammered again, lurching to her feet and standing in the midst of them like a white queen. Or a devil, judging from the way they were looking at her. She circled the room, making a small, senseless pattern in the dirt—no, it wasn't dirt at all. She looked down. Rugs. No, pelts. Sheepskin pelts butted up against each other all over the floor to cushion their sore feet. Her circling had knocked the edges up to curl over themselves like burned paper.

On one side of the room there were a few cots, the kind that stack on top of one another like bunks, probably for the children since they didn't appear sturdy enough for adults. In fact there were two bundles on them that looked like sleeping babies. Stacked on one of the cots were folded woollen blankets. Nearby was a basket, a big one, brimming with miniature ships, tiny horses carved from ivory and wood, rag and husk dolls, and a miniature wagon well enough crafted that the wheels turned.

The room was a rectangular one shaped roughly like the main area of the pub above it. Two of the walls were dirt, and two brick. In one brick wall was a small dumbwaiter, no doubt leading up to Matthew's kitchen. Perfect—food delivered without arousing suspicion.

Her hands flopped down against her skirt. Her shoulders fell. "Oh, Cordelia . . . look at them."

"I see them," Cordelia's voice threaded through the little door, though in the odd light her face was mostly hidden. She made no move to come into the hideaway.

Abbey turned around in place, then around again, absorbing each terrified face, her palms flattened against her skirt. "Don't be afraid," she said gently. "How long have you been here?"

They refused to speak. The children pressed into the heavy breasts and skirts of the young women or hid behind the young men. No one would answer.

"You were in the jail, weren't you? Some of you," Abbey said. "I know you were," she added, pointing at the young slave she herself had protected from a beating that first day on the wharf. "And you . . . and you . . . but not all of you. Not these children. Have you been hidden down here all this time, or longer?" Her tone must have intimidated them, because they cowered, pressed up against the wall like sticks inside a spinning bucket, and no one would speak to her. Some of them stared at the short door and Cordelia.

"Why don't you come in?" Abbey called then. "You're making them nervous."

Cordelia paused, then her skirt moved, which was all that could be seen for now. One glance had evidently been enough for her. "No, I'm happy here, thank you. Conduct your business. I'll just keep an ear out."

Abbey turned to what appeared to be the oldest of the young men and asked, "Do you know of a man named Pollock? I think he was going to transport you. He was going to resell you, did you know that?"

Wide black eyes widened still more, and each face in the room that was old enough to understand instantly matted over with horror. If Negroes could pale, these were very frightened people. Obviously they hadn't known what was going on.

"Oh, poor Jake," she whispered.

"Pardon?" Cordelia's voice filtered from the tunnel.

Abbey sighed and shook her head. "He saw me beating on that slaver and he knew I'd get myself into this if he told me about it. He's right, too, I would have. And I'd probably do something rash just because I do things like that. Poor Jake . . . God, I love that fellow. Even I didn't know how much until this moment."

"For running slaves, you love him?" Cordelia's disembodied voice asked.

"For shielding them. Look here." Abbey fanned her arms around the room. "A fire for warmth, food stacked in the corners, sheeps' pelts on the floor instead of bare dirt . . . toys for the children every bit as fine as the ones Luella plays with . . . they're wearing sweaters over their rags . . . heavy shawls . . . and none of these people has a shackle on. They could have walked down that tunnel and out the hatch at any time. He's not holding these people. He's protecting them."

"So kindhearted," came the muffled comment.

Abbey gave a short ironic laugh. "Yes. He refused to deal with Pollock, but he couldn't seek Dominic's help, could he? Even in concealing these people, he's still breaking federal laws regarding runaway slaves. Pollock tried to trick him by promising to transport them. When Jake saw through his plan, Pollock tried to beat their location out of him. Just imagine it. Imagine it!"

"I can," Cordelia's voice muttered formlessly. "But I wonder why they didn't simply leave them in jail until they were ready to take them off the island. No one would have noticed, then."

"Oh, Cordelia, they're not just doing a job. They're on a quest, don't you see? The jail is cold and damp. The children would have become sick, perhaps died."

"No one in Nantucket would let children die, even in jail. Mostly we let our convicts go home at night, even." She paused. "Not escaped slaves, of course."

"Oh, of *course*. They're crime is unforgivable, this wanting to be self-governing. Such a dangerous notion, I'd want them off the street!"

She looked around at the dark faces that understood only the surface meaning of her words and none of her sarcastic tone. She clamped her lips tight and tucked them in, biting them to keep herself quiet.

"Abbey," Cordelia softly called, "if you don't mind, I'll slip back topside. The mustiness is making me nauseous. Should I meet you out on the street?"

Abbey smiled at Cordelia's unstoppable politeness. "Of course. And take the lantern, Cordelia," she said.

"No, thank you. I'll leave it for you. The way out is easy enough. I'll be waiting."

Abbey turned back to the slaves. "Do any of you know what's been going on? Tell me if you do, because I'm here to help you. You must be gotten off the island as soon as possible. As long as Thomas Pollock knows you're here somewhere, he'll never give up trying to find you." She pressed her hand to her head and imagined the weeks they had spent living cooped up like this. "Sakes, you must be going stir-crazy! Where was Mr. Ross going to move you to? Do you know?"

A small boy brightened, and before his young mother could pull him back he stepped forward, blurting, "Canada."

He bounced into his mother's heavy skirts as she pulled him against her.

"It's all right," Abbey told the terrified girl. "I'm going to make sure that Canada is where you end up if I have to sail you there myself."

Something in her voice must have spoken her conviction more eloquently than her words could, because the young teenaged buck she'd saved on the wharf suddenly bolted from his place at the wall, stooped to peek into the tunnel for some reason, then straightened up and hurried back toward Abbey. Nervously he wiped his hands on his battered trousers.

"Missy . . . missy, I gots to tell yawl somethin. Yawl gots t'know!"

"What is it?" Abbey asked.

"Dat lady . . . dat lady out yonder . . . she no good, missy. She no good!"

Abbey slammed her fists into her sides and demanded, "Oh, now, what are you talking about? She's our housekeeper."

"No, missy, she ain't no housekeeper. I dun saw her in No'th Ca'lina afores dey brung me here. Miss, she a fed'al slave agent. We knows 'bout her. Missy . . . missy, yawl gots to bleeve us, she no good!"

"Are you talking about Cordelia? How could you know? She didn't even come in here!"

The boy straightened. "Yes'm," he said. The panic went out of his voice. "Dat's why she don't come in."

Cold dread washed over Abbey. Dread and realization. A federal agent, hidden here on the island.

Nantucket—a station for the Underground Railroad.

How many slaves had been rerouted out of here by Jake and his cousins, only to be headed off and returned to their owners? Desperately she tried to remember how long Cordelia told her she'd been living on Nantucket. Long enough to build an ironclad guise.

Now two other runaways came forward, a chubby woman in her twenties and another teenaged boy.

"He right, ma'am," the woman said. "Dat lady, she go round breakin' up freedom stations and roundin' up 'scape slaves. She work for plantation owners and de gub'ment."

"Yes'm," the boy agreed. "But we hear tell only 'bout half de slaves gits back to dere plantations. Dem others, dey jus' disappear."

Abbey pressed her hand over her eyes. "Disappear . . . and I led her here." Her own words hung on her with the weight of a ball and chain. "Oh, God . . . oh, God . . ."

Her shoulders drooped and suddenly she was the one who was nauseous. The slaves made room for her on one of the cots as she sank down and slumped against the brick wall beside the dumbwaiter, whispering self-deprecations over and over again.

One of the women left her children behind and brought Abbey a cup of hot milk from the stove. Abbey stared into the warm drink, seeing only the starkness of what she had done.

"You din know, miss," the woman said. "We knowed we wuz in trouble, mind. We shoulda been outa here long time past, and wees still here. We knowed somethin' gone wrong. Ain't your fault."

Abbey stood up abruptly. "Is there anything in here that could be used as a weapon? Anything at all?"

The slaves turned their heads back and forth, sharing glances, then looking around the room, but there was little more than blankets and toys. Abbey looked around, too, and as her eyes passed over the dumbwaiter beside her, they suddenly stopped. She turned fully to face it. "Where does this go?"

"Upstairs, missy," the woman answered. "But it ain't big enough for you."

"But it's big enough for one of the children, isn't it?" Abbey looked around at the children and said, "Is one of you brave enough to ride up to the kitchen and take a message? Is there a pencil here?"

"Yes'm, we gots a pencil," a girl about eight years old piped up and dove for a bunch of pencils and paper on the floor. She supplied Abbey with a pencil and a piece of paper, and said, "I goes up for you, ma'am." And she looked scrawny enough to do it.

Abbey paused as she scrawled a note. "Can you?"

The girl was plainly terrified of the prospect as she glanced at the tiny, coffinlike dumbwaiter, but she straightened and said, "Yes'm, I kin go."

"Take this message to Jacob Ross. No one else, do you understand? Jacob Ross."

"Yes'm, I understands." The girl held her hand out flat for Abbey to put the paper in her palm, then clutched it tight and squeezed into the dumbwaiter, her knobby knees tucked against her chin.

Abbey watched, the breath holding tight in her body, as two young men wordlessly hauled on the dumbwaiter line and, stroke by stroke, lifted the little girl into the shaft within the wall. The rope strained and squeaked as though an omen.

There was nothing left for her to do. She was as trapped as these people were, caught between the brick wall and Cordelia. Cordelia, of all people. A perfect position, Abbey realized coldly, to have a station in the very house of the magistrate, where every conversation could be overheard and every paper examined after dark. It made perfect sense.

"I have to get out," she blurted. The young Negroes looked at her, their fates determined by her presence. "I have to confront her. And if I do that out there, at least she won't come back down the tunnel. If there's a fight, it shouldn't be where the children are. I'm going. All of you stay here."

They didn't argue, having been taught all their lives never to dispute the decision of a white person. If they were inclined to try to protect her from her own foolishness, they showed no sign of it. They assumed she knew what she was doing. It was a good thing, too, because her logic could have been shredded with a butter knife.

Before she knew it she was in the tunnel again, lifting the heavy lantern. As the light slithered along on the wall, she paused.

She put the lantern down and left it behind her. The tunnel was straight, and she had been down it once before. Once was enough. She didn't need the light.

She bumped the wall twice because she couldn't see it. It jabbed against her shoulder and reminded her that the trouble of this night had just begun.

And she had given it a push. Why didn't she tell the child to give the note to Matthew or Elias? Or anyone? That child would hunt and search until she found Jake, and that could take all night. She had Jake on her mind, that was her problem, and it could be her undoing before this night was over. She prayed that someone would be smart enough to wonder why a Negro child would show up in the dumbwaiter. Her heart begged for someone to be in the kitchen when she came up.

The tunnel opening was quiet, deathly quiet. The quiet of death on the way, the last breaths of chance. When she saw the pewter outline of it against the pitch darkness she knew she had been right to leave the lantern behind.

She crept to the opening and listened.

The sea washed against the pebbles and pilings. A quivering wind brushed the tops of Nantucket's trees. Wooden hulls scratched, grated, whined against their bumpers. Masts groaned. Sail bags rattled. In the distance horses' hooves rattled over the cobblestones, chased by the racket of wheels.

And, faintly, under it all, was the creak of footsteps on the dock above. Footsteps that went nowhere, came from nowhere. Footsteps that made the moves of waiting.

When Abbey heard the steps, the shell of her fear crumbled. From the nest rose unabridged insult and a sustaining kind of anger. She didn't need a weapon.

Her astonishment and disbelief had thawed halfway back in the tunnel. When she looked upon the smallish face and severe hair of a woman who had minutes ago been a stalwart companion, she could see only the fact that she had been used. Professionally used.

She came out of the tunnel, pressing close to the bank. From the gritty bank she dug out a handful of sand and closed it in her fist. Seaside darkness provided a cloak, and Abbey skipped quickly along, using the pilings as cover. The dock planks creaked above her as Cordelia paced, the gray skirt swishing over Abbey's head. Cordelia—

—who was there, holding a gun.

A gun. Somehow she had hidden a pistol in her nightclothes. Who knew how long she had kept it with her, slept with it, swept with it, made food with it tucked in her clothing, waiting for the moment when Abbey would lead her to her prize. Of course, it had become obvious early on that Abbey would provide the key in uncovering the runaway slaves. This interest in Jake Ross fell beautifully into the hands of the government agent—a double agent. A criminal herself if the Negroes were right.

Abbey hated herself as she watched the dark form of Cordelia move above her through the cracks in the dock.

The wad of sand bit into her skin. When the skirt above her swirled outward and moved toward the dock's edge, Abbey stepped out and flung her wad upward, letting instinct do her aiming.

Sand and pebbles smacked Cordelia's chin. Her head snapped back and she staggered, her free hand clawing at her face. Even the gun hand went up, falling off its aim to press against her spattered cheek.

Abbey vaulted up onto the dock, tangled for a horrible moment in the folds of her own skirt. With a great wrenching howl she pulled her skirt free and lunged toward Cordelia.

Strangely it wasn't the gun that finally convinced her. It was Cordelia's fighting back. Abbey's assumptions about eastern women shattered in the blow that struck the side of her shoulder and cast her cleanly down onto the dock. Or perhaps Cordelia wasn't an eastern woman at all.

By the time Abbey rolled over, she was staring into the barrel of the pistol, and Cordelia was spitting sand from her mouth. She held the pistol extended in one hand and backed off a few steps to gain an advantage.

"I was afraid one of them might recognize me," she finally said, in a tone prohibitively calm. "You're smart, not to announce yourself with lanternlight."

"I knew you wouldn't willingly give me an advantage," Abbey told her, rolling to her feet.

"Correct there." Cordelia wiped grit from the corner of her eye.

Abbey parted her lips to speak, but a hard thump on the dock behind her drew both their attention. She turned, and her glance met a pair of moon-shadowed eyes.

"Jake . . ." she whispered. Aloud she said, "You *had* to come alone?"

He moved to her side, staring at Cordelia. Something in his eyes said he wasn't surprised that this snag had developed, only surprised that the snag was Cordelia.

"Mrs. Goodes," he said, his tone saying *Of course.*

"You're under arrest for illegal transport of runaway slaves, Mr. Ross. I'm a bonded agent with the United States Federal Government, and I'm taking charge of the slaves down that hole. Don't interfere, Abbey, or I'll have to arrest you as an accomplice."

Abbey stepped in front of Jake and spoke as soon as she felt his warning touch on her arm. "Then you'll have to arrest yourself, Cordelia. It's also illegal to take possession of runaway slaves under the pretext of returning them to their owners, only to resell them at some vulgar profit."

Cordelia's face hardened, her secret revealed. From behind Abbey came Jake's cursing breath.

"What are ready-made, trained, English-speaking darkies going for on the hidden market?" Abbey demanded. "You know, I don't suppose the U.S. government will be too approving of how you're using your authority." Abbey waited to see if she read the situation right, to see how far she could push Cordelia, and in which direction. She licked her lips. "Let us go, Cordelia. Let the slaves go this time. Or you'll never hear the end of it from me. Either none of us go to jail, or all of us do."

Cordelia's hand tightened on the pistol, and her tongue pressed against the insides of her lips. She had nothing to say to the open accusation and the solemn dare from a woman she knew would make good on her promise.

"Abbey, are you sure of this?" Jake whispered, anxiety giving a hiss to his voice.

"Look at her face," Abbey said by way of an answer.

Cordelia snapped an angry glare at her, proving Abbey was right.

"Judas," Jake murmured.

"I told you they wouldn't go for it," another voice popped from the darkness behind them, and there was a clutter of footsteps with it.

Jake and Abbey spun around. Pollock. Behind him were Sumner and Maynard.

Instinctively Jake pulled Abbey against him, partially to protect and partially to keep her from diving into impossible odds.

Pollock made a broad shadow on the dock, his face shaded by the brim of his hat, bracketed by his two accomplices.

Cordelia snapped, "Damn you, why must you make things worse? I told you to stay away."

"Don't worry about her," Pollock said, his voice wrapping around Abbey coldly and tightly. "She'll be sent so far from here she couldn't find her way back with a guiding star. I know where I can get a sky-high price for someone like her.

Sucking in a breath, Jake pressed against Abbey, ready for a fight, but Abbey dug her fingers into his sweater and held him back just long enough for sense to sink in.

"Don't be a pig," Cordelia blurted, a spray of saliva giving body to her contempt for her associate. "I'd kill her first."

"Why?" Pollock demanded. "She remind you too much of yourself?"

He was astonishingly cold. Such coldness mystified Abbey as she listened. Cordelia was somewhat agitated, but Pollock was impassive. That doubled, then tripled the insult of his being here, of his being the one to get the upper hand on her, of his being the one to engineer her defeat and perhaps even her death.

As the insult burned within her, Abbey decided—no, she *knew* that she would refuse to give in to him. She would claw and fight her way back from hell if necessary before allowing Thomas Pollock to win. Obstinacy rose around her like a shell.

And beside her, rigid and just as adamant not to be taken easily, was Jake. Beside her, where he had belonged from the beginning, as she had somehow known. Beside her for whatever was to come. She wouldn't be separated from him anymore by these people nor by his own goals. If the slaves in the cellar room died or found even worse fates on the plantations of people who would deal with such as Pollock and Cordelia, if Abbey and Jake found only this one moment of true unity, so be it—but Abbey was sure as she stood here that she was indomitable, that she and Jake couldn't be completely defeated tonight. They may be vanquished, for certainly the fight was yet to happen, but they would forever have won something for the sake of honor. There would always be the glitter of chance turning their way, if only in the futures of the little slave children down there who had seen clearly that there were white people on the face of this earth who would give up life so black hands could know the sensation of holding coins they'd rightfully earned.

With all this behind her and Jake behind her, too, Abbey squared her narrow frame and gave Thomas Pollock a glare that would burn him for the rest of his life. She felt Jake's hands take hold of her upper arms as though he knew, and without looking she was certain he was spiking Pollock with the very same glare—a horrendous unity for the two of them, something that would never leave them. They were invincible.

"Get rid of them," Cordelia tonelessly ordered.

Pollock stepped aside. Sumner and Maynard pounced upon Jake and Abbey and dragged them from the wharf.

High night winds howled over Nantucket. Nature, for all its flamboyance, is perpetually thoughtless and, the late-hour chill belied the fact that it was summer. Wind coming down from the Arctic. Either that or Abbey simply could not feel warmth in the world right now.

She and Jake walked side by side through downtown Nantucket, flanked on their right by Sumner. Maynard walked in front of them, his small head swiveling from side to side, watching the empty street. Several paces behind, Pollock himself walked with Cordelia, discussing their plans for the fates of the slaves in the cellar room. Abbey strained to hear and before long had heard enough. Enough to know that the families were to be broken up, the children taken from their mothers, so that in time all of them would forget and there would be no thread of unity left. In time the names of Cordelia Goodes and Thomas Pollock would flicker and wink away from the Negroes' memories because they would be forever alone, so desolate and despairing that their will to fight back would be snuffed out. And even if they did mention those names, what was the difference? They would be owned by people who had done business with these despicable people. There would be no one to listen.

Horrible. Horrible. Unthinkable and unforgivable. Cordelia especially, who used her position to deceive and profit. She who carried the sanction of the law. To steal was one thing, but to be trusted and use that trust for corruption—she was worse than Pollock. At least Pollock had never pretended.

Jake strode beside her, glancing periodically at the man who flanked them several paces away and the one who led the way through the sleepy streets. "That was a thickheaded thing to do," he said privately.

"I know," she said.

"I love you for it."

"I know."

His lips turned up at one corner, and he smiled at her in spite of the situation.

"Quiet, you two," Maynard barked from in front of them. His thin shoulders and long arms and gangling gait gave no hint of the power given to him by his own viciousness, which Abbey had experienced firsthand on the wharf. She owed him a small remuneration as well, didn't she?

She leaned closer to Jake. "What are we going to do?" she whispered.

"Get killed, probably." The cool breeze pulled at his yellow hair, teasing his eyes.

She looked at him, ready to rail him for giving up, and was met with a little wink that told her he was going to do no such thing. A warmth folded around her hand as he tightened his grip. She squeezed back, flooded with sudden passion. Of all the hours she'd spent wanting him, she never wanted him more than at this moment when his hand took hold of hers and drew her against him to walk beside him into the face of their plight.

"We've got the whole island," she whispered lower than before. "Just break away—"

He shook his head. "Can't. People below."

Abbey let out a long, tight sigh. "I hate it when you're right."

"Shut your mouths!" Maynard ordered, his pointed face swiveling toward them in profile.

"Split up," Jake whispered, hardly more than a breath now. He waited until she looked up at him again and counted on her to read his lips. "Draw off . . . I'll empty the tunnel."

Without nodding, she let her eyes agree with him. They fell silent and continued the ominous march. Abbey concentrated on listening to Cordelia and Pollock talking as they brought up the rear of the procession, and even dragged her feet a little until she felt the jab of Sumner's pistol in her ribs.

She dared not guess where they were being taken. Somewhere to be murdered, of course. Sequestered until their bodies could be dumped and not found before their killers were safely off the island with the hapless slaves shackled in the hold.

Abbey had no intention of allowing herself to be led to such a place, to go there under her own power. At the moment she was stalling, and she knew Jake was playing the same game. She wasn't even afraid of the pistols, for they were only iron and bullets and she had wrath on her side.

"Get ready," came a soft breath at her left. His voice was a buoy.

Her arms involuntarily tightened against her sides. She worked to keep her pace from wavering and giving them away. There was no point in being afraid. Fear would just get her killed. If they were going to kill her anyway, she might as well fight. Pollock's coldly murderous ways and Cordelia's inflexibility gave Abbey nothing to lose.

They were walking past a closed dry goods store. In front of the store were two empty barrels. As they passed these barrels, Jake suddenly spun around. He shoved Abbey forward into Maynard—a rough move, but it worked—then continued his spin and kicked one of the barrels into Sumner's legs. Another whirl, and he had the second barrel by the rim and was heaving it into the air.

Abbey lost her balance when he pushed her forward, and for a split second she resisted when her shoulder rammed into Maynard's back. But her anger bore her up, and she pointed her elbow and buried it into Maynard's lower back. He grunted and catapulted forward off the clapboards, sprawling headlong into a stack of firewood. By the time Abbey caught herself on an awning pole and hauled around, Jake loomed with his barrel over his head like some great colossus about to heave its thunderbolt.

Cordelia shrieked and forgot she was holding a gun. She raised her hands to protect herself and reeled backward as Jake heaved the barrel toward her and Pollock.

Writhing to one side, Cordelia stumbled off the sidewalk and let Pollock take the full force of the barrel alone. Force struck force, and Pollock was driven to the ground, dazed and confused.

Jake wobbled on the clapboard porch, regaining his balance, searching for some kind of weapon. On the cobblestones, Sumner was gathering himself after the initial surprise. He was raising his gun and aiming it.

Abbey didn't hesitate. She grabbed one of the logs from the pile where Maynard now lay senseless and hurled it at Sumner. It struck him butt-end in the shoulder. His pistol clattered to the cobblestones with a dull ring.

Pollock was getting to his feet. Jake saw him and was about to lunge into the big man when a pistol shot boomed through the night, worse than thunder. Abbey yelped instinctively, frightened by the sound, but it was Jake who stumbled.

"Jake!" she shrieked.

A protective rage boiled up in her, and she dove headlong into Cordelia with a growl much more like an animal's than a woman's. Cordelia's eyes widened when she caught sight of Abbey coming toward her, arms outstretched, hands clawed, and she brought the smoking gun around.

Abbey's hands closed around Cordelia's throat, the flesh soft and giving, muscles beneath it corded with terror. The power that started in the factory of her heart now came flooding out the tips of her fingers, piercing Cordelia's neck with an unbreakable grip and a threat that couldn't be ignored. Abbey paid no attention to the pressure of the pistol barrel trapped flat against her side, a hot shaft scorching her dress. She pushed Cordelia back, back, back toward the awning pole until it slammed between the woman's shoulder blades. Then Abbey started pulling and pushing, bashing Cordelia's head against the squared wood.

There were sounds behind her—more fighting—but she was ghostlike in her persistence. Relentlessly she fought against Cordelia's struggles and the cold threats that poured from Cordelia's mouth, but finally the threats fell away and the housekeeper went limp. If there was any sympathy in Abbey for the struggling woman, it dissolved in the look of contempt from Cordelia's eyes as consciousness slid from them.

Abbey threw the woman down and spun around, reaching for Jake.

He stumbled toward her, one hand pressed into a bleeding shoulder. Behind him on the clapboards, Pollock was rolling over and reaching for a discarded pistol someone had dropped.

Dazed by his bullet wound, Jake let Abbey pull him away, off the porch and across the cobblestones toward the dark south side of the street. Behind them was a clatter of motion and the clap of gunfire, and Abbey ran for her life and for the life of the man she needed as a drum needs a beat.

Chapter Seventeen

LAMPLIGHT TOTTERED IN every window as folk were pulled from their beds by the sound of gunshots on the streets of Nantucket. Or was it only the thunder of an off-island storm? No one was sure, for the sounds made no encore after the first two. The men who came out to check the street found nothing, no one. Nothing but the toppled barrels and scattered firewood in front of Simon Parkhurst's dry goods store. Assuming a stray goat or ram had become frightened and done the damage, they restacked the wood and righted the barrels before going back to bed. If the loud noises were thunder from some incoming squall, better not to be caught out of doors.

Abbey dragged Jake around the corner to the cadence of Pollock and his confederates' footsteps clapping after them in the moonshaded night. They had a good head start, but Jake was still stunned by his new wound and she was caught between wanting to let him rest and knowing rest would be the death of them.

She pulled him between two buildings and pressed up against a brick wall, listening.

All she heard was her own panting and Jake's wheezes. Her hands were cold as she searched for her handkerchief and pressed it against Jake's shoulder. He accommodated by moving his hand, then holding the handkerchief in place himself. He closed his eyes for a moment, groaned softly, then took a steadying breath.

"You're bulldog willful," he commented. In spite of his wound the words were steady and his tone strong-hearted. "I like that in a woman."

"You had to get shot, didn't you," Abbey muttered. "You couldn't have stepped out of her way."

"I never step out of a woman's way, you know that."

"Why did you come alone?"

"Same as before," he told her, breathing heavily through a dry mouth. "The little girl found me halfway down Broad Street. I sent her after Elias and Matt, but I came on my own, anyway. Maybe she couldn't find them. Maybe she got scared, I don't know . . . oh, that stings."

"Hold your hand over it. That's right. They're coming—I hear them—"

Jake caught her hand and this time he led the way through the alley and out onto the next street.

The sound of pursuit was closing upon them. Pollock's voice barking orders, Maynard swearing revenge, and finally even Cordelia's shrill accusations. So she wasn't dead. Too bad.

Half a block. A quarter block. Closing. Store after store, all closed up tight, fanned by.

"Jake, wait!" Abbey drew up short. "This way!"

"What?" Jake teetered beside her.

"The hat store! We can hide there!"

"How can we get in?"

"Lucy's spare key." She scrambled to the door of the Geary Hat Store, dropped to one knee, and searched under a rock in the little porchside garden. By the time she overturned the rock where Lucy had hidden the key, her fingernails were black with soil and her knuckles raw. Her hands were cold, terrified.

Yes, she was afraid now. Running was much scarier than fighting, especially when your adversary was nipping at your heels.

The door opened and closed in a breath.

Abbey and Jake ducked behind the counter and tried to control their panting.

They could hear the heavy clodding of boots on the clapboard sidewalk outside—a big man. Pollock.

An instant later, Maynard and Sumner together. Then Cordelia.

The clattering on the sidewalk was deafening, deadly.

Then, quite miraculously, it passed them by.

Other sounds now, farther away. Pollock's muffled voice blurting orders to the men. He and Cordelia arguing.

Abbey twisted and coiled her arms around Jake's neck, heedless of his shoulder. "Why didn't you tell me? Why didn't you tell me? I could have helped you."

He caressed her back and her hair. "Because you're pigheaded, that's why. And, as you see now, it's a dangerous business."

"It's a necessary business," she said sharply, pulling herself back to look into his eyes. "It was no fair to keep me out, Ross."

"How did you find out about the tunnel?"

"I followed Elias." She sat back on her ankles and pressed her hand to her lips. "Oh, Jake . . . I led Cordelia there. I had no idea she was—"

"We had an idea," he said resentfully. "We knew there was a federal investigator on the island, but we didn't know who it was."

Abbey was silent for a moment as all the pieces clicked together in her mind. "Is that why you didn't want to tell me? Did you think it was me?"

Jake licked his dry lips. After a paused he rasped, "I told you—we didn't know who it was."

"But it could have been me."

"Yes," he admitted. "It could've."

The wind howled against the stubby building's facade. Abbey gazed at him through the layered darkness. Somehow the pattern of the windowpane resting across his face in the grainy moonlight endeared him to her. It was a badge of his effort. Quietly she told him, "A smart assumption. I would have thought the same."

Jake sighed and then grinned sadly. "I'll admit you did throw me off a mite when you stepped off the ship and immediately set to throttling that slaver. But we've learned the hard way not to put anything past the people who want to bust the Underground Railroad. Deception's one of their best skills. They know we're sly, so they've learned to be twice as sly."

"Cordelia's of a worse breed than that, even," Abbey said. "She's one who resells them. Bad enough to put shackles back on children and have the government pay her, but she turns a second profit from plantation owners. She's a greedy woman."

"Only the seediest of plantation owners would deal with her ilk, Abbey," Jake mentioned generously. "That's what my cousins and I concentrate on—the slaves who live under the worst of conditions. Most don't have it so bad. Most have a roof over their head and food and clothing, which is more than plenty of white folk have when times are bad. But Matt, Elias, and I go after the ones whose owners don't figure slaves for people at all. We've done pretty fair off Nantucket so far, too. We've funneled almost three hundred slaves since last year."

"Gracious," Abbey whispered. "It makes me ache to be part of it!"

Jake shifted his legs, and with a wince readjusted the bloodsoaked handkerchief against his shoulder. "I fancied it would," he drawled.

"You fancied," she scolded. "Fancy this."

With a handful of his sweater she pulled him against her and pressed her mouth to his. It was a kiss of passion, of thanks, of respect, of apology, of admiration, even of playfulness in this dangerous moment. Their lips made a soft wet smack and they were both lost in it, until a wave of weakness came over Jake and he almost fell against her.

"Jake," Abbey whispered sympathetically, holding onto him.

"I'm full of holes, aren't I. . . ." he muttered, squinting at his shoulder in the dimness.

"Medals of honor," she told him.

He gazed warmly at her and smiled. "Must you be such a cussed optimist at every turn? You're tuckering me out."

"Sorry. What are we going to do?"

"I don't know," he wheezed. "I've got to clear those slaves off the island . . . problem is, Matt set it up for Pollock to come through with a boat to transport them. By the time I put a bridle on the arrangement, it was too late to round up another boat for this week. There's no way to get them to the Continent."

Abbey had opened her mouth to speak when sounds from outside the door cut her off. Together they looked at the closed, locked shop door.

Her heart snapped when she made out the clear outlines of Pollock and Cordelia through the thin linen curtain on the door window.

"Oh, God!" she gasped.

"Shhh—" Jake pulled her deeper behind the counter.

"Cordelia! She must have thought of the store! She knew I'd come here! Damn me!"

Jake clamped his hand over Abbey's panicked whispers and drew her back still farther. "Is there a back room?"

Abbey nodded furiously, driven to shakes by Pollock's rattling the shop door. An instant later the lock was being blown off by Cordelia's pistol at close range, a bitter reminder that Abbey had failed to pick up the gun when she had had the chance. By the time Pollock was battering his way in through the shattered door, Abbey and Jake were shutting the door to the storeroom—but not before Cordelia's victorious yelp told them they'd been spotted.

Jake used his whole weight to clamp the door shut while Abbey fumbled with a heavy shipping crate and maneuvered it into place before the door. As the door creaked and groaned under the slamming of Pollock's shoulder, Jake found a broom and wedged the handle between the crate and the wall. Now Pollock couldn't get in, but . . .

"We can't get out," Jake choked, looking around the tiny shelved room. The only light came from two tiny windows through which moonbeams came in like pencils.

"Then we'll fight," Abbey shot back, burying his announcement. The idea of fighting fortified her. A streak of irrationality came over her, and she began pawing through the stored dresses and hats for anything that could be used as a weapon. A hanger, a pin—

"Abbey—" Jake covered the small room in two steps and stood behind her. "Abbey."

She found a hatpin and held it before her eyes to check the length of it, the strength of it—

"Abbey!"

He clasped her shoulders and wrenched her around to face him.

She hadn't realized that her breathing had become so jagged with panic. As she stood there rigid in his grip, blood from his hand smearing her sleeve, her lips hung slightly open as the air rasped in and out of her lungs. She stared up at him, and the fear began to creep back.

"Abbey, we could die tonight," he said. "We can't just decide against it. Being pigheaded doesn't stop a bullet."

"We won't die," she gasped.

He shook her. "We might! You've got to accept it."

"Why should I?"

"Because it just hurts more if you don't. Abbey, I've seen death," he said, his brows pulling together over those nutshell brown eyes, which were glazed by moonlight and the determination to make her understand him. "I've seen it, I've smelled it coming."

She stepped back, pulling out of his grip, and smacked his hands away with sudden wickedness. "I've seen death too, Jacob Ross. I know something about it." Her words came like a blade born on those ragged breaths, and with the declaration, her fear abated. "Don't tell me what I have to accept. I wasn't made to just accept. And I don't plan to wait around through life like some cautious granny, cowering away and hoping to die insensible in my sleep. I might go, but I'll go spitting. Get away from me. I've got things to do."

The pounding on the other side of the door called her with its pulse now, just as moments ago it had repelled her. With a hatpin in her fist, she struck the door.

"All right, Mr. Pollock," she called. "Stand aside. We'll come out."

"Abbey," Jake warned, wondering if she'd finally gone mad. Yet there was a strange approval in his tone this time and the faintest touch of a smile tugging at his lips.

She turned, and winked at him.

His smile broadened. He moved forward and helped her remove the crate and the broomstick from the doorway.

Pollock had stopped battering the door. There were muffled voices from the outer room.

They would be stepping out into the barrel of at least one gun.

Jake took her hand again. Together they stepped out of the storage room.

Pollock and Cordelia stood side by side near a rack of dresses. Each held a pistol, and Cordelia now held a large lantern, which cast a deceivingly warm glow over the entire store.

"Better," Pollock said impassively.

Jake and Abbey came out into the glow and said nothing.

"I'm sorry you have to die," Cordelia told them, but her tone said she was only being polite.

"I'm not," Pollock stampeded her. "We've got a business to run. No sense being soft about the job at hand."

"You can shoot us, obviously," Abbey said immediately, "but if you do, you'll never get off the island. I imagine murder leaves a particularly ugly trail in a quaint place like this, where everybody knows everybody else's nature. I've told everyone about you, Thomas. You're no secret anymore. Even if you should get away, neither of you will do business for long on the Continent. The slaves recognized you, Cordelia. They'll tell the Colberts, and word will spread like brushfire. A business like yours needs secrecy, and you won't have it anymore."

A deadly silence came over the hat store. Abbey tightened her hand around Jake's and tucked the other hand behind her skirt, the hatpin hiding in her fist. She straightened her shoulders, forcing herself not to think of the fact that she was using a hatpin to face down a gun.

Pollock's mouth was set like rock. He was a conniver, but he had his dull-witted side, and it was this side to which Abbey addressed her logic, the side that held his pomposity at bay and forced him to be aware of the kind of circles he ran in. His eyes grew small with rage. He raised his pistol level with her head.

Jake pulled her behind him in a last moment of defiance, but it was Cordelia who nudged Pollock's arm downward.

"Stop it," she said. "She's right. They've got to die drowned or something. Something not so obvious as shot. We need time to get off with the blacks."

Pollock glowered and fumed beneath the brim of his hat. He paused for one indecisive moment, clearly longing for the perfect violence of blowing their heads off, but then he tucked his pistol into his belt, inhaling to make room for it next to his barrel belly. "Fine," he growled. "Fine. We'll do it nice and ugly. Drowning don't hurt enough."

Jake's arm tightened around Abbey. There wasn't room to jump before Cordelia could fire her own six-shooter, and she wasn't going to trust them again. She hadn't taken her eyes from them once, nor had she wavered with her gun.

Pollock reached to his side, to Cordelia's lantern. He held it before his face, and his face became a golden mask. Using only this thumb and forefinger, he worked the hot glass globe from the wick and rolled it onto the store counter. The light's consistency changed, becoming bare flame now, burning from the short wick. With quiet deliberation he turned the crank until the wick came up and up, burning and roaring. He winced as the heat singed his face.

He moved the lantern in a rotating motion, then grinned as he heard and felt a full tank of oil sloshing around inside the reservoir. He appeared to like the sound.

"Burn my boat, will you," he snarled. He raised the lantern.

"No!" Abbey screamed. Jake dragged her backward toward the storage room.

The lantern crashed to the floor and skidded across the wood, leaving a snake of fire in its path. Two racks of dresses immediately burst into flames. A room that seconds ago had been drab now suddenly had turned hellish. Some shadows were destroyed by the monstrous light, others created by it, sharp black shadows defying the violent yellow flame.

The heat came only an instant later, scorching the fine hairs on Abbey's face as Jake dragged her backward to avoid incineration.

Every dress, every hat in the store became a torch, the room itself a furnace. Any chance of escaping through the front door was grilled as the flames climbed higher and lit the draperies. The small linen curtain on the door shriveled and was devoured.

Suffocating against the back wall, Jake and Abbey shielded their eyes against the heat and watched with pure bitterness as the two who would laugh upon their graves slipped by the window outside, and were gone.

Chapter Eighteen

The FIRE QUICKLY ate through the older side walls of the Geary Hat Store, chewing its way slat by slat to the stores on either side, devouring the merchandise to nourish its growth, a crawling demon out to swallow the business district. Soon the fire was sucking from every building on the block. Its great crackle had become a roar, a wave of searing mutilation that branded its shape on the skin of Nantucket. The gunshots which had been pegged as distant thunder were forgotten as buildings began to collapse and flames licked the night sky.

But the back wall, the newly built stock room in back of the Geary Store, held.

Even as the fire ate through the side walls and consumed the block building by building, the stock room became a flameless furnace in which smoke and heat were much more the threats than bare flame.

Jake smashed out the two small windows right away. He and Abbey put their faces up against them and sucked at the fresh air, but even the air from outside was quickly polluted by billows of smoke from out front. The smoke was black and stifling, in every way the antithesis of its radiant source.

"They can't get away! They *can't* get away!" Abbey shrieked, a demonic rasp raking out of her throat. She kicked and kicked at the outer wall, drowning in her own rage. Sweat poured down her face and down Jake's heat-rushed cheeks as he struggled beside her, working to pry away the wall boards with the tip of the broomstick.

"Don't use up the air," he said, deceptively calm. He got the broom handle deep into a crack between the wall boards. Using his weight carefully, he bore down upon it. The boards screamed, the broom handle bent to an impossible point, and blood poured from the bullet wound in Jake's shoulder, but he was unrelenting. With an awful snap, the first board gave way. Beyond it was the cedar shingling of the outside wall in back of the store.

"All right, all right . . ." Abbey pushed back her sweat-soaked hair and rummaged around the room looking for another broom or anything else that could be used as a lever. As she searched, she accidentally pressed her hand to the store wall—and leaped back. The wooden wall was as hot as coals. Beyond it, she heard the laughter of the fire. Smoke was pouring in the crack underneath the store room door. She immediately began stuffing dresses into the crack to save their air.

In the outer room, with a sound as terrible as any gunfire, the ceiling collapsed, crashing into the fire, providing more fuel. Abbey clamped her arms over her ears and whimpered through quivering lips as the sound came through and took half their ceiling with it. Above her now, flames licked their way into the store room. She looked up and bellowed, "No!"

Jake called her name, but didn't leave his job of breaking the wall away. "Abbey, get away from there! Come by me! Now! *Now!*"

She covered her head with her arms and stumbled toward him just as the second and third planks broke away. Jake ignored the blood flowing down his arm, driven on in his task by something beyond the limitations of his body. He had taken over Abbey's fury when it began slipping from her and used it now to batter his way through the cedar shingles until the night air seeped in through an open hole. "Come here!" he shouted over the thunder of the fire. Through funnels of black smoke he reached for her and pulled her to him. "Can you get through? Try."

Abbey forced her stinging eyes to find the open part of the wall. It looked impossibly small, but Jake was pushing her toward it.

Like a baby, she went headfirst into the world. Nails and splintered spears of wood tore at her skin and her clothing. For an instant she was trapped between hell and heaven, but an unsympathetic shove from Jake smashed her through the hole and she tumbled into a struggling garden that now would never grow.

She fell a full three feet to the ground, and the air slammed out of her, leaving her gasping and aching. Delirium set in as the first sucks of fresh air went immediately to her head, but an instant later came the nightmarish realization that Jake was still trapped. She turned on her hip and struggled to her feet, looking up just in time to see the whole roof of the store plunge inward. Flames struck out like petals of a giant yellow rose where a moment ago there had been structure.

"Jake!" Abbey clawed at the shingles. "Jake! Jake, come on!"

There was no sign of him.

She shrieked his name deliriously in a voice so panicked it didn't even sound human.

The building was hot to her touch. Half the wall above her head now fell inward, sprinkling like bread crumbs onto the flaming innards of the store. She kept on screaming his name and pulling at the warm cedar. The heat caressed her fingers. The touch of death.

"Jake!"

Her scream reached up to the incinerated rooftops that were crumbling and turning to cinders before her very eyes. The entire block was now roaring. All around her firebells clanged and men ran with hand pumps and buckets. The meager Nantucket fire brigade was joined by citizens, more and more, flooding from the houses by the dozens. Some had dragged a hose from the fire cistern on Water Street, but it would not be enough. Nothing but the ocean itself could be enough now. Nothing, nothing.

Abbey pummeled the edges of the hole in the cedar wall with her fists. "Jake!" Tears poured from her eyes, tears of horror, grief, and the sting of the smoke.

From inside there was no answer; nothing but the subtle shift of collapsed roofing on the floor. Before her she saw a wall of yellow and orange fire, eating its way toward her, toward Jake.

She grabbed a garden rake from where it leaned against a picket fence, heaved it over her shoulder, and began smashing it against the cedar. The shingles splintered under the teeth of the heavy rake, but every blow was enough to sap the power of the next blow from her arms.

"Jake!" Her voice was little more than a screech now, raped by smoke and its own tearing at her throat, its sound destroyed.

Why wasn't he moving? Where was he, where was he—

Two great smashes from either side of her crushed the wall to bits. The cedar disintegrated and fell away, leaving only a pile of smoldering refuse and a wall of fire beyond it.

Someone pulled Abbey back away from the wall, but the smashing continued. She felt herself being handed over to another pair of hands, and she was leaning against a soft presence that held her on her feet and wiped the soot and grit from her eyes.

"'Old toight, mum, 'old toight, Abbey—over there! I see 'im!"

Abbey clung to the familiar voice and the strong, narrow arms, blinking desperately. Her vision cleared enough to catch the forms of Matthew and Elias crashing their way through the wall and charging into the burning wreckage. Orange sparks flew and glowing cinders leaped up and swirled around them as their feet churned through the char, and they pawed the wreckage aside like children raising minnows in a stream. All at once they dove for the same spot. They lifted a mess of Jake from the kindling. He gasped and coughed, clawed at his shoulder and leaned on Elias, but he walked out under his own power. They lifted him from the collapsed store, moving slowly and carefully as though to taunt the blaze behind them.

Abbey tried to call his name again, but it gagged her. She stumbled from Lucy's arms and into Jake's as his cousins supported him on either side.

Jake crushed her against him, feeling the intense heat still pressing at his back, and he looked up. His head reeled.

The business district was an inferno. The fire was spreading impossibly fast, giving luster to the ocean and glare to the night sky. Fire bells and the clatter of hooves and wagon wheels added a heartbeat to the horror.

"God—" he choked. "Matt! Look at it. . . ."

Matthew had his arm around Jake's shoulders and was shielding him and Abbey from the floating sparks. Elias was there, too, beside Lucy, captured by the balefire before them.

"We got to get out of here before the air goes," Matthew said sensibly.

Jake grabbed his cousin, getting a handful of collar. "The tunnel! The slaves! They'll roast!"

"And do what with 'em?" Matthew demanded. "Hide 'em where?"

"I don't know! Come on!" He pulled on Matthew and Abbey both, stumbling through the little garden.

Elias reached out and caught Jake. "Not you. Look at you. You're scorched and shot and what else—"

Jake put a palm against Elias's chest and shoved him away. "Get your hands off me. We're getting those people off this island—tonight."

The younger cousin's face flushed, and he stepped forward again, but Abbey wedged between them and pushed them apart, snarling at Elias, "You heard him. Let's go."

The fire crackled and flew in the air above them. Orange sparks and curling bits of burning paper and wood gave a hellish splendor to the night.

Matthew said, "Let's go."

Jake didn't wait. He hobbled off into the night, pushing past the men of Nantucket who were crashing through the streets with their buckets and hoses and horses and crates of sand. Elias set his lips and followed, with Matthew, Abbey, and Lucy close behind.

Lucy caught at Abbey's sleeve as they ran. "Nicky's coming to meet us, Abbey—"

"Oh, Lucy!" Abbey hauled up short and grabbed her hard. "He can't! There are escaped slaves to get off the island! He can't get involved!"

"You underestimate him, Abbey," the cockney girl insisted. "You jus' don' understand him."

"That may be true, but you know how he is about smugglers and slavers! He's bound to feel the same about the Underground Railroad. Stall him, Lucy! Stall him, please! Please! I'm begging you!"

"But, Abbey . . ."

"Please!" Her final request was hardly more than a squeal as she pressed her point home on Lucy's narrow shoulders and dashed off into the crackling night after Jake and his cousins.

Behind them, the Geary Hat Store and all its adjacent colleagues crumbled and were consumed in a hail of orange glitter.

• • •

Abbey and the three men were forced to take the long way through town to the end of Steamboat Wharf, turned back several times by the fire as it spread. There hadn't been rain in two weeks. Everything was dry. Everything burned.

The town had gone into an organized flurry in its attempt to curb the fire, but buckets and cisterns and desperation were not enough tonight. The Nantucket Fire Brigade discovered its own impotence that night. With water all around them, they could only burn.

The tunnel was wet, and it was hard to breathe, hard to drag heavy, moist air down their scorched gullets, but they stumbled down it toward the cellar hideaway without as much as a candle to light their way.

Jake plowed into the cellar room first and collapsed against the bunks, staring. Abbey came after, then the cousins.

Abbey gaped and choked out, "Where are they?"

The room sprawled before them, its bales of hay no longer serving as chairs, the sheepskin rugs cool now, the toys scattered as though kicked about, everything broken and in disarray. Even the bundles of sleeping children were gone from the bunks, with only blankets left discarded on the floor. A struggle, clearly. Stolen. Against their will.

"Oh, Jake—" Abbey gasped. "They got here first! They took them!"

"But where?" His gentle face was smeared with black soot, his eyes tortured. "Where do we even begin to start looking?"

Abbey staggered toward him and filled her fists with his sleeve. "I destroyed Pollock's ship! I destroyed it, I tell you!"

"He'll steal another. Do you think he won't?"

"They probably started a few extra fires downtown just to cover their tracks," Matthew suggested.

Abbey spun on him. "Standing here doesn't get them stopped. Let's get out of here!"

Elias ducked back out the short opening and they all followed. Matthew waited behind to help Jake, but Abbey was consumed, obsessed, with something else.

How many times would the core of her heart be threatened before she reached her point of intolerance? She'd seen Jake nearly die twice now, and that was too much. She'd felt his death nipping at her ankles and stinging her fingertips, and she knew unequivocally that she couldn't live without him. But he was with her now, only paces behind, and she felt him as fully as if they were pressed against each other beneath the covers, separated only by a thin film of perspiration. She reached back and caught his hand as they went through the tunnel, and the enthusiasm she felt in his grip drove her onward as though she were no longer earthbound. He was pushing her on, so intense was his presence there. In moments he had caught up with her, and they were running side by side through the tunnel, bursting out onto the sandy shoreline against the flames that washed the sky.

Poor Nantucket Town suffered under a swift and merciless hand of flame. What had been a nightmare when they entered the tunnel was the portal to Hades when they emerged. Silhouetted between black shapes of buildings and the pearl-gray sky, the fire possessed a kind of horrid resplendence.

"Which way?" Matthew asked.

"Christ knows," Jake growled. "I'll find them if I have to pull every strand of shoregrass on this island."

"No need," Abbey said, standing firm on the slanted bank. "I know where they are."

Jake pushed past Matthew and gripped her arms, a flood of both warmth and desperation.

"They needed time to corral a boat," she said. "Where's the one place in town to hide the slaves where nobody'll look?"

"Abbey, don't toy around!"

"The jail. Jake, the *jail.*"

"We've no time for guesses."

"It's no guess. Something Cordelia said in the tunnel—never mind. Follow me."

The town was hot, plain hot. The air itself moved with a terrible smothering presence as they ran through town. A block away the businesses of Nantucket handed fire from one to the next. Through the town, down the little warm streets, to the most innocuous jail ever built by any man's hand, a tiny jail that was almost sweet in its smallness and its lack of security. A simple bolt on a big wooden door kept the jail locked; no key, just a bolt.

And none of them was more surprised than Abbey herself when

Elias and Matthew hauled aside the big bolt and pulled the door aside to find a row of stunned black faces gawking out at them.

Jake grabbed Abbey and pulled her against him, spinning her around until her skirt opened like a bell, and he howled, "I love you!"

Abbey laughed and howled back, "I know! I know!"

For what she hoped would be the last time, she found a need to squeeze out of his arms and plow into the jail, into the coven of dark faces she was so relieved to see.

The rush of delight and any smugness she might have enjoyed were snuffed, though, as three of the young women stumbled into her, clutching her, begging her, wailing and blubbering in misery, incoherent. At first Abbey took the blubbering as gratitude and the delirium brought on by renewed hope, but then she caught the key words—

Babies . . . dem chillun . . . never seen again . . . took . . . stole . . . gone . . . skipjack . . . Steamboat Wharf . . .

Coldness dropped over her. The waves of heat from the town fire weren't enough to warm her as the meaning sank in.

"Jake!" Abbey shoved her way through the clinging women to where Jake and his cousins were giving each other congratulatory hugs. "Jake, the children!"

The three men looked up at her cry, and even in the unnatural orange glow of the great fire, she saw the color drop from their faces.

"The children are gone!"

"What's a skipjack?"

"It's a cutter rig," Matthew supplied. "Small."

"That must be why they took only the children," Abbey gasped.

"That," Jake said hurriedly, his eyes wide with near panic, "and they're easy to smuggle, easy to scare into keeping quiet, easy to resell—a year from now they'll be so changed their own parents wouldn't know them—damn it to hell! Damn it! Steamboat Wharf, is that what you said?"

Jake's strength was rapidly waning as the blood continued to seep from his shoulder. A pallor had come across his features, and the depth had left his eyes, but he struggled onward with frightening doggedness, his mouth set hard and his eyes narrowed.

Abbey longed to hold him, to make him lie back in the shoregrass and draw him into her lap, caress him and soothe him and tend his wounds and stroke him as she had when he was healing before. To remind him of other sensations. Other compassions. The one thing they'd never had was enough time. She could have done it, done it in a minute. She could have forced herself to dismiss Cordelia from her priorities, even to let Pollock disappear into the past if it meant a future with Jake, well and whole again, his body healed from the battering that had violated his smooth flesh. She could have brought herself to forget everything and move forward, gladly, with relief, with her one great prize—Jake Ross against her heart where he belonged.

Except for the slave children. Except for those trusting, frightened little faces looking up at her through a clear glass memory. They had trusted Jake and he had stuck with them, no matter the trouble it had caused. Abbey had been the one to stumble over his well-laid plans and scatter them. This was her fault, and she would see it out.

"The stables," she said all at once. "We can't just run all over town, but we surely can ride."

She started off toward the nearest stables. Behind her she heard Jake bark an order.

"Matt, you come with us. Elias, get those people down to the shoreline, away from the fire."

"And then what?" Elias snapped back. "We got no boat!"

"Shut up and do it!"

Then there were footsteps racing after her.

Matthew helped Jake keep moving, kept him from falling when he wavered, but knew better than to argue with this ferocious determination that had come over his cousin and this woman who had battered her way into his life.

It was one thing to fight when you didn't have a hole in your shoulder, and something else to keep up when you did. Abbey swelled with adoration for Jake as she heard his effort to keep up with her. Somehow he was right at her side when she pulled three skittish horses from the neat little stable down the street and yanked their bridles on faster than she thought she could. The horses were mulish now, agitated by the smell of fire and the looks of it against

286

the dark buildings around them. Certainly by now the fire could be seen from many miles out at sea, and from close up it was that much more a terror.

At the last moment, as Abbey climbed up on the edge of a stall and dropped onto her horse's back—a fat, well-fed horse, nothing like the lean animals of the range—Jake paused and dropped his forehead against his horse's broad red flank. Exhaustion showed in his face now, and he couldn't get onto the horse without Matthew's help.

"Jake," Matthew began, "why don't you—"

"No," Jake said, lifting his head. "No, I'm going. Get me up there."

Matthew shrugged and did as he was told.

"You lead, Abbey," Jake said, drawing himself straighter as he gathered the reins. He was trying not to appear weak as he sat the horse and they steered out of the yard. "You're the best rider. You know how fast a horse can go through the streets."

"On cobblestones?" she blurted back. "I'll just be guessing!"

With that, the last cheer left her mood and pure anger settled in. Pollock's face wobbled before her in the rising heat over the town, with Cordelia's right behind him. She urged her horse through the streets with Jake's on the right and Matthew's on the left. Even the horses seemed to catch their sense of purpose.

Through the burning streets of Nantucket they rode, their horses' hooves clattering a riot across the cobblestones, making another din within the roar of the fire. Then the clatter changed instantly to a loud drumming, and they knew they were on the docks.

What a sight they made to Thomas Pollock and Cordelia Goodes from the wide transom stern of their skipjack as it pulled away from the dock under the power of a half-raised sail. Frantically they tried to urge the little boat away from the riders who broke right out of the flames and thundered down the dock toward them.

When Jake saw the skipjack moving against the end of Steamboat Wharf, he could tell the little boat was making good its escape. He'd brought no gun to shoot with, and a man could only jump so far. Bitterness struck his soul as he envisioned himself, Abbey, and Matthew forced to haul rein and watch as Pollock and Cordelia and their henchmen urged up the broad triangular sails and skimmed out to sea, forever getting a head start.

"Abbey, slow down!" he bellowed over the din of their hooves. "It's too late—we can't get out to them."

Matthew pulled his horse up, but even as Jake drew his own reins in he saw that Abbey was lifting her elbows for a final order to her mount.

"Abbey, we can't reach them!"

But her jaw suddenly set itself and she shouted back, "You just don't know how to sail a horse!"

Her elbows came down and her legs dug into the horse's shoulders. She sent the end of her reins down with a slap on the animal's flank, and, like lightening, the horse bolted forward between Jake and Matthew.

The edge of the dock rushed up beneath her, and at the last second she gave the horse a signal that it instinctively understood—*now*.

The horse gathered itself and stretched out over the water, its mass passing between dock and boat with the grace of a bird.

However, it landed like a horse. Hard.

The skipjack floundered under the terrible sudden weight and wavered sickly in the water, fallen off the breeze. The horse hammered the deck, shrieking at the unfamiliar sensation of the floor moving beneath its hooves, and it stumbled into a pile of tools on the foredeck. The tools scattered across the deck with a terrible racket.

Abbey had no weapon, so she used her horse as one. She drew back hard on the reins, making the beast rise on its hind legs. Forehooves pawed the air inches from the faces of Sumner and Maynard, who stumbled wide-eyed against the rail and then toppled into the water with two great splashes.

Without a moment of hesitation—both Pollock and Cordelia carried guns—Abbey twisted the horse back across the flat deck and scooped up the nearest rope, hoping it was long enough. It was no lariat, but a rope was a rope. Abbey wrestled the coil into place in her hand, swirled it over her head, and let it fly back toward the dock. It writhed outward, playing toward Jake. He reached out with his good arm and caught the coil. He and Matthew wound it around the nearest piling and began hauling the skipjack closer and closer to the dock.

Cordelia was still on the stern, knocked aside by Abbey's insane jump. She held desperately onto the mast and watched numbly. But it was Pollock who wasn't surprised, Pollock who had spent enough of his life around horses and range riders that he could act against her now without the handicap of shock.

For a moment Abbey lost sight of him as the maddened horse twisted beneath her, but then he appeared—holding a Negro girl no more than two years old.

Holding her high in the air.

"No!" Abbey shrieked. But too late. Pollock knew the one thing that would call her off him.

He heaved the toddler hard into the sea.

Abbey spun from the horse's back and landed on the deck at the same moment Jake let loose a roar of anger. But she was much closer than Jake, and he couldn't swim, anyway.

Couldn't swim. Yes, that's good.

"Can you swim?" she raged at Pollock, scooping up a sledgehammer from the nest of tools on the deck. She swung it over her head and brought it down sideways into Pollock's right knee. Bones splintered.

Pollock's mouth fell open with a soundless gasp of pure agony. Abbey pushed him back, his right leg flopping at an impossible angle, and together they plunged into the cold, engulfing waters of the Atlantic.

She pushed him aside and dove for the struggling child. The toddler was gulping chunks of air, her little black face almost impossible to see in the dark ocean water, visible only by virtue of the skittering lights from the fire in town as they ran across the swells. Abbey dove for her and got her hand around a thin arm just as the child slipped under a swell. She pulled hard, the water dragging against her.

From behind her a hand clawed at her hair. Pollock—gasping and bellowing in pain, unable to tread water with a shattered leg. He caught her shoulder and dragged her down under the water. It was all she could do to maintain a grip on the spindly little arm while she fought off Pollock's hard grip. In the chill darkness underwater, she kicked at the big man, landing a few lucky blows on flesh, and finally he fell away beneath her. When she finally struggled to the surface, she heard only the echoes of his terrible shrieks.

She shook her wet hair to one side and pulled the sputtering child up against her. She was disoriented. She couldn't find the skipjack, couldn't find the town, couldn't find the dock, couldn't find the island. But she had the child, she had the child. Why was it so dark? Where was the fire?

Firm hands took hold of her arms. She twisted and fought them off with a maniacal shout.

"Abbey! Don't—it's me, it's Jake. . . . I've got you."

She surrendered instantly, as she had always dreamed of doing. The child was lifted from her arms, and finally she was pulled from the water. A moment later she was pressed against him, ringing wet, slumped against his chest as they knelt together on the dock. And there it was. The great fire. Still burning.

"Jake," she whispered. "We did it. . . ." She melted against his warm throat, pressed her face beneath his chin, and buried herself there.

Beyond expression, Jake simply moaned his relief and caressed her against him. "I didn't think you could surprise me any more," he said softly, "but you did."

Beside them, the skipjack grated against the dock, and Matthew tied it up without a word. The muffled sobs of children from the closed hold were their simple victory chimes.

Abbey pressed the salty water from her eyes and forced herself to think. "Maynard . . . Sumner . . . don't let them get away. . . ."

"They won't get away," a strong voice said from behind them on the dock—an unwelcome voice.

Jake pulled Abbey to her feet and they turned.

"Oh, Dominic," Abbey murmured. "Please . . . not these people. Please."

"Save your breath, young woman," Dominic said flatly. His trousers were pulled hastily on over his nightshirt, and he was scorched and dirty, but still possessing the stateliness that made him who he was. Beside him, Lucy stood somber and resolute in her own way, cuddling the sopping Negro child. Behind them, a handful of men awaited orders.

Dominic made a gesture, and the six men he had brought with him instantly dispersed to pull Sumner and Maynard from the water and to take possession of Cordelia, who was still hugging the skipjack's mast.

"Dominic," Abbey said hoarsely, "I'm begging you."

"Don't beg," he said. "It's undignified." He gazed at her, at Jake, at Matthew, and he listened to the sound of sobbing from inside the skipjack hold. "Well, what are you waiting for? Get moving before I see you getting away."

Jake stepped toward him. "What?" He and Dominic stood facing each other, two handsome men, both sooty and tousled, somehow commanding a mutual grandeur as Abbey stared at them.

"Am I under arrest?" Jake asked, barely above a whisper.

"You are, shall I say, officially requested to leave the island," Dominic said, "with all your . . . possessions. Tonight, or there's little more I can do. Will that suit your needs?"

Speechless, Jake could only nod in his befuddlement.

Dominic raised his red brows in a shrug. "Well, I have to do my job," he said, "but I needn't do it particularly well all the time, must I?" He tolerated their gawking at him for several seconds, gloating really, then he said, "Why do you think I hired those two buffoons? I couldn't officially help you—"

"So you unofficially didn't hinder them," Abbey finished. "Oh, Dominic . . . oh, Dominic." She plunged forward and threw her arms around his neck. As she pressed her ear to his shoulder, she saw Lucy beside him, her funny face curled up in a grin.

Jake came up close to them. "What about Mrs. Goodes?"

Dominic reluctantly pulled back from Abbey as though forcing himself to do so. He swallowed hard, then gently urged her back into Jake's arms. After a moment he said, "She'll be held on the island, pending trial. I'll remand her over to the custody of the U.S. Government. Federal authorities will find the necessary evidence to see that she never sees the light of freedom again, I'm sure."

"But she's not going to keep quiet. What'll that do to you?" The sudden softness in Jake's tone belied an unexpected concern for Dominic, as though somehow they had known all along that they were secretly on the same side.

Dominic's lower lip came up in a kind of shrug. "She's a corruptionist, and she attempted to do murder. She mishandled her authority . . . oh, a dozen things, I'm sure none for the first time. We knew someone was reselling slaves off the East Coast islands, we simply didn't know who. What she has to say about me will pale, I'm sure. You forget, Mr. Ross, this is the North. We disapprove of slavery. And I am a northern official." He looked down at Abbey now, and with his thumb he smeared a tear from her already wet cheek. "If you go down to the salt meadows between the wharves and Goose Pond, I suppose you'll find a seaworthy though elderly schooner moored there, just big enough to transport several people off the island. I'm sure it won't be missed."

"My God . . . thank you," Jake whispered.

"No, no," Dominic said, dismissing the subject with a flutter of his fingers. "Take care of Abbey," he said. "However, I think it only fair to warn you that neither you nor I can keep her from doing her will. Jacob," he added, extending his hand, "you will be welcome back on Nantucket the day you become heroes instead of criminals. That day is coming, I'm sure."

Still overwhelmed, Jake found himself grasping the hand of the island's highest official and sinking into a completely unexpected brotherhood.

As Abbey watched, choked to tears, the two men shared a warm camaraderie for the first and last time.

"Now if you'll pardon me," Dominic said, wrapping his arm around Lucy's shoulders, and gazing down at the cockney girl's tear-streaked face, "we have a town to save."

The slave families were rowed out to Dominic's schooner by the hellish light of a fire that was out of control. Abbey sat with Jake and Matthew in the salt marshes near the shore, waiting for Elias to bring the rowboat back for them.

Matthew silently tended Jake's shoulder as best he could and managed to get the bleeding to stop, which for now would have to do.

Jake sat still, hugging Abbey's hand to his chest, and gazed longingly back at the blazing horizon of Nantucket Town, now a panorama of flames reaching toward the marble clouds. Abbey came up beside him, touched him, felt him, drew her hands over him. The rowboat was on its way back for the last load—them.

"You like Nantucket, don't you, off-islander?" Abbey murmured.

"I feel like I'm running out on them," he whispered, the fire patterning his face.

She placed her hands on the sides of his warm face and turned it toward her, to let her become his world. "Nantucket will survive. It always has," she said.

"Yeah," Matthew said, "as long as the pub don't burn."

Jake looked up at his cousin and smiled sadly, a small and limited smile of great warmth, soon broken by a wince that rammed his eyes shut and made Matthew pull his hand away from Jake's shoulder.

"Sorry," Matthew murmured. "You're a mess, cousin."

Abbey helped pull Jake's sweater back over his head and get his sore arm into the sleeve, mentioning, "I don't know how you ever survived without me."

The sweater popped over Jake's head, leaving his hair tousled, and his eyes squinted at her. "Before I knew you," he said, "I didn't get shot once a week."

She bobbed her eyebrows. "Every relationship has its little adjustments."

He hung his head and shook it wearily, his lips widened in a grin.

"Elias'll go with you to help master the schooner," Matthew said. "Take all the time you need with him, then shove him back this way on a southbound packet. By then, everything should have cooled down a mite."

Jake nodded. "It'll be good to have him along. You . . . I'll miss." He tugged on Matthew's arm sentimentally.

Matthew gave Jake's good arm a squeeze and dismissed the moment with, "Don't get slimy on me, Ross. Nantucket ain't seen the last of you, I reckon."

"I presume not," Jake agreed.

"Spoken like a true islander. I'll get the rowboat."

Matthew left the two of them alone on the salt marsh while he waded out to the returning rowboat.

Abbey sat quietly beside Jake, reading his eyes as he hesitated. He didn't seem to want to stand up, to start the next leg of this unusual adventure she'd plowed her way into. He felt her gaze.

"It's a dangerous life we have before us if we keep this up," he said softly.

Without even giving him time to finish his sentence, Abbey said, "Better than a deaf and dumb one. We could do worse. Canada's waiting, lighthouse keeper. And there's a whole South full of slaves who need the Underground Railroad."

He squinted at her in the moonlight, saw her framed by the fire on shore, and whispered, "Nothing frightens you."

Abbey poured herself into his embrace. Against his injured shoulder she murmured, "Life without you frightens me. Everything else is just shadows. I've never been afraid of shadows." She pulled herself away, keeping her hands on him. "Let's go. Before we become afraid, let's just go."

She helped him to his feet, and they slipped their arms around each other, standing side by side as Matthew pulled the rowboat into the shallows and they heard its keel grate on the sandy bottom.

Puzzling at the expression in his eyes as he caught sight of the rowboat grating on the beach behind her, she asked, "What else? Is there something?"

He forced down a swallow. "I . . ."

"Jake," she gently prodded, "tell me."

"Well . . ."

Abruptly she shook her head and pinched both his cheeks, deriding, "Why, you! You don't want to get in that rowboat, do you? Didn't you think you'd ever have to leave the island?"

He shifted his feet. "I was hoping I'd be caught and put in a nice warm jail before that happened."

She sank into his arms, he lost himself in her, and they fell together into the kiss that had been waiting all this time to happen.

The town burned, but the fire was their own.

Author's Note

THE GREAT FIRE of 1846 destroyed most of the business district of Nantucket Town. The island of Nantucket never entirely recovered from the spoilage and would never again regain the grandeur of her past. The fire spread with lightning speed through the stores and houses, fed by storage casks holding tons of whale oil. All told, the fire spread over almost forty acres and destroyed 360 buildings, including the majestic Atheneum and the Tudor-arched Trinity Church with its Gothic windows, spired belfry, and pinnacled buttresses. Some time afterward, it was determined that the spark had ignited in the William Geary Hat Store.

By this time, partly because of the prohibitive sandbar that spanned Nantucket's main harbor, the whaling industry had already shifted to ports like New Bedford and Martha's Vineyard, where the harbors could handle the deep-draft spouters. The shift away from Nantucket had begun in the 1810s and now had reached the point of no return. Nantucket's legacy as a seaport would quickly wane. All that would remain of her days as the queen of American whaling would be the charming Quaker homes and Greek Revival buildings that somehow escaped the Great Fire, which consumed one-fifth of the town.

Another major economic blow came when most of the island's young men emigrated to the Continent to seek their fortunes on the opening western frontier during the great California Gold Rush of

1849. Gold fever ran through Nantucket with every bit the ruination of the Great Fire.

This coffin received another nail almost coevally, in 1852, when a process was discovered to refine earth oil for lamps and candles. It burned cleaner and cost less than whale oil and dealt a killing blow to the whaling industry's former mecca. Since then, technology has provided us with ways to synthetically provide every product that once came only from the bodies of living whales. We no longer need to tear the skin off these intelligent creatures in order to light and warm our homes.

The shot to the heart for Nantucket was the American Civil War. Confederate commerce-killers like the famous cruiser *Shenandoah* patrolled the northern coastal waters, burning or sinking any Yankee ships. There would be no more whaling on the scale that had once made Nantucket the third wealthiest city in Massachusetts. With this coda, the legacy of Nantucket slipped peacefully into legend.

Nantucket's part in the Underground Railroad continued on a small scale until the advent of the Civil War, of which slavery was the only good casualty.

The stateliness of the past has also gone out of whaling in these modern times. As an author and a historian, I am touched by the Melvillesque images of old-world spout hunting, and indeed I describe it to you as the grand and honorable pursuit it once was, but I caution readers to keep whaling in perspective. In those days of old Nantucket, whaling ships went out with a handful of men, sought hard and long for the sight of a pod, embarked in tiny whaleboats with hand-held harpoons, and collected comparatively few whales for the effort. It was enough upon which to build an industry, and the industry naturally waned when there was no more need for it. This is healthy economics, and we should not mourn.

In present times, however, we have the same handful of men hunting a dwindling population of great whales, but hunting them much more diabolically—with faultless radar and explosive-tipped, rifle-propelled harpoons. They take in whales by the thirties and fifties, often wiping out whole pods in one voyage.

I prefer to remember whaling as it was in those hard-working post-Colonial days, when man and whale went equally in the oceans of Earth, and I hope this novel, rather than romanticizing a ghoulish industry, will call to mind the days of old Nantucket. Perhaps soon our memories of whaling as an industry will be replaced by open-sea sightings of living, thriving whales, and we'll sail on by and wave hello.

Today, Nantucket thrives again. It is a place where you and I can go, walk upon the cobblestones, drink grog, breathe sea air, sing chanties, count masts, and remember things of those past days as though we too were there.